THE
SHADOW LAMP

Other Books by Stephen R. Lawhead

A Bright Empires Novel
Quest the Fourth:

THE
SHADOW LAMP

STEPHEN R.
LAWHEAD

Thomas Nelson
Since 1798

NASHVILLE DALLAS MEXICO CITY RIO DE JANEIRO

Published in Nashville, Tennessee, by Thomas Nelson. Thomas Nelson is a registered trademark of Thomas Nelson, Inc.

Scripture quotations taken from the NEW REVISED STANDARD VERSION of the Bible. © 1989 by the Division of Christian Education of the National Council of the Churches of Christ in the U.S.A. Used by permission. All rights reserved.

Page design by Mandi Cofer.

Thomas Nelson, Inc., titles may be purchased in bulk for educational, business, fund-raising, or sales promotional use. For information, please e-mail SpecialMarkets@ThomasNelson.com.

ISBN 978-1-40169-020-5 (ITPE)
ISBN 978-1-59554-938-9 (TP)

Library of Congress Cataloging-in-Publication Data

Lawhead, Steve.
  The shadow lamp / Stephen R. Lawhead.
    pages cm. -- (Bright empires ; Quest the 4th)
  ISBN 978-1-59554-807-8 (hard cover)
  I. Title.
PS3562.A865S53 2013
813'.54--dc23

                                    2013009866

HB 12.22.2017

For Margaret,
my favourite mother-in-law

"Coincidence is the word we use
when we can't see the
levers and pulleys."

— EMMA BULL, AUTHOR

Contents

Important People

Anen—Friend of *Arthur Flinders-Petrie*, high priest of the temple of Amun in Egypt, Eighteenth Dynasty.

Archelaeus Burleigh, Earl of Sutherland—Nemesis of *Flinders-Petrie*, *Cosimo*, *Kit*, and all right-thinking people.

Arthur Flinders-Petrie—Also known as *The Man Who Is Map*, patriarch of his line. Begat *Benedict*, who begat *Charles*, who begat *Douglas*.

Friar Roger Bacon—The early philosopher, scientist, and theologian of Oxford in the mid-1200s; he has been called *Doctor Mirabilis* for his wonderful teaching.

Balthazar Bazalgette—The Lord High Alchemist at the court of *Rudolf II* in Prague, friend and confidant of *Wilhelmina*.

Benedict Flinders-Petrie—The son of *Arthur* and *Xian-Li* and father of *Charles*.

Brendan Hanno—Attached to the Zetetic Society in Damascus, an advisor to ley travellers.

Burley Men—*Con*, *Dex*, *Mal*, and *Tav*. Lord *Burleigh's* henchmen. They keep a Stone Age cat called *Baby*.

Cassandra Clarke—A post-graduate palaeontologist who accidently gets caught up in the quest for the Skin Map.

Charles Flinders-Petrie—Son of *Benedict* and father of *Douglas*, he is grandson of *Arthur*.

Cosimo Christopher Livingstone, the Elder, aka Cosimo—A Victorian gentleman and founding member of the Zetetic Society, which seeks to reunite the Skin Map and learn its secrets.

Cosimo Christopher Livingstone, the Younger, aka Kit—*Cosimo's* great-grandson.

Douglas Flinders-Petrie—Son of *Charles* and great-grandson of *Arthur*; he is quietly pursuing his own search for the Skin Map, one piece of which is in his possession.

Emperor Rudolf II—King of Bohemia and Hungary, Archduke of Austria, and King of the Romans, he is also known as the Holy Roman Emperor and is quite mad.

Engelbert Stiffelbeam—A baker from Rosenheim in Germany, affectionately known as *Etzel*.

En-Ul—Elder statesman of River City Clan.

Giambattista Becarria, Fra Becarria, aka Brother Lazarus—A priest astronomer at the abbey observatory on Montserrat, and Mina's mentor.

Gianni—See *Giambattista Becarria*, above.

Giles Standfast—*Sir Henry Fayth's* coachman, *Kit's* ally, and erstwhile servant of *Lady Fayth*.

Gustavus Rosenkreuz—Chief assistant to the Lord High Alchemist and *Wilhelmina's* ally.

Lady Haven Fayth—*Sir Henry's* headstrong and mercurial niece.

Sir Henry Fayth, Lord Castlemain—Member of the Royal Society, staunch friend and ally of *Cosimo*, and *Haven's* uncle.

Jakub Arnostovi—*Wilhelmina's* wealthy and influential landlord and business partner.

J. Anthony Clarke III, aka Tony—Renowned astrophysicist and

Nobel nominee, he is *Cassandra's* concerned and protective father.

Rosemary Peelstick—Zetetic Society host, colleague of *Brendan Hanno*.

Snipe—Feral child and malignant aide to *Douglas Flinders-Petrie*.

Turms—A king of Etruria, one of the Immortals, and a friend of *Arthur's*; he oversees the birth of *Benedict Flinders-Petrie* when *Xian-Li's* pregnancy becomes problematic.

Wilhelmina Klug, aka Mina—Formerly a London baker and *Kit's* girlfriend, she owns Prague's Grand Imperial Kaffeehaus with *Etzel*.

Xian-Li—Wife of *Arthur Flinders-Petrie* and mother of *Benedict*. Daughter of the tattooist Wu Chen Hu of Macao.

Dr. Thomas Young—Physician, scientist, and certified polymath with a keen interest in ancient Egypt, he is also referred to as *The Last Man in the World to Know Everything*.

Previously

The number of individuals now caught up in the quest to unravel the meaning of the scrap of human parchment known as the Skin Map has increased: Cassandra, the newest member of our intrepid group, is rudely wrenched from her work as a jobbing archaeologist and pitched headlong into a veritable maelstrom of new ideas, experiences, and alarming revelations when she inadvertently discovers ley travel—that ferociously unpredictable interdimensional mode of transportation employing the regions of geomagnetic force that encircle the planet and radiate through the cosmos known, for brevity's sake, as ley lines. While a life of academia may have left her unprepared for the realities of a multidimensional universe, she is nevertheless well placed to exploit the phenomenon. Our Cass is tough-minded and centred, and not easily overwhelmed by her new life as a questor. It was Cass who made contact with the clandestine organisation known as the Zetetic Society, thereby fast-tracking her education in all things related to the quest and its attendant possibilities and difficulties.

Attentive readers will recall that this same society was mentioned

1

quite early in the proceedings by Cosimo Livingstone and Sir Henry as a group to which they belonged, and of which they were esteemed and active members. The Zetetics, headquartered in the timeless city of Damascus, exist to provide support, information, and sustenance for the active questors and are currently led by Brendan Hanno and the redoubtable Mrs. Peelstick. They have taken Cass into the fold and put her to the task of finding out what has happened to Cosimo and Sir Henry, whose fates are a mystery to them, if not to readers of previous volumes of this saga.

Sir Henry Fayth, it should be noted, was a founding member of the Zetetic Society and, lacking a direct heir of his own, he had hoped one day to pass the baton of membership to his niece, Haven. That same Lady Fayth, having become entangled in a complicated relationship with the nefarious Lord Archelaeus Burleigh, has, we are happy to report, succeeded in making a clean break and is now freely pursuing her own interests. Something of an enigma, to be sure, she has forged a shaky friendship with Wilhelmina; the two have conspired to thwart Burleigh's plans on at least one occasion, and have thus far prevented Mina from falling into the hands of the man Haven calls the Black Earl, a rogue of the first order.

Unfortunately, the wicked earl and his Burley Men are not the only ones labouring for their own dire purposes. Another such is Douglas Flinders-Petrie, son of Charles and great-grandson of Arthur Flinders-Petrie, the possessor of the original Skin Map, which, as we all should know by now, records the coded destinations of various ley portals scattered throughout the multiverse and which is thought to provide the location of the treasure everyone is seeking. Douglas has shown himself fully as ruthless as he is resourceful and has enlisted the aid of a medieval scholar of great renown—none other than the venerable Friar Roger Bacon, the thirteenth-century Oxford poly-math. In one of those odd historical quirks, it turns out that Bacon (affectionately known as Doctor Mirabilis, the Wonderful Doctor) has written extensively about ley travel in a book called *Inconssensus Arcanus*, or *Forbidden Secrets*—a tome of such incendiary content that it had to be inscribed in an unreadable cipher: the same in which the Skin Map is encoded. Thus Douglas, aided by his truculent assistant, Snipe, is well on his way to learning the secret of the map and the location of the treasure, which we have long suspected is not merely monetary in nature.

As for our old friends Kit and Wilhelmina, it is pleasant to report that a glad reunion has taken place in the unusual, albeit strikingly beautiful, setting of the Abadia de Santa Maria at Montserrat, high in the Spanish Pyrenees. The abbey, like so many sites of religious significance, is part of a sacred landscape that is simply heaving with telluric energy; thus it is a place well suited to the needs of a ley-leaping priest such as Giambattista Becarria, an Italian monk who also happens to be a first-rate scientist with an intense inter-est in and understanding of astronomy and physics. Fra Beccaria came to Montserrat Abbey to escape an increasingly awkward past; Wilhelmina came on purpose to find a man she hoped could help her learn more about the fundamentals of ley travel. She found that and more. In Brother Lazarus—the name he assumed to better protect his ley-leaping secret—Wilhelmina has gained a sympathetic friend and mentor.

Before returning to our story, all that remains is to mention Kit's experiences in the Stone Age, which would appear to have made him not only sturdier and cannier, but also more determined to see the quest to its conclusion come what may. Far from being a meaningless cul-de-sac on the way to greater things, Kit's sojourn in the Stone Age may yet pay big dividends for all concerned. Certainly, it was there that Kit learned the significance of the Bone House and became the only one of the questors to have actually visited the miraculous Spirit Well. And while the meaning of that fabled place is yet to yield itself to the fullest inquiry, readers could be forgiven for thinking they are beginning to perceive the faint glimmerings of a revelation that could dramatically alter the fortunes of not only the individual questors but the entire universe as well. For, as we have seen time and again in the preceding pages, even the smallest events can have enormous consequences.

PART ONE

The Ghost Road
Revisited

CHAPTER 1

In Which Next Steps Are Contemplated

Kit stood gazing at the burnt-out ley lamp still sizzling at his feet. The heat from the metal carapace had singed the dry grass, sending tiny tendrils of white smoke drifting up to assault his nostrils with a harsh metallic scent. Overpowered by the energy coursing around and through the enormous tree before them, the devices had expired in a burst of heat and blue light.

"I guess that's that," he concluded.

Brother Lazarus bent over Mina's hand, inspecting the burn.

"We know the ley is here—no doubt about it," said Kit, taking in the yew's gargantuan trunk, hard as iron and big as a house, growing right in the middle of the ley. "Now all we have to do is figure out what to do about this whacking great tree."

"I think that will have to be a problem for another day," said Wilhelmina, withdrawing her hand and shaking it gently. Raising her eyes, she indicated the circle of sky above the clearing; the clouds now held a dusky tint. "We're starting to lose the light. What do you want to do now?"

"We could stay here and make camp," suggested Kit, "and then try to establish contact with River City Clan in the morning." He saw the glint of dissention in Wilhelmina's dark eyes and quickly added, "Or we could think of something else."

"How about this?" she said. "We could see if the Valley Ley is active and use it to get back to Prague."

"What about Burleigh? I thought we were trying to stay out of his way."

"I doubt he's still hanging around. He's probably long gone by now."

"But if he's there waiting for us?"

"There's an element of risk, I admit," she said. "But standing around gawping at the problem"—she gestured towards the colossal yew tree before them—"isn't going to help. Anyway, it isn't as if that tree is going anywhere."

Brother Lazarus, who had been pacing the circle formed by the needle-drop of the yew's spreading branches, stepped into view and announced something in German. He spoke in a quaint, Italian-inflected *Deutsche* all his own; Kit could follow nothing of what he said, but sensed a note of excitement in his tone. Having delivered his message, he marched off around the tree once more.

"Well?" Kit asked, watching the priest count off the paces.

"He says that you were right—judging from the size of the tree and the diameter of the trunk, it has been at least a thousand years since you were here last—give or take a century or three. Your Stone Age pals are ancient history, I'm afraid." She gave Kit a sympathetic pat on the shoulder. "Sorry." Turning again to the rapidly fading sky, she said, "There really is no use in staying here now. Let's go back to Prague and I'll buy us all a nice dinner—schnitzel and beer, the best you've ever had. What do you say? We can sleep between clean sheets tonight, and tomorrow we'll put our heads together and figure out our next steps."

"Right." Kit took a last look around the clearing, then agreed with some reluctance. He stooped and gingerly tested the heat of the ley lamp case. It had cooled enough to touch without burning, so he picked it up and then retrieved Mina's. "We best not leave these lying around. You never know who might trip over them."

Shrugging off his pack, Kit stuffed the broken devices into it, nestling them down beside his furry tunic retrieved from the cave mouth. The shirt—cut from skins and stitched by hand using a crude bone needle and strands of dried gut—was no treasure; he would have ditched it long ago but for the priceless object sewn into a pouch inside: Sir Henry's green book. How he had managed to hold on to that through his ordeal was a minor miracle, and Kit was not about to lose it now. Shouldering the pack once more, he smoothed the front of his borrowed cassock, gave the voluminous sleeves a tug, and said, "Okay. Let's see if we can navigate our way back to Prague before another thousand years have passed. Think you can find the ley?"

Mina glanced around at the white limestone bluffs barely visible through the trees to the south. "Shouldn't be a problem," she said. "Anyway, if we stay here we'll probably get eaten by something big and hairy."

"It's this way then." Kit led them back to the rim of the gorge and the long downward trail that contained the ley. They descended into the valley and into deepening shadows. The chiselled rock face rose sheer on the left-hand side of the track, and the right-hand side angled off sharply into heavy brush and the tops of trees growing farther down the slope.

"I could never catch it when it was open, you know," he told Mina as they started down. "I tried as often as I could, but without success, until I finally gave up. I had your lamp and figured if I ever stumbled across another ley, the lamp would tell me."

"Like it told you about the Spirit Well?"

"That was a total surprise," Kit allowed. "Last thing I was expecting, really. Something very strange and"—he gave a shrug—"maybe profound was going on in the Bone House. I'd give a lot to know what it was that En-Ul was really doing."

"What do you *think* he was doing? Any ideas?"

"I got the impression . . . The clansmen don't use language as we do, remember, it's more a mental thing—you get impressions and images, so you have to picture what you mean and hold it in your head. It's weird, but it works." Kit stopped walking. "Anyway, the closest I was able to get to it was that he was in some way *dreaming time.*"

"You mean *creating* time?"

"Maybe, or maybe the Old One was seeing what time would bring and somehow interacting with what he saw. Like I say, the finer points escaped me. All I got was an impression of sleep and dreaming all mixed up somehow with time and creation and . . . I don't know . . . *being.*"

Wilhelmina saw that Kit had halted and pulled up. "Why have we stopped?"

Kit put out a hand and pointed to a bench-like rock jutting from the cliff face. "This is where I landed when I first arrived."

Mina nodded. "I recognise the place—from my experimental

travels." She pointed down the narrow trackway. "But I always landed farther down the path. So maybe this is where it starts."

"Whatever," said Kit. He glanced at the sky and the shadows deepening across the canyon. "It should be active any moment now—if it is going to operate at all."

"Don't say that," Wilhelmina chided. "You might jinx it."

Brother Lazarus said something to which Wilhelmina gave an answer. The priest stepped forward and held out his hand, spreading his fingers wide. He paced off three more steps and then turned with a grin and spoke again.

"He says the ley is active now—not full strength, but enough," she explained.

"He can tell by *feel*?"

"It's something he's developed over the years—experience, I guess." She moved to join the priest on the path. "Don't you ever feel anything when you make contact with a ley?"

"There's the throwing up," Kit replied, falling into step with her. "Violent motion sickness, dry heaves, dizziness, disorientation—that sort of thing. Sure."

"Besides that, dummy. *Before* you jump—don't you feel it?"

"A little, I guess," Kit conceded. "A kind of tingle that makes the hair on my arms and neck stand up sometimes. Not always, but often enough."

"Same here."

They continued down the track. In a moment, Kit did feel that unmistakable swirl of energy around him; static electricity seemed to dance across his skin with the faint tingling sensation. Brother Lazarus stopped and held out his hand to Wilhelmina, who reached out to Kit. "Shall we go?"

Kit took a last look around, as if fixing the place in his memory. Wilhelmina took his hand, saying, *"Auf Schritt zählt sieben."* To Kit she repeated, "On step number seven. Ready?"

"Wait!" said Kit, pulling his hand away. "I can't. Not yet."

"What's the matter?"

"I'm sorry, but what if we're wrong about the tree and all? What if the clan is still around?" He glanced back down the path as if hoping to catch a glimpse of them. "Look, thing is—I can't leave without seeing for myself if they're here or not."

"But that could take some time," Mina pointed out. "The ley won't be active all that long and—"

Kit cut her off. "Then we'll come back tomorrow. Look, we've come all this way, and it's important to me to find out."

Wilhelmina could see there was no arguing him out of it, so she gave in gracefully. She explained Kit's reluctance to Brother Lazarus, then said, "Okay, sure—why not? Let's go see your friends."

Kit thanked them both for understanding and started off.

They proceeded down the ramp-like trail, taking care to break stride every third or fourth step until the trail curved around a bend and passed beyond the ley line's zone of activity. Once they reached the valley floor, Kit led them along the bank of the slowly flowing river.

"River City camp is about six miles or so from here," he told them. "It's still early enough in the year, so that's where they'll be. If they *are* still around, you're in for a treat. Being with them is like nothing you've ever experienced. It's like . . ." Words failed him just then, and he realised living with the primitive clan was simply beyond any comparison he could make or think of; he could describe it, after a fashion, but not capture it. "You'll just have to see for yourself."

Brother Lazarus, who had been listening to this exchange, cast a quick glance around and asked something in German. Mina listened, then looked around too. Kit saw the apprehensive expression on her face. "What?" he asked.

"He was wondering if it is entirely safe. It *is* safe, right?"

Kit gave her a lopsided smile. "Safe as it ever is," he said. "Stick with me, Toots, and you should be okay."

"It's just that we're not exactly equipped for being out here among primitive creatures, defenceless and all."

"Defenceless?" Kit laughed. "We're not defenceless."

"No?"

Kit shook his head. "We've got *me*!"

"Oh, *that's* reassuring." She rolled her eyes. "Seriously."

"Seriously." Kit nodded. "There are bears and lions and such, true. But they tend to stay clear of humans unless challenged in some way, or sick, or desperately hungry."

"So as long as we don't run into a sick and starving lion, we'll be right as rain—is that what you're saying? Well, thank you, Tarzan, you've been a big help."

"You can count on me." Kit laughed again, and it occurred to Wilhelmina that it had been a very long time since she had heard him do that. Perhaps, in some odd way, the boy really was in his element in the Stone Age. She smiled at the thought. Who could have guessed?

The suggestion of stalking lions and ravenous bears did cast a pall across the mood, however, and they proceeded with a bit more caution and quiet. The afternoon sun sank below the rock rim above, casting the gorge in shade. After a while, they paused and drank from a clear pool at the river's edge and rested a moment before walking on. The shadows deepened around them and soon stars were appearing in the sky directly overhead. The valley echoed with the calls of flocks returning to their roosts in the higher branches of surrounding trees, and the lower thickets shivered with the furtive rustlings of small creatures making their nests for the night. Aside from that, the only sound to be heard was the liquid lap and splash of water slipping over and around the stones that lined the river's course.

"Is it much farther?" asked Mina at one point. "I can hardly see my hand in front of my face. Maybe we should stop."

"We're almost there," Kit assured her. "It's just up around the next bend."

A few dozen paces later they reached a place where the river made a wide sweep around a sharply angled bend, forming a small peninsula of land. Surrounded on three sides by water, this bend in the river was the place Kit had dubbed River City. He stopped and, scrying into the gloom, surveyed the place for any sign of habitation. He sniffed the air, but scented only the river smells of stone and mud and water plants.

"It's pretty quiet," Mina whispered; she glanced at Brother Lazarus next to her. He shrugged. "I don't think there's anyone here."

"You wouldn't see them unless they wanted to be seen," Kit replied. "Come on, let's check it out."

He led them farther into the river bend and to the heart of the primitive settlement site. Thrashing through brush and stands of birch saplings, they came at last to the farthest tip of the peninsula, where Kit stopped. "This was where we spent the warm months," he said, gazing around the little clearing. "If the clan was still intact, they'd be here."

Mina caught the note of melancholy in his tone. "I'm sorry,

Kit. I am." She put a hand on his arm. "But we knew it was a long shot."

"Yeah," he sighed. "Still, I hoped . . . we'd find something, you know?"

"You can always come back later. You might have better luck locating them next time."

"I guess."

"What now?"

"We'll stay the night," he told her. "There's no better place around here to make camp. We can get some sleep and head back to the ley line in the morning."

"And back to Prague? Schnitzel and beer?"

"Back to schnitzel and beer—and Engelbert's extraordinary strudel."

Kit showed them how the clansmen made their crude huts from bent branches, and in the dark did his best to construct a shelter for them. Brother Lazarus found some blackberries and gathered a few handfuls for each of them, and they passed a comfortable night—as comfortable as a night without food, fire, or even much sleep would allow—and roused themselves again well before daybreak so they could reach the ley line in time.

As they approached the trail leading up and out of the gorge, Kit paused. "Thanks for going along with me," he said. "Both of you. It meant a lot to me."

"We didn't do anything," Wilhelmina countered and translated for Brother Lazarus, who agreed.

"You were willing," he said. "That was enough."

As the sun touched the high ledges of the ravine's rim, setting the white limestone ablaze, Kit turned his face to the trail. "Shall we?"

15

"Onward and upward," answered Mina, stepping between them and holding out her hands. "Step lively, gents. Breakfast at the Grand Imperial awaits and I don't know about you, but I could use a strong cup of coffee right now."

CHAPTER 2

In Which Concern
Quickens to Action

"Look here," said Tony Clarke, his voice rising, "my daughter has been missing three days! No one has turned up a single trace of her. You were the last person to see her——"

"Not the last person," Friday corrected. "Her friends saw her."

"True," allowed Tony, trying to keep his temper in check and his tone even. "I'll give you that—her friends saw her at the Red Rocks Café. I spoke to her on the phone later that same evening, and she said she had been out in the desert with you."

"That is true."

"She told me something extraordinary happened." Tony watched the tall, lanky Arizonan for any telltale sign of emotion, recognition, or even interest. "She told me you took her with you on something she called the Ghost Road—that you and she visited another world, or at least another location in this one."

"Your daughter talks a lot."

"She does, yes—when she is excited. I could tell on the phone that she was terribly excited—unnerved, frightened even—which is rare for her. She said you had shown her a phenomenon beyond ordinary human experience, scientifically speaking. She asked me to come and help her learn more about it." This last part was not strictly true. It was he himself who had insisted on coming to Sedona to check out Cassandra's story—but he felt the summons was implied in his daughter's act of phoning him in the first place. "That is why I am here."

"You said you were here to find your daughter."

Ignoring the man's pigheadedness, the physicist tried to keep himself focused on the main task. "Cass said she had discovered something incredible and life changing."

"She didn't."

Tony stared at the obdurate Indian. Was Friday *trying* to provoke him?

"Come again?" said Tony. "Then what did she mean? What happened out there in the desert that made her think she had seen something that overwhelmed her powers of description?"

"The Yavapai have always known about the Ghost Road. Your daughter did not discover it."

"Right. Point taken. Cassandra found this Ghost Road and she didn't know what it was—it was new to her, she had never seen one before—so then what happened? Where did you take her?"

"I did not take her," countered Friday. "She followed me."

Tony was slowly getting the measure of this fellow. He might wear a feather in his long braid of black hair and sport the faded denims and chambray of a modern cowboy of the Southwest, but this recalcitrant Native American was a match for every lab-coat-wearing, literalist pedant Tony had ever encountered in his years as a research physicist. Like his academic counterparts, Friday stubbornly insisted on the precise meaning of his words, making not the slightest effort to grease the wheels of communication.

"Okay. She followed you," said Tony. "Cass told me of a place called Secret Canyon. I've located it on the map. Is that where the Ghost Road can be found?"

"Yes."

"I want to see it. I want you to take me there."

"No."

"Why not?"

"It is not for you."

"I don't care. My daughter is missing and I'm going to find her. Secret Canyon seems to me a very good place to start looking." He fixed the reluctant guide with the stare of a father not to be crossed or denied. "And you, my friend, are going to show me."

Friday's expression did not change. He might have been carved out of oak. "No."

"Let's look at this another way," suggested Tony, assuming a more reasonable tone. "You can show me exactly what you showed Cassandra on the last day anyone in Sedona saw her, or you will show the police after I tell them about you taking Cass for a walk in the desert."

That made an impression. Tony saw a glint of concern flash in the hooded black eyes.

"Yes," Tony continued, nodding slowly. "This is the bargain. Either you take me out to see the Ghost Road now, or I go to the police with this information. They have been extremely helpful up to now, but they have done all they know how to do. Imagine their excitement when I tell them about you and what you did with my daughter."

"I did nothing with your daughter."

Tony had struck a nerve; he could hear it in the altered timbre of Friday's voice. He pressed his advantage. "If that's your story, just tell them what happened. No doubt you will be able to explain every detail to their complete satisfaction. In fact, I'm sure they'll want to know all about the Ghost Road too."

Defeated, Friday dropped his head. "I will show you."

"Good." Tony's spirits rose on this small victory. "Time is a'wasting. Let's go."

They drove through Sedona in Tony Clarke's rental car and out to the site of the dig. The archaeological works had been temporarily suspended while forensic investigation of Cass' disappearance continued. About fifty yards from the site entrance on the highway, Tony pulled off the road. "We'll walk from here," he said. "The police won't thank us for contaminating the area."

Friday said nothing, but slammed the door and started off down the highway.

Tony locked the car and hurried after the long-striding fellow. "Tell me about the Ghost Road."

"What do you want to know?"

"Well, to begin with—what is it? How does it work?"

"I don't know."

"Look, I thought we had an understanding that you were going to be helpful."

"It is true. I don't know how it works. I only know that it exists and that it has been used by my people for many hundreds of years."

"Who uses it? What do they use it for?"

"The shaman uses the Ghost Road to cross the Coyote Bridge."

Tony sighed. Getting information was going to be like pulling teeth. But this thought was followed by another: he was dealing with an indigenous culture's description of a genuine marvel. Naturally they would cast it in terms they could understand—words that meant something to Friday and his people. They likely did not have another vocabulary, or even, perhaps, another way of thinking about the phenomenon. In any case, what Tony was being told lined up with what Cassandra had said in that late-night phone call that had put him on the next plane to Arizona.

Alarm bells had begun ringing the moment he stepped off the jetway and tried to call Cass from the Flagstaff regional airport. Her cell was off and she did not answer the phone at the motel. He had collected a rental car and driven down to Sedona where, after a quick stop at his motel, he had hurried out to the dig site—which was shut down for the day owing to some local political stunt he had yet to understand. Back at the motel, he got in touch with two of Cass' co-workers who told him that, yes, they had all seen his daughter at Red Rocks the night before. But, no, they had not seen her since.

It took a few hours to learn that one of the white vans used by the diggers was missing from the parking lot. As the dig was suspended for the day, it had taken that long for anyone to notice the vehicle's absence. Nevertheless, the van was quickly located at the excavation site tucked in behind a mound of debris bags; the vehicle was unlocked, the keys beneath the floor mat. It did not take a rocket scientist to put two and two together: Cass had driven out early that morning in the van, parked it in the shade, and gone off to investigate the Ghost Road again.

He had immediately informed the police about his daughter's

disappearance and her mention of a visit to Secret Canyon. After the obligatory bureaucratic delay, the canyon had been thoroughly searched late the next day by national park rangers and two members of the local K-9 corps. The search turned up very little; though the dogs raised a scent leading from the van, they lost it once inside the gorge.

Now Tony and Friday would carry the search forward into other realms.

The two men walked along the shoulder of the highway until they reached a place where they could cross a weed-choked ditch and strike off into the desert. Tony listened to the crunch of the dry, gravel-strewn earth beneath his feet and cast his mind back to what Cass had told him about her encounter with a force or phenomenon she could not explain. He could still hear her voice, slightly aquiver with uncertainty, as she said, "Dad, I think I travelled to a different dimension. One second I was in the canyon being pelted by sand and wind and rain, and the next I was . . . Dad, I was standing on an alluvial pan of volcanic cinders—no canyon, no cacti, no nothing—only lines stretching to the horizon in every direction . . ."

When he pressed her for details, she said, "Lines, you know—they looked like someone had taken a snow shovel and dug a shallow trough through the cinders across the plain, but not arbitrarily or haphazardly. These lines were absolutely straight, and they went on for miles."

Her description put him in mind of the ancient patterns scratched into the volcanic pan of the Nazca Desert in southern Peru. A quick perusal of available reference books tended to confirm her description; it was, he reasoned, what one would see from the ground if dropped into the middle of the Nazca plain.

Tony Clarke, the father, believed his daughter had undergone a very powerful experience that had rattled her normally rational view of the world. J. Anthony Clarke, the scientist, hypothesised that she had undergone an experience of translocational perception induced, perhaps, through the clash of electromagnetic forces wrought by some of Arizona's unique physical geography.

Known famously as the Sedona Vortexes, these telluric energy emanations could produce singular effects. Could they, he wondered, significantly affect cognition and awareness? He had read abstracts of experiments where volunteers subjected to intense magnetic fields experienced altered states of consciousness. Was this what had happened to Cassandra?

Of course, mental dislocation was one thing; physical disappearance was something else entirely. A good scientist, J. Anthony Clarke refused to speculate until he had more facts at his command. And that was why he had sought out Friday on this bright, fresh morning.

"Okay, so you don't know how the Ghost Road works," Tony conceded. "But how do you manipulate it? Where does it go? I want to know anything you can tell me."

A faint smile passed Friday's lips. "You are just like your daughter."

"Thank you. I'm waiting . . ."

Friday briefly described his experience of the Ghost Road, saying that the so-called spirit paths could only be found at certain times in the morning and evening, and that one must be initiated into their use by another traveller. He hinted that various destinations could be reached by linking path to path, thereby allowing a traveller to jump from one place to another. He said shamans who used the mysterious pathways seemed to age very slowly, if at all, and that there was great wisdom to be gained from travelling the Ghost Roads.

Tony realised he was receiving a crash course in interdimensional travel and absorbed everything that was said; his understanding grew by leaps and bounds as his quick mind made instant connections between what he was being told and the science that had been his life's work.

As they talked, the red stone cliffs drew nearer, rising abruptly from the surrounding plain, stark and imposing in the bright morning light. Before the sun had cleared the towering rock stacks to the east, his guide had led him to the half-hidden entrance of the dry gorge known as Secret Canyon.

Casting a last glance at the sky, Friday said, "We are in time."

Tony looked around. Steep walls of deep-red sandstone formed sheer curtains on either side of a narrow gully, the floor of which was mostly smooth and level. The valley interior between the two undulating walls was steeped in shadow. "What happens next?" he asked.

"We walk."

"After you."

Friday nodded and started into the canyon; a step behind, Tony followed. It took a few moments for the hiker's eyes to adjust to the dim light filtering down from the sky high above. The air held a mineral tang—that of stone and water and ozone created by the dry desert wind as it passed over the canyon rim. The two followed the smoothly curving path through the ravine until they came to a place where the trail straightened. Friday picked up his pace and lengthened his stride.

Tony, watching his native guide, imitated the long, loping gait as closely as possible and, a moment later, felt the light breath of a fresh breeze wafting over them. A few more steps and the shadow deepened even more. Glancing up, he saw that they had passed into an area of misty fog hanging up along the canyon rim. A second or two later he felt the first spits of rain on his neck and hands.

The breeze freshened, whistling among the high rocks, sending a light drift of pebbles down upon them.

"Stay close and watch your step," Friday instructed.

"Is this part of it?" asked Tony.

"Yes."

Without seeming to move any faster, Friday's stride came quicker. He reached out a hand to Tony, who grasped it and was almost instantly blown off his feet by a terrific gust of wind. Or at least that is what he imagined had happened. For at the same moment the wind hit him, the canyon floor offered up a change in levels—a mere half step, but enough to throw the scientist off his stride. He lost his balance and would have pitched forward onto hands and knees if not for Friday's steadying grasp.

Everything became a little confused. The hanging fog seemed to pass in front of him and Tony felt a slick of mist on his face. Then the cloud vanished and he was standing in full daylight in the desert. Thinking at first that they had merely exited the canyon, Tony looked back fully expecting to see the red rock walls behind him. What he saw instead took his breath away and set his mind reeling.

The signature sandstone stacks of Sedona were nowhere to be seen, nor any of the saguaro, yucca, or barrel cacti. Instead, he saw that they stood on a vast, empty plain, flat as a pan to the horizon, which showed an uneven band of hills in the blue distance. He stood in a shallow trench that had been carved from the loose volcanic pumice that covered the plain; this trench stretched before and behind them, straight as a surveyor's line as far as he could see.

Friday stopped walking and dropped Tony's hand. "We are here."

"Where?" asked Tony, gazing around in wonder. It was much as Cassandra had described it on the phone. "What is this place?"

25

"This is *Tsegihi*," he replied. "You would say 'the Spirit World.'"

"It may be the Spirit World, but it looks like Peru to me."

"If you say so."

Tony gazed around, feeling the sun hot on his back and head. "This is where you brought Cass—" he began, then was overwhelmed with a sudden and violent nausea that doubled him over and left him heaving into the dust.

"That happens," observed Friday.

Tony raised his head and gave his guide a dark look. "You might have warned me," he said, dabbing his mouth with a sleeve. He drew air deep into his lungs and the waves of seasickness slowly receded. He straightened once more. "What do you do here?"

Friday returned his gaze but made no attempt to answer.

"Okay. Let me ask you this, then—what did Cass do when she came here?"

"Nothing," replied Friday. "We looked at *Tsegihi*, and then I took her home."

"That's all? That's it?"

"That's it." He turned his gaze to the far mountains, drew a deep breath, exhaled, and said, "Now I take you home too."

"Not so fast, my friend. If Cass came here alone, she probably left a trace of some kind—she may still be here somewhere. We're going to look for her."

Friday made no reply, so Tony turned and surveyed the plain on which they stood. There was not another living thing in any direction as far as the eye could see. If there had been anyone, or anything, moving out on the pan, they would have seen it. Assuming Cass had arrived at roughly the same place as the two of them, what did she do next?

"Are there other lines around here?" Tony asked.

"Many."

"Do you know where they lead?"

"No. They go everywhere. It is dangerous to travel where you do not know."

Tony considered this. "If she just kept walking, would she ever reach a town or village or anything?"

Friday gave a curt shake of his head.

"Then I think it is likely she tried to get back home," Tony concluded. "Knowing her, that is what I think she would have done." He glanced around at the lines etched into the pumice gravel of the plain. "Am I right in thinking that these lines mark different spirit roads or pathways?"

Friday swept the empty plain with a stoic gaze. "Some of them."

"Since she would have no way of guessing which lines might be active pathways, the most logical thing would have been simply to retrace her steps. Am I right?"

Friday said nothing.

"Let's assume for the moment that my assessment is correct." Pointing to the trail on which they stood, he asked, "Does this road lead back to Secret Canyon?"

"No."

Tony considered this. He looked up and down the length of the shallow trench, nodding thoughtfully. "Okay. So where does it go?" he asked at last.

His reluctant guide hesitated in a moment's indecision, then confessed, "I do not know."

"Well, Friday, my friend, we are about to find out."

CHAPTER 3

In Which Cass Takes a Quantum Leap

Weary, footsore, feeling very much like an old, tread-bare tyre leaking air, Cassandra came to stand before an immense wrought-iron gate guarding the entrance to a stately house at the end of a city street. There were no streetlights, no lights from the surrounding houses—no lights at all, save the last gleam of daylight swiftly dying in the west.

Brendan's directions had been faultless; however, his description of travelling into seventeenth-century England left a lot to be desired. But then, probably nothing he could have told Cass would have done justice to what she had experienced in the last . . . how long? One day? Two? It seemed like a lifetime already.

Then again, where do you start, she wondered, *to describe a world at once so familiar and yet so strange?*

Before her stood the imposing red-brick mansion of an English aristocrat with its gabled eaves and multiple chimneys, each with a different pattern and design; the mullioned windows with tiny diamond-shaped blown-glass panes; and the ornate iron railings around the entire property perimeter with the broad-limbed plane trees forming a darkly patterned backdrop. In the road behind her, a herdsman with a willow switch led four cows down the middle of the street; a man stood on the corner ringing a bell and shouting at the top of his lungs; and women in long skirts with wicker baskets on their heads walked hand in hand, chatting blithely as they passed.

Cass took in the utterly dream-like quality of the scene with a long, slow shake of her tired head. If William Shakespeare appeared on the doorstep to greet her, it would not surprise her in the least. Certainly, the people she had met on the way and those walking about the streets appeared to be right out of a Shakespearean play. In dress and habit the people seemed like they would have been comfortably at home in the world of *Merry Wives of Windsor*. They talked like characters from Shakespeare too—which was another thing Brendan might have warned her about with a little more force: the language, unless followed with excruciating attention, was very nearly incomprehensible. She struggled through even the most obvious and simple exchanges and kept these to a minimum. *It's English, Jim*, she thought, *but not as we know it*.

This, added to all the other shocks and alarms that landing in the alien world of 1660s London had thrown at her, had worn Cassandra to a frazzled nub. She wanted nothing more than to curl up with a warm drink, rest, and regroup. Unfortunately, any such comfort would have to wait. Just now she stood on the brink of her greatest challenge thus far.

Stepping through the gate, she started up the curving walk to the front door, where she paused to gather her thoughts. Drawing a breath, she put her hand to the big brass doorknocker. "Here goes nothing," she murmured and gave the door three solid taps.

She waited. Fatigue seemed to come seeping up through the ground into her blood, sending a jumble of the day's events cascading through her mind.

The day had started well before sunrise with a speed course in ley travel conducted by Brendan Hanno—the Chief Zetetic, as she now liked to think of him—her mentor and guide in this brave new world of interdimensional exploration.

"You'll want to keep in mind a few very basic general guidelines," he had told her as they bumped along a lonely Syrian road into the arid hills north of Damascus. "The nearer one is to the beginning of a line, the closer one seems to be in relation to its origin point in time. It is well to keep that in mind, but don't trust your life on it—there are too many exceptions."

"That's another thing," said Cass, taking a big bite of the sticky sweet roll that was her breakfast. "What makes the ley lines in the first place? How are they created?"

"If we knew that," laughed Brendan, "we would probably have completed the quest years ago. The creation of the leys is one of the many splendid mysteries of our unique endeavour."

"Maybe that can be one of *your* contributions to the quest," suggested Mrs. Peelstick from the backseat. "Another sweet roll, dear? I also have some very nice pears."

"We're almost there," Brendan announced, slowing the vehicle. "We'll stop just along the road and I'll walk you to the ley. I don't think there's anyone around, but you never know."

They reached the valley and arrived at a crossroads identified by an old stone marker. There was a small farm surrounded by olive trees a few hundred metres to the west and another a few hundred metres beyond that. Otherwise, the place was deserted. Brendan stopped, pulled on the hand brake, and switched off the engine; Cass stepped out of the vehicle and into a cool, fresh morning. The sky was showing a frail pink light in the east.

Mrs. Peelstick opened the rear door and joined her in the road. "I will be praying for your safety every step of the way, Cassandra," she said. "Go with God."

Cass gave her a brief hug, made her farewell, and fell into step beside Brendan. "That marker," he said, indicating the milestone beside the road, "is Roman. If you look real hard you can still make out the distance."

"Distance to where?"

"Rome, of course," replied Brendan cheerfully. "All roads lead to Rome, you know. The ley we want is not far from here." He headed up the hill towards the rising sun. "Old Reliable, I call it."

"Because it never lets you down?" Cass, dressed in her sturdy walking shoes and long peasant skirt, blouse, and blue-checked shawl—Mrs. Peelstick's valiant attempt at approximating Ye Olde English fashion—lifted her hem and climbed the rising path, picking her way among the chunky rocks littering the ground.

"Because it is unfailingly stable—a sign that generally indicates a very old ley line. When you find a ley marked by successive epochs of human culture—standing stones, Neolithic burial mounds, sacred wells, churches, that sort of thing—all strung out across the landscape, then you can be reasonably certain that the ley is not only quite old but also very stable."

"Stable," wondered Cass. "As in . . . ?"

"As in, unlikely to pitch you into the soup."

"So the older a ley line, the more reliable it is destination-wise."

"Generally speaking. There are exceptions."

Cass shook her head. "Where would we be without exceptions?"

They walked across a scrubby wasteland of sparse grass and rocky soil of the kind that in Syria passed for lush pasture. The sky continued to grow brighter, spreading red gold along the eastern horizon. The air was fresh and cool but held a hint of latent heat; it would be hot later. But then, Cass reminded herself, by that time she would be somewhere else, and some*when* else. "So tell me about London in the seventeenth century," she said.

"Your ultimate destination is London, yes," replied Brendan, his long legs covering ground in easy strides. "From here it is a three-jump journey, but if all goes according to plan, you should be able to make it in one day, relatively speaking. You will be moving backwards in time, aiming for the year 1665—although anytime between 1663 and 1667 will probably be acceptable."

"That exact? Really?"

Brendan laughed, his voice ringing clear in the early morning air. "If only! That *would* be something." He glanced at her, enjoying her guileless reaction. "The temptation to show off for you is almost irresistible. But no, I claim no such expertise. We can be reasonably certain in this case because London at that time is the home of Sir Henry Fayth. Cosimo Livingstone is a Londoner too, as it happens. As members of the society, Sir Henry and Cosimo have travelled back and forth to enough society functions over the years to establish and document the way very well." He smiled at her. "You simply follow in their footsteps."

"Almost literally," Cass remarked.

"The notes I gave you are from the directions Cosimo Livingstone placed on file. They lead to Clarimond House—Sir Henry's home in London. Follow them to the letter and you shouldn't go too far astray." He glanced sideways at her. "I would go with you, but Society business keeps me here just now." He offered her a reassuring pat on the back. "Don't worry. By the time this is over, you'll be giving lessons in ley travel."

"Let's hope." Cass thought for a moment, then asked, "So what is the mechanism involved here? What is it that drives ley travel?"

"That is the million-dollar question," began Brendan. "The short answer is we still don't know. We have theories." He gave a small laugh. "Many good and useful theories."

"Pick one."

"Well, the best current thought is that where two different dimensions of a multidimensional universe impinge on one another, they form a line of force on the physical landscape."

"A telluric energy field," said Cass.

"You know about telluric energy—good. To us earthlings, it manifests as a straight line, but there is reason to suspect that in reality this energy field is anything *but* straight. If we had the physical apparatus to perceive this field of force in its actual multidimensional representation, I suspect it would look very different." Brendan glanced at Cass. "Ever seen the aurora borealis?"

"Only in pictures," said Cass.

"In the northern lights you have these tremendous swirls and snarls of high-energy particles whipping wildly through the upper atmosphere by a violent solar wind. The phenomenon appears to observers on the ground as an enormous shimmering curtain of ghostly light wafting gently in an unfelt breeze." He glanced at Cass, concluding, "If we could see a ley line as it really is in time and space, *that* is what I think it would look like."

"And this chaotic whiplash movement is what makes them so unpredictable, I suppose," ventured Cass. Brendan nodded approvingly. "But," she quickly countered, "we travellers do not experience anything like that when we make a leap. For me, at least, it is more like a blink of the eye—one moment you're one place, and the next moment you are someplace else with nothing in between. You don't really travel any distance at all."

"It's funny," replied Brendan, "but most people hear the term *quantum leap* and think it an enormous, superhuman jump, but actually it is nothing of the sort."

"The very opposite, in fact," said Cass. "An electron pops from one level to another in its orbit around the nucleus of an atom— simply passing from here to there instantaneously, and without traversing the incredibly miniscule space in between."

"Correct. In that analogy, *we* are the electrons. When we interact with a ley, we jump from one dimensional reality to another without traversing any distance in between—though I suspect that in space-time terms the distance actually travelled may be mind-numbingly vast indeed—whole galaxies or universes away." He was silent for a moment, then gave another laugh. "Or maybe not. We may never know." Pointing to another stone marker just ahead, he said, "There is the beginning of the ley."

Cass looked where he indicated and saw a rounded stump of

stone—like that of a broken column set on a much-eroded base. A shallow ditch stretched from the pillar stone, merely a scant indentation in the rough earth; easy to miss if one was not looking for it. Another stone stood a hundred metres or so away, and beyond that the smooth round hump of an earthen mound—a *tel*, in local parlance.

"I can see it," said Cass. They stopped at the pillar stone and looked down along the arrow-straight line of the ley. She gazed along the narrow path and gave a curt nod of determination.

"Any questions?" asked Brendan. She shook her head. "Then off you go."

"If all goes well, I'll be back before you know it." Cass started for the path. "Bye for now."

"God be with you, Cassandra," he called after her.

She gave him a wave and walked to the starting point, then paused. "Right," she said, preparing herself for the unpleasant travel-sick sensation awaiting her on the other side. That fleeting queasiness was nothing compared to the psychological dislocation involved in leaping from the 1930s to the 1660s.

What followed, although convoluted, was detailed on two hand-written cards in easy-to-follow steps that led her across two different worlds—of which she saw almost nothing—to the very outskirts of a version of London Samuel Pepys would easily recognise, if not, at this moment, actually inhabit.

Now, quivering on the point of mental and physical exhaustion, Cass waited for a heavy wrought-iron-clad door to be answered and the next challenge to begin. She knocked again and was just at the point of lowering herself onto the doorstep in utter collapse when she heard the sound of footsteps on the other side. There was the click of a latch being lifted, and the door opened.

A man in a long black coat, white shirt with a soft collar knotted in a tie, and white stockings below his short, knee-length trousers stood holding a brass lamp. "Yes?" he said dryly, gazing at Cass with the bored expression of the habitually unimpressed.

"Good evening to you, Villiers," said Cass, using the name Brendan had supplied.

The servant raised the lamp and held it closer. "I fear I am disadvantaged, Miss . . . ?"

"My name is Cassandra Clarke," she replied. "I have come a very great distance to speak with Sir Henry Fayth. Is he at home this evening?"

The valet stared at her more closely, taking in her travel-stained clothes, before answering. "His lordship is not at home," he replied at last and began closing the door. "I wish you a good night."

"Villiers?" came a voice from somewhere inside. "Is there someone? I thought I heard the door."

A moment later a figure emerged from the gloom of the interior, and Cass found herself in the presence of an almost radiantly beautiful young woman. Dressed in a long gown of glistening blue satin edged with cream-coloured lace at the throat, wrists, and hem, her long russet hair spilling abundantly over slender shoulders, she stepped into the light cast by the oil lamp, an expression of sincere interest on her lovely face.

"A beggar woman seeking Sir Henry, my lady," intoned the servant stiffly, his hand still on the door. "I have informed her that his lordship is not in residence. She is just leaving."

"To be sure," replied the young woman. Turning to Cass, she said, "It is true, my uncle is not home at present. Perhaps I may be of some small service? Is it food you want? Or work?" She smiled sweetly. "Forgive my forthrightness, I beg. I am Lady Fayth."

CHAPTER 4

In Which a Reasonable Chariness Is Overcome

The two young women stared at one another for a long moment as, slowly, the light of recognition came up in their eyes—each seeing in the other something only another ley traveller could identify. For Lady Fayth it was not the scuffed shoes and dusty clothes of the young woman on her threshold, nor her curious way of speaking the King's English—with the same clumsy intonation and construction of Kit and Wilhelmina—it was more an attitude, a quality of having experienced something, of possessing a secret. Ley travel itself seemed to impart an air or energy other sojourners could sense.

Haven knew, without being told, that the dowdy creature before her was a fellow traveller. Still, she was not ready to admit a stranger into the secret sisterhood just yet. "Pray, forgive my ill-mannered presumption," said Lady Fayth, "but in what manner are you known to my uncle?"

"I was given Sir Henry's name by a mutual friend—Mr. Brendan Hanno. Perhaps you know him?"

"I must confess that I have not had the privilege of the gentleman's acquaintance," replied Lady Fayth. "Am I to understand that this Mr. Hanno is also a friend of Sir Henry's?"

"It is my understanding that they are indeed very good friends," answered Cass, trying to adapt to a more archaic style of speech. "They are fellow members of the Zetetic Society. I am here representing that society in a matter of some importance."

"Are you indeed?" The young woman favoured Cass with a look of piercing appraisal, then, as if making up her mind to accept her visitor, she opened the door a little wider. "I am Haven Fayth, Sir Henry's niece. It has fallen to me to keep this house in my uncle's absence."

Cass, her last reserves of strength running low, swayed on her feet as Haven finished speaking.

"Oh, my dear thing!" exclaimed Haven. "You must think me a very barbarian. I can see that you have travelled a very great distance. I expect you are thoroughly spent."

Cass nodded. "You are very gracious, I'm sure. And yes, I have come a . . . an unbelievably long way."

"It is not meet that we stand here on the steps gabbling like fishwives," replied Lady Fayth lightly. "You must come in and allow me the honour of offering you succour." Turning to Villiers, who stood silently by, she commanded, "Tonight's table is to be set with an extra place, and bring wine and cheese to the library at once." Then, taking the lamp from the steward's hand, she turned to her guest. "Pray follow me, if you please, Cassandra. Rest and refreshment are at hand."

Lamp held high, Lady Fayth conducted Cass into the great house's cavernous interior and down a corridor steeped in heavy evening shadows. She opened a door and led Cass into a room lined floor to ceiling with shelves of books, pausing to light candles on two side tables. "Please be seated," she said, placing the lamp on a large desk nearby. As Cass settled gratefully into a large leather armchair beside the empty fireplace, Lady Fayth said, "I feel this room has a chill. If you will excuse me but a moment, that will soon be put right."

Haven disappeared, leaving Cass alone. She closed her eyes and luxuriated in the blessed comfort of a chair that seemed to hold her tired body in a fond embrace. Against her will, she drifted off to sleep—awaking when a teenage girl entered the room with a pan of red-hot coals and proceeded to make a fire. She closed her eyes again and dozed, rousing again to find Lady Fayth and a young man standing over her.

"It is a very pity to wake you," said Haven softly, "but there is refreshment and I think it would restore you wonderfully." Turning to the young man, she said, "Giles, would you mind?"

A young man stepped to a side table on which rested a silver tray with a decanter and crystal goblets. He poured three cups, then returned with two of them, which he offered to the ladies.

"It is my pleasure to introduce you to Giles Standfast."

The young man bowed from the waist.

"Giles, this is Cassandra Clarke, an acquaintance of Sir Henry's through a mutual friend." To Cass, she said, "Giles was coachman and body servant to Sir Henry."

"My lady," said Giles with a nod. "A nasty, grievous affair, no doubt."

"Pardon?" said Cass, looking from one to the other. "I'm not sure I understand."

"She does not know, Giles," said Haven, touching his arm as if to restrain him from saying anything more.

Giles lowered his head. "I apologise, my lady. I have spoken out of turn. I thought—" He lapsed into silence.

Haven said, "Perhaps you might explain your interest in contacting Sir Henry?"

"Your uncle and a Mr. Livingstone were expected to attend a recent meeting of the Zetetic Society. They failed to arrive and, apparently, no one has had any communication from either one of them for some time. There is concern on the part of the members that something may have happened to them."

"Yes, I see." Lady Fayth's expression grew sorrowful and her voice took on a sombre note. She paused, then drew a breath and said, "I would to heaven there were a more salubrious way to relate this . . ." She hesitated, then blurted, "It grieves me full well to say that Sir Henry is dead and Cosimo with him. Both were struck down by vile enemies while on a journey to Egypt." She dropped her head. "It was a sad and terrible end to two truly noble lives."

Though Lady Fayth was the very picture of sorrow, Cass nevertheless sensed that the young woman standing before her was being less than candid, perhaps as if she were reciting scripted lines from a play. *Shame on you, Cass,* she told herself. *Behave yourself.*

"I am sorry for your loss," replied Cass after a moment.

Haven raised her glass. "Let us drink to their memories."

Cass lifted her goblet and took a drink; the wine was very raw and sour on her tongue, but it was stimulating. The three sipped quietly for a moment and Giles passed the plate of cheese. The food and drink did revive Cass, and after a moment she felt better prepared to face whatever came next. "Would you mind very much speaking about what happened? I am certain the society will want to know whatever I can tell them."

"To be sure." Lady Fayth proceeded to give a careful yet oddly perfunctory explanation of what had transpired in Egypt: how she, Kit, and Giles had tracked Cosimo and Sir Henry to the wadi containing High Priest Anen's tomb, and how they had fought the Burley Men but were overpowered and imprisoned with Cosimo and Sir Henry, who were already quite seriously ill by that time.

"There must have been a rank miasma in the air of the tomb, and both men were mortally sickened by it. We would have caught the contagion too, if we had not been rescued in time," Haven concluded. "As Giles was present when Sir Henry met his demise, he will happily answer any further questions you might have regarding the tragic circumstances of his death." She tilted her head to one side. "Was there something else you wished to know especially?"

Cass thought for a moment, then said, "Lady Fayth, you mentioned the younger man—Cosimo Livingstone's great-grandson, Kit? But you have not said what happened to him. Perhaps Giles can tell me what became of him."

"Indeed, my lady," replied Giles. There was a slight hesitation and he glanced at Lady Fayth. Something passed between them, Cass could tell. "We were all together when we were taken captive," he said simply. "Mister Kit and I escaped to safety together."

"Is he with you now?" asked Cass. "Could I meet him?"

Again Giles glanced at Lady Fayth, who nodded, encouraging him to answer. The servant's mouth twitched into a frown. "The ones who killed Sir Henry and Cosimo found us again. They gave chase.

Lord Burleigh was mounted and had possession of a pistol." He presented a bandaged arm. "I came away wounded, but Mister Kit made good his escape."

"In the confusion, Kit was lost," Haven added, "and no one knows where he has gone—at least, his whereabouts are not known to us at this time."

Brendan and Mrs. Peelstick had warned Cass of dark forces and the mysterious enemy known as Lord Burleigh, but this was the first mention of an actual attack and violence. "This Lord Burleigh and his men—the people who chased you—are you quite certain they were the same ones who killed Sir Henry and Cosimo?"

"Aye, my lady." Giles gave a sharp nod; his voice took on a defiant tone. "They are always lurking about, waiting for opportunity to wreak havoc with anyone who gets in their way. They fear neither man nor God, and quail at nothing to work their wicked will. They did for Sir Henry and Cosimo, no mistake."

A thoughtful silence settled on the group. "What is to happen now?" asked Cass after another fortifying sip of wine.

"I suppose that is for us to decide," replied Haven. She cocked her head to one side and regarded Cass with a frank expression. "May I be so bold as to ask how you came here?" When Cass hesitated, she pounced. "It is a perfectly simple question. By what mode of transport did you effect your arrival at this house?"

"I came on foot—mostly," Cass hedged.

Haven sniffed. "And whence came you?"

"Pardon?"

"The place of your departure—from where did you come?"

"I came directly from Damascus—more or less," she said. "Where the society has its headquarters."

A subtle smile turned up the corners of Haven's lips. "How did you come to know Lord Burleigh?"

Cass frowned. "But I do not know him at all," she protested. "I have only heard the name, nothing more"—she nodded at Giles—"until just now."

"How long was your journey?"

Again Cass hesitated. Why was she being subjected to this interrogation? "Look," she said finally, "I think we both know how I came here. I travelled on what some call Ghost Roads—regions of electromagnetic power. I think you know them as ley lines. That is what Brendan called them."

Lady Fayth and Giles exchanged a glance, and Giles nodded. "She is a ley leaper," he said firmly.

"Verily," agreed Haven. To Cass she said, "Pray, forgive my crude enquiry. But for all we know, you might well be in the employ of the Black Earl and have been sent here to deceive us."

"And the Black Earl is . . . who?" wondered Cass, setting aside her glass.

"The aforementioned Lord Burleigh," answered Haven. "He is entitled the Earl of Sutherland, and his machinations know no bounds. His greed is exceeded only by his arrogance, which is great indeed. And as Giles has said, he quails at nothing to have his way—even if that means cutting the throats of anyone he perceives as a rival."

Cass accepted this and said, "Well, considering all that you have been through, I can understand your reluctance to place trust in a stranger. I will be only too glad to reassure you in any way I can." She spread her hands. "You'll have to tell me where to start."

"Your demeanour speaks for itself," said Lady Fayth. "Yet, for our present purpose, I would hear more about this society you have mentioned. Let us begin there." She glanced at Giles, who was still standing by the table. "Pray, take a seat. We may be here awhile, and I would not have you tire yourself overmuch."

"Thank you, my lady," replied the coachman. He made a slight bow as he spoke, and Cass caught a strong whiff of the class divide between them. "I will stand if it is all the same to you."

"But it is *not* the same to me," Haven countered quickly. She patted the cushion of the chair beside her. "If we are to be partners in this quest, we must not allow the differences in our station to impose unnecessary constraints. You have been wounded and require recuperation. It does no one any good to have you less than robust and full of health." She patted the cushion again. "Now come and sit. I will hear nothing more about it."

Giles gave a reluctant nod and acquiesced to his mistress's wishes. The incident left Cass in no doubt that Lady Haven Fayth was a woman very much used to having her own way, and the pretence of egalitarianism was nothing more than the assertion of privilege. When Giles was seated, she turned to Cass and smiled. "You may begin. You were going to tell us more of this society, I believe?"

"As good a place to start as any, I suppose," said Cass and explained about meeting Mrs. Peelstick and Brendan in Damascus, the Zetetic Society headquarters with its *genizah*, which she described as a library of sorts containing old books and obscure manuscripts the society deemed useful even if, as was apparently the case, only vaguely understood. She told about some of the other members she had met and offered a general explanation of the work of the society as she understood it.

Haven and Giles listened to all she had to say, nodding now and then and exchanging covert glances as they assessed what she was telling them. It was a loose and somewhat rambling recitation and included many superfluous details: descriptions of the courtyard in Damascus; Fortingall Schiehallion's odd book, *Maps of the Faerie*; the Old Straight Street market; Brendan's charming Irish accent; and Mrs. Peelstick's habit of infusing mint leaves in the tea.

Winding down at last, Cass finished with a report of the council at which the absence of Sir Henry and Cosimo was raised with some concern and it was decided that she should embark on a mission to find out what could be discovered of their disappearance.

"I suppose you could say my mission has been successful," she concluded. "I learned what I came to find out."

Lady Fayth, chin in hand, considered this, then rose abruptly. "Pray, excuse us," she said and summoned Giles to attend her. The two moved to a corner of the room where, backs turned to Cass, they held a brief private conversation that concluded with a definite nod on the part of Giles, whereupon the two returned to their places.

Haven smoothed her dress with her palms as she resumed her seat and said, "We have digested what you have told us and find the tale, like its teller, wholly creditable. In short, we are prepared to accept that you are who you say you are, and that you mean us no harm." She smiled. "You will forgive us for being chary—when dealing with the Black Earl it is better to err on the side of caution."

"I understand," replied Cass; she had felt no real anxiety over this point, but it was still nice to know that she was accepted.

"Now that you have learned what you came to find," Giles said, addressing Cass directly, "what will you do?"

"Take word back to the others, I suppose," she replied. "I know Brendan—Mr. Hanno, that is—and Mrs. Peelstick will appreciate news as soon as possible. I expect they will want to make plans of some sort."

"You might do that," suggested Haven, "or you could come with us."

Lady Fayth glanced at Giles and said, "Mr. Standfast and I have already determined to return to Prague. That is where we must raise the trail if we are to continue the quest."

"It is the last place Kit was seen," Giles expanded. "There are folk there who can perhaps help us to find him."

"Well, I don't know . . ." said Cass, her attention flagging once more. She was much too tired and hungry to be making any firm decisions. "As important as it may be to find Kit, the Zetetics are waiting for word of my mission."

"May I suggest," began Haven, rising from her chair, "that we adjourn the discussion and revisit the matter in the morning? Supper is soon ready, and after we have eaten, you may retire to your rest. We can reconsider the question when you are refreshed." She smiled warmly. "Would that be agreeable to you?"

"Most agreeable, my lady," replied Cass. Realising she had slipped into a servant's form of address, she bit her lip in embarrassment.

Haven merely accepted this appellation as her due and held out her hand to Cass. "Come, we will find some clothes for you which will be more suitable. No doubt you will want to bathe and refresh yourself after your long journey today."

"Thank you," said Cass, accepting her hand, a little uncertain of the protocol. "I would like that, yes."

Haven patted her hand and led her from the room. "Ley leaping is always such an adventure, do you not find it so?"

"I am not very experienced," Cass confessed. "I fell into it by accident . . . gosh—only a few days ago, I guess. But it feels like years."

"Oh, indubitably. Time ceases to run a normal course for ley travellers," replied Haven. "It can become monumentally confusing. Is that not so, Giles?"

"Very true, my lady," he said. Taking up the candle tree from the table, he closed the door to the study and followed the women into the corridor, adding to himself, "It is nothing if not confusing."

CHAPTER 5

In Which Kit Returns to the Scene of the Crime

On the seventh step Kit felt the ground give way beneath his feet. Instinctively his toes reached for another foothold, stretched, and found purchase. In the same moment, a stiff breeze kicked up grit from the path. He shut his eyes, and when he opened them again he was standing in the middle of an arrow-straight, tree-lined parting between two fields—the same tree-lined path to which he had been directed by Wilhelmina on the night of his slender escape from Burleigh.

"We're back," he said, swivelling around to find Mina and Brother Lazarus. "Everybody okay?"

"Never better," answered Wilhelmina, brushing bits of leaf from her hair. Brother Lazarus, directly behind her, patted dust from his priestly robes; he smiled and said, *"Es war gut Sprung."*

"Jawohl!" Mina agreed. She gazed around, orienting herself to the landscape. "The river road is behind us. It's early yet, so we should be

able to hitch a ride from one of the farmers heading into the city." She started down the tunnel-like groove of the tree-lined trail. "I wonder what day it is."

"Or what year, more like."

"In my experience," Mina told him, "as long as I make the jump on the seventh step from the marker stone on the Big Valley ley, I'm rarely more than a day or two out. You'd never believe how long it took me to learn that."

"Does that concept work everywhere?"

"Mmm." She thought. "I believe so." Turning to Brother Lazarus behind them, she rattled off a long sentence in German and the two held a brief conversation, punctuated by complicated hand gestures on the part of Brother Lazarus, who occasionally lapsed into Italian.

"We'll have to do something about that," mused Kit as he listened to their exchange—of which he grasped only a fleeting word or two. "So what'd he say?" he asked as Mina turned back.

"He says that it appears to be possible in a very general sense for a traveller to adjust his arrival by the method I've just explained— allowing for such variables as stride length, relative speed of motion, and so forth. However, it would be unwise to mistake what is possible for what is likely."

"Right." Kit nodded thoughtfully. "Rule of thumb, not universal law. I'll try to keep that in mind."

Shouldering their packs, the three travellers proceeded down the trail and came in sight of the road and, glimmering in the near distance, the silvered glint of the Moldau River. Upon reaching the road, they stepped out of the shaded path and into the sun-warmed air of a fine autumnal afternoon. On the road ahead they saw a hay wain heading for the city.

"There's our ride," cried Mina, starting after the horse-drawn wagon. "I think I know this farmer; he'll take us to my front door."

"Wow, Mina—you've got this whole place sewn up."

She was already away. "Hurry!"

Wilhelmina streaked off to catch the wagon, leaving Kit and Brother Lazarus to scramble in her wake. *"Guten Tag!"* she called. *"Hallo! Guten Tag!"*

The driver looked back and the wagon slowed to a stop. "We're in luck," she called as the two men joined her. "He's on his way to the hostler in the city. Here, help a lady up."

A few moments later all three were seated on bundles of straw and listening to the slow *clop, clop, clop* of the horses as the wagon rumbled along, past newly harvested fields on one side and, on the other, the slow river snaking its smooth way along banks of tall grass gone to seed. While the other two chatted in German with the farmer, Kit turned his attention to the countryside. Something about the air, or light, or the familiar Olde World feel of the place induced in Kit a reverie, and he soon found himself brooding over the events of his slender escape from Burleigh on the night Giles was shot. It was on this same road—perhaps near this very spot, the scene of the crime, as it were—that it had happened. They were on foot and Burleigh was on horseback; moreover, the earl had a gun. Unable to outrun their mounted pursuer, they had tried to unhorse Burleigh and Giles had taken a bullet in the arm, allowing Kit to escape in the confusion.

Kit had not spent any substantial amount of time thinking about that night; no doubt getting lost in the Stone Age and living amongst River City Clan had presented him with such a host of new and alarming dangers that Burleigh and his dire schemes shrivelled into insignificance by comparison. But the ruthless Lord Burleigh and his thugs occupied Kit's thoughts now, and the notion that they might still be lurking down some dark alley waiting to pounce filled him with renewed dread. What did they want with him, anyway? More to the point, why did they want him dead? Was it simply to keep him out of the way? Or was there something more to it?

Contemplating these things cast Kit into a melancholy mood that lasted until he saw the city walls rising in the distance. As soon as the wagon passed through the city gates, however, his mind turned to the special supper Wilhelmina had promised them. Thinking about a tasty schnitzel and cool flagon of foamy beer made his mouth water and banished all thoughts of Burley Men and midnight chases.

The wagon trundled up the narrow rising street from the gate to the market square in the old city. There Wilhelmina bade the driver to pause while they grabbed their rucksacks and disembarked; she told him to come to the Grand Imperial Kaffeehaus when he finished his business and there would be a nice hot cup of coffee and fresh strudel waiting for him.

"*Danke!*" called the farmer and snapped the reins to urge his team on.

Strolling across the square towards the coffeehouse, Kit wondered, "How many days do you imagine have passed since you were last here?" Recalling their previous discussion, he added, "Or maybe I should ask if you have left yet?"

Wilhelmina laughed. "That's never happened in Prague. Not yet. But if I had to guess, I'd say it's two or three days since I left. Rarely more than four. I was gone for a week once, but that was a mistake." She lifted one shoulder in a light shrug. "We'll find out soon enough."

Hurrying to the door of the Grand Imperial, Mina darted inside.

Kit and Brother Lazarus entered behind her to find a room full of patrons at their morning cups and green-and-white-liveried servants ferrying pots of coffee and plates of pastries to the tables in an atmosphere redolent of fresh-baked bread and pleasant conversation. The mood was cheery and light, and Kit was again reminded what a success Wilhelmina and Engelbert had made of the place.

Mina stood in the entryway, surveying the scene with obvious delight. "Make yourselves at home," she told them, shedding her pack and heading directly for the kitchen. "Etzel!" she called. *"Ich bin zurück, mein Schatz!"*

As she reached the counter, the big man himself stepped from the kitchen, a floppy green hat covering his curly hair, his round face red from the oven. *"Liebling!"* he cried, throwing his arms wide. Mina's slender form disappeared in his bear-like embrace, and she was lifted bodily from the floor and whisked out of sight into the kitchen.

"I guess he's glad to see her," mused Kit. He and Brother Lazarus exchanged a knowing glance and then took in the room. Their arrival had been noticed by the shop customers, some of whom smiled and nodded in their direction. Kit wondered at this reception until, glancing down, he realised that what the diners saw was a pair of unfamiliar priests in dark clerical robes and backpacks. Kit nudged Brother Lazarus, who raised his hand in a vague benediction, and the customers returned to their chat and coffee.

Mina reappeared with Etzel in tow. *"Engelbert, dies ist mein Freund, Giambattista Becarria."*

Etzel swiped the shapeless hat from his head and gave the priest a tidy bow; Brother Lazarus returned the bow, then shook the baker's hand.

Turning to Kit, she said, "Kit, I'm sure you remember Engelbert."

"Of course." Kit, in turn, stuck out his hand. "*Hallo*, Engelbert. Good to see you again."

"*Hallo, Herr Livingstone! Ja, es ist gut Sie zu sehen!*" He offered Kit an affectionate pat on the shoulder. The big baker's hand was dry-powdered with flour and left a large handprint on Kit's black robe.

"First things first," said Mina, becoming crisply officious. "You two can have the spare room upstairs. The beds are good and there's a chest where you can stow your bits. I'll tell one of the maids to bring some more blankets," she said, repeating it in German for Brother Lazarus. "Go on up now and make yourselves comfortable. I'll have some hot water brought so you can wash and make yourselves presentable—because I'm taking us all out for dinner tonight to celebrate our safe return." She saw the fishy expression on Kit's face and said, "What?"

"These clothes——" he began. "Do you think I could get something a little less . . . *religious*?"

"Tired of the priesthood already?"

"Please," Kit insisted. "Anything will do."

"Okay, I'll send one of the lads out to find something more . . . *you*." Taking Engelbert by the arm, she led him away; switching smoothly to German, she said, "Come along, Etzel. I want to hear what's been happening around here while I was gone. Tell me everything."

"Thanks, I'll owe you one," called Kit as they disappeared back into the kitchen. "See you later, Engelbert."

He turned his gaze back to the room and tables of contented customers, his nostrils filled with the fresh-pastry smell of the bakery. "This way, Brother Lazarus," he said, indicating the stairway at the back of the room. "It may not be the Ritz, but the food is good and you get a genuine feather bed."

CHAPTER 6

In Which Vows Easily Made Are Easily Broken

The next morning Kit awoke vowing he would never eat again, a heartfelt resolution that lasted until—washed and dressed in the new, very baggy trousers and fine linen shirt that now formed his wardrobe—he wandered down into Etzel's kitchen, where a fresh batch of honey-and-walnut rolls was just coming out of the oven. The divine aroma overthrew his resolve and he succumbed without a fight, drawing up a chair to the worktable as the big baker, beaming encouragement, placed a fresh hot roll on a clean plate before him.

"Etzel, you are a genius," Kit enthused around a mouthful of the meltingly toothsome pastry. "A true artist."

"*Es ist gut?*" wondered Etzel, watching Kit's reaction.

"*Ja! Sehr gut!*" Kit replied, virtually exhausting his small store of German vocabulary. The baker returned to his oven, humming happily.

The night before, Kit had been equally impressed with the schnitzel served up at the best chophouse in the city. Wilhelmina had arranged for her business partner, Herr Jakub Arnostovi, to take them to Saint Hubertus' Hall, Prague's most fashionable dinner club—a request the astute man of business was only too happy to oblige. There, in a valiant attempt to match the seasoned trencherman Engelbert bite for bite, Kit outdid himself, downing a mound of coleslaw and sauerkraut while demolishing a lightly dusted, seasoned, and fried slice of veal that not only covered the plate but lopped over the edges—and this while guzzling a heady *Dunkelweissbier* from a seemingly bottomless jar. Hence his short-lived resolution upon rising the next morning.

As Kit was savouring his sweet roll and a hot cup of coffee, Wilhelmina came breezing in. "Good afternoon," she said, pausing to cast a critical eye over him. "Are you among the living at last?"

"Hi, yourself," replied Kit. "Is it late? What time is it?"

"Doesn't matter," she said. "How's the pastry?"

"Divine. Etzel is an angel in a baker's hat." Kit took a sip of coffee. "Am I the only slugabed? I haven't seen Brother Lazarus—is he around?"

"Been and gone," Mina told him, swirling coffee in a small pewter pot before pouring it through a strainer into one of the Grand Imperial's signature cups. Raising the cup, she inhaled and then took a sip—much as a wine steward sampling a newly opened bottle. "He said he had errands."

"Oh?" Kit forked in another mouthful of pastry and chewed thoughtfully, wondering what errands the priest could possibly have. "You've known him a long time, right?"

"Long enough to know he can be trusted to the ends of the earth and back—if that's what you mean. Don't worry, he'll return when he's finished, whatever he's doing."

In fact, Brother Lazarus was gone three days, returning on the morning of the fourth so changed that Kit hardly recognised him as the avuncular priest he had come to know. Gone were the ankle-length, heavy cassock and knotted cincture; in their place was a plain, well-cut black suit, worn with a black shirt and white priest's collar; the sturdy sandals had been replaced with beautifully polished black brogues. His hair was cut very short, his beard trimmed to a stylish point, and his old steel-rimmed glasses had been exchanged for new ones of similar design, but in gold. A sleek leather satchel on a thin strap and an ebony walking stick with a silver top completed the ensemble.

"*Buongiorno! Buongiorno*, everyone!" he called as he strode into the dining room of the Grand Imperial Kaffeehaus. He stood for a moment, searching among the tables.

Kit, who was idling over a second cup of coffee while waiting for Wilhelmina to finish her duties so they could sit down together and discuss what to do about the missing priest, heard the familiar voice and glanced up. "What the . . . ? Brother Lazarus?" He stood abruptly, almost knocking over his chair.

The nattily dressed priest made directly to the table nearest the kitchen where Kit was seated. "My errands are completed," Brother Lazarus announced, "and I have returned—refreshed, renewed, and ready."

Mina emerged from the kitchen just then, saw him, and ran to greet him. "I was beginning to worry——" She stopped suddenly, taking in his dramatically altered appearance. "Look at you! What on earth have you been up to?"

"Ah, *Signora* Mina." He gave her a bow, kissed her hand, then held it while he spoke. "I have had the most wonderful time. I have been to Rome and enrolled in a language school."

"And learned English, I see."

"*Certamente,*" he said. "The Jesuit Language School is second to none. I have a facility with languages, as you know." His smile grew wide with pleasure. "I was a star pupil."

"You don't say." Mina shook her head. "You've also been to see a tailor."

"A small indulgence." He turned in a slow circle. "You like it?"

"Very smart," she replied approvingly. "Dashing, even."

"Excellent. I am content."

"You did all this in three days?" wondered Kit. "I *am* impressed."

"No, no, Mister Kit," offered the priest with a cautionary wag of his finger. "Three days of your time in this place, perhaps——but almost four years for me."

"Of course," mused Kit, appreciating the audacity and acumen displayed in such purposeful manipulation of ley travel. As Mina had demonstrated, by careful calibration of the jumping-off point, a traveller could return within a few days of leaving, no matter how long he or she had been away. *So this*, he thought, *is where Mina learned it.*

"If we are going to be working together," the priest continued, "it only makes sense that we should be able to speak to one another in a common tongue. It was most logical that I should learn English in the modern idiom. We have much work before us."

"Are you hungry?" asked Mina.

"Famished!"

"Come, sit down. I will have some food brought and you can tell us all about it." She hurried off to the kitchen.

"Such a delightful lady, no?" said Brother Lazarus, watching her bustle away.

"You're not so bad yourself," said Kit. He led the way to the table and resumed his seat. "I can't believe you did all this. I think I may have underestimated you, Brother Lazarus."

"Please, call me Gianni," replied the priest. "From now on, only Gianni."

"New clothes, new language, new name," observed Kit. "That makes sense, I guess."

Presently Wilhelmina returned, followed by a green-liveried serving girl with a tray of coffee, cups, and a plate of little sausage-and-cheese sandwiches. "Tuck into these," she said, taking her place. "I am thinking of offering savouries in the afternoons. Have some and tell me what you think." She passed around the plates while the serving girl poured coffee. "*Vielen Dank*, Margareta," she said, dismissing the girl to her duties. "Now then, Brother Lazarus, I want to hear all about your adventures in Rome."

"It is Gianni now," Kit told her.

"Is it? You don't say."

"Please, it was my mother's pet name for me," the priest explained with a smile. "It is what my family and friends called me when I was a boy."

"Gianni it is," Mina agreed. "I like it, but why the change? Why now?"

The priest waved a hand airily. "Brother Lazarus had grown old and set in his ways. He had served his useful purpose and it was time to give him a well-deserved rest." Gianni paused, becoming thoughtful. "Indeed, you dear people have rekindled my sense of adventure. You have renewed in me my vocation."

"As a priest?" mused Kit, wondering how they had managed to do that.

"I have always been a priest, and a priest I will always be—that is my calling. But my vocation is to pursue knowledge of what some have quaintly called the hidden mechanisms of the universe. This, I believe, has been ordained by God. I have been hiding away on my mountaintop, and while it has been a time of fruitful enterprise, the world has turned. I was a man asleep, but I have awakened—and not a moment too soon."

"Gianni, old son, you are one amazing chap," Kit told him.

"No, my friend," the priest countered, growing suddenly serious, "I am merely one to whom much has been given. See here, we have important work to do and nothing must be allowed to impede us. We must by all means return to the Spirit Well. I cannot say why at this moment, but this, I feel, is of utmost importance."

"Hear! Hear!" Kit thumped the table with his hand. "Let's do it. First, we have to find a way back to the Bone House."

"Maybe easier said than done," Mina pointed out. "There is that giant yew tree to get 'round, you know."

"Where there is a will, *signorina*, there is a way—this I know." Gianni raised his coffee cup in triumph. "Bless you, dear friends, it has been a long time since I felt such excitement."

"Wait until you see the Spirit Well," Kit told him. "*Then* you'll have something to get excited about."

"Okay," said Wilhelmina, "walk us through that. I want to understand it better."

"Well, first off, I think we have to find a way to get back to the time when River City Clan occupied the valley *before* the yew tree was there. That would make everything a whole lot simpler," Kit suggested. "The ley line leading to the great gorge . . . there's something fishy about it, and that's a fact."

"I never had any trouble with it," Mina pointed out.

"Maybe, but I couldn't get it to work at all. I never got so much as a quiver of static electricity from it in all the time I was there." He sipped his coffee thoughtfully. "I had no difficulty getting to the valley—but once there, I just couldn't get back. Until I stumbled over that ley line inside the cave, I was pretty much stuck in the Stone Age."

"Ah, my friends!" cried Gianni. "Speaking of the cave—I am reminded that I took photographs when we were there, *si?*" Reaching for his satchel, he put it on the table and, opening the flap, produced an ordinary manila envelope from which he withdrew a number of glossy black-and-white photos. "While in Rome I took the opportunity to have the film developed." He began arranging the photos on the table. "These are the photographs I took inside the cave. As you see, the images are crisp and clear—very good representations, if I do say this myself."

"It worked! Amazing," remarked Kit, leaning over the array of photos. In black-and-white, and flattened by the photographic process, the painted symbols took on a finer definition and contrast than could ever have been perceived in the dim light of a Stone Age lamp. "These are fantastic. You can see every little dot and squiggle."

"Hold that thought," said Wilhelmina, rising and hurrying from the room. She returned a few minutes later with a flat, linen-wrapped package bound with a scarlet ribbon. "Let's compare, shall we?" She handed the parcel to Gianni and said, "Be my guest."

Placing the package on the table, he pulled on the strip of cloth that served as a ribbon to close the bundle and then carefully, fold by fold, unwrapped the object within to reveal a papery scrap of parchment so thin as to be almost translucent. The smooth surface of the parchment was embossed with a spray of bright blue pictograms—squiggles, lines, spirals, and dots—each about the size of an egg or walnut.

"Madre di Dio!" cried Gianni, rising to his feet so fast his chair rocked backwards. Leaning forward on his hands, he stared at the ragged portion of the Skin Map before him. He snatched up a photograph and held it against the original, discarded it, and picked up another and another in swift succession—matching each to the parchment before setting it aside. With the fourth photo he stopped. *"Voilà!"*

Kit and Mina drew close to examine the match. "Spectacular," Kit said, his voice hushed as if in the presence of a great mystery. "They're the same—exactly the same."

It was true. Not only were the symbols from the walls of the cave the identical style and description, but, as rendered in the photos, they were the same size in relation to each other. Many of them appeared to be an exact match down to the precise sworl, zigzag, squiggle, and dot.

"This is significant," concluded Wilhelmina. "Whoever made those marks in the cave must have seen the original and copied them exactly."

"We must also consider the possibility," suggested Gianni, "that both sets of symbols were made by the same hand—so to speak."

"Arthur Flinders-Petrie, you mean." Kit regarded the Skin Map and then the photos. The correspondent similarities between the two were staggering. "You are suggesting he was there?"

"How else?"

"I've got an idea," said Kit. "Let's check them against the ones in Sir Henry's green book. It's up in the chest—I'll go get it."

He disappeared up the stairs and came running back a few moments later with the small, handwritten book bound in green leather. The slender volume contained various jots and musings of its owner, Sir Henry Fayth, on the nature and meaning of ley travel. Most of what was written was opaque philosophy to Kit, but in the margins and on a few random pages, Sir Henry had drawn diagrams and symbols, meaningless to Kit until he saw the Skin Map.

He flipped through the book to a certain page, then put the book flat on the table for the others to see. The tiny diagram Sir Henry had drawn in sepia ink was very like one of the symbols in the photographs. "Almost, but not quite," said Kit.

They tried a few more, but found no direct match among the few scattered marks Sir Henry had recorded. "Maybe the marks in the book relate to a different portion of the map," suggested Wilhelmina. "One that we haven't seen yet."

"Or perhaps," suggested Gianni, "they serve some other purpose. We shall put our minds to work on this."

"Well, however those marks came to be painted in that cave, our man Flinders-Petrie was there," declared Mina. "I'd bet the store on it. Whether he painted them himself or not, he was in that valley among those people."

"May I propose an experiment?" said Gianni. "It is that inasmuch as is possible we re-create the conditions of that first ley journey—retrace your route step for step as precisely as we can. Perhaps this will give us insight into what happened the first time."

"What if the same thing happens again and we can't get back?" wondered Kit.

"Then we can use the ley inside the cave," replied Mina. "That one that leads to Spain, right?" She spread her hands on the tabletop. "Whatever else happens, we can always get back to the abbey. What do you say?"

It took Kit all of three seconds to pass judgement on the plan. "Fantastic," he agreed. "When do we leave?"

They fell to discussing preparations for a return trip to the Stone Age—what they would bring and what to expect when they got there. Kit was a fair way into describing life with River City Clan when he noticed Wilhelmina had stopped listening. "Am I boring you with this?" he asked.

"Hmm?"

"You're miles away. What's wrong?"

"Oh, nothing, really. I just realised we're proposing to do all this without our shadow lamps. I think that's a problem."

"Not a huge problem." Kit glanced from her to Gianni and back. "Is it? I mean, we know the locations of all the relevant ley lines. We'll be fine."

"Sure, what could possibly go wrong?" She flashed him a sarcastic smile.

"We'll be fine," Kit insisted. "And another thing—why do you call them shadow lamps anyway?"

"Because of the *shadow*. Why else?"

"Not following you . . . What shadow?"

"The new model ley lamp—the upgraded one I was using—has a few significant improvements, along with some slight differences," Mina explained. "For one, there is a distinct dimming of the surrounding light when you interact with a ley line. Just before you make the leap, everything goes a little dark—like when the sun goes behind a cloud or when you step into a shady place. Everything gets all shadowy."

"And then?"

"Then it brightens up again and—*voilà!* You're there." Wilhelmina's smooth brow furrowed as her eyebrows knit together in a look of concern. "I hate to say it, but I don't think we should make another assault on the Stone Age or the Spirit Well without a lamp to guide us."

"You really think it's that important?"

She nodded and Gianni spoke up. "I will trust Signorina Wilhelmina's heart in this. Obtaining a replacement will delay our journey only a little, and it may save us much difficulty in the end."

Now it was Kit's turn to frown.

"It would be better to have them and not need them, rather than the other way 'round," Mina pointed out. "Gianni's right, it will only delay things a little while, and it could make the difference between success and disaster."

"All right," conceded Kit. The urge to return to his River City friends was so strong he could feel it like a blade between his ribs. But clear-headed, ever-practical Mina was right: they were about to venture into the unknown and would likely need all the help they could get. "It's a fair point. We don't want to go charging off half-cocked. Do whatever you have to do to get us a replacement shadow lamp. But do it quick, okay?"

"We'll be on our way before you know it," Wilhelmina told him. "I'll get on to Gustavus up at the palace and tell him we want to see him right away."

"And what are we supposed to do in the meantime?"

"Relax," Mina advised. "Rest up for the adventure ahead and eat plenty of Etzel's extraordinary strudel."

"Now that," said Kit, cheering slightly, "I can live with."

CHAPTER 7

In Which Official Doors Swing Wide

There were nine of them: each one a criminal condemned to the hulks or destined for transportation to Van Deimen's Land. In the words of the 1776 Criminal Prosecution Act, these prisoners were the more "atrocious and daring offenders" and so were to be subjected to a more "severe and effectual punishment" than otherwise afforded by His Majesty's legal system. Whether Tasmania-bound or relegated to a mouldering prison hulk, these nine desperados were going to be spending a lot of time in the belly of a filthy, stinking ship.

Burleigh had for several months availed himself of the court records known as *The Proceedings of the Old Bailey*, searching for just those cases that might provide him with suitable candidates. Once he found a likely suspect, he studied the individual case, ever narrowing his search from scores to a handful, then winnowing that lot further until he had just nine. These men he wanted to interview in person.

Extraordinary though the arrangement may have been, and it was that if nothing else, it nevertheless took surprisingly little effort to effect, requiring only the liberal application of spendable money. Wealth in the form of silver, gold, diamonds, or any other convertible commodity was something Burleigh now possessed in virtually unlimited supply. It never ceased to impress the self-made earl how even the most "impossible" things could so easily be accomplished with a little common bribery. The more generous the contribution to the unofficial coffers, the wider official doors swung open. And where the prison system was concerned, its agents and employees seemed to regard under-the-table payments as a regular, expected, and necessary component of their meagre wages.

In his pursuit of a few useful men, his lordship was given to reflect on how very thin was the line separating the gaoler from the gaoled: in many cases, that stripe was so slender as to be well nigh invisible. Save for the fact that one fellow stood in chains, the end of which the other fellow held in his fist, a casual observer would have been hard-pressed to tell the difference. With a regularity that was both remarkable and depressing, Burleigh noted that the wretch being packed off to an Australian penal colony had been convicted of a crime far less serious than the official accepting the bribe.

Depressing, too, was the fact that the men he read about in the Old Bailey *Proceedings* were from precisely the same class and background as himself—a few from the very same slum neighbourhood in London—and were inevitably hobbled by the same lack of education, skills, social connections, or reasonable prospects. In reading about these men and their crimes, he could have been reading about himself. If not for Granville Gower, Earl of Sutherland, young Archie Burley would have been one of the miserable multitude with a one-way ticket to a short life of brute labour Down Under.

Still, the men Burleigh was interested in were neither saints nor angels unaware. He was not interested in petty serial offenders or poor unlucky mugs who, for lack of better police work or proper legal representation, might have walked free; or any whose crimes might well have been mitigated by circumstance if the facts of the case had been allowed full rein. None of these was suitable for his specific needs. As the earl pored over issue after issue of the Old Bailey's broadsheet, he scanned for a rare class of individual: genuine brigands. His lordship wanted bona fide malefactors and miscreants, authentic outlaws, dyed-in-the-wool, unapologetic troublemakers of a high order. Only these, he reckoned, could he trust with the charge he intended to place upon them.

He strode through one of the lower corridors of the Justice House where prisoners were confined, awaiting the final resolution of their individual cases. Those who saw him might easily have taken Burleigh for the Prince of Darkness or one of his senior assistants—dressed all in black with a black riding cape lined with crimson satin, tall black boots, and a black felt slouch hat pulled low over his long face; his beard short and pointed as a poker, his dark eyes hidden in shadow—he did at least look the part as he glided along the deserted byways of the prison. In the pocket of his coat, his lordship carried his carefully prepared papers, one for each of the men he had selected as worthy of further consideration. Each detainee in residence had been sentenced and every last one of them knew what fate awaited him; none were happy men and none had reason to hope for anything good. Thus a pervading atmosphere of gloom and despair hung as a stagnant cloud in the darkened corridors through which Lord Burleigh, a lavender-scented handkerchief pressed to his nose, was led by a warden with a lantern in his hand.

"Do you have the list of names I sent you?" asked Burleigh, his voice pinging along the steel doors lining the corridor.

"Aye, sir," mumbled Warden Jacks, selecting a key from the large ring in his hand. "I do have it."

"Were you able to get all of them?"

"All saving one, sir. And he won't be missed, if you pardon my sayin' so. Won't be missed by a mile."

"Which one?"

"Burdock," replied the warden. "Was found dead with a shiv in his neck this mornin', so he's been scratched from yer list."

"Unlucky fellow," replied Burleigh. "Oh well—one down, eight to go."

The warden turned the key in the lock and opened the door. "A table and two chairs—as ordered, sir," he said. "I'll leave you to settle while I fetch the first one in. Anyone particular you'd like to start with?"

"Just bring them as they come to hand, Warden," replied Burleigh, moving into the cell.

"As you will, sir."

Burleigh took the chair behind the table where a pair of lighted candles burned in cheap tin holders. The air in the cell was rancid and close. Removing his gloves and folding his handkerchief, he put them to one side and withdrew the sheaf of papers from his coat pocket, placed them neatly on the table before him, then folded his hands to wait. Presently he heard the patter of footsteps outside and the door opened once more. Warden Jacks and the first prisoner appeared.

"Sit there and don't you twitch a muscle," cautioned Jacks. "I have you in my eye."

The prisoner took his seat and regarded Burleigh with the wary expression of a man who could not decide whether the prospect before him augured good or ill.

"Name?" said Burleigh.

"Thompson," replied the man. "Thomas Thompson."

Burleigh searched through his papers and withdrew a single sheet, holding it to the candlelight. "Murder—is that right, Thompson?"

"It's a lie. I never killed nobody. I wasn't even in t'pub at the time."

"Is that right?" That mitigating ambiguity was probably why Thompson was not destined for the gallows. Burleigh raised his eyes and gazed at the prisoner across the table, his angular face keen in the candlelight. "Tell me why I should believe you."

"I've got a wife and three littl'uns, see? I'm their only support. I go to prison and they all starve. They're on the street already. I don't rightly know where they are."

Burleigh glanced at the warden, who was shaking his head.

"Don't listen to *him*," whined Thompson. "He don't know nuffin' an' that's a fact." He leaned forward, raising manacled hands. "You gotta help me, mate. I got duties an' obligations, see? I gotta get outa' here. I gotta help me family."

Burleigh nodded, glanced at the page one more time, then held it to the candle flame. "I'm finished with this one," he told the warden as the paper caught fire. "Bring in the next." He dropped the flaming page to the floor.

"Okay, you," said Jacks, putting a hand to the convict's collar. "Out."

Thompson was led away, still protesting his innocence. His voice could be heard ringing down the hallway; the pleading was silenced by the slam of a door, and a few moments later the warden appeared with another prisoner. This candidate was dark and slender, and much younger than Burleigh had expected. "Name?" he asked.

"Marcus Taverner," replied the man in a clear, forthright voice.

"Why were you convicted?" Burleigh shuffled through his papers once more and brought out a single sheet.

"Robbery with grievous assault."

"Did you do it?"

"I did."

"Why?"

"Cove owed me money for a job well done and refused to pay up."

"So you took it."

"Oh, I took it, boss. For a fact I did—and gave him something to think about besides." A slight smile touched the young convict's lips. "Call it interest on my investment."

"Where are they sending you?"

"Ganymede," replied Taverner.

"Pardon?" Burleigh glanced up in surprise. "Did you say *Ganymede?*"

"The HMS *Ganymede*," explained Warden Jacks. "A seventy-four-gun frigate captured from the Frenchies, sir. Now a prison hulk anchored in Chatham Sound."

"What do you think about your sentence, Taverner?" asked Burleigh, turning once more to the prisoner before him.

"Not much." He shrugged. "Reckon I'll weather the storm right enough."

Burleigh made a mark on the page with a stub of pencil, and without looking up said, "That will be all. Bring in the next one."

The warden took the prisoner away, returning with another man in manacles a minute or so later. This one, like the others, was dismissed after a few questions, and a fourth criminal took his place, followed in quick succession by numbers five through eight—each in turn questioned by Burleigh, who made slight notations on the page before him.

"That's the lot, sir," announced Warden Jacks after removing the eighth prisoner. "Any you want to see again?"

"That won't be necessary, Warden, thank you." Burleigh took the last page, creased it, and wrote something while the official waited. "These are the men I've chosen. They are to be transferred to the prison ship HMS *Discovery*."

Jacks looked at the paper, holding it close to his face. "The *Discovery* is at Deptford, sir."

"That is true, Warden. How very astute." Burleigh pushed back his chair and stood. "They are to be transferred tonight."

"But—see here, sir—"

Burleigh stuffed the sheaf of papers into his coat pocket and stepped around the table. "Is there some problem, Warden? Or—could it be that the money you expect to receive should be given to someone else?"

"That's not much time, sir—if you don't mind my saying so."

"No, Warden Jacks, it is not much time. But you are a clever and resourceful fellow. I have no doubt you will find the time to make the necessary arrangements." He tapped the paper in the warden's hand. "They must be aboard no later than midnight tonight."

"If it is all the same to you, sir, what difference does—"

"It most assuredly is *not* all the same to me, Warden. You will abide by the terms of our agreement, or I will find someone prepared to do so without question."

"Beg pardon, sir. The prisoners will be there."

Burleigh departed Justice House, rejoined his coach, and ordered the driver to make his way down to the Isle of Dogs in the docklands. The coach rumbled down streets of increasing dereliction, each one grimmer and dirtier than the one before, until arriving at the Millwall Docks where the driver was directed to a pub called the Black Spot. Burleigh disembarked, saying, "Have the horse fed and watered, and get something for yourself." He passed the driver a stack of silver shillings. "Then come back here and wait. I do not know how long I shall be."

In fact, it was still early afternoon when the man Burleigh had come to meet entered the Black Spot. The clock in the church at Chapel House had just gone three, and the fellow, pausing on the threshold to allow his eyes to adjust to the low, fuggy light inside the tavern, was immediately spotted by Burleigh. A serving boy was dispatched to fetch the sailor to the alcove where his lordship had taken up residence. Burleigh thanked the lad and ordered beer and food to be brought.

"Sit down, please, Pilot Suggs. I trust you have been able to secure a suitable vessel for our use?"

"Not one to beat about the bushes, are we, sir?" observed the seaman. "Very well." He glanced around the near-empty room as if expecting to be overheard, then said, "In answer to your question"— he looked around again—"a dog could die of thirst in this place."

"I have ordered a jug of their best and some food for you," replied Burleigh, waving aside the man's impertinence. "It will arrive shortly. You were saying?"

"Yes, sir. I have secured a craft that answers right well to your particular requirements. She's a single-masted river runner, going by name o' *Rose of Shar*—"

"Do not trouble me with irrelevant details, Pilot," Burleigh interrupted. "If you are happy that you have met the standard to which I shall hold you, then that is the end of it."

The seadog's eyes narrowed and he sniffed loudly. "I was just in the way of making polite conversation—begging your pardon."

The boy arrived with a plate of bread and sausages; on his heels came the landlord bearing a foaming flagon and two jars. Burleigh thanked the publican and dismissed him with a few pennies. When the two were alone again, he said, "I have given my crew instructions that we are to weigh anchor no later than midnight." He pushed the plate of food nearer the pilot, who helped himself. "Are we in agreement?"

"Tide flow." Suggs nodded. "As agreed." He took a big bite out of a sausage and chewed thoughtfully, then washed it down with ale. "And I am to be paid in coin—as agreed?"

"To be sure." Burleigh took a long drink and then reached into an inner coat pocket. He brought out a small leather bag and hefted it in his hand as if weighing its contents, or trying to decide what to do with it. In the end, he tossed it to the seaman. "There is your payment in ready silver, and in advance."

Suggs eyed the money bag but made no move to pick it up. "What is to stop me just taking the money and leaving you dry-docked?"

This brought a smile to Burleigh's lips. "Not one to beat about the bush, pilot?"

Suggs sniffed again and took another bite of sausage.

"I'll tell you *why* then, since you ask," Burleigh said, taking another drink. "Fulfill the rest of the bargain and I will give you twice what is in that bag when I accept delivery." He nodded as the river pilot scooped the silver off the table. "Call it a bonus for a job well done. You can divide it with your men however you will."

"I'll be there before midnight—providing your bluebottles show with the cargo."

"That goes without saying." Burleigh slid from his bench in the snug and stood. "I am satisfied that we are in accord. I will leave you to your dinner. I shall be aboard the *Percheron* from nightfall. Do not keep me waiting any longer than I must."

"Never fear, sir," replied a happy seadog. "You can count on Smollet Suggs."

PART TWO

Many Unhappy Returns

CHAPTER 8

In Which Strong
Temptation Is Resisted

Xian-Li stood in the yard with her favourite blue bowl, letting the dry kitchen scraps sift through her fingers. Surrounded by her flock of brown speckled hens, cackling and scratching as she flung bread crusts and apple peels to them, she felt a sudden chill and gave an involuntary shiver. The day was bright and blustery, so her long black hair was gathered in a red scarf. She watched her shadow on the ground; the trailing ends of the scarf waving in the breeze made it seem as if the shadow itself were alive.

Though the sun was warm on her shoulders, the chill struck her again a minute or so later—this time accompanied by a feeling of oppression or dread so strong that she paused in mid-throw, a handful of pea pods in her fist. She turned around, expecting to find someone watching her . . . but there was no one. The yard was empty, the servants inside or otherwise out of sight.

The feeling of foreboding passed in a moment and Xian-Li continued feeding the chickens. She soon emptied the bowl, shaking the last crumbs onto the ground. Tucking the crock under her arm, she started back to the house. As she reached the back door she glanced up, and there he was: Benedict, her precious son, standing in the open gateway. His hands were empty, hanging at the end of limp arms; he wore no coat or hat, and the look on his face was one of utter desolation and emptiness. The blue bowl slipped from her grasp as she ran forward.

"Beni!" she gasped as she gathered him into her embrace. "Oh, Beni! You have returned." She pushed back and held him at arm's length so she could see his face. Something in his aspect had changed; he seemed older than his thirteen years. "What has happened?" She glanced behind him, looking for Arthur. "Where is your father?"

"Mother, I——" Benedict broke off, unable to finish. Xian-Li saw then that he was in pain, his flesh pale, his eyes dark-rimmed.

"Are you hurt?" She looked him over, feeling for injuries with her hands. "What has happened?"

Benedict drew a deep breath and said, "He is not coming."

"Not coming? Arthur is delayed?"

"Father is not coming home," Benedict corrected, his voice quavering. "He is never coming home again . . ."

Xian-Li searched his ashen face for clarity. "I don't understand. Is he hurt?" She straightened, as if preparing to fly to her stricken husband's aid. "We must go to him." She made to press by him.

"Mother, wait!" Benedict seized her arm. "Father is not injured. He is dead."

She halted, her back stiffening.

"Father is dead," he repeated. "He is not injured. He is dead and buried in a tomb, Mother, and he is never coming home."

All strength fled in that instant and Xian-Li collapsed as if life and breath had been jerked from her body. She lay like a thing discarded—a bundle of refuse carelessly tossed aside.

Benedict stood unmoving, watching, as it seemed, from a distance and not knowing how to cross the awful chasm that had opened between them. Finally he stumbled forward, knelt down, and, taking her by the arm, helped his mother to her feet. They clung to one another in their sorrow.

How much time passed while they stood in the yard could not be measured, for time had stopped. When Xian-Li lifted her head and opened her eyes once more, it was to look out on a world completely and radically changed. Never again would it hold for her the satisfactions and delights that she knew and loved. Never again would it be her home. How could it? The man she loved, who was her life, was gone.

Weeping at the fearful, gaping wound that had suddenly ripped through her soul, Xian-Li allowed herself to be led into the house, where she fell into a chair at the table in the kitchen. The cook and housekeeper scurried around trying to find ways to comfort their mistress. Xian-Li, numb to everything around her, did not resist, but met their efforts with the calm acceptance of the condemned who at last understand that time is short and life fleeting and that nothing matters except that which is eternal.

The cook, tutting and fluttering, produced a brown bottle and poured a small measure of sour cider into a cup, which she placed in her mistress's hands. "Get some o' this down you," she advised. "You'll be t' better for it."

Xian-Li, without thinking, raised the cup to her lips. The astringent cider assaulted her mouth and throat and made her cough, but helped clear her senses. She gazed around as if waking from a dream, saw Benedict and reached for his hand, took it, and squeezed hard as if to reassure herself that he at least was still solidly alive.

"I am sorry, Mother. They did everything they could—no one could have done more." He knelt beside her chair, the tears so long held back falling freely now. "I did everything I could too."

Xian-Li gathered him into her arms and held her son—a young man now, really, but not too old to refuse the comfort of her embrace—as he emptied the well of his sorrow and lifted his head at last. She gestured to the cook to bring more cider and then sat Benedict down in a chair beside her. "I want to know what happened," she said, her voice raw. "I need to know everything."

"He was hit on the head—there was a fight, and he was hit—" he began.

"Shush!" His mother placed her fingers against his lips, then handed him the cup of cider the cook had poured. "Drink first. Then start at the beginning. Do not rush. There is no reason to hurry."

Benedict obeyed, taking a long sip of the sharp-tasting liquor, forcing himself to step back mentally to the time and place the tragedy began. "We arrived at the temple and dined with Anen," he began, his voice finding strength as he relived the events. "During the meal Anen told us there was trouble of some kind—the people were angry—and we discussed whether to stay or go home. I wish we had come home . . ." His eyes sought her face. "I wanted to come home, but—"

"You could not know," Xian-Li told him. "Go on."

"The priests were going up to the pharaoh's new city to speak to him—to see if they could settle things. We went along with them. The pharaoh met us, but he refused to listen and then, as we were leaving, a riot broke out. The people loyal to the pharaoh became very angry for some reason and they attacked the priests—throwing bricks and rocks, mostly, and pushing and shouting. Everyone started running, trying to escape. We made it through the gates to the river, but Father went back to help Anen and the high priest." Benedict turned tear-filled eyes on his mother. "That is when he was hit—a brick, a stone, something hit him on the head and he fell to the ground."

"He was killed then?" asked his mother, her voice low and soft.

Benedict shook his head. "No. He was badly injured, but alive. We fled to the boats. Some of the priests were injured too, but we were able to escape. On the boat, the high priest's physicians tended Father, and I thought he would get better." The boy paused, took another swallow of cider, licked his lips, and continued, "But by the time we got back to the temple, he was no better. Anen said they had to perform an operation—they had to open his head to get out pieces of bone and clean the wound."

Xian-Li nodded. "I know they can do this. They are very skilled."

"I did not watch them, but Father was awake and I talked to him before they started. He said good-bye and told me to take care of you. His last thoughts were of you, Mother. Then later, after it was over, Father woke one last time and called me—" Here Benedict faltered, unable to continue.

"Please, Beni," said Xian-Li. "I need to hear it all."

"He wanted me to take him to the Spirit Well," Benedict said, putting his face in his hands.

Xian-Li was silent for a long moment. "That is what your father did for me," she replied at last. "Did you know that? Did he ever tell you that I died of fever there in Egypt—this was before you were born. Did your father ever tell you?"

Benedict shook his head glumly. "He said once he had a secret to tell me. I asked him what it was and he said it was—" He paused, remembering the exact words. "He said that it was a good too wonderful to tell."

A sad smile touched Xian-Li's lips. "Yes, he would say that."

"I asked him what could be too wonderful to tell? But he just said I must wait until I was older." Benedict looked to his mother. "What did he mean?"

"I think he was speaking of the Spirit Well—and what happens there." Her eyes flicked to the doorway where the servants huddled, nervously clutching their hands. Ignoring them, she urged, "Tell me what happened after you spoke to your father the last time."

"He said he wanted me to take him there—to the Spirit Well—but I did not know what it was or where to find it." Benedict dropped his gaze to his empty hands. "He tried to show me—one of his tattoos—but . . ." His voice faltered again. "By then it was too late—he just closed his eyes and died."

"Was there pain?" asked his mother.

Benedict shook his head. "I think he was beyond pain. The priests did everything they could for him, but the injury was too great." He raised doleful eyes to his mother. "Anen ordered his body to be embalmed and buried, but because of the troubles, I did not see Father again after that night." He shook his head sadly. "I would have done anything he asked—anything. You must believe me."

"I do believe you, Beni dear. I have no doubt that if the temple physicians could not heal him, then there was nothing more to be done."

"But why did he want to go to the Spirit Well? What is it?"

"It is a place of great healing—and more," replied Xian-Li. "It is where your father took me when I failed to recover from the fever."

"Then I might have saved him? If I had known where to find this place, I might have saved him?" His head dropped again as misery overwhelmed him once more. "If only you had been there, Mother— if you had been there, we could have saved him."

"You must not think that," she told him, her voice firm. "Even had I been there it is doubtful I could have done anything more to help. I remember nothing about what happened when I passed from life. I only remember going to sleep in one world and waking up in another. What I know of the Spirit Well was told to me by Arthur." She reached for her son's hand and clasped it. "Whatever happened there is now lost forever."

"Why?" asked Benedict.

"Because your father is gone, my son. All that he knew—the worlds he visited, the places he loved . . ." She shook her head sadly. "Gone."

"It is not gone, Mother." Benedict rose from his chair, saying, "Wait there a moment."

He disappeared into the next room, returning a moment later carrying a cylindrical parcel wrapped in linen and tied with a woven raffia cord. He carried it across his palms and placed it in his mother's lap as if making a sacred offering. She regarded the package and raised questioning eyes to her son.

"Open it," he instructed.

Xian-Li untied the cord and withdrew the linen wrapper to reveal a scroll of thin parchment, which she placed on the table before her and unrolled. One glimpse of the surface and what was written there caused her to sit bolt upright. She gave a startled cry, her hands fluttering to her face.

She stared at the parchment roll with wide, horrified eyes, then at her son. "Is it . . . ?"

Benedict nodded.

"But how?"

"It was not my doing," he said, and explained how in asking for a copy of his father's tattoos his request had been misunderstood owing to his inability to speak the language. "This is what they gave me instead."

"His skin?" she said, shaking her head in disbelief as she stared at the object. "How could they do this?"

"I cannot say, but it is done." Kneeling down beside his mother, he said, "You see what this means?"

Xian-Li reached out a tentative hand and gently smoothed the thin papery object with her fingertips.

"Mother, it means nothing is lost. We still have hope."

She remained still, silently contemplating the loose scroll as it lay on the table. Such a strange, unnatural thing; it filled her with fascination and revulsion in equal measure.

"Mother?" said Benedict, still on his knees beside her.

"No," she said with a sigh, whether of resignation or regret Benedict could not tell. "No, my son. This is part of Arthur and must be allowed to die with him."

"Why? I do not understand."

Xian-Li made no reply but continued to gaze upon the parchment document that was her husband's tattooed skin.

"Tell me," pressed Benedict. "Why must we give it up? It is almost as if we were meant to have it, to keep it and use it. Maybe Father meant for us to save it so we could continue his work."

Xian-Li considered this. Certainly, it was a strange and unnatural thing, and yet . . . here it was. Beyond anyone's thought, plan, or desire—an indelible record of Arthur's life's work, faithfully preserved and dropped into her lap.

"Oh, Beni, it is so dangerous, and you are so very young," she said, grief settling its full weight upon her once more. "It is a mistake—a temptation, and we must resist. Do you not see that? The secrets of his work are a danger to any who possess them. It brings nothing but pain and grief. You have seen what can happen." She raised a hand to her son's cheek and turned his face to hers. "You know what I am saying is true."

Benedict, still wounded by the loss of his father and the circumstances of his death, accepted his mother's verdict but was reluctant to give in. "I know, but it doesn't seem right. Father endured so much and learned so much—that it should just end like this . . ." He waved a hand at the pale, flat parchment on the table. "He deserves better than that."

Xian-Li was silent for a long moment, gazing at her son. "Perhaps you are right," she conceded. "Perhaps we can do better. I want to say farewell to my beloved in the traditional way. I want to see his tomb, to know where he is buried and pay the last respects of a wife to her husband."

"Return to Egypt, you mean."

"We will return to Egypt," continued Xian-Li, "and we will take the parchment with us. We will return it to Arthur. That is where it belongs." She gathered Benedict in a motherly embrace and they held on to one another for a time, each drawing comfort from the living warmth of the other. "You must make me a promise, Beni," Xian-Li whispered.

"Anything," replied Benedict.

"You must promise never to reveal the secret of your father's work to anyone—not even your own flesh and blood."

When he made no reply, she insisted. "Promise me, my son." She pulled away to look him in the eye. "I want to hear the words."

"On my life," Benedict said, taking on a solemn tone, "I promise never to reveal the secret of Father's work to another living soul."

She raised a hand and pressed her palm to his face. "Then it is agreed. We will return the skin to Arthur, and when that is done, that will be the end of it."

CHAPTER 9

In Which a Coffeehouse Summit Is Convened

A return to the Bone House meant finding a way back to the Stone Age, and Kit was determined to be better prepared for the journey this time around. Knowing what he knew about the conditions to be faced, he determined to outfit himself as best he could and decided a stout pair of shoes was first on the list. He had in mind something sturdy with high tops and heavy soles suitable for rambling. In this the cobblers of Prague were more than happy to oblige; however, as Kit quickly learned, it was not so simple as picking a pair off the rack and popping them on for a waltz around the shop. And while Kit had numerous variations from which to choose—each cobbler had samples and specialties—his purchase would be handmade to order and the finished product would take a few days to manufacture.

In the end he selected an amiable craftsman with a line in hunting boots, allowed his naked foot to be measured, and, stressing through gestures and mangled German the importance of a good thick sole, left the shoemaker to his work. His mission accomplished, Kit was sloping across the square when he thought he heard an all-too-familiar voice calling his name. "Kit! Kit Livingstone!"

The sound brought him to a halt. He looked around, and there stood Haven Fayth sprung, apparently, from the damp brown flagstones of the square.

"Upon my word," she said, her voice a honeyed purr. "This is an entirely agreeable surprise, I must say."

"Haven . . ." Kit intoned dully. "Where did you come from?"

"Bless me, Kit, is that how you would greet a friend?"

"I'll let you know when I see one," he said, eyes searching reflexively around the square for Burley Men. "What are you doing here?"

"We have only just arrived."

"We? Is Burleigh with you?" Kit intensified his survey of the square, searching left and right for any sign of a looming dark figure. "Where is he?"

"I honestly cannot say, Kit. The Black Earl and I parted company just after your disappearance." She gave him a quick glance head to toe. "But look at you, my dear fellow. You appear to be in rude health."

"No thanks to your friend the earl."

"Oh, Christopher," she tutted, adopting the tone of a parent chiding a disobedient child, "you cannot for a moment believe I would wish any harm to come to you. Indeed, when I discovered what Lord Burleigh had done, I did my utmost to thwart any success he might have had in discovering your whereabouts. You may ask Wilhelmina; she knows very well how I flummoxed his plans. Or," she said, indicating the two figures advancing across the square behind her, "you can ask Giles. He will tell you the same."

"Giles!" cried Kit, stepping around Haven to greet him. "Giles, you're here." Seizing his hand, he shook it with vigour. "How are you? How's the arm? Are you healed?"

"Hale and hearty, sir," replied Giles, wincing with pain under Kit's enthusiastic greeting. As Haven had done, he took in Kit's altered appearance with approval. "You, sir, have given us some concern. But I see you have fared very well indeed."

"Fresh air and healthy living, that's all," Kit told him. "I'll tell you all about it."

Aware that they were being joined by another young woman, Kit turned to the stranger.

A couple inches shorter than Haven, her face half hidden beneath a broad-brimmed hat, she was gazing at him with intense interest in her large dark eyes. "*You* are Kit Livingstone?"

"I am indeed," he said. "Have we met?"

"No," she said quickly. "It is just that we have come here hoping to find you and . . . well, here you are—the first person we meet."

"Pray allow me the pleasure of introducing you to Miss Cassandra Clarke. I am certain you two are going to get along famously," gushed Haven. "Cassandra, this is Christopher Livingstone, who much prefers to go by the name of Kit, heaven knows why."

"Glad to meet you, Kit," said Cass, extending her hand.

"Charmed," Kit replied, accepting her hand. "What part of America do you come from?"

"It is *that* obvious?"

"Sorry, it's a bad habit of mine. An English girl would have offered her cheek," he told her, then leaned close and gave her a quick peck. "Very happy to meet you, Cassandra."

In contrast to the willowy Lady Fayth—and judging merely from what he could see beneath her long woollen coat—the newcomer gave the impression of being more substantial somehow. Perhaps it was her compact, athletic body or the no-nonsense cut of her medium-length brown hair or her expressive dark eyes, which hinted at unfathomed depths; none of these attributes was remarkable in itself, but taken together her features combined to form an entirely pleasing whole.

Kit caught himself staring and blurted, "So, how did you happen to fall in with these two?"

Before Cass could reply, Haven interrupted. "All will be revealed in good time. Just now, however, might it not be best to move our glad reunion inside and away from prying eyes?" She gave an involuntary glance around the square. "Marry, do you think we might repair to more convivial surroundings? Somewhere warm, perhaps? We have been travelling a very long time."

"This way," said Kit. "Mina will want to know you're here."

"One could wish for a more fulsome welcome," said Haven, taking his arm.

"Wish away," replied Kit, gently but firmly removing her hand.

Lady Fayth drew breath to speak, but thought better of it and held her tongue, allowing Kit to lead them to the Grand Imperial Kaffeehaus and usher them inside. "After you," said Kit, holding open the door. Giles was last and Kit snagged his arm; leaning close, he said, "What is Haven up to?"

"Sir?" wondered Giles.

"Is it true she has split with Burleigh?"

"Indeed, sir. To the best of my knowledge, she has escaped his clutches—much as yourself, sir. My lady returned to London and has been very beneficial to my convalescence."

"Do you believe she is sincere?"

"She has given me no cause for doubt," replied Giles.

Kit nodded. "Well, I want us both to keep an eye on her anyway—just in case."

"I understand, sir," Giles assented. "You are rightly chary, but I cannot think there is any cause for concern."

"All the same," said Kit. "After what happened, I don't want to take any chances where Her Ladyship is concerned. Just promise me you'll keep an eye on her, okay?"

"I will make it my special concern," Giles assured him.

They entered the coffeehouse, where Wilhelmina was already greeting the new arrivals. After the introductions were made all around and a table requisitioned for a chat over coffee and cheese sandwiches, it was decided that a proper discussion of the state of affairs should take place as soon as possible.

"Since we are all together for the first time," Wilhelmina announced, "I propose that we hold a council so everyone can meet everyone else and we can all get better acquainted. A few things have lately come to light that the rest of you should know. I suggest we meet tonight after the shop is closed."

"A coffeehouse summit," said Kit. "I like it."

There were nods of agreement all around.

"I must consult Engelbert, of course," continued Mina, "but I think we can close the coffeehouse a little early in order to have plenty of time for discussion. I'll arrange to have some food brought in and we'll make a night of it. Okay?"

Again there was general agreement and no dissenting voices.

"Then it is decided," said Kit. "I want to hear what some of you others have been up to while we were apart." He looked narrowly at Lady Fayth.

Wilhelmina then busied herself with making arrangements for housing the newcomers. The inn on the square was thought to be too risky in light of Burleigh's penchant for holing up there when visiting Prague. "The last thing we need is tripping over Burley Men while we're here," was how Kit put it.

"There are other places," Mina told him. "Leave it with me."

Once the doors were closed, the curtains drawn and windows shuttered, and the serving staff sent home, Etzel and his helpers busied themselves in the kitchen, and Kit and Gianni cleared a space at the far end of the dining room. They pulled the largest of the round tables into the space and dragged chairs around for everyone. As it was her venue, Wilhelmina undertook to preside over the gathering, assuming a formal style she thought suited the occasion.

"I declare this meeting open," she began as soon as everyone was seated. "To begin, I want to say you are all welcome here. I expect this will be a long night, as we all have a lot to share and there is much to discuss. If no one objects, I will act as chairman to keep things on an even keel." Mina passed her gaze around the table. "No objections? Good." Putting out a hand towards Cass, she said, "I see that most of us know most of us, but some don't know others, and others probably know hardly anyone at all."

"Try saying *that* ten times real fast," whispered Kit to Giles, and received a disapproving look from Mina. "Don't mind me," he told her. "You're doing fine."

"As I was saying . . . Since new members have been added to our group, I think it will save time in the long run if we take a moment to go around the table and introduce ourselves. Since Kit seems to have a lot to say, we'll start with him." She gave him a sour smile. "Tell us how you came to be here."

"Right." He nodded, thought a moment, then gave his full name and a brief-to-the-point-of-brusque report of his experience of meeting his long-lost great-grandfather in a London alley, and how Cosimo introduced him to ley travel and told him about the Skin Map and the race to find it.

Lady Fayth spoke next, offering a precise and forthright account of her tutelage under her uncle, Sir Henry Fayth; she was followed by Giles who, clearly uncomfortable, gave only the barest explanation of his experience.

Cassandra came next and told about her accidental introduction to ley travel while working in the Arizona desert, getting lost, and, providentially, making contact with the Zetetic Society. The mere mention of the society pricked everyone's curiosity and there were lots of questions, but before the meeting could be derailed, Mina intervened, saying, "I'm sure we all want to hear more about that—and we will come back to it shortly. But for now, let's move on."

Then all eyes turned to Gianni.

Folding his hands on the table, he leaned forward slightly and began. "My name is Giambattista Beccaria—Gianni, if you will—and let me say what an honour it is to be included in such a delightful company," he said, natural charm warming his Italian tones. "I am a priest of the Ordo Sancti Benedicti, beginning in Sant'Antimo and later at the Abadia de Montserrat in Spain. Although a priest, my vocation has been that of astronomer." He smiled, his round glasses glinting. "Thus, in more ways than one, a man with his head in heaven."

As he spoke, Kit could feel the group falling under the spell of a man who seemed to exude benevolence and humility mingled with a genuine, unforced grace. It was proof, if any were needed, that Wilhelmina was wise to choose him as her mentor.

"One day, many years ago, I discovered what you all are pleased to call ley travel. At the time I did not know what it was that I had discovered, but being of a scientific mind, I studied it and eventually succeeded in learning how to manipulate it for my own purposes. Never in my studies did I imagine that it might serve some greater goal. In this, *Signorina* Wilhelmina has been my instructor—for it is she who told me about the Skin Map and its unknown treasure. And now, my friends, I believe we are very close to plumbing the depths of this great and sacred mystery. For, if our suppositions are correct, the object of our quest has been found."

This declaration caused a small sensation among those at the table who had not yet heard the news. Haven was first to find her voice. "Forgive me, Brother Gianni, but am I to understand that the Skin Map has been found?"

"The Map of Skin, no, *signorina*," replied the priest. "That remains beyond our reach at present. I was speaking of the Well of Souls—and my belief that this is the secret that the map conceals."

"And how, I beg you, was this feat accomplished without the use of the map?"

Extending a hand towards Kit, who was sitting directly across from him, the priest said, "For that, we have Mr. Livingstone to thank. It is he who discovered the way—or, perhaps, *one* of the ways by which this miraculous place may be reached."

"By my faith! Kit, is this true?" Haven spun around to regard him with an expression of sceptical appraisal. "Are we to understand that *you* have found the Spirit Well?"

"I did." Kit offered a judicious nod. "At least, I think I did. If not, then what I found is something equally amazing. But we cannot be sure it is the Well of Souls until we can return and make a thorough investigation."

"That is without doubt the best news I have heard," enthused Lady Fayth. "I fail to see what is preventing us from going there right this instant." She appeared ready to leap out of her chair and race off in completion of the quest. Sensing the others did not share her joy at this revelation, she added, "Yet there *is* something preventing us, I fear." She looked to Kit and Wilhelmina. "Pray, what is it?"

"The problem," Kit replied slowly, "is the *way* I discovered it—that is, the means I used to reach the place where I found it."

"Yes?" demanded Haven. "Speak, sir! What is this fearsome difficulty you are so obviously loath to mention?"

"There's a problem with the pathway, or portal, or whatever," replied Kit irritably. "The Bone House is gone."

"Bone house?" Haven threw herself back in her chair and crossed her arms over her chest. "And what, I implore you, is a *bone* house?"

"It is a house, a shelter, made of bones, and it—"

"A *house* made of *bones?*" She tossed her head in derision, her tone high and haughty. "Do you honestly expect anyone to believe this unabashed claptrap? Or is this merely your lumbering way of discouraging the rest of us from participating in your discovery?"

"Look here," snapped Kit. "I'm not making this up. It is real, it exists—at least, it did exist. If you don't believe me—" He glanced at Mina and Brother Gianni, looking for confirmation. "Tell her."

"Haven, this isn't helping," said Wilhelmina. "Kit is telling the truth."

"My friends," interposed Gianni smoothly, "if I may be allowed to suggest a simple explanation." He turned to Haven. "Lady Fayth, it appears that our friend has found a portal that leads directly to a world containing a phenomenon that he has with good reason identified as the Spirit Well, yes? This portal was marked, as is so often the case, by the ancient inhabitants of the region—in this instance not with stone or earthworks, but with an edifice constructed of the bones of deceased creatures. *Prego!* The Bone House."

Haven glanced at Kit. "Is *that* what you were trying to say?"

"More or less," he allowed.

"Are we all on the same page now?" asked Mina, glancing around the table.

"In future, one could hope for more linguistic precision," replied Haven, undeterred. "At all events, it would seem the most prudent course would be to return forthwith to what you believe may be the Spirit Well and verify these conjectures of yours. If that is what you propose, then let us be about it at once."

"That *is* the proposal on the table," Kit replied testily. "And if you had only given me half a chance—"

"Not forgetting we have a major complication," Wilhelmina interrupted, trying to keep the discussion on track. "As Kit has explained, direct access to the portal no longer exists. So the quest has become a little more complicated. We have to find a way back to the Spirit Well without using the Bone House." Satisfied with her summation, she gave a nod and sat down, adding, "Something tells me it won't be easy."

"The best things," Cassandra observed to herself, "rarely are."

CHAPTER 10

In Which a Solemn, Sacred Deal Is Struck

S o, your dad is an astrophysicist?" said Kit. "What's that like?"

"Out of this world," replied Cass. Kit gave her an appreciative smirk. "That's what I used to say whenever anyone asked. To me, he's just a typical dad."

"Does he know where you are?"

"Don't ask," Cass sighed. "He's probably called out the National Guard by now. The last time I spoke to him, he was about to jump on a plane and come to help me investigate this odd phenomenon I thought I had *discovered*."

"Ley leaping?"

"The man who showed me called it 'crossing the Coyote Bridge.'"

"That's a new one."

"He is a Yavapai tribesman, and he was helping us with the dig where I was working." Cass went on to explain about finding what

Friday called the Ghost Road located in Secret Canyon near Sedona. "Have you ever been to America?" she asked.

"Not even close," admitted Kit. "One day, maybe. I've always wanted to see Hollywood and New York."

"That's what everyone says," Cass laughed, and Kit decided he liked the sound so much he would try to make it happen again. "They're only about three thousand miles apart," she told him. "But sure, why not? Where else?"

"Disney World, or Graceland." He lifted his palms as if weighing options. "I can't decide. It's a toss-up."

"Oh, Disney World—definitely," she advised. "You'd look good in mouse ears."

In an effort to clear his head and keep out of Haven's reach, Kit had decided to take a walk and invited Cass to join him. She had a capable, uncomplicated, and forthright manner that he found refreshing, and was rather fetching in a long skirt with a high-laced bodice and crisp white blouse borrowed from Wilhelmina's wardrobe. Thus, they sauntered along a pleasant stretch of riverside outside the city walls, content in one another's easy company.

"Palaeontologist, eh?" he said after a moment. "Old bones and all that? Fossils and rocks?"

"Pretty much."

"What do you think of Prague?" he asked. "It's jolly old."

"I love it. Don't you feel like you're in a fairy tale?" She told him about being sent to London to find Sir Henry. "That was fascinating too—but nowhere near as charming as this."

"You were at Clarimond House?"

She nodded. "That's where I met Haven and Giles. They suggested we should come here and—to make a long story short—here we are. But now I need to get back to Damascus and give them a report. Have you ever been to the Zetetic Society?"

"Afraid not. My great-grandfather mentioned them once or twice in passing. He had plans to take me to one of their meetings or something, but that, like a lot of other things, just didn't happen."

"Because he died?"

"And Sir Henry along with him. Giles and I were with them at the end."

"I'm sorry." She gave his arm a sympathetic pat. "I had to ask— it's one of the things I was sent to find out."

"Well, you can tell them it was Burleigh and his goons. They're to blame. In fact, they seem to be responsible for most everything bad that happens around here."

"That's what Haven said—'stricken down by vile enemies.'"

"She's right about that, but don't believe *everything* she says," Kit cautioned. "You can't trust her."

"I wondered."

"Let's just say that Haven Fayth looks out for her own interests first, last, and always. But yes, she was there too, and on this occasion she's telling the truth." Kit then launched into a description of events in Egypt leading up to their capture by Burleigh. He concluded, saying, "This is news to you? Burleigh and his toadies?"

"Oh, Haven told me about them, but I guess I thought they were just tomb robbers or something. I didn't really understand that they were after the Skin Map or what they were willing to do to get it."

"They're murderers. And they have this way of showing up exactly when they need to, and when they can do the most harm. I used to wonder how they did it, but now I think I know." He paused and glanced at his agreeable companion. "They use a device—a shadow lamp. Has anybody mentioned that yet?"

"What is it?"

"It's a gadget that can detect ley lines and portals and such." He went on to describe what it looked like and how it worked and how Wilhelmina had secured a prototype of the instrument for herself behind Burleigh's back. "Mina has started calling it a shadow lamp. It emits this sort of glowing light, and then apparently everything goes a bit dark right before you make a ley jump."

"Does Mina have the only one?" Cass asked. "Can I see it?"

"Well, I used to have one—Mina's old model before she upgraded. It got wrecked just before coming here when we encountered that portal we were talking about—near the gorge I mentioned? Anyway, this portal was pumping out a massive amount of energy. Our gizmos couldn't handle it. They overheated and burned out. We didn't know they would do that."

"Can they be fixed, or can you make more of them? If so, maybe we should all have one," suggested Cass. "If we're going to be working together, it would be good for us all to have the same tools."

"We don't make them. Mina got them from a contact at court who makes them for Burleigh. It's a secret. But I think you're right; it would be good if everybody had shadow lamps." He stopped walking and took in a view of the river sliding silently along its grassy banks. "I could keep walking for miles on a day like this, but we should get back before they send out the bloodhounds."

Cassandra drew a deep lungful of the clean country air. "I like it here—and it's been good to get outdoors. I'm not used to being cooped up all day." She gave Kit a sunny smile. "Thank you. This has been nice."

They turned to stroll back to the city, the warm autumn air already beginning to chill as the sun slanted towards the horizon. Kit asked about her life and work in Arizona, and she told him about the dig and discovering traces of the rare theropod Tarbosaurus, which she called a real coup for the university.

"Do you miss it?" asked Kit. "Your old life, I mean?"

"Truthfully? No. I haven't thought about it much. Since all this began, I've been completely consumed and overwhelmed by the experience."

"It has that effect."

"How about you? Do you miss your old life in London?"

"To be honest, there isn't that much to miss," Kit replied. "I had a boring, nowhere job and not much else. Looking back on it now, I see that Cosimo did me a huge favour by bringing me into the family business, as he called it." Kit gave a sharp, scoffing laugh. "Some business! I was stuck in the Stone Age for three years—maybe more. I lost count."

"Get out of here!"

"It's true. You didn't know?" Cass shook her head, so Kit continued. "The Bone House we were talking about—that's where it is. Smack in the middle of the Stone Age. There's a ley line near here that leads to this incredible gorge—sheer cliffs of white limestone with a river flowing through it. To make a long story short, Burleigh was after me and I tried to escape using the Valley Ley, as Mina calls it—but something went wrong. I landed in the Stone Age with a clan of primitive people. I don't mind telling you it was the most amazing, frightening, exhilarating, and rewarding thing that has ever happened to me. I am absolutely itching to get back there."

Just thinking about it brought Kit to silence. He paused and his vision grew unfocused as the memories flooded through him.

"Kit? Are you okay?"

When he answered his voice had taken on a note of longing. "It's hard to describe, but when I was there I was more than myself—as if being around the primitives made me better than I am, somehow." He shrugged. "Now I feel like I've lost a limb, or a brother, or something. I liked who I was when I was with them—if that makes any sense. That's why I want to go back . . . why I *have* to go back."

"I want to hear every single detail." Cass stopped walking, looked directly into his eyes, and fixed him with her gaze.

"Better still, I'll show you," offered Kit. "As I was saying, the expedition to find the Spirit Well starts from there. I guess I just assumed you would be coming along too. But now you say you have to get back to Damascus—" He felt himself floundering. "Do you? Do you have to go back right away, I mean?" The intensity of her look unnerved him slightly, so he lightened the mood. "I'll introduce you to the clan, show you a real, living mammoth—not just bones! And who knows? If you're good, maybe a cave lion too, and how to hunt with a sharp stick."

"Done!" she said. Cass spat into her palm and extended her hand. "Spit and shake." Kit did as he was told and they shook hands. "There," she said. "It is a sacred, solemn deal. You can't renege on it."

"I wouldn't want to renege on it," Kit told her.

The moment stretched too long, becoming awkward, so they resumed their walk in silence. When that became uncomfortable too, Kit blurted, "So tell me more about Sedona."

Cass shrugged. "Sedona is a decent enough place, I suppose. I love the red rocks and canyons. But truth be told, I was really taken with Damascus—something about the place . . . or maybe it's the people."

They talked about the surreal contrasts of their lives old and new, and the unimaginable bounces the life of a ley traveller could take at any turn. Eventually they passed through the massive town gates and up the steep street now sunk in shadow. Upon reaching the Old Square, they entered the sunlight once more and proceeded to the Grand Imperial Kaffeehaus.

As they sauntered into the square, Cass paused to take in the great gothic edifice fronting the square. "What is that building?" she asked, indicating the looming presence rising before her.

"That's the Rathaus," Kit explained. "Nothing to do with rodents, happily—unless the rat catcher has headquarters there. It's like a civic centre. Administration, local government, city offices—everything, even a prison."

"It looks like the kind of place Dracula might hang out in. Kinda creepy."

"You know, you're right." Kit smiled. He had enjoyed the day and Cass' company far more than he imagined when inviting her for a stroll in the country. But now it was over and he was considering how to keep the moment alive when they reached the door of the Grand Imperial.

"Thank you for taking me with you, Kit. Maybe we can do it again sometime?"

"No problem," he said and instantly cringed inside. *No problem?* Was that *really* the best he could do?

She put her hand on his arm, warming the spot she touched.

Kit was on the cusp of thinking a kiss on the cheek might be in order when the coffee shop door opened and Wilhelmina appeared, holding a compact parcel the size of a loaf of bread. "Oh, there you are," she chirped. "Not interrupting anything, am I?"

"Just got back from our walk," Kit said. "What's in the bag?"

"Coffee grounds," Mina replied, hefting the bundle.

"A gift for one of your many admirers?"

"Yes, actually," she said. "In exchange for this rare and important commodity, I gain certain favours from my alchemist friends."

"Nice." Kit nodded appreciatively.

"Are there really alchemists around?" wondered Cass.

"Oh, sure," Mina confirmed. "They've been most helpful to me—one in particular. I'm sending this up to him with a note requesting a visit. But it's got to get there before the clock strikes six."

"Because he morphs into a dormouse?" said Kit.

Mina rolled her eyes. "Because that's the changing of the day guard, and entrance to the palace becomes tedious and unnecessarily complicated after that."

"What do they do with the coffee grounds?" asked Cass.

"Who knows? Experiments of one kind or another. The thing is, it's valuable stuff on account of its scarcity, and I'm happy to keep the lines of supply open because sometimes I need a favour."

"Like shadow lamps," Kit guessed.

"Like shadow lamps," confirmed Wilhelmina. She made to move off. "So if you two will excuse me . . ."

"Mina," said Kit quickly, "Cass and I were talking about that. What are the chances that you could get enough lamps for each of us to have one?"

"I don't know," Mina said. "But it's a good idea. I'll ask Gustavus and see what he says."

CHAPTER 11

In Which a Line of Succession Is Elucidated

Douglas Flinders-Petrie dashed the water out of his eyes and then grabbed his knee. The path underfoot was rougher than he had anticipated and, blind from the leap, he had taken a tumble. The palm of his left hand was grazed and he had torn a hole in the knee of his trousers. "Good work," he muttered. "Capital."

He heard a grunt and glanced back over his shoulder as he straightened. Snipe was two steps behind him with a wicked smirk on his big, bland face. "Not funny," Douglas growled.

Rubbing his knee, he straightened and looked around. They appeared to be in a trench cut into a thick stratum of brick-coloured stone. Closer examination revealed that the rock was tufa—the soft, porous volcanic rock that covered much of central Italy. Smooth terra-cotta-coloured walls bearing the hatch marks of the tools used to carve them rose to the height of two or three metres on either side, creating a sunken pathway: a Sacred Road.

From his research Douglas knew that these hidden byways seamed all throughout the region, but he had not imagined them so big, nor so deep. A few dozen steps ahead he observed a doorway carved into the trench wall, the spiral lintels decked with a garland of fresh flowers; at the threshold stood a clay jar decorated in black and red.

"It worked," he breathed happily to himself. "It bloody well worked. We're here." Turning to Snipe, he said, "Come on."

They started along the trench, pausing briefly at the decorated door. It was a tomb, as were all the chambered nooks lining the length of the Sacred Road. The floral decoration told Douglas that a deceased someone had taken up residence inside and that the funeral had been recent. He paused at the tomb. The door was also tufa stone, and both it and the lintels had been freshly painted vivid blue, the Etruscan colour of death and eternity.

Douglas regarded the door and then, stooping, took up the jar. It was sealed, but he broke the seal and raised the vessel to his mouth. "Here's to immortality," he said, then drank a long, satisfying draught. The wine was sweet and warm. He drank again and passed the jar to Snipe. "Let's go see who we can find."

They followed the path until they came to a T-junction. A flight of steps had been carved into the wall at the join and, mounting these, the two travellers emerged into a classic Tuscan landscape of gently mounded hills accented by slender dark cypress trees that stood like exclamation points. A simple dirt track led from the now-hidden Sacred Road. To the west lay a low rise of grain fields, green beneath dazzling, cloud-scudded skies; to the east, a forest of live oak and pine, covering the gentle swells like a prickly green blanket.

As he stood taking this in, a pair of local farmers appeared on the track a little distance away, leading a young bullock. They slowed as they approached, taking in the strangers' outlandish mode of dress. The farmers—father and son, by the look of them—wore pale-red knee-length tunics, sandals, and wide-brimmed straw hats. Douglas wore black trousers and a loose-fitting white shirt. A man in a three-piece business suit at the beach would not have appeared more out of place.

There was no disguising his foreignness, so Douglas embraced it. Raising his hand in greeting, he called aloud, "Hello! We are travellers." The two rustics exchanged a puzzled glance. Knowing he would not be understood, Douglas boldly plunged ahead. "What land is this?"

The elder of the two natives said something in a language unlike anything Douglas had ever heard; certainly not Latin—which he had hoped to use—and it was definitely not Italian. The farmers looked him up and down, then regarded Snipe, who was at that moment pulling the legs off a grasshopper. With a final glance at one another, the two hurried on their way, giving the strangers a wide and wary berth.

Douglas' elation over having successfully deciphered and used one of the symbols from his scrap of the Skin Map faded as he watched the farmers walk away. Clearly, reading the symbols was only half the battle. Add that to the fact that this time Douglas had a wealth of insider knowledge: he knew from boyhood stories that his great-grandfather Arthur had lived some years in old Etruria; he knew about the Sacred Road and the burial customs of the Etruscans. He knew the story of how Turms the Immortal had been instrumental in healing his great-grandmother and making the birth of his grandfather Benedict possible. Knowing all these things enabled him to guess his whereabouts ... *this time.*

Next time it might well be an altogether different story. If he was to succeed in finding and reuniting the scattered pieces of the original map, he could not count on guesswork, no matter how astute. He would need more—much, much more. At the very least he would require a key of some kind, some way to gain even a little foreknowledge of his destination before embarking. What shape or form that key might take, he had no earthly idea. There were seventeen tattoos on the section of map in his possession. Visiting each place and working out not only where it was but also when, and all the other attendant details, would require time, patience, and, above all, dogged persistence.

Thus, Douglas concluded gloomily, unless he found a key to orient the symbols to their destinations, he was in for an exceedingly long and tedious stretch of trial-and-error.

"Put down that grasshopper, Snipe," he grumbled and started down the trail. "We might as well find out what we can before heading home."

Pausing only long enough to make a little cairn of stones to mark the location of the tufa trench containing the ley line, Douglas struck off along the track. The countryside was pleasant and deserted. They met no one else, and the sun was high overhead when they stopped at a ford some time later. As they stooped to drink, Douglas heard voices and, looking downstream, saw three women washing clothes. He watched them for a moment, listening to their speech; he could sense a rhythm to it, and this time the vowel sounds seemed similar to what he knew of archaic Latin. He was on the point of risking a word or two when there came a tremendous splash.

A curtain of water descended over him and he leapt to his feet. "Snipe! You fool!" he spluttered. Whirling around, he saw the young misanthrope lifting another large stone to heave into the stream. "Drop that rock!"

Snipe obeyed, letting it fall heavily into the water. The women heard the commotion, of course, and saw the two weirdly dressed strangers lurking nearby. Douglas smiled and raised his hands, trying to show he meant no harm, but the damage was done. They all jumped up and one of them ran away, shouting as she disappeared into the brush lining the stream. The remaining washerwomen picked up stones from the bank and held them in readiness. Douglas, still smiling and waving, backed away from the ford, pulling Snipe with him. As soon as they were out of sight of the women, he turned and began trotting back the way they had come.

Soon there were shouts behind them. A rapid look over his shoulder confirmed that they were being pursued by a posse of agitated locals—some of whom carried sticks or clubs. Douglas doubled his speed and began searching for a place to hide, but the countryside was open field on either side of the trail. Their only hope was to dive into the hollow of the Sacred Road and try to lose their pursuers there—a slim hope, but the best he could muster under the circumstances.

On they ran—the chase edging closer with every step. As the first stones began to strike the path around them, Douglas pulled up. Shoving Snipe behind him, he turned to face the crowd, raising empty hands high. *"Amabo!"* he shouted, hoping Latin might at least slow down the rush to judgement. *"Ego nullam iniuriam!"*

The desperate feint worked. The crowd—numbering a dozen or so, mostly men—halted and began arguing—quarrelling, he guessed, over what to do with the intruders now they had caught up with them; this was an improvement in that they were no longer being pelted with stones. The dispute ended and one of the men stepped forward. He pointed to Douglas and addressed him directly; the fellow seemed to be inviting him to respond in some way. *"Amabo,"* Douglas repeated in Latin. *"Amabo.* We mean no harm."

The Etruscan spokesman made a gesture that left Douglas in no doubt that he and Snipe were to come along meekly or face unpleasant consequences. Douglas, his smile shading into a grimace, made a show of compliance. Gathering Snipe under an arm—more for the natives' benefit than for Snipe's—he allowed himself to be led away.

They were conducted by the crowd to the foot of a hill where the dirt track was met by a long, straight upward path that led to an imposing, official-looking structure—a temple, Douglas decided, or perhaps a palace, or something of the sort—with a roof of terra-cotta tiles; deep, shadowed eaves; a spacious, open portico lined with stately columns painted blue; and a copper-clad door. A double row of cypress trees shaded the rising path to this edifice; the flanks of the hill were planted with olive trees and rampant with tiny yellow wildflowers and blood-red poppies.

At the bottom of the ascending path the crowd halted. The hill was very symmetrical—much too symmetrical, Douglas thought, to be natural, and the building too perfectly placed. The combination suggested the site held ritual significance. "This has got to be the place," he murmured to himself as Snipe bent and with a lightning-quick grab snatched up another grasshopper.

Surrounded by their captors, they were made to wait while the self-appointed spokesman climbed the hill and sought entrance to the structure. Douglas watched as a round man in a yellow robe appeared on the portico, and a brief discussion ensued, following which the spokesman descended the hill and took his place with his fellow Etruscans once more.

Presently the yellow-robed priest, if that was what he was, and another, somewhat younger priest appeared on the temple steps; they were joined by a third man in a long crimson robe, and all three proceeded down the long path to the bottom of the hill.

"Stand easy, Snipe," Douglas breathed. "Put down that grasshopper and don't make trouble."

The portly priest—the senior cleric, Douglas surmised—ordered everyone to step back and form a more orderly assembly. The rustics obeyed, leaving the two captured strangers exposed before the man in the crimson robe. The red-robed one regarded them for a fleeting moment, his large intense eyes taking in the details of their exotic appearance, and made up his mind at once. Raising his hand to his people, he spoke a few words in a calm, reassuring voice and received a respectful, even obsequious, reply with nods and little bows of acquiescence. Then, addressing two yellow-robed ones, he spoke a command, turned, and retraced his steps to the temple.

His assistants took up positions on either side of Douglas, and one of them indicated that he and Snipe were to follow their leader.

Up the steep path they passed between the long rank of finger-thin trees on either side and arrived at the steps to the temple portico, where the travellers were forced to remove their boots before they were allowed inside. Barefoot, they were then conducted into the temple—which, Douglas quickly realised, was less a temple and more a residence. The walls were painted in shades of pale green and decorated with a broad band containing a series of hunting scenes. There were banks of overstuffed cushions scattered around a large, low table of dark polished wood and iron tripods holding painted pottery jars in red and black. From somewhere the lilting music of a flute sounded like running water.

Two servants in short green tunics came running with a large camp chair, which they unfolded and lined with cushions. The crimson-robed man lowered himself into the chair with the air of an Oriental potentate taking his throne. Meanwhile, the yellow-robed lackey Douglas assumed to be the junior assistant directed the visitors to kneel before his master, who studied the strangers with intense interest—much, Douglas imagined, as a collector might study a new species of beetle. The silence grew and stretched, and still the red-robed one neither spoke nor was spoken to by any of his evident minions. After a time, the rotund senior priest returned, this time accompanied by two men—one older and bald-headed, the other much younger; each was dressed in a long white tunic with a wide braided belt of golden cord. They, too, fell to studying the strangers with an interest that matched that of their red-robed master.

Moments later, the servants returned—one bearing a copper tray with a jar not unlike the one from which Douglas had drunk outside the tomb; also on the tray were three shallow bowls and a dish of almonds. The senior priest directed the servants to pour the wine, which they did and then, bowing low, retreated without a word. The yellow-robed assistant passed a filled bowl to his master, then handed one each to Douglas and Snipe, who immediately drained his bowl and held it out for more. The servant stared at Snipe, then glanced back at his master, who merely nodded. Snipe's bowl was refilled and Douglas whispered, "Do *not* guzzle that."

Snipe gave him a dark look and dipped his tongue.

The man in the chair raised his bowl as if in offering to the gods on high, then, pronouncing a word, inclined his head and drank.

Douglas recognised this as his invitation to drink too. He took a swallow of the bittersweet resin-infused wine—a taste he recognised but had never acquired. He forced a smile, and the man in the chair gave him a nod of approval before turning to one of the white-garbed onlookers, who bowed, then turned to address Douglas. The fellow rattled off a few words and paused to regard Douglas expectantly. Douglas merely shook his head, whereupon the fellow spoke again in another language that sounded very like Greek. Douglas gave his head another slight shake and said, *"Ego"*—he tapped his chest with a finger—*"narro latin nonnullus."*

This produced an immediate response. The man loosed a string of words that sounded somewhat familiar, though different enough from the Latin Douglas knew that he could not make head nor tail of what the fellow was saying. He smiled and shook his head. "Latin," he said.

"Latica," replied the servant.

"Haud Latica," offered Douglas. *"Non narro Latica."*

The servant turned to his master, put out his hand, and spoke a word that snapped Douglas to sharp attention: "Turms," he said, and repeated, "Turms."

In response, the red-robed man placed his hand to his chest and repeated the word, producing in Douglas the fervent hope that he was possibly in the presence of the one man he had most hoped to encounter on this journey: Turms the Immortal, Priest King of the Velathri.

"Turms," Douglas said and offered a formal bow. Speaking Latin, he added, "Greetings, Turms of the Velathri."

The king nodded indulgently and waited with an expectant look. Douglas placed his hand on the head of his glowering companion and said, "Snipe." He repeated the name, then placed his hand on his own chest in imitation of the one Turms had used and said, "Douglas." He patted his chest, saying, "Douglas Flinders-Petrie."

Now it was the king's turn to be astonished. Pointing to Douglas, he loosed a string of words Douglas could not make out, then added, "*Arturos.*"

It took a moment for Douglas to work out that he had just been told the name by which his great-grandfather had been known among these people. Douglas nodded his understanding, saying, "Arthur Flinders-Petrie." He then engaged in a simple pantomime in which he described stair steps, or levels, each one a little higher than the last. "Arthur," he said, his hand describing the lowest level. "Benedict." His hand described the next level higher. "Charles," came next, and then the rising hand came to rest on his own head. "Douglas."

Turms stood up from his chair and in two quick strides crossed the distance between them. Raising both hands, he placed them on Douglas' shoulders and looked deeply into his eyes—holding the gaze longer than Douglas found comfortable. Even so, Douglas sensed he was in the presence of a wise and munificent soul, one with enormous power and intelligence. He returned the gaze as steadily as he was able.

In a moment the great king tapped both hands on his shoulders and contact was broken. Turms turned his head and rattled off a string of commands to his senior assistant, who bowed, approached Douglas, took his arm, and began leading him away. The king called after his departing guests, and Douglas offered him a similar bow of respect and added his thanks—though for what, he did not yet know.

The king's steward led them out through another room to a side door onto another portico where two guards in light armour with thin, wicked-looking iron spears or javelins across their laps were sitting on wooden stools. They jumped to attention at the appearance of the servant, who offered a brief explanation of, Douglas guessed, the king's commands; then Douglas and Snipe were led down a short flight of steps and away through an olive grove to a small house a few dozen metres distant from the king's residence. They were shown into the house, which was sparsely furnished in two rooms—the first an all-purpose room combining a living space with a table and chairs for eating. The second, smaller room at the rear of the lodge was furnished with stools, a lamp, and several thick mats and cushions for sleeping.

They were, Douglas understood, being offered the use of these quarters, which he appreciated. The presence of the armed guards, however, cast something of a shadow over the transaction. He did not have time to wonder about this, for the bald steward, after showing them the rooms, turned to face Douglas and said, *"Latica Etruii."*

The steward then placed his fingertips on his own lips, said the words again, then touched Douglas on the lips.

"Latica Etruii," Douglas said, nodding. Was he to be taught to speak the language? Placing his palm on his chest, he said his name, then pointed to the servant, raising his eyebrows in expectation. "What is your name?"

The steward smiled with pleasure, tapped himself on the chest, and pronounced, "Pacha."

"My thanks, Pacha," Douglas told him in Latin.

The servant departed then, but not before posting one of the guards at the door of the guest lodge.

"I do not like the look of this, Snipe," Douglas muttered, watching Pacha the portly assistant and the other guard disappear into the olive grove. Douglas waited until they were gone, then decided on a simple test. He stepped boldly from the house onto the narrow porch. The soldier merely watched him. It was only when Douglas made to step off the porch onto the path that the guard actively intervened; he called a word and gestured for Douglas to come back. When Douglas failed to heed his command, the guard moved from his post and retrieved his charge, bringing him back to the portico.

"*Stati!*" said the guard, much as one would command a straying dog.

Douglas nodded his understanding and walked back into the house. "Well, that much is clear at least," he announced. Snipe, who was poking at something in a corner of the room, did not deign to look up. Douglas pulled a chair from the table and sat down.

No use getting worked up about it, he thought. The situation, though highly inconvenient, could easily have been worse. Apparently they were to be taught the language of Etruria. And lest there be any doubt or mistake, they would remain the guests of the king until they learned it.

CHAPTER 12

In Which a Shocking Hypothesis Is Mooted

For J. Anthony Clarke, the internationally renowned astrophysicist, interdimensional travel was a mind-blowing revelation on a par with discovering the Grand Unified Theory, the God particle, life on Mars, superstrings, and the Loch Ness monster all at once. Every fibre of his being vibrated with the knowledge that he had experienced a phenomenon of unrivalled transformational power. Ecstatic as he was over this game-changing discovery, he immediately put aside every scientific interest and concentrated instead on his overriding domestic concern. For Tony Clarke, anxious father of a missing daughter, the experience was merely confirmation that he was on the right track.

This leap between dimensional worlds—or what had Cass called it? The Ghost Road?—this radical shift in both location and time was something he could happily spend the rest of his life studying and documenting. Already the physicist in him was formulating the ways and means of quantifying certain aspects of the phenomenon that could lead to a testable hypothesis. Shocking as it might be to the scientific establishment—shocking, mind-blowing, consciousness-altering as it was to himself—exploring the phenomenon would be his life's great work.

But first he had to find his daughter.

For that, Tony had to trust the services of his guide, Friday. Laconic, disapproving, pedantic grudge that he was, the Yavapai native was nevertheless a man of his word. He had agreed to help and, so far, that was what he was doing.

From the Nazca desert the two had made a jump to another place—a world, or at least a region of small farms and villages linked by dirt roads—vaguely reminiscent of Eastern Europe, although Tony couldn't tell for sure. In any case, it was not Antarctica and it was not Peru. At first blush the place seemed to hold out some promise as a destination Cassandra might have discovered. But after the better part of a day of wandering around to no effect, Tony concluded that it was highly unlikely that his daughter would have found much in the way of help or even interest here. "I'm guessing she went back the way she came," Tony said, though less certain than before as the fingers of doubt steadily tightened their grip.

"That is what I would do," Friday concurred.

"Then we go back," Tony decided, a note of defeat edging into his normally buoyant tone. "And on the way you can tell me about how to recognise a Ghost Road when I see one. What are the telltale signs?"

Reversing their course, Friday led them back along the river to where a track from the rocky bluffs joined the road that wound alongside the riverbank. The sun lowered in the afternoon sky and the air was growing perceptibly cooler as they climbed the hillside to the cleft in the rocks through which they had emerged into this pastoral, if uninteresting, world. While they walked, Tony contemplated the awful possibility of not being able to find his daughter. What would he do then? He had no idea.

"We are early," Friday announced. "It is not time."

Tony glanced up and looked around to find that they had indeed arrived back at the hilltop ravine by which they had entered this world. He gazed at the river valley spreading out below them—had they really climbed it that quickly? Lost in thought, he had been completely oblivious to their hike. He glanced at the narrow gap in the rocky escarpment before them, then looked at the sky, judging the time of day. "How do you know? How do you sense when the Ghost Road is . . . um, *active*? Once it is active, is there any way to tell where you will end up? That is, where the Coyote Bridge will take you?"

"You ask a lot of questions."

"It's my job."

While they waited for the Ghost Road to open, Friday schooled his insatiable pupil on the finer points of what Tony now thought of as Ghost Road and Coyote Bridge navigation. Finally Friday raised his eyes to the sky. The sun had sunk behind the hilltops, casting the rocky ravine in shadow. The air streaming through the rift in the rocks was cool with the breath of evening and the moon was breaching the horizon to the east. He nodded. "We can go."

"Well then," Tony replied, taking a deep breath to steady himself, "let's get on with it."

Friday turned and stepped into the narrow divide between solid walls of wind-eroded stone. Tony followed, keenly attentive to every move and action on the part of his guide, memorising the sequence for further study: first a little walk down a path until arriving at the active part of the path, the bridge; then moving into or through the force field created by the line of force, which was signalled by an atmospheric disturbance—rain, or wind, or fog, or all three at once—in greater or lesser measure. If successful, these actions resulted in the instantaneous translocation to a new reality or dimension of the universe without crossing any distance between—a true quantum jump. The journey, so swiftly accomplished, came at the cost of a little motion sickness. But the nausea soon passed; moreover, Tony noticed his body was growing accustomed to these leaps and the resulting sickness was gradually lessening—which he took as a sign that the malady would decrease with repeated experience until it was no longer a feature to be dreaded. Friday, for example, did not appear in the least affected by this intense, yet transitory, kinetosis.

Ever the observant scientist, Tony was enumerating all these things when the mist-laden clouds closed around him and he lost sight of Friday just two steps ahead of him. There was a splash of cold rain on his face and the bite of a chill wind, then a blur of confused motion and . . . silence.

He landed on his heels with a jolt that travelled up his leg, causing him to jam his knee. He took a hobbling step and the knee seized, almost pitching him forward onto a path of cobbled stone. The next moment the motion sickness caught up with him and slammed him hard. His empty stomach bunched into a tight ball and he retched with dry heaves.

Steadying himself against the near wall, he raised his head and looked around to find that he was in what seemed to be an alleyway between two whitewashed walls so narrow that, standing in the middle, he could have touched both sides with outstretched hands. The air was humid and hot, and the scaly branches of a sycamore tree overhung the alleyway. From beyond the nearby walls, dogs were barking. At one end the path terminated at a blank wall; at the other, a stone archway gave onto a sun-filled expanse beyond which Tony could not see.

Nor could he see any sign of Friday.

He waited for a while, trying to decide what to do, then waited some more. When Friday failed to appear, it occurred to Tony that perhaps his taciturn companion had arrived ahead of him and was waiting somewhere nearby. In any case, he decided, it would not hurt to have a look around. He moved to the mouth of the narrow alleyway and peered out onto a street unlike any in his experience—save from films, or old black-and-white newsreels. But here, shimmering beneath a blazing hot sun, in living colour, was a scene his grandfather and great-grandfather would have recognised—if, that is, either one of them had ever travelled beyond the family farm in Pennsylvania.

The people he saw moving about were dressed in long, flowing robes of bird's-egg blue or coffee-coloured beige, lightweight stuff that gave them a floaty aspect. The women wore headscarves in bright patterns; there were striped pantaloons, ample white shirts with black vests, and red fezes for the men—and the few vehicles that were not either donkey carts or handbarrows were sun-bleached automobiles of 1930s vintage. The street itself was lined with shops and booths under faded maroon-and-white-striped awnings.

The fact that the inhabitants of this place appeared to go about their business without a glance in his direction gave him a fair bit of courage to venture a few steps from the alley—at least far enough to see if he could spot Friday somewhere on the street. To the left he saw a row of vendors' stalls and tiny shops——fruit, leather goods, cloth, spices——and mingling patrons, women with net bags in twos and threes drifting leisurely along the stalls and shop fronts. Ahead, some distance down the road, he saw an archway of classical design in antique white marble and beyond it another arch——this one of banded black-and-white flanked by wide timber doors. It was, he recognised, the entrance to one of those rambling covered markets abounding in Middle Eastern countries——a souk, or bazaar——a busy place, judging by the numbers of shoppers passing in and out through the entrance.

As he stood taking this in, he became aware that he had come under the scrutiny of another. At the same moment, he felt a tug on his sleeve. Looking down, he met a pair of bright brown eyes set in the round, smiling face of a boy with wiry jet-black hair——a lad of perhaps eight or nine years, dressed in dirty cream-coloured trousers that were too short and ragged at the knees and an oversized tunic of the same stuff, frayed at the collar.

"Hello there," said Tony. "Do you speak English?"

The boy glanced behind him, and Tony saw that he was accompanied by a young girl who could not have been more than a year or two older. Like her grubby companion, her simple dress was stained and bedraggled, but her face and hands were clean, and her hair was neatly combed and braided beneath a bright blue scarf. Aware that he was about to be accosted by beggars, Tony patted his pockets for some change.

"I'm afraid I don't have any money," he began, then realised the lad was holding out a piece of paper to him. "Oh? What's this?"

The boy urged the bit of paper on him. Tony took the scrap, a little bigger than a business card, turned it over, and saw a message written in English. It read:

Lost? Lonely?
Looking for Something to Believe In?
We Can Help

For Information
Come to 22 Hanania Street nr.
Beit Hanania

The Zetetic Society

Tony read the paper again. An advertisement? He passed the message back to the boy, who merely shook his head and pushed it back at Tony. "No? You want me to have it?" he said. "What does it mean?"

"Come with us, mister," said the girl, stepping up.

"You speak English?" said Tony hopefully. "Is this where I am? Damascus?"

"You come with us," she said again and stepped away, paused, and beckoned him to follow.

Aware that he was probably a fool falling into a local scam of the kind perpetrated on unwary foreigners, Tony was sufficiently intrigued by the enigmatic note to follow, at least until he found whatever it was the youngsters were selling. "All right. I'll come with you," he said. "But no funny business."

The young boy fell into step beside him, and the girl led them into a dizzying tangle of tiny streets and paths and byways through neighbourhoods of open-air kiosks and little workshops like tiny factories turning out wooden bowls and spoons and chairs; here a potter making jars and cups; there a rug maker weaving grass mats; and just beyond, a woman making lace tablecloths and bed coverings . . . and on and on. The passersby paid Tony and his small escorts no attention whatever; he might have been invisible for all the notice he received. Apparently foreigners were such a common presence as to be beneath regard.

Down one street after another they went. At each turn Tony felt more foolish for having agreed to come along, and more certain it would all end badly. Finally, as they entered a quiet street lined with larger, more imposing buildings fronted by black-and-white stonework doorways, he decided that the goose chase had gone on long enough. He stopped. "Okay," he declared. "This is it. I am finished."

The girl stopped in the middle of the street and turned around. "You come."

"No." Tony shook his head. It was late afternoon and hot, the sky above had the faded quality of worn denim, and he was tired and thirsty and longing for some small confirmation that he would not be beaten and robbed by bandits. "I quit. I'm not going any farther."

"You come," insisted the girl. She turned and walked to a nearby doorway. "Is here."

"Sorry." Tony shook his head slowly.

The little boy tugged on his sleeve and pointed at the door where the girl waited. "No, sorry. I'm going back," said Tony, glancing over his shoulder. "*If* I can find my way."

The girl, still watching him, rose up on her tiptoes and, taking the brass knocker, rapped loudly on the door. She knocked again and gestured for Tony to come along. He refused—

—and was still refusing when there came the click of a lock, the door opened, and the kindly face of an elderly woman with a severe haircut peered out, squinting behind her wire-rim glasses into the bright sunlit street.

"Oh, hello, Afifah, have you brought me a visitor?" she asked in a gentle Scottish accent.

"There," replied the girl, pointing at Tony, still standing in the street.

The woman stepped from the door. "Hello, Fadi." She waved to the boy. "Who have you brought me?"

The boy tugged on Tony's sleeve and pointed to the woman, urging him to go to her.

"Come along with you," she called. "I won't bite."

Tony, deciding that he had little to fear from a white-haired old woman, took a few steps closer. "Hello," he said. "I'm not sure there hasn't been some mistake."

"You'll have to come closer. I'm not going to shout."

He moved to the doorway where the stout, tweed-skirted old dear waited with folded hands. "Was there something you wanted?"

"My daughter," Tony blurted without thinking. "I'm looking for my daughter. She is lost and I'm trying to find her."

This was not how he had planned to begin any potential conversation, but the accumulated strangeness of the day's events finally overwhelmed his natural detachment, and his emotional control finally gave way to the moment. He abandoned any attempt to reverse his headlong plunge and concluded, as if by way of explanation, "I've come from the United States."

"Oh my," replied the woman in her buttery Highland brogue. "Then you had better come in, if you've come that far."

As she stepped back and opened the black-painted door a little wider, Tony saw the polished brass plate engraved with the words *Zetetic Society.*

CHAPTER 13

In Which Landlubbers
Take to the Sea

The *Percheron* was a durable, compact ship rescued from the breaker's yard by a shipping agent in the hire of Lord Burleigh. The double-masted, square-rigged vessel had started out life as a twenty-four-gun French brigantine, which had been captured during a brief skirmish in the Bay of Biscay. Because of its wide hull and generous hold, the craft was converted to a storeship and spent the next few years hauling supplies around to its larger sisters of the British fleet, the mighty ships-of-the-line. Badly damaged in an early autumn storm off Land's End, the vessel was judged by the admiralty as not worth the cost of repair and was condemned to be sold for scrap and fittings. Upon being alerted by the agent, Burleigh stepped in, purchased the wounded ship, and had it towed to a private shipyard in Southampton.

The reconstruction had cost a princely sum, but far less than a new ship that, for the price, would have been a smaller, lighter craft; and inasmuch as his lordship planned to take up lengthy residence aboard ship, comfort, safety, and overall seaworthiness were of primary consideration. And in Burleigh's thinking, the value of a sturdy seagoing fighter was not to be disparaged. Against that, money did not enter the list. Thus no expense was too great, and none was spared. The result was a ship that was both highly manoeuvrable and tight as a drumhead. What she may have lacked in speed was more than made up for in comfort, not to mention the cavernous cargo capacity. Fully laden—as it was just now—the *Percheron* would be able to spend up to thirty-six months at sea, which suited Burleigh's designs.

Now, as his lordship strode the deck, feeling the damp night air on his face and neck, with the faintly foul river scent in his nostrils, he could not wait to weigh anchor. He ran his hand along the newly polished rail, turned, and walked back to the wheelhouse, which he had enclosed and covered to provide shelter for the helmsman.

"Where are they, Mr. Farrell? Any sign?" It was a needless question, but Burleigh could not help asking.

"Just gone nine by t' bell in yonder church tower," replied the captain around the long-stemmed pipe in his mouth. "River's running high t'night. Reckon they'll be along smart enough. We shall make tide, sir." He gave a sharp nod of assurance. "Never fear."

"And the crew?"

"Below in quarters—but ready to haul away as soon as I ring stations." He paused, still trying to gauge the measure of his new employer. "They are chosen men, my lord. Twelve o' the best—as requested. And you've a jemmy ship—bright as I've ever had t' pleasure to helm. We'll get on right enough."

"The men I'm taking on tonight, Captain," offered Burleigh.

"They're not trained to the sea as such. To be blunt, they have no training whatsoever."

"So you've said, sir. So you've said." Mr. Farrell removed the pipe and gave the bowl a tap against the ship's wheel. "Not to worry. I've weaned pups before. Three months with me and my crew and they'll be salt-licking seadogs right enough."

"I am counting on it, Captain."

"And so you may," affirmed Farrell. "Though they be t' sorriest landlubbers that ever staggered a deck, they'll be fit for His Majesty's Navy as of this time next year." He gave the pipe another tap and stuck it in his mouth. "You can lay odds on that."

"I will leave you to it, Captain." Burleigh moved off towards the stern to wait.

"One small matter arising, your lordship," Farrell called after him. "Would you mind telling me where we're headed?"

"Once everyone is on board and we're under weigh—then I'll tell you."

"I only mention it because it might help to have a course in mind before we make Greenwich."

"Before Greenwich it is," agreed Burleigh as he continued on his way.

The raised quarterdeck of the stern had been re-planked and still smelled of wood shavings and oakum. Burleigh settled on one of the balustrade benches he had installed—another of his own designs—pulled his coat around him, and, stretching his long legs before him, leaned back to wait. He was soon reflecting on how well sound carried over water—especially at night, it seemed. He could hear conversations among crewmen of other boats as they passed, the dip and slosh of oars, and the odd sound from the shore—a shout, the slam of a door, the barking of dogs, raucous singing from a wharfside pub, a catfight, a breaking bottle, a baby's cry, a sudden eruption of laughter, the endless wash and ripple of the river waves against the mud-slick shore: a varied tableau of sound, an aural reminder of all that made life in the docklands so various.

Presently a church bell marked the hour and Burleigh counted ten tolls; the clear, melodic tone was still echoing across the water when he heard another bell—four quick chimes coming from the wheelhouse—followed by a hailing shout. Rising, the earl quickly made his way to the bow, where three crewmen were already lowering a rope ladder to a boat that had come up alongside. Looking over the rail, he saw a tender with a knot of men huddled on the centre benches.

At Burleigh's appearance, the crewmen ceased what they were doing and snapped to attention. "Carry on," he commanded.

"Permission to come aboard," called a man standing in the stern.

Burleigh recognised his man Suggs and waved him in. "Here we are, all correct and proper," announced the pilot, swinging his leg over the rail.

"Any trouble?" asked Burleigh.

"Narry a feather out of place," replied the riverman, coming to stand before Burleigh. "I flapped your bit o' paper in their fat faces, and the rozzers never raised a peep. Then I sprinkled a little silver on 'em—as specified in your particulars—and they went away cheerful, happy fellas."

"Any of them twig to our ruse?"

"No, sir." The pilot gave his shaggy head a shake. "All they know is I saved 'em a tiresome trip to Deptford in the middle of the night."

"Well done, Suggs. You have earned yourself that bonus." Turning to the crewmen standing by, he said, "Bring up the prisoners."

Pilot Suggs leaned over the rail and called down to his men. "Unchain 'em and let 'em up—one at a time, mind. We don't want anyone falling in the drink."

Burleigh watched as the first prisoner was unshackled and allowed up the ladder. "When all are assembled, bring them aft. I will address them there." Turning back to Suggs, he passed a bag of coins to him, saying, "I may have need of you in days to come."

"Always at your service, sir," replied the pilot, touching his hat in salute. "My distinct pleasure."

Burleigh dismissed the riverman and returned to his place at the stern rail to wait. A short while later there came the thump of heavy street shoes on the planks and he rose, folding his arms across his chest. The four newcomers, uncertain what to make of this turn in their fortunes, stood tentatively before his lordship's calculating gaze—a general inspecting green recruits.

"My name is Archelaeus Burleigh," he said abruptly. "I am the Earl of Sutherland, and this is my ship. You are here tonight because I have saved you. Each one of you has been rescued from imprisonment or exile because you are chosen men—chosen by me for a particular enterprise that has been long in the planning." He levelled his gaze at each one in turn, then declared, "Now the time has come for *you* to choose. Swear loyalty to me and I will, in due course, grant you all your freedom. Serve me well and I will enrich you beyond your most fevered dreams of avarice—"

"What if we choose not to swear loyalty?" asked the man called Taverner.

"If that is your choice, I respect it. You will be taken back to Justice House, where I have no doubt you will serve out your sentence—possibly with twenty years added for attempting to escape."

"Not much of a choice, is it?" grumbled another of the men.

"Perhaps not—I grant you that," replied Burleigh in a reasonable tone. "But, as you are men of limited prospects, I think you must all ask yourselves if you are likely to receive a better offer in the next few minutes. Because, you see, the tide is beginning to run, and this ship sets sail on the tide. Have I made the alternatives clear enough?"

The prisoners glanced at one another, and the one who had raised the question received an elbow in the ribs from the one closest to him. "Clear as bells, m'lud."

"Well then," continued Burleigh, "I urge you all to choose the path to wealth and eventual freedom in my service." He moved to stand before the first man. "What do you say, Taverner?"

"I'd sign on with the devil himself if he got me out of that plague hole."

"Welcome aboard," replied Burleigh. He moved on to the next man. "How about you—Dexter, is it? What do you say?"

"Yes, sir. You can count me in."

Burleigh welcomed him and moved on to the next man. "It is your turn, Connie Wilkes. Are you with me?"

"Aye, sir," replied the man. "One good turn deserves another—as me old mam'd say."

Burleigh likewise welcomed him and then turned to the last man. "That leaves you, Malcolm Dawes. Time to make up your mind."

Glancing at his fellows, Malcolm shrugged and said, "If they're in, I'm in."

"Good," said Burleigh after welcoming the last of his new gang. "We are putting to sea at once. Your first chore will be to aid Captain Farrell's crew. Tomorrow we will begin your education."

"What education is that?" asked Taverner. "Begging your pardon, sir."

"An education in what I expect from those in my service," replied the earl. "An education in the way the world really works." He paused, then added, "An education in how and where to find the riches I have promised you."

The ship's bell rang again and a voice called from the foredeck.

"They are ready to weigh anchor. You are dismissed to help them. Mr. Farrell is captain of this ship, and you will obey his every command—without question. In the days to come, he will teach you to sail. When you have completed your chores tonight, you will be shown to your quarters. We will speak again tomorrow."

The convicts looked at one another uncertainly, then Taverner said, "You heard the boss. Let's get cracking. The sooner that anchor is up, the sooner we leave Ole Blighty behind. I don't know about the rest o' you, but that can't be soon enough for me."

Malcolm turned on him. "Listen, sunshine, you ent top dog here. I don't take no orders from the likes o' you."

"What was that?" sneered Taverner. "Did I hear a rat squeak?"

Burleigh watched but made no move to intervene in the power struggle between them.

"Leave it out, you two," snarled Dexter, stepping between them. "He's right, Mal. The sooner we get under sail, the better it is for all of us. Last thing we want is bluebottles buzzing 'round, right?"

"'Course I'm right," Taverner gloated. "Come on, lads." He hurried away and the others fell into line behind him.

Burleigh smiled as the gang tramped off. They were raw, oh yes—very raw. He did not allow himself to imagine for a moment that it would be an easy task to forge them into serviceable shape, but at least the first challenge had been made and met, the first crisis of leadership peacefully resolved.

He moved to the aft companionway and went below to his quarters—a suite of panelled rooms of extreme opulence. The cabin boy had lit the candles for him and turned down his bed. From a decanter on his sideboard, Burleigh filled a cut-glass beaker with fine port and sat down to toast the day's success. As he sipped the sweet liquor, there came a knock on his cabin door and, upon invitation, a crewman put his head in. "Begging your pardon, my lord," said the sailor, "Captain desires the satisfaction of knowing where the earl would like his ship to go."

"Ah." Burleigh swirled the drink in his cup and held it to the candlelight, studying the deep velvety colour. "Tell Mr. Farrell to set course for Gibraltar and the Tyrrhenian Sea."

CHAPTER 14

In Which an Alchemical
Difficulty Is Compounded

N ever heard of the Magick Court?" asked Kit. "Really?"

"I'm not much into tennis. Or basketball," replied Cassandra. "Professional sports leave me cold."

"Fair enough," allowed Kit, grinning. "Actually, it's nothing to do with tennis."

"I'm really not all that much into magic either."

Wilhelmina and Gianni, sitting opposite them in the carriage, were deep in a conversation of their own. Kit was happy to play tour guide. "How about Mad Rudolf—ever heard of him?"

Cass shook her head.

"We need to improve your education, American girl."

"Yeah, right," she scoffed. "So what's so important about this magic court, Professor Livingstone?"

"For starters," replied Kit, adopting the smug manner of a junior lecturer, "the Magick Court is not really about magic at all. It's all to do with Emperor Rudolf's search for the Philosopher's Stone—"

"Got this one," said Cass. "Alchemy, right? Changing lead into gold."

"Partly," allowed Kit. "It *is* alchemy, but they're not trying to change lead into gold, they're searching for the formula for immortality. Emperor Rudolf has brought the best and brightest scientific minds of the age here to help crack it." At Cass' expression he laughed, enjoying the all-too-rare occasion when he actually knew something useful. "I'm serious. They're all up here beavering away like mad things, and Emperor Rudolf pays the bills."

"Real, live alchemists," Cass mused, shaking her head lightly. "I *am* living a fairy tale."

"No kidding," agreed Kit. "But then, this *is* the age of fairy tales, remember. The Brothers Grimm live just around the corner."

"Really?" Cass said—before catching herself. Kit nodded in mock sincerity and she gave him a gentle push. "Liar."

The red carriage jounced over the bridge separating the imperial precinct from the lower town, and Cass caught a glimpse of a structure that appeared, in her view, almost defiantly dull. Where she might have anticipated a grand, castellated edifice with towers and parapets and arches, what she saw was a blockish bulwark that prefigured post-war brutalist architecture by a good three hundred years. Emperor Rudolf's palace was, it had to be said, an extremely depressing barn of a building, devoid even of a barn's prosaic appeal.

Sharing the plaza-sized courtyard was a cathedral of such inspired grandeur of vision that it seemed to have been dropped onto the square from another, altogether more refined planet for the sole purpose of showing up the deficiencies of its ugly sister opposite. Where the palace hulked and brooded, breathing an air of drear despond, the cathedral soared and scintillated, its delicate, graceful spires and the swelling copper dome catching light from every available angle and giving it back as golden fire—transmuting earthly matter into substance fitted for heaven.

Before Cass had time to dwell on the meaning of this visual parable, the carriage jounced through the gates and swayed to a halt; the door was opened by a servant in royal red livery. She followed Mina and Gianni as they disembarked and found herself standing before an entrance dominated by a great pediment featuring what could only be the most realistic statue of Saint George and his dragon that she had ever seen. The heroic knight stood with one foot firmly planted on the thrashing creature's sinuous neck, his broadsword sweeping down for the *coup de grâce* as the odious thing raked the air with its scimitar claws and gnashed its rapier teeth before Saint George's resolute righteousness.

"Gosh," she murmured.

"I know," said Mina. "I felt the same way first time I saw it."

"Will we meet the emperor?" wondered Cass. "Or any of the royal family?"

"I don't think so," Mina told her. "But you never know. Rudolf is always around—kind of like a ghost drifting through the corridors. But he doesn't mingle much."

"Have you met him?"

"Once. He seems a nice chap—a bit eccentric, but not half as mad as people make out. It's possible we might meet Docktor Bazalgette, though. He's the Lord High Alchemist and, just so you know, he takes his position very seriously. If we see him, a bow and curtsey are in order. And whatever you do, do not mention the Turks. Oh, and be sure to call him *Herr Docktor*. He insists."

Cass gave Kit a look that said, *Pinch me, I'm in a dream*, and Kit returned it with a glance that said, *You cannot make this stuff up.*

From the palace emerged a man in a coat and knee breeches of green satin, white stockings, and shiny black shoes. *"Ich heisse Sie alle willkommen zu Ihnen alle,"* he said with a perfunctory bow. *"Kann ich Ihre Vorladung sehen?"*

Wilhelmina produced the summons she had received, and they were conducted straightaway through the enormous vestibule and into Grand Ludovic Hall. They crossed a space that could have served as a municipal skating rink and were met at the far end by another servant. At a word from his superior, the footman led them up a wide staircase and then another, down a succession of corridors and long connecting hallways to a dusty back wing of the palace.

"Here is where the alchemists hang out," Mina told the others.

They stopped at a brass-studded, leather-bound door. The footman gave a quick, officious rap on the doorframe, and there issued a muffled voice from within. *"Einen Moment, bitte!"*

As the footman disappeared back down the corridor, the leather-lined door opened to reveal a slender young fellow dressed as if he were attending a costume party as the Sorcerer's Apprentice—complete with a fur-trimmed cloak of dark purple and a pancake-shaped velvet hat that lopped over his ears. *"Och!* Here you are." He opened the door wide. *"Kommen Sie herein."*

"I hope you don't mind," said Mina in English. "I brought some people along." She made short work of introducing the others.

"Willkommen to my laboratory, *meine Freunde,"* he said. "Forgive my poor English, I am begging you. Gustavus Rosenkreuz is at your service."

Wilhelmina explained, "Herr Rosenkreuz is the chief assistant to the Lord High Alchemist." She gave his shoulder a friendly pat. "He is second to Docktor Bazalgette in the palace, but a first-class genius in his own right."

The fair-haired young man inclined his head modestly but smiled with pride at Mina's effusive recognition. "You are too kind."

He smiled and removed his floppy hat. *"Begrüssen Sie, alle."*

He then shepherded his guests into the lab. Cass entered first and was met by a sight and a stench that stole her breath away. In the massive fireplace at the far end of the room stood a huge black cauldron; the massive horned head of an ox was bubbling merrily away in a steaming bath, the noxious sulphurous vapours of which stung the nostrils with the aggressive rancour of rotten eggs.

The chamber itself resembled a storeroom for the Museum of the Weird. There were shelves everywhere and all of them stuffed, so far as she could tell, with jars, boxes, crocks, and cages, veritably groaning with all variety of curious objects—everything from ostrich eggs to silk worm cocoons to desiccated lizards and lumps of coal. There were tools of exceedingly arcane construction whose uses could not be guessed, as well as beakers and pots, mortars and pestles, tongs, pinchers, knives, and spoons of every size.

"Please, come this way," said Gustavus. "We can speak more privately."

He led his little troop of visitors through the lab towards a book-lined chamber beyond. If the laboratory was a branch of Ye Olde Curiosity Shoppe, Cass decided, then the study was its rare book room. Not at all a large space, it was made even smaller by the floor-to-ceiling shelves lining every wall, each shelf crammed to groaning capacity with leather-bound tomes of all sizes; a table stood in the centre of the room, and it was heaped with books, papers, and scrolls. There were three chairs at the table and a bench on one side. Gustavus offered

Wilhelmina and Gianni each a seat; he took the third, and Kit and Cass shared the bench.

"Thank you, Gustavus, for agreeing to see us. We'll try not to take up too much of your time," began Mina.

"Please, Fräulein Wilhelmina, my time is yours."

"I will come to the point," she replied. "You know those instruments you have made for me? The shadow lamps?"

"Of course, yes," replied the young alchemist. He leaned close and with a sly smile whispered, "It remains our secret—of that you can be certain."

"I fear I must presume upon your discretion further," Mina told him. "We want you to make some more of them."

"Six of them," added Kit. "To be precise."

Gustavus peered at them doubtfully and sucked his teeth. "So many?"

"We experienced something unexpected," offered Mina. "Something extraordinary." She went on to describe what had happened when she, Kit, and Gianni encountered an extremely powerful field of telluric energy—a region of such force that it destroyed the devices. "The lamps grew so hot they almost melted in our hands."

Impressed by this information, the alchemist nodded appreciatively. "That would be extremely hot, as you say."

"Stranger still," Kit put in, "the energy was not confined to a line—it seemed to be contained in an absolutely enormous tree. And it was so powerful it completely destroyed the lamps. Burned them out. *Phhtt!*"

"The device is *kaput?*" wondered the alchemist.

"Stone-cold dead," replied Kit. He pulled his defunct ley lamp from his pocket and passed it to the alchemist.

"Both of them," said Mina. "Kaput."

Gustavus examined the device, its bright brass carapace now dull and distorted, warped by the heat of the power surge that had destroyed it. "That must have been very exciting," he observed.

Cass suppressed a smile at his heavily accented English: *wary eggs hiding*.

"It was astonishing," granted Mina. "I had no idea they would do that."

"Do you have your lamp with you?"

"Mine was the newer version, you remember," she said, handing him her shadow lamp. "But it burned out too, just like the other one."

Gustavus turned the ruined gizmo over in his hand, sniffed it, shook it, and listened as it gave off a faint rattle as if it had a few grains of sand trapped inside its hollow shell. "So now you wish me to make more such devices." He glanced up to inquire, "Six, you say?"

"Six," confirmed Kit. "I know it is a lot to ask, but we could really . . ." He trailed off because the alchemist was frowning.

"Is something wrong?" asked Wilhelmina.

"*Es tut mir leid,*" replied Gustavus, placing the ruined instrument on the table before him. "I cannot. I am lacking the materials."

"We will happily pay for the materials," suggested Mina quickly. "Whatever you need—"

"I have everything required to make these little devices," said Gustavus, "all the materials *except* that which is the most important, *ja*? The substance that animates the mechanism."

"What is the substance?" asked Gianni. "Perhaps we can get it for you."

"I do not know what is the substance," the alchemist replied, shaking his head. "This is the problem."

The four questors looked at one another. Kit spoke up. "So you're saying we don't have enough of whatever it takes, and we don't know what that is or where to get more," said Kit. "Yeah, I guess that's a problem, all right."

"A classic compound problem, I'd say," echoed Cass.

"Always Herr Burleigh brings me the special material," explained Gustavus. "I use what he brings to make his devices, and then I make the copies *mit* what I have saved." He blushed slightly as he confided, "So, maybe I do not tell him exactly how much is required to make a lamp like this."

"Do you have any of this material left over from the last shadow lamps you made?" said Mina.

"A very little." Gustavus rose and started for the door. "Come, I will show you."

He led them back into the main laboratory where, from behind some jars labelled in Latin, he withdrew a wooden container about the size of a cigar box, which he placed on the nearby table. Opening the box, he took out a small glass bottle containing a grainy grey substance like dull, metallic sand. "This is the animating matter after preparation," he explained. Producing a second, slightly larger bottle, he said, "This is how it comes to me." Inside were small blobs that looked like dirty brown chalk. "It must be heated and treated with chemicals to refine it. Only then can it be used."

"May I?" Kit took the jar containing the pale-grey powder, pulled out the stopper, and raised it to his nose. He took an exploratory sniff. "It smells like . . . I don't know—rocks?"

He offered the bottle to Cass, who gave the glass a shake and sniffed. "I get traces of talc and maybe oxidised aluminium." She passed the vial to Gianni, who took an exploratory sniff.

"Definitely metallic," he said, passing the jar to Mina.

Wilhelmina put her nose to the opening and then shrugged. "To me it just smells like minerals." Handing the jar back to Gustavus, she said, "What do you think it could be?"

"I have no idea," he confessed. "The material is like nothing I have ever seen and, as I said, it is always supplied by the earl himself—the same with the basic plans for the device. They are from Herr Burleigh, although I make very good copies for myself."

"Okay," said Kit. "So first off we need to find out what the special ingredient is—that will tell us where to get more." He looked to the others. "Any ideas?"

Cass said, "I know a few basic chemical analysis techniques. I could do some tests and see what turns up." She tapped the jar lightly. "Who knows? We might get lucky."

"I can help you with this, if you like," offered Gianni.

"Or we could ask Burleigh," suggested Wilhelmina.

Kit gave her a look that expressed his opinion that she was wildly and woefully mistaken if she imagined that to be in any way a reasonable idea. "Maybe *you* could ask him," he suggested tartly. "Last time *I* met him, his earldom did his talking with a pistol."

"I'm not saying it would be easy," Mina muttered.

Kit gave her another look and turned to the alchemist, as if seeking a more rational ally. "How much of this stuff do we need, anyway, Gus? How much of the special powder does one lamp contain?"

"Twenty drachms," replied the alchemist after a moment's thought. He made a calculation in his head. "*Jah*, twenty drachms is correct."

"That's about thirty grams," said Mina, translating for the others. "So that's 180 grams altogether."

"More would be better, I'm guessing," said Kit. Turning to Cass and Gianni, he asked, "So what do you two need to test it?"

"Give us some time to think about it," replied Cass.

Gianni added, "We'll make a list of tools and equipment."

"Then it is settled," concluded Wilhelmina. "Gustavus, if you will allow us to take a sample of the stuff, we will test it. And if we can determine what it is, then we can probably find out where to get it."

"How about it, Gus?" said Kit.

The alchemist quickly agreed. "I will personally aid you in any way I can." He made a small bow of deference, then added, "However, I make one . . . ah, *Bedingung* . . ."

"Condition," translated Wilhelmina.

Gustavus nodded. "I make one condition—that I should be allowed to accompany you on one of your astral expeditions."

"You want to make a ley jump with us?"

"Please." The alchemist gazed at the group hopefully. "It is my most sincere wish."

"Well," said Mina, "in light of your past service and present involvement, that seems reasonable." She glanced to Kit for support. "I don't see how we can refuse you, Gustavus."

"Then we have a deal," said Kit. "Where do we start?"

PART THREE

Hide and Seek

CHAPTER 15

In Which a River Becomes a Flood

"For the last time, Giles, I did not *steal* the book," Lady Fayth insisted. "It belongs to me. It was my Uncle Henry's, and so it rightfully should have passed to me when he died. Therefore you need have no more qualms about it." She gave him a stern look. "At all events, we will most certainly return to Prague before anyone can form the slightest notion that we have been away for even a moment."

Giles, still frowning, passed a dubious gaze at the surrounding landscape: an empty plain of low hills covered with grass in all directions as far as the eye could see. A fitful breeze, cool out of the north, blew over this prairie sea in rippling waves. "You are confident our travel can be reckoned so precisely, my lady?" he asked.

"To be sure, Giles. I have done it before." She started walking in the direction of the dull white glow of a sun slowly burning through heavy grey clouds.

"Where are we now?"

"This place? I cannot possibly say. It is merely an intermediate point on the way to our destination." She glanced back with an expression of mild exasperation. "Any more questions?"

Giles knew better than to gainsay his mistress. "No, my lady."

"I am heartily glad to hear it." She quickened her pace. "Do come along. The next ley is some little distance, and we must be there and ready before the sun sets. I do not wish to spend the night out here in this"—she flung a hand around at the treeless, hillbound wilderness around them—"this godforsaken desert."

They walked for a time in silence, listening to the hiss of the wind over the hills and the swish of their feet through the coarse grass; the occasional cry of a high-flying hawk fell from the empty heights above with a lonely shriek. The morning passed and afternoon wore on in a series of low hills, each the same as the other. At the crest of each hilltop they paused on the high ground to look across the rolling landscape, hoping to spot one or more of the standing stones that marked the ley for which Haven was searching. All that met their gaze was an endless undulation of treeless steppes, the green ocean-like swell of a limitless sea of grass.

"My lady," said Giles after one such pause, "it occurs to me that we—"

"Listen!" Haven cocked her head to one side. "Do you hear that?"

"I hear noth—"

"Shh!" she snapped. There came a sound on the breeze, a faint riffling rumble on the wind. "What is that?"

"Thunder?"

The odd sound grew louder. Instinctively both travellers looked to the sky to see a small dark object streaking through the low cloud-cover, leaving a trail of grey smoke behind. The thing fell with blinding speed, smashing into the flank of a hill across the valley in front of them. Between one heartbeat and the next, the peace of the steppe was rent by an explosion that heaved fire and dirt and smouldering fragments into the air.

Giles and Haven glanced involuntarily at one another. Then Giles turned and started running for the hilltop. "Hurry!"

"Giles, no!"

But he was already racing away. Haven had no choice but to follow. By the time she reached the summit, Giles was bent low, hands on knees, gazing down into the shallow bowl below at a number of tent-like dwellings ranged along the small stream that coursed through the valley. Men and horses were running away from the crater made by the impact of the mysterious thing that had exploded in the midst of their encampment.

"What in the name of all—"

"Get down!" rasped Giles harshly. He pulled her down beside him. "They'll see you."

"Who are they?" she wondered aloud.

At that moment, the sound of distant thunder ruffled the air and another of the infernal salvos fell from the sky. They looked up to see the telltale signature of smoke as the thing streaked to earth, landing a short distance from the still-smoking hole left by the first one. Again there was a brief hesitation—time enough only for those closest to the object to throw themselves to the ground before the deadly fountain of fire and smoke and glittering fragments erupted once more.

"What *are* those things—those sky bolts?" she asked. "Have you ever seen the like?" Haven glanced back down at the encampment where those under this strange attack were attempting to escape—with much shouting and wailing—fleeing back along the valley course—most on foot, others on horseback—all of them abandoning their camp in desperate flight.

"We dare not stay here. We cannot risk getting caught up in this attack." He looked right and left along the ridgeway. "Which way should we go?"

Haven's face contracted in thought. "That way . . . I think." She pointed in a northeasterly direction. "In all honesty, Giles, I cannot say."

Giles scanned the landscape around about. "If we follow the ridge to there," he said, pointing to a place where the hill line ended half a mile or more distant to the southeast, "that should not take us too far out of our way."

Before they could move, the dread whiffling sound cleaved the air, swiftly becoming a scream as another of the awful things plummeted, driving itself into the soft earth. A bare breath later it erupted, shaking the camp, destroying three of the tented dwellings, sending wreckage into the air. Amid the smoke and sparks, small clods of dirt and debris rained down all around. People fled the destruction, screaming and wailing as they ran.

"We have to move." Giles started away. "Now!"

They raced down the hillside, putting the flank of the hill between themselves and the strange sky-born weapons. Two more explosions in quick succession reverberated behind them as they ran, but they did not look back. When, after a time, no more eruptions were heard, Giles slowed, allowing them to catch their breath.

"Those poor people," gasped Haven, pressing a hand to her side. "How unspeakably horrid. What in God's good name were those ghastly, terrible things?"

"I cannot say, my lady. But there is trouble here, and we best get to the ley line and make our jump before anything else happens."

Haven agreed, and they moved on at a more reasonable pace, using the broad slope of the hill as a shield between them and whatever tragedy was unfolding on the other side. They moved along quickly, pausing now and then to listen, but they heard no more airy thunder or explosions. All was quiet—as if the chaos and destruction witnessed in the last minutes were already half a world away. As soon as Giles judged it was safe to proceed, they climbed to the top of the ridge once more and, crouching low so as not to be seen, took a good long look around.

As Giles had seen, the long, sloping ridgeway descended into a fold of the valley, merging and blending with two smaller hills to form a two-pronged fork of two narrow finger valleys: one leading away to the north and one to the southeast. "If the ley is that direction"—Giles pointed towards the southeast—"then it must lie somewhere beyond that rise."

Haven, coming up slowly behind him, made no reply.

"Did you hear, my lady? I said—" Giles took one look at the chalky pallor of her skin and seized her hand; it was clammy to the touch. "I think we must sit down a little and—"

Just then her eyes rolled back in her head, showing white; a juddering sigh escaped her lips and she collapsed. Giles caught her as she fell and eased her to the ground, then knelt beside her, rubbing her hands and calling her name. "Lady Fayth!" He snapped his fingers in front of her face. "Wake up, Lady Fayth!"

A moment later her eyes fluttered open; she saw Giles looming over her and the cloudless sky beyond. "Giles Standfast! Whatever are you doing?" she demanded. "Let me up! Let me up this instant!"

She made to rise but was overcome by dizziness and sank back once more, closing her eyes.

"There now. You rest easy." Giles continued to chafe her hands.

"What has happened?" she asked, her eyes still closed.

"You have had a swoon, my lady. Lie still but a moment and regain your strength."

"It would seem that I have come over very weak and unsteady of a sudden—a most peculiar feeling." She opened her eyes and offered a wan smile. "You are most attentive. If not for you, I surely would have suffered an injury."

"Your kindly opinion is welcome," replied Giles, "but in truth, if I had been more attentive, I might have seen that you have had nothing to eat or drink and we have been walking all day."

Haven sat up slowly, clutching her head. "It is true—I am somewhat famished."

"We must find water." Giles stood up and looked around as if hoping to catch a sparkling glimpse nearby. "That, I think, must come before we attempt another leap."

"You are right, of course." She raised a hand and he helped her to her feet. "We should have reached the ley long before now, I do readily confess it." She looked around at the wide and unvarying landscape and the sun now beginning its downward descent towards the west. "I cannot think where we might have gone wrong." She turned to him. "Poor Giles, I fear I have led us both astray. It is all my doing and I most heartily regret it. I am sorry."

"Let us find water first," he said, brushing aside her apology. "Then we can think what is to be done."

"Very sensible. Lead the way you think best."

"There appears to be a higher hill just beyond the near coombe."

He pointed to the north, where a short distance away a broad plain rose above the surrounding hilltops. "Perhaps we might see more from there."

He led and Haven followed. They reached the bottom of the shallow valley and were just about to start up the long, sloping hillside when Haven gave out a sighing, "Oh-h-h!"

Giles swung around just in time to catch her again. This time he did not ease her to the ground, but bore her up into his arms and proceeded to carry her to the top of the ridge, where he laid her down in the grass.

She stirred then and came to herself once more. "Oh," she sighed. "This is most discomfiting, and I do apologise. I am much obliged for your care."

"You need water is all, my lady. That will put you right as rain."

"If I may rest a little—" She stopped. Giles had turned his face away to the northwest. "What is it? Did you see something?" She pushed herself up on her elbows. Giles was gazing along the floor of the valley they had just quit; his jaw was set and face hard.

Haven turned to see what he was looking at: six riders on horses little larger than trap ponies were galloping at speed down the valley towards them. The dull thump of the horses' hooves on the soft earth reached them, and a moment later they were staring into the faces of six hard-eyed men covered in black hair in the form of fur caps, long braids, and drooping moustaches; all carried short curved swords, spears, and knives strapped to their chests. The warriors appeared to be astonished at what they had captured.

"Who can they be?" whispered Haven, a shudder passing through her.

Giles made no answer but took Haven's arm and pulled her behind him as the riders pounded to a halt at the foot of the hill.

Aside from the swords, knives, and pikes—each with a wicked, serpentine blade—three of the war band also had small bows made of horn and quivers of arrows attached to their saddles; all of them wore heavy leather jerkins that covered them from neck to knee. This crude armour was bedecked with iron discs or overlapping plates like fish scales. The warriors' faces were dark and ruddy, creased by wind and sun to leather, and half hidden beneath the large pointed caps, the flaps of which hung down over the ears and nape of the neck; their almond-shaped eyes, set above high cheekbones, were small and black, hard and sharp as obsidian.

The warriors made no move but remained on their mounts, staring at the strangers with a kind of wary wonder. The only sound was that of the wind and the horses' heavy breathing. This tense silence lasted until Giles raised an empty hand in simple greeting. "We are travellers," he announced, speaking loudly and clearly. "We mean no harm. Let us pass in peace."

The riders exchanged glances and one of them—a swarthy fellow with a round, hide-covered shield slung over one shoulder—spoke a command to the others in a rough tongue, whereupon one of their number wheeled his mount and galloped back down the valley. The shield-bearing leader then lowered his pike and thrust it at Giles' chest. He barked a command halfway between a growl and a yelp, jerking the honed blade of the pike towards the rising flank of the hill. When the two captives made no move, the warrior gestured with the pike again and barked his command more insistently. So his captives would not fail to understand, two of his riders moved to take up positions on either hand. The leader warrior turned his mount and started up the hill; the flanking riders shouted and pointed, indicating that Giles and Haven were to follow.

"I am not going anywhere with them," Haven declared, her defiance thin and uncertain.

Giles stood his ground and spoke up, saying, "We need water." He knew the warriors would not understand but repeated his demand all the same. The nearest rider prodded him with the butt of a pike and, with a grunted command, urged the prisoners to fall in line. But Giles, mindful of the danger, refused to budge. Pointing to the flat leather bag hanging on the rider's saddle, Giles pantomimed a drinking motion. "Water," he repeated. "We are thirsty. We must drink."

The swarthy fellow understood the gestures; he opened the waterskin and passed it to Giles. "Thank you," said Giles and, under the gaze of the riders, swallowed down three big mouthfuls.

Haven watched him with an expression rare for her: respect. "Sorry, my lady," he said, handing the skin to her. "I thought best to try it first. It is warm but good."

Haven was no longer listening. She snatched up the skin and put her lips to the hollow bone opening and sucked down a large mouthful so quickly she almost choked on it. She took the next two swallows more slowly and finished by wiping her mouth on the back of her hand, then smearing the moisture on her cheeks to cool her face. "Thank you," she murmured, then drank again and reluctantly relinquished the skin, whereupon the warrior wheeled his mount and repeated his command to move out.

"That was very brave, Giles," whispered Haven as the troop started away. She gave his hand a squeeze. "I would have perished save for your boldness."

"At least we know they don't mean to kill us outright," replied Giles. "We will get on better now that we have a little water in us." He regarded her doubtfully. "Can you walk?"

"If I must," replied Haven.

One hill led to another, and another after that. Descending each rounded slope was taxing enough, but climbing them took all of Haven's swiftly diminishing strength. When at last she could go no farther, one of the riders took her up behind him on his mount. The other riders trotted on ahead, leaving two to guard the prisoners. Giles, beside his lady, stumped on in grim determination as the day faded into a silvery haze that slowly deepened and darkened, thickening with the approach of twilight.

As they crested one of the higher hills, Giles, his arm around his mistress to keep her from falling from the horse, exclaimed, "Look!"

Haven raised her eyes and glanced down at his face, stained red by the glow of the setting sun. She followed his gaze, and her breath caught in her throat.

The downward flank of the hill fell away, leading onto a view of an enormous, shallow valley with a wide river coursing through it, the water glinting like quicksilver. Yet, thirsty as she was, it was not the shining river that seized her attention and caused her breath to catch. Spread out before them, filling the great bowl of the valley on either side of the river, was a massive drove of people and animals: men, women, children, horses, dogs, cattle—in knots and clots by the hundreds, thousands, and more—an entire nation on the move, heading west into the dying light.

"God help us!" gasped Haven, taking in the sprawling spectacle. "What is . . . who . . . ?" She left off as words failed her. She turned to Giles. "Whatever are we going to do?"

Their captors descended the slope and joined the migration. Hemmed in by the riders, Haven and Giles were kept a little apart from the greater mass of people on foot, but were close enough to observe that they were a squat, hardy race with straight black hair and black almond eyes set in faces round as the moon and flat as dinner plates. Their limbs were short and well muscled, and from what could be seen beneath the thick folds of their heavy felt clothing, they appeared to be stocky rather than lithe. For shoes they wore strips of hide bound with leather strapping so that, despite their immense numbers, they moved with an almost unnatural quiet. No one spoke, no dogs barked, no child murmured, no horse whinnied—all this mass of humanity and livestock flowed over the land as silent as the river beside them.

While the greater population remained unaware of the foreigners in their midst, every now and then Giles and Haven caught someone eyeing them with undisguised curiosity. Clearly, those nearest these two strange, tall, pale folk took notice, but none breathed so much as a murmur; the greater mass of people trundled on with heads down and eyes fixed on the next step ahead, and the unearthly silence prevailed.

And it soon became apparent why this should be.

As the leading edge of the great throng reached a bend in the river and started around, there came the fearful sound of a skybolt sizzling through the darkling sky. Giles and Haven, like those around them, halted in midstep and looked up to see a fireball streaking through the heavens, whistling as it came nearer. It arced overhead and fell to earth some distance behind them, striking near the riverbank. An instant later the thing erupted in a deafening, dazzling barrage of smoke and flaming fragments, heaving sparks and mud into the air.

Even before the explosion, the mass of people surged away from the strike, fleeing for their lives. Swift on the trail of the first, two more fireballs lit up the twilight sky, trailing white smoke and flames and filling the air with a vicious shriek. The explosions struck closer this time, and with the eruption of sparks and hot metal came the screams of unlucky victims.

The leader of the war party that had captured Giles and Haven appeared out of the confusion; he came shouting commands, and the warrior who carried Haven pushed her off his mount and into Giles' arms. Then all three riders departed, abandoning their captives, joining the greater cavalcade of warriors streaming up the flank of the hill. Whatever war this people was waging, the enemy had found them again and battle had resumed.

More of the hateful, hellish missiles fell to earth, each one striking nearer. As the latest plunged towards them, Giles grabbed Haven by the arm and turned her away from the impact, placing his body between her and the explosion. "Whatever happens," he shouted, "I will protect you!"

"Pray it does not come to that," Haven replied, her words drowned by the thunder of the explosion.

Within a heartbeat, the river of humanity flowing around them was transformed into a fast-moving torrent.

"It already has!" shouted Giles as the surge engulfed them. It was join the surge or be dragged under. He pulled Haven away and held on tight. Hand in hand, they entered the flood.

CHAPTER 16

In Which a Snarky Attitude Is Discouraged

You speak English." Tony Clarke regarded the elderly woman in the doorway.

"After a fashion," she replied, her soft Scottish accent a pleasant purr. She had straight white hair and keen dark eyes behind round, steel-rimmed glasses. "Those of us brought up beyond the wall have a facility with languages."

"The wall?"

"Hadrian's Wall, dear man," she said. "But did you come to discuss ancient history, or was there something else you were wanting?"

"Oh yes. Sorry—I was just so surprised to find someone I could talk to that I seem to have forgotten my manners." He sighed as relief washed over him. "You wouldn't believe the day I've had."

"Never mind," the woman said. "Please, do come in. You'll catch sunstroke out there without a hat."

As Tony moved towards the door, the Scottish woman fished a handful of coins from a pocket and offered them to Tony's young guide, who stood quietly by. "Thank you, Afifah. Here you are."

The young girl accepted the coins and thanked her patron.

"That will be all today. Run along home now, you two. I'll see you tomorrow."

The children darted away and the woman smiled to see them go. "We employ them to watch for travellers," she explained, turning to Tony. "Are you coming in, then?"

"Yes, thank you." Tony stepped into what appeared to be a modest bookshop with shelves lining three walls. There was a grouping of soft chairs with a reading light and a small round brass table. "I really don't mean to bother you—"

"And yet here you are all the same."

Tony did not catch the devious twinkle in the old lady's eye and stumbled over himself apologising.

"Don't mind me, dearie," replied the old woman lightly. "I was just having a bit of fun. Of course, you are here because you were brought here by our little reception committee. Welcome to the Zetetic Society. I am Mrs. Peelstick. Would you like a cup of tea?"

"Glad to meet you," replied Tony, extending his hand. "I'm Tony—Tony Clarke."

"Are you?" said Mrs. Peelstick, eyeing him intently. "Are you, indeed? Younger than I would have guessed—but then everyone is these days." She smiled, but her eyes remained keenly sharp behind her glasses. "I expect you are here about Cassandra."

"Yes!" He gazed at her in astonishment. "How could you possibly know that?" Before she could answer, he said, "Is she all right?"

"Which question to answer first?" Mrs. Peelstick chuckled. "Your lassie was the very picture of perfect health the last time I saw her. And I know who you are because Cassandra told us that you would be looking for her. We expected we might see you any old time. She was in good spirits and fine form—a darling girl."

"Thank God!" He sighed and felt the weight of anxiety lift away, leaving him feeling lighter than air. He swayed on his feet.

"Oh dear!" exclaimed Mrs. Peelstick, moving quickly to his side. "You'd better sit down." She steered him to one of the comfy chairs. "Just you park yourself there and I'll go fetch that cup of tea." He collapsed into the chair as she scuttled off. "Won't be a moment."

"Thank you, I—" But she had already dashed from the room. He sank back and closed his eyes, relaxing into the knowledge that his beloved daughter was safe and well. He heard the clank of a kettle and the clink of glass and a mildly tuneful humming.

His eyes were still closed when Mrs. Peelstick returned bearing a tray with a pot, glasses, and a plate of sweet Syrian pastries. "Here we are," she announced, placing the tray on the little brass table. The glasses, Tony noticed, contained fresh green leaves onto which his host poured hot black tea. "We serve it with mint in this part of the world," she told him. "I think you'll find it very refreshing. Please, help yourself to sugar."

"Is this how Cassie found you? Serving mint tea and cookies?"

"Sesame and pistachio biscuits—delicious, have some." She stirred the leaves around in the glass and then handed it to her guest. "Yes, I think Cassandra and I did share a glass of tea that first day she was with us. It is something of a ritual with us."

"She stayed here with you?"

"She stayed at the convent nearby. It seemed to suit her better."

"But she's not here now?"

"Not at the moment, no." Mrs. Peelstick spooned sugar into her tea and regarded her guest with benign interest. "She is on a mission, I suppose you would say, for the society."

"I don't understand. Why would she leave? Where did she go?"

"You're not a traveller, are you, Mr. Clarke?" She regarded Tony's expression. "No, I can see you're not—at least, not before today. Isn't that right?" Tony just stared, unable to think what to say. "In that case, why don't you just sit back and enjoy your tea? Rest a moment."

"I'm sorry, but that won't do." Tony put down his glass. "I have travelled—God knows how—across several different dimensions, or worlds, or whatever to find my daughter. I want some answers."

"And we will answer all your questions, never fear."

"We?"

"My colleague, Mr. Hanno—he is the current director of the society. I'm sure he will be most anxious to meet you, and he can best explain. He is on an errand but should return shortly. In the meantime, why don't you simply relax a moment and enjoy your tea?"

Though she offered an old woman's saintly smile, Tony sensed cold steel beneath the grandmotherly appearance. Less than satisfied, he retrieved his glass, blew on the hot brew, and sipped lightly— buying a little time to take a breath and regain his composure. "Very well," he agreed in a more measured tone, "perhaps you might at least tell me about this Mr. Hanno, whoever he is."

"Brendan Hanno is the elected head of the Zetetic Society and its Director of Operations."

"And he lives here?"

"In Damascus? Yes. In this house? No."

"You said he is Director of Operations—what sort of operations would those be?"

"Why, the various operations of the society."

"And those would be?"

The white-haired old lady with the will of iron gave him a sly smile. "I am not at liberty to say just now. Perhaps when——"

"I know," said Tony. "Perhaps when Brendan gets here, he will tell me."

"That's right, dear." She raised the pot gingerly from the tray. "More tea?"

"A warm-up, please." He offered his cup. "Then, by all means, tell me about the Zetetic Society——if *that* is allowed."

"No need to be snarky, Mr. Clarke," chided the woman. "I am only acting in the best interest of our members. After all, I only have your word that you are indeed Cassandra's father. Why, you might be anyone at all. You might be someone who wishes her harm——a kook, a stalker, or the like. Why, you might be a pan-dimensional murderer! How would I know?"

The thought had not occurred to Tony that the woman's obfuscation might serve the higher purpose of protecting his daughter's well-being. "You're right, of course. I apologise. Forgive me for being——what was it?"

"Snarky."

Accepting his apology, Mrs. Peelstick directed her guest's attention towards the society's extensive collection of Middle Eastern literature and maps and explained the origin of the society's name and a little of its history. "*Zetetic* means 'seeker,' don't you know."

Tony Clarke listened politely as the redoubtable Mrs. Peelstick passed the time, giving very little away. "Interesting," he replied when she finished. "And Cass has joined the society, you say?"

"We are having something of a surge in membership recently,"

Mrs. Peelstick told him. There was a sound at the door—a key being inserted and a lock being clicked. She glanced across to the doorway and said, "Well, if I'm not mistaken, here is Brendan now."

A moment later a tall thin man in a cream-coloured linen suit and wide-brimmed Panama hat entered the room. He paused on the threshold and then, seeing Mrs. Peelstick and her guest, crossed the room in quick strides. "You must be Anthony Clarke," he said, holding out his hand. "How do you do? I am Brendan Hanno."

"Glad to meet you," said Tony, shaking hands with the fellow. "But how do you know my name? Have we met?"

"I met little Afifah and her brother in the street. She told me someone had come, and I guessed it might be you." He waved Tony back to his chair. "And if there was any doubt, you are the very image of your daughter—rather, it is the other way, I suppose. In any case, I would know you anywhere."

"Really? Mrs. Peelstick here is not so sure about me."

The steel-rimmed glasses flashed. "No need to get—"

"I know. Snarky. Sorry."

"Please, sit down. Would you like some more tea?" Brendan glanced at Mrs. Peelstick and caught a look from her that Tony could not decipher. "No. You've been through a lot today, no doubt. Something stronger is called for, I think. Perhaps we might indulge in a wee dram? The society stocks a particularly good single malt. If you would follow me to the courtyard?"

"You two go on," said Mrs. Peelstick. "I will see to supper and leave you alone to talk. I warn you, Brendan, Mr. Clarke has a million questions and means to ask them all."

"Now who is being snarky?" said Tony, offering a smug smile.

Brendan did not catch the exchange, or chose to ignore it. Indicating the doorway opposite, he said, "I am so glad you're here. We have much to talk about."

"My daughter, for one thing," put in Tony, falling into step behind the tall man. He was led through the bookish reception room along a short corridor to a vestibule with French doors that opened onto a spacious courtyard decked with potted palms and a fountain.

"Please, make yourself at home," said Brendan, who disappeared back inside to sort out the drinks.

A large umbrella shaded a table surrounded by cushioned chairs; stately rows of peach-coloured canna lilies grew in narrow beds along one wall, and grapevines climbed another wall to an overhead lattice, shading half the paved yard with cool green shadows. Tony immediately liked the secluded garden. He examined the fountain and found the surface of the water covered with yellow rose petals; the lightly trickling water sent a subtle fragrance into the air.

"Here we are!" announced Brendan, reappearing with a drinks tray a minute or so later. Tony followed him to the table. "We'll soon put the world to rights."

Placing the tray on the table, Brendan took up a crystal decanter and splashed a pale amber liquid into two small cut-crystal glasses, then dribbled in a drop or two of water from a pitcher. "Try this," Brendan said, handing his guest a glass. "*Slàinte!*" He raised his glass.

"Cheers!" replied Tony. They both took a sip of the smooth sweet fire and Tony tasted a hint of smoke in the spirit.

"As I say, I am glad you are here," said Brendan, settling his long frame into a chair. "Your timing is extraordinary—impeccable."

Tony could not see how this could possibly be, since before the day began he could in no way have guessed where he was going or whether he would arrive anywhere at all. As for Friday, his erstwhile guide, it was anyone's guess what had happened to him. But as there was absolutely nothing Tony could do about it, he decided to withhold judgement and see what happened next. "Happy to oblige," he replied, sipping his malt. "Now, about my daughter—"

"Cassandra is a bright spark," Brendan said. "I can tell you that when last seen—oh, seven days ago, I think—she was in good health and high spirits, and eager to get on to the quest. She did have some concerns about contacting you to let you know that she was safe and happy, but now that you are here, I hope you will consider yourself reassured regarding her welfare."

Tony considered this for a moment. "I certainly don't mean to be, in Mrs. Peelstick's term, snarky—if I seem that way, let's chalk it up to parental concern and exhaustion brought about by utter . . . disorientation and a massive paradigm shift. But how can I be certain that you don't have Cass stashed in your basement or locked in an attic somewhere?"

Brendan smiled. "Like father, like daughter. You two are cut from the same sceptical cloth, no mistake." He shook his head at the wonder of it. "Let me reassure you by whatever means at my disposal that Cassandra is not locked away in any attic, basement, or dungeon. Put yourself in our shoes for a moment. If we had malign intentions towards her, would it not have been far easier to merely feign ignorance of her existence? A simple 'Never heard of her, sorry, mate,' and you'd have been on your way none the wiser. Nor, I venture, would we have gone to the trouble of leading you here in the first place."

"Leading me here? I don't think you understand how . . ." He paused as he saw Brendan's glance sharpen. "Oh! The kids on the street handing out the cards. That was you?"

"We prefer to keep a low profile whenever possible."

"You have succeeded," Tony granted. These people might be crackpots of the highest order, he could not yet tell, but he sensed a growing bond of trust. In any case there was no point in antagonising them; that would get him nowhere. He decided to play along. "Still, I have to ask."

"Of course. Tangible proof will come in due course, believe me. But right now, I ask that you accept my assurance that we have only the best interests of all our society members at heart."

"Yes, your Mrs. Peelstick said something similar. Am I to understand that my daughter has become a member of the Zetetic Society—a seeker?"

"Oh, indeed. Cassandra has joined the society and has undertaken what I hope will be the first of many profitable quests on our behalf. We expect great things from her."

Tony puzzled over this. "There is that word *quest* again. What sort of quest are we talking about, exactly?"

"The usual sort," Brendan replied cheerfully. "A search for treasure of one kind or another."

"But you cannot say more because I am not a member of your society," concluded Tony.

"Succinctly put."

"We will return to that later." Tony took another sip of single malt and savoured the smoky-sweet taste as it slid like liquid gold down his throat. "You said you were anxious to talk to me—and I gather it was not about Cassie, so . . . ?" He raised his eyebrows expectantly as he took another drink. "This is very good, by the way."

"It is a forty-two-year-old Speyside." Brendan picked up the decanter and added another slug to both glasses. He returned the container and carefully replaced the crystal stopper. "Now then, Dr. Clarke," he said, his tone taking on a note of gravity, "what can you tell me about the expansion of the universe?"

CHAPTER 17

In Which Final
Respects Are Paid

*I*t was clear to Benedict that the return to Egypt was harder on his mother than she let on. The physical journey was taxing enough—she had not made a ley jump in many years and the portal crossing from Black Mixen Tump had been rough—but the emotional impact exacted a brutal toll all its own. Returning to a place so freighted with unhappy associations and yet so bound up with the family's fortunes would have tested the sternest soul, and it surely tested Xian-Li. Nor was Benedict untouched by the same turmoil his mother experienced. Upon seeing the long double row of ram-headed sphinxes stretching off into the ochre desert and the white arid hills rimming the vast horizon, Benedict heard his mother gasp; his throat seized and his hands grew clammy.

Xian-Li stopped on the path and clutched Benedict's arm.

"Are you well, Mother?" he said. "We do not have to continue. We can go back."

Her eyes closed, Xian-Li shook her head. "No. I want to see the end of this." She opened her eyes and looked at her son, the sadness visible in every line of her face. "There must be an end."

Benedict nodded and, adjusting the strap of the leather bag on his shoulder, he led them on without pausing again until they gained the heights and could at last look down upon the broad green strip of fertile valley on either side of the great blue river that coursed its way through the illimitable Egyptian barrens. There on the broad banks, Niwet-Amun, the City of Amun, gleamed white in the dazzling light of the sun blazing in a cloudless sky.

"Not far now," said Benedict with some relief. What he did not say was that at least the city was still there. After what had happened during his previous visit, when Habiru masons attacked and threatened to tear down the temple, Benedict had feared they would find the place a crumbling ruin and their friend Anen a casualty of conflict.

Yet there it was, its pylons rising sedately, red banners fluttering from poles outside the entrance, its walls intact, its columns erect. No columns of smoke rising from heaps of burning rubble, no wasteland of scorched palm and tamarind trees, no desolated fields lying fallow—in fact, none of the things Benedict secretly imagined, and secretly dreaded, to find. The temple and its surrounding city appeared drowsily serene through the placid shimmering haze of humid river air. Calm lay heavy and deep over the Land of Isis' Children.

"Is all well?" asked Xian-Li, her hands cupped round her eyes to shade them. "It seems peaceable enough."

"I think it is well. I wonder what we shall find at the temple?"

They moved on, descending the tight serpentine trail down through the rock-bound hills to the verdant valley, arriving at the outskirts of Niwet-Amun where fields of sesame gave way to smaller patches of turnips, beans, and melons, and the vegetable gardens gave way to mud-and-thatch dwellings. A single road ran along the river-bank and into the centre of the city whose heart was the temple. By the time they reached the large square before the temple entrance, they had attracted an entourage of curious children, dogs, and a few idle white-haired elders. Benedict offered the greeting his father had taught him, but received only stares or silent nods in return.

The doors of the temple stood open and people passed in and out of the temple precinct; those going in carried bundles or baskets containing their offerings—cabbages, figs, leeks, and other vegeta-bles. One or two bore cages with doves or small songbirds; those coming out of the temple wore a double stripe of holy oil on their foreheads.

The travellers passed through the gate under the surprised gaze of temple guards with long ebony rods, and were well into the com-pound when one of the soldiers sprang into action. He shouted something at them and ran to apprehend the strangers, placing him-self in front of them to bar the way.

Smiling, composed, Xian-Li turned to the man and offered a few words of greeting that shocked the guard even more. He called to his fellows, and soon Benedict and his mother were surrounded.

"Peace be upon you, lady. May your shadow never diminish," called a voice from the quickly gathering crowd.

Benedict turned to see a tall, bearded man in a red headcloth pushing through the knot around them. Though his hair and beard were grey and he was a little thicker through the middle now, Benedict recognised him at once. "Tutmose!" he cried. "Tutmose, it is me—" He patted his chest and spoke his own name slowly. "Ben-e-dict."

Xian-Li glanced at her son. "You know him?"

"He is the commander of the guard. Or he was when we were here before."

"Peace of heaven upon thee," offered Xian-Li, answering in Kemet, the language of the Nile Valley. "And peace upon thy house."

Benedict stared at his mother, who saw his astonished expression. "I once lived here, Beni," she said.

The commander spoke a word of exclamation, then took her hand and, bowing at the waist, touched the back of her hand to his forehead. "Be welcome here, my friends." To Benedict, he said, "It gladdens my heart to see you once again."

Following his mother's translation, Benedict suggested, "Ask him if Anen is still here."

Xian-Li said, "Tutmose, my son would like to know if Anen is still in residence at the temple."

The bearded commander's smile widened to a grin. "Where else should the high priest be found but at his temple?" Tutmose gave a command to the other guards, who reluctantly began dispersing. "Come, I will take you to meet him. I know he will be pleased to see you."

"Not only is Anen here," Xian-Li told her son, "he is now the high priest. I think some years have passed in this world since you were here."

They were led to one of the larger buildings in the compound—a low square structure with red pillars and a large statue of a man in a kilt wearing a royal collar, armbands, and a crown surmounted by an orb and two gigantic feathers. The kilt was real, as were the collar and armbands, which were made of gold. As they approached the entrance to this building, two priests in white robes emerged leading a group of young boys with shaved heads. The boys gawked at the strangers, but the priests passed by without a glance. A third priest rushed out, scattering the group in his haste.

Upon seeing the strangers he gave out a glad cry, threw his arms wide, and rushed to meet them. He said something in Kemet, but it was not until he said his name that Benedict recognised him. Older, his shaved fuzz of hair white now, he was also fatter, with a plump, round face and belly and chubby legs—but it was Anen, the high priest himself.

What his mother said was true. For Benedict, only a year had passed since his tragic visit—it had taken that long to settle the affairs of their estate following his father's death and for his mother to prepare herself to return—for the Egyptians, however, it seemed that many years had elapsed. His father, Benedict appreciated, would have been able to narrow that gap so that they might have arrived within a few days of his last visit. Sadly, Benedict lacked that ability, and because of his vow to give up ley travel when this last task was completed, he would now never possess such skill.

"They told me that the wife and son of my dear friend Arthur had come, and my heart leapt for joy within me," Anen declared. "Xian-Li! Benedict! May the peace of this house soothe your soul, and may your sojourn in the land bear much fruit."

Of this, Benedict only heard his name; the rest, his mother translated for him, then replied, "The peace of God bless your soul and may His wisdom comfort you—" That was all she got out before being engulfed in a glad embrace. Then it was Benedict's turn, and before he knew it they were being ushered into the high priest's residence.

"Anen, my friend, it is pure delight to see you again. The years have been good to you," said Xian-Li when they were seated in the audience chamber. Like many of the rooms in Egyptian palaces, this one was open on one side, allowing the air to circulate through gauze-thin curtains hanging in strips of blue and white. A pool outside cooled the air somewhat, and date palms and fragrant sprays of jasmine shaded the high priest's private courtyard. Temple servants in green kilts produced trays of dried figs, dates, and slices of melon and handed around tiny cups of water infused with aniseed and honey. Benedict sipped his drink and assumed the role of spectator, watching as his mother and Anen chatted happily to one another—the anxiety and emotional turmoil of their return to Egypt forgotten, at least for the moment.

Eventually talk turned to the reason for their visit, and here his mother began translating for him, switching smoothly between languages—so easily that Benedict began to wonder just how many years his parents had spent in Egypt. However many, her mastery of Kemet was impressive, and with her running commentary he was able to follow the conversation.

"Arthur's death was a great shock to me," she told Anen. "I still cannot fully understand the loss—it grows ever greater with each passing day. I am in mourning and learning to live through my grief. But you see, it has only been a year in my world."

Anen nodded sadly. "The death of my friend saddens me too—though for me it has been more than ten years."

They spoke about the odd anomaly of time slippage between the worlds; Anen seemed to accept and understand the phenomenon. Judging from the way his mother related their conversation, Benedict wondered whether the high priest was also a traveller like his father.

"I must thank you for your care of Arthur following the accident,"

Xian-Li said. "I know in my heart that no one could have done more." She offered a sad smile. "I also thank you for taking such good care of Benedict and sending him back to me. As ever, we are obliged to you, Anen."

The high priest made a sour face. "Obligation—this word has no meaning between friends. Had I the power of Osiris, I would restore your husband to you and resurrect Benedict's father and redeem my friend from the bonds of death." He shook his head. "Alas, the high priest has no such power. Our reunion must wait until the next life. Then we shall all be together once more. In the meantime," he sighed, "we must learn to live through our grief—as you have said."

They exchanged memories of previous visits—happier times they both remembered—and Anen asked, "Would you like to see his tomb?"

"I would, yes," said Xian-Li. "I would like that very much. It is one of the reasons we came."

"Then I will arrange it at once." He lifted his chin and turned his head. Instantly a servant stepped forward in anticipation of a command. The two exchanged a brief word. The servant departed and the high priest said, "We can go whenever you wish, but as the City of the Dead is some distance from here and the heat of the day is soon upon us, may I suggest we embark in the morning at sunrise so that we may enjoy the journey while the cool of the night still clings to the hills?"

Benedict cleared his throat to announce that he was being left out of the conversation.

Xian-Li explained, "He is offering to take us to see the tomb where Arthur's body has been laid to rest. Anen ordered a boat for us. I think the tomb is on the other side of the river."

"We will happily accept your wise counsel," Xian-Li told him. "But you are the high priest and must have many claims on your time. We would not expect you to make a special journey for us."

"As it happens, the final decoration of my tomb is nearing completion, and I have been meaning to go inspect the work. Moreover, it would be a particular pleasure to show you my home for eternity. I myself never tire of visiting it, for there I am reminded of the many blessings I have received over the years." He said this with the evident pride of a man who is pleased with his life and accomplishments.

"Thank you, Anen," replied Xian-Li. "We are grateful for your kindness."

Benedict added his thanks when his mother explained, whereupon Anen said, "Just now, my friends, you will allow me to offer you some refreshment. After we have dined, it would please me to show you the delights of Niwet-Amun. We have done much building work in the city since you were here. You will enjoy this very much, I think."

The high priest's servants provided a fine meal of fruit, flavoured breads, and a thick milky paste made of almonds and honey. After the meal they were taken by chariot all around the city, making stops at statues and monuments and shrines and markets. At every stop people congregated—as much to see the high priest, Benedict thought, as to get a glimpse of the foreign visitors. Clearly Anen was held in great regard by the people, and as his guests Benedict and Xian-Li gained considerable status.

They spent a pleasant evening and a restful night, rising before the sun to begin the journey across the river to the high priest's tomb. The boat turned out to be a vessel built on the lines of a royal barge, but smaller; it was rowed and served by a complement of slaves who, as soon as they reached the opposite shore, disembarked and became chair bearers for the trip inland.

Benedict had never ridden in a chair before—though they could still be seen on occasion in England, mostly employed by elderly grandees—and at first found the swaying, gliding sensation slightly disconcerting. He soon grew used to the motion, however, and even enjoyed it. The three chairs, each borne by four slaves, led the way; following them were four priests on foot and, behind them, six more slaves carrying baskets containing food and drink for the day.

They travelled up from the flatland along the river and into the empty desert hills rising just a mile or so beyond the wide green strip of irrigated fields. Once into the desert they turned south, skirting the foot of a steep, craggy bluff to enter a wide wadi, or canyon. The farther they went, the narrower the gorge became—almost scraping the sides of the chairs at one point before reaching a wider place where the wadi split into two large ravines.

Here the high priest's entourage stopped. In the wide basin formed by the three channels stood a large tented structure and several smaller huts; other dwellings lined the wider of the two branches—all of them made of coarse cloth stretched over light wooden frames and roofed with dried palm fronds. These were the shelters for the workers, the artists and masons engaged in decorating the high priest's tomb. The entrance to the tomb itself was a simple rectangular opening carved into the limestone wall of the gorge.

"Kings and queens have their sacred valleys," Anen explained cheerfully. "This one is mine." He waved an imperious hand over the canyon. "This is where my *ka* will live until time ends and paradise returns to the world of men."

"What happens after that?" wondered Benedict when his mother had translated Anen's thought.

"Forgive his impertinence, but my son would like to know what happens after?" asked Xian-Li.

The high priest laughed at the question. "What happens? We will live in paradise!" Indicating the doorway to the tomb, he said, "Would you like to see it?"

CHAPTER 18

In Which Temptation Is Removed

Anen, high priest of Amun, stood shielding his eyes from the sun as he gazed beyond the gleaming cliff tops at a vulture circling high overhead. The shadow rippled as it passed over the wadi wall below. "This," he declared, "will be sealed until the end of time. Then I shall emerge to take my place among the company of the immortal."

Xian-Li translated for her son, who nodded and asked, "Are we allowed to go in?"

"It is the sole purpose of our visit!" replied Anen with a laugh. He signalled one of the servants to bring lamps and rushlights, and sent them ahead to light the way. Then, stepping carefully over the raised threshold, he led his guests through the doorway and down a steep flight of steps to a lower level and a small, closet-like vestibule leading onto what was either a short tunnel or a very wide threshold that opened onto a large rectangular room with a high, flat ceiling. The entire room had been carved out of the soft limestone; its walls had been smoothed and plastered, and the hard white surface decorated with colourful scenes of life on the riverbank: boys fishing, a man washing a big-horned buffalo, girls herding geese, women making bread and beer, slaves harvesting and threshing grain, and more. Everywhere they looked were pictures. Any surface not covered with images was painted with hieroglyphs or words.

"It is wonderful!" gasped Xian-Li, then said the same in Kemet for Anen's benefit.

"It has taken a very long time," said the priest, "and the expense has been great. But I feel very fortunate to think my *ka* shall spend its days among such pleasant and industrious people."

A second doorway opened off this room into another. Pointing to it, Benedict asked, "What is in there?"

Xian-Li translated the question and Anen said, "Ah! This is my special place. Come, I will show you."

They moved from the main chamber into a much smaller one, also filled with paintings. Unlike the others, however, these were contained in room-sized murals, some of which were finished, but others still in progress: four painters were at work under the supervision of a master artist who moved from one to another correcting the odd wayward line—the shape of a calf here, the curve of a horse's neck there—using a piece of charcoal in one hand and a lamp in the other. The artists worked by the light of small oil lamps and larger rushlights; other workers smoothed plaster onto the walls, mixed paint, or prepared brushes. The close, unmoving air smelled of palm oil and the metallic tang of lime plaster and cut stone.

A simple sarcophagus sat off to one side; unadorned, hewn not of granite but of white limestone, it seemed almost inconspicuous amongst the busyness of the painters and their creations.

At the sudden appearance of the high priest, the master artist barked a command and all the workers put down their tools and, to a man, turned and knelt before their exalted patron. Anen raised both palms shoulder high and spoke a few words; the artists and their master got up, bowed, and resumed their work. And what work it was!

The room's ceiling had been stained a deep blue and dotted with six-pointed stars; the walls were divided into sections, each section containing a large rendering of a scene from Anen's life. One depicted the high priest as a young man with a slender waist and wide shoulders, standing in a boat—fishing for yellow-bellied perch with a barbed spear while lazy green crocodiles and blue-grey hippos looked on from a nearby sandbar. Another showed him standing in the temple before Amun, who was handing him an ankh of immortality.

As stunning as these pictures were, it was the third panel that arrested Benedict's attention. This one featured Anen and another man, the second one pale-skinned and dressed in boots, trousers, and even a jacket—rendered in a curiously stylised form by artists who had never seen such dress. Even so, the light-skinned man bore more than a passing resemblance to his father.

Benedict nudged his mother and pointed to the image. As she turned, his eyes fell on the next mural in line and his heart leapt to his throat. It depicted the high priest holding an irregular, oblong-shaped object something like a papyrus sheet or sheepskin, the surface of which was covered with the distinctive blue symbols of Arthur's devising: the indigo tattoos he had worn in life to guide his explorations and journeys. In the painting, Anen held the irregular, oblong-shaped parchment with one hand pointed to a bright star rising in the eastern sky.

"This is where my casket will rest," the high priest was saying. He glanced at his guests and regarded their alarm. "In these you see the chief events of my life—those high moments I wish to be remembered. Meeting my dear friend Arthur—this is one that is precious to me."

"And this one?" asked Xian-Li, pointing to the third panel.

"Oh, sister," he said reverently, "this one is to remind me of the way to the world to come—the world as it was once, long ago, and will be again. A world where all evil is banished, and where there will be no more time, no more age or infirmity."

Anen's voice grew husky; his eyes gleamed with tears. "My friends, there will be no more hardship or disease. Death will no longer haunt our dreams and drain the happiness from our best days. There will be an overflowing abundance of health and life and joy made perfect . . . forever."

"Heaven," murmured Xian-Li quietly. To Anen she said, "The paradise you describe, we call it heaven."

Anen considered this. "It is a good name. For the Children of Isis and Osiris it is called *Aaru*." He sighed then and said, "Alas, not many believe in paradise anymore. As high priest I have done my best to teach them, to tell the people what I know to be true. How do I know this to be true?" His smile grew wide. "I know because I have seen it. Arthur showed it to me."

Turning once more to the painting, he pointed to the star portrayed as a disc with spikes of light radiating from it. "Aaru is there—in the realm of the Dog Star. The paradise I spoke of—that is where I have seen it. I have been there—did you know that? I have been there and seen it with my own eyes." His gaze grew intense. "My sister, I think you have seen it too."

Xian-Li confessed that this was so. "Arthur called it the Well of Souls," she told him.

Benedict, feeling left out of this exchange, interrupted. Pointing to the plain white sarcophagus, he said, "Mother, ask him if that is where father's remains are kept."

"You are right," confirmed Anen when asked. "I am honoured to have a friend rest beside me."

Benedict moved to the large, chest-like object and gestured to the top where a series of hieroglyphs had been carved. "What are these?" he asked. "What do they say?"

"It is Arthur's tomb name," Anen explained and then said a word that to Benedict sounded like *Say-Neti-Up-Uatu*.

"The Man Who Is Map," Xian-Li translated. She smiled sadly. "Arthur would have liked that." She traced the carved glyphs with her fingertips, then let her hand rest on the sarcophagus. To Benedict, she said, "It is time, son."

Taking the leather strap from around his neck, Benedict opened the bag's flap and drew out the slender parcel, still wrapped in its linen covering and tied with the scarlet thread.

"What have you there?" inquired Anen. "Is it a grave offering?"

"Yes," Xian-Li told him. "We wish to place it in the tomb with Arthur." She traced her fingertips across the stone lid. "May we?"

"Let it be as you say." He turned and gestured to the master artist and spoke a command. Instantly the workmen downed tools and came scurrying to the sarcophagus. They lined up two on each side and two at the head of the stone casket, and with brute strength raised the heavy lid an inch or two and slid it down and away to reveal the linen-bound mummy of Arthur Flinders-Petrie.

A fine trace of the narcotic, dulling cloy of myrrh lifted from the linen-bound corpse and caught in the back of the throat. Xian-Li coughed and put the back of her hand against her mouth, but then lowered the other hand, hesitantly, to rest upon the rounded chest of her husband's body.

Benedict had expected to feel some surge of emotion at the sight; yet he gazed at the elegant wheat-coloured wrappings and the pristine, body-shaped form, and so far removed were they from anything he had known of his father in life, he felt nothing. Even so, he stood holding the flat parcel between his hands, unwilling to commit it to the tomb.

Xian-Li placed a firm hand on his. "It is time, Benedict. Remember your vow, son."

Still he hesitated.

"Benedict, listen to me. If we are ever to know peace, this temptation must be removed."

His resistance melted, and the young man gently lowered the parcel onto the mummy's rounded chest. The bulge created by hands bound over the chest caused the wrapped parchment to slide off to one side and down. After he tried a second time to balance it, Anen said, "Will you allow me?"

Xian-Li nodded, and Benedict delivered the parcel into the priest's outstretched hand. Anen spoke a word, and two of the workmen reached in and lifted the mummy slightly, allowing the priest to slide the thin package under its head as a small, flat pillow. He looked to the young man and his mother for approval.

Benedict offered a grunt of satisfaction; Xian-Li closed her eyes and bowed her head in silent prayer. After a moment she opened her eyes and raised her head once more, took a last look at the mummy, then turned and made her way from the tomb. Benedict followed.

Anen gave the command for the sarcophagus to be closed once more and then, filling his gaze with the wonderful paintings being lavished on his final resting place, commended the master to his craft, and work resumed.

"Thank you, my friend," Xian-Li said to the high priest when he rejoined them outside. "Your indulgence is greatly appreciated. You have been most kind."

"Yet I would do more," said Anen thoughtfully. He brightened as an idea came to him. "Will you allow me to take you to meet Pharaoh? It is only two days to Thebes by boat and a most enjoyable journey, and the king's new summer palace is a splendour to behold."

He watched Benedict's stricken expression as his mother translated the invitation. "No! No! Do not misunderstand," he said quickly, and explained. "There is a new pharaoh now—Tut-Ankh-Amun. The old one, the one you remember—Akhenaten, who caused such trouble—is gone many years now—he and his queen and children and the troublesome Habiru with them. Do not worry, there will be no riots this time, I promise."

"If it would upset my son, I think—" Xian-Li began.

Benedict was quickly reassured that the troubles were indeed long past. "We should go, Mother. This is the last journey of this kind that either of us will ever make, and I would like a better memory to place alongside the last one if that is possible."

His mother smiled her acceptance and replied, "Your offer is kind and generous. We would be happy to accompany you to the royal palace."

"So shall it be done." Anen led them back to where the slaves and chairs were waiting in the shade of a canopy. "We will return to the boat, and I will send word to Pharaoh's court that we will come to him at his summer palace in three days' time." He raised his hands palms outward in the gesture of official pronouncements. "My friends, it will be a journey you will never forget."

CHAPTER 19

In Which the Observer Effect Is Expanded

$\mathcal{E}$xpansion of the universe—" Tony Clarke regarded his host with a mystified expression, his glass halfway to his mouth. "What an odd thing to ask."

In the pleasant surroundings of a tranquil walled garden shaded by fig trees and potted palms, with a fountain playing gently in the background, sitting beneath a blue umbrella, sipping good single malt Scotch in the Old Quarter of a version of Damascus in the 1930s . . . the question seemed especially incongruous. It took Tony a moment to change gears mentally.

"A little odd, perhaps," allowed Brendan lightly. "But it is something the Zetetics have been watching with keen interest for some time, and it has some bearing on our discussion."

Tony took a sip. "Well, then you will probably be aware that many, if not most, astronomers and cosmologists where I come from accept that the universe is indeed expanding—and at an absolutely enormous rate."

Brendan was nodding. "And by some calculations that expansion may even approach the speed of light itself." He smiled. "I seem to recall that you wrote something on the subject, Dr. Clarke."

"You sly dog," Tony laughed. "You knew all along that this is one of my special interests. Yes, I've written a few papers on the subject of cosmological expansion. But you will also be aware, of course, that this remains an area of considerable debate, since there are so many variable and competing models. It largely depends on which horse you back in the race to reality, but at present no one has the slightest idea what is causing this expansion—that is, the force driving it, powering it."

"Dark energy is *your* best guess, if I recall correctly," suggested Brendan, swirling the Scotch in his glass.

"You *are* well informed. I take it you study . . . shall we say—widely?"

"Oh, I pick up bits here and there. What else can you tell me?"

"Dark energy could be the driving force—or dark matter, whatever that might be. The problem, as I see it, is that this phantom stuff was dreamed up to explain cosmological expansion in the first place. In the race to find an explanation, that fact is often ignored.

"The point is, I think, not only do we lack even the foggiest idea what is causing the universe to expand at such incredible speed, there is good reason to believe that the expansion is actually *accelerating*." He took another sip from his glass. "Again, we don't know why. Thus, the search is on for this mysterious dark matter and dark energy that the various formulas and models suggest *should* be there."

"But cannot be found."

"True, but if either of those things could be proven to exist, then we might begin to get a clue to what's actually going on in the universe. And by that I mean we might at last begin to understand the origins of the universe and—who knows?—maybe even the nature of reality itself." He savoured another swallow of his whiskey and added, "Of course, all this is mere conjecture. The scientific equivalent of thinking out loud. We have no proof at all, nor even the glimmer of a testable hypothesis. Only speculation." He smiled. "Anyone is free to speculate."

"Then perhaps you will allow me a little of that speculation?" Brendan drained his glass and set it aside. "What if we accept that the universe is indeed expanding at a truly alarming rate? Further, what if the cause of this accelerating growth was not some exotic unknown dark matter out there in the cosmos, but something very much closer to home? Or, put another way, perhaps the source of this mysterious dark energy resides right here on earth."

"You've got my attention," said Tony. He emptied his glass and put it down on the table beside Brendan's. "So what's your theory? Let's have it."

"Suppose we say that dark energy is driving the expansion of the universe, and that this is actually linked to human consciousness?"

In the silence that followed, Brendan watched his guest to see how an eminent scientist would receive his amateur suggestion. The tinkling sound of the fountain and the fragrance of jasmine filled the air; the lowering sun stretched the shadows, casting the courtyard in blessed shade. Resisting the impulse to speak, Brendan allowed his guest the courtesy of a moment's quiet contemplation.

"An unorthodox speculation, but not—as some might think—completely outrageous," Tony concluded. "Given that quantum forces at some level govern events in both the cosmic and microcosmic realms, there may be some heretofore undiscovered link." He nodded thoughtfully. "Yes. All right, let's accept that human consciousness is somehow involved. Where does that get us? Go on."

"Let us further suppose that what we call ley travel is one tangible manifestation of this involvement between human consciousness and the accelerated growth of the universe."

"Interesting," allowed Tony; both his expression and tone were noncommittal. "How is this supposition to be derived?"

Brendan rose from the table. "I think much better when I'm moving. Would you mind if we walked a little?"

"I wouldn't mind if we juggled eggs while standing on our heads. You have me hooked, Professor. Lead the way."

Leaving the society headquarters, they entered the mazed streets of the Old Quarter, keeping to the quiet byways shaded by overhanging grapevines and fig trees. After walking awhile, Brendan said, "As a physicist you will be familiar with Schrödinger and his famous cat."

"The unfortunate animal that is both dead and alive at the same time—in limbo awaiting its fate—depending on *who* is peeking into the box, or *when*, or maybe *both*," answered Tony.

"The very cat."

"I assume you know that Herr Schrödinger proposed that thought problem to ridicule the core theories of quantum mechanics?" observed Tony. "He was upset about the uncertainty principle, among other things, and wanted to point out how utterly absurd it all was."

"Yes, and like a lot of other ridiculous notions it came closer to describing what might actually be happening than its more serious rivals. That poor cat got sucked into the black hole of quantum theory and has been trapped there ever since."

Tony laughed. "Black hole. I like that."

They passed tiny shops selling bread and others selling spices, or olives, or soap, or vegetables. Housewives in colourful scarves and drab chin-to-ankle robes carried their shopping in hessian bags bulging with yellow peppers, pomegranates, or greens; one or two, with both hands full, carried stacks of flatbread on their heads. The scent of cumin and oregano drifted from the carefully tended mounds arrayed before the spice merchant's shop.

"For the theory we are constructing, let us suppose that Schrödinger was right about what has become known as the Observer Effect—that human beings somehow influence the outcome of certain interactions simply by their participation—but on a scale far greater than he or anyone else has yet imagined."

"On the cosmic scale," Tony guessed. His supple mind ran ahead to possible conclusions. "Are you suggesting that in certain circumstances, human beings create the reality they observe? That idea has been kicking around for some time—as a philosophical speculation."

"I am suggesting that, yes, but I want to push the old idea a bit further. What if, through our participation, we not only create the reality we observe . . . we also create an alternate reality that we do not observe?"

"Again, an old chestnut. We used to throw it around in undergrad physics classes. It's the idea that gives rise to the multiverse theory—that for any given event where the outcome could go any of a number of different ways, they *all* spring into existence. Flip a coin, for example—in one universe the coin lands heads, in another it lands tails. Both things happen."

"When you look in Herr Schrödinger's box to check on your tabby you find it dead in one world—yet in the alternate world you will find it very much alive. Both things happen, yes." Brendan paused and stopped walking. Tony stopped to face him. "But now," he continued, "there are *two* different worlds—both very much alike in many ways, but slightly different because in one, Schrödinger's much-put-upon moggy is dead, and in the other the creature is still alive and purring."

"I think I see where this is going."

"I'm sure you do," agreed Brendan. "If you extend the model to include every human being on the planet—where each and every decision, each and every possible outcome to those decisions brings a new world or dimension, or even a new universe into existence—"

"You have exponential expansion," Tony finished the thought. "With the creation of each new dimension, the universe itself must expand to contain it."

"The more conscious human agents on earth, the more decisions being made, the greater the expansion and the faster it expands. But not only that, in each of those new dimensions people will be making decisions that bring other new dimensions, new worlds, new universes, into existence"—his hand described an airy circle—"and so on and so on and so on."

"Faster and faster," concluded Tony. "Resulting in the ever-increasing acceleration of the expansion of the observed universe."

"Human consciousness *is* the dark energy driving the expansion of the universe."

Tony was already nodding. "I like it. Intellectually, it is a stimulating idea. As a hypothesis it might win some adherents. But for it to become a genuine theory, it must have parameters that can be tested." He glanced at Brendan, who was smiling at him. "What?"

"You are so much like your daughter."

"Or the other way around. In any case, I'll take that as a compliment."

"I meant it as one. But yes, for our speculation to become anything more than an intellectual exercise it must be testable, and those tests must produce results that can be replicated." Brendan started walking again. They passed a coffee shop where men sat smoking hubble-bubble pipes over little cups of bitter black coffee. "That," he declared, "is where ley lines come in."

"I'm still with you," said Tony. Unaccountably, he felt his pulse rate rise on a buzz of excitement. "Do continue."

"Since we've gone this far in our suppositions, let us further suppose that the alternate dimensions created by the interaction of human consciousness with matter are everywhere—scattered throughout space and time."

"They would be," granted Tony.

"But some of these dimensions—perhaps the earliest ones, or merely those closest to us—actually intersect our world. Where two dimensions intersect, they form a line, an electromagnetic line of force on the landscape. These lines are what we call ley lines. Various instruments can detect them, and people sensitive to them can feel them. Certain rare individuals can even manipulate them."

"Using them to travel from one world or dimension to another." Tony gave a low appreciative whistle. "I've got to hand it to you, Brendan, you got there in the end. I don't mind telling you I was beginning to wonder if you had wandered off into fantasyland, but you brought it home. Bravo!"

"What do you think of it? As a hypothesis at least—what do you think?"

"Intriguing, audacious, quirky—those words come immediately to mind." Tony shook his head. "But on balance, it is no weirder or more outlandish than many other hypotheses currently making the rounds. And I admit it has more going for it than most."

"I should hope so," chuckled Brendan. "It is, after all, my best explanation of how you came to be wandering the byways of Damascus."

Tony, speechless, nodded as he contemplated the implications of all he had been told. Could it really be true? If it was true, it very well could be the explanation for ley lines . . . *and* for a whole lot more besides. "Given what I know by my own experience of ley travel—which, for the record, I am still struggling to get my head around," Tony said, his eyes narrowed in thought, "I am forced to conclude that your hypothesis has what we physicists call legs."

"In that it accounts for certain observable conditions?"

"In that it carries a higher force of description for certain observable conditions than many rival explanations," Tony told him. "Moreover, it accounts for those facts in a simpler, more elegant way—if anything about all this could be said to be simple."

Brendan grinned. "I am deeply relieved to hear you say that."

"As a theory, I like it," Tony declared. "Moreover, I want to explore it." He offered a slightly bemused smile at his own enthusiasm. "Well done, Professor Hanno. There is plenty of meat here to make a meal."

"Thank you, Dr. Clarke," replied Brendan. He touched the brim of his Panama hat in salute. "But I did not bring up the topic merely to bend your ear. I have a far more serious motive."

"Oh? And what would that be?"

"We have been speaking of the expansion of the visible universe—but what if I told you that the universe is no longer expanding?"

"Are you likely to tell me that?"

"I have very recently received evidence that the rate of expansion has slowed overall, and in some quarters may even be reversing."

"You don't say," mused Tony.

Brendan offered a solemn nod.

"I would have to ask you where you obtained this evidence," said Tony. "It would have to be verified, of course, and I would wonder why no one has detected this before."

"As you may know, the upgrading of the Jansky VLA telescope— much needed and much delayed—is now complete. I have contacts in New Mexico who have reliably informed me of certain observational data recorded during the recalibration process. At first, these anomalous observations were dismissed as mistakes, interference, or something of the sort. But it is just now beginning to appear that those initial readings are not mistakes at all, that something very strange is going on at the farthest reaches of the universe—"

"The expansion is slowing . . ." Tony mused. "That's what they're saying?" He ran a hand through his hair. "I know some of those guys at the VLA. I could call them and verify everything you've said. We could get the latest data."

"It is a possibility. But assuming that their calculations did confirm all I've told you and that everything I've said is true?"

Tony regarded him for a lingering moment before answering. "If what you say is true," he replied at last, "then I would say we have a problem. A very . . . big . . . problem."

CHAPTER 20

In Which Unwanted Attention Is Aroused

*H*alf a league! Closing fast, Captain," called First Mate Garland, his voice falling from the upper rigging in sharp staccato blasts.

Lord Burleigh cupped his hands around his eyes and gazed into the too-bright sky. He could make out the silhouette of a man high up in the dizzying tangle of ropes and cables that spread like a web from the top of the mast. The white expanse of canvas billowed, full-bellied, before a good wind driving them towards the dark eminence of land on the horizon. The course was set for the Gibraltar Strait, the mouth of which they had hoped to clear before the evening tide flow made navigating more dangerous.

Many ships, arriving too late to chance passage in the dark, chose to wait in the Atlantic overnight—which made the region a prime location for pirates to ply their vile vocation. This was what had

Captain Farrell and his crew muttering oaths and maledictions under their beards.

The *Percheron* was a tight and ready ship, but fast she was not. She rode too heavily in the water and carried only one mast, which limited the amount of canvas she could raise. In short, she was a sturdy, well-bred workhorse, not a racer: robust, resilient, handsome in her own way, but no one would ever call her sleek or fleet of foot.

"This is most worrisome, sir," Farrell told him when Burleigh joined the captain in the wheelhouse a few moments later. "I own that I am deeply concerned."

"And the nature of your disquiet, Captain?" inquired Burleigh.

"I ween that schooner abaft is following us with malicious intent. That is my apprehension."

"Is it not just as likely they are merchantmen making for the strait and just as eager to reach it before nightfall as are we ourselves?"

"Aye, the possibility has occurred to me," allowed Farrell. He tapped his pipe against a wheel peg and then put it back into his mouth. "Indeed, sir, it is greatly to be wished. And if we were in friendlier waters, I would not feel that sentiment ill placed."

Burleigh heard the unspoken qualification in the seaman's voice. "However?" he asked.

"We best be on our guard, sir. That's all as needs sayin' as of this present moment."

"Your concern is duly noted, Mr. Farrell." The earl cast a last glance over his shoulder at the white speck that was the trailing schooner. "Unless you require my presence, I will be in my cabin. Please do not hesitate to summon me should the situation alter."

The seaman raised his hand and touched his temple with a knuckle in the traditional seaman's salute. Burleigh went down the steps of the aft companionway to his chamber where he pulled off his boots, stretched out on his bed, and was soon sleeping the sleep of the dead. When he awoke some hours later, he returned to the quarterdeck to see that the sun was lower in the west and the dark smudge off port side had grown to a sizable mass. Burleigh detected a faint, earthy smell of land on the wind. The mystery ship on their tail was now much closer.

"How do we fare, Captain?"

"Here you are! Saves me sendin' for to fetch you, sir."

"The other ship is very much closer, I see." Burleigh cast a sideways glance behind him.

"Aye, she is," agreed the seaman. "Can't be helped. We are spankin' along smartly enough, but yon schooner is a fast gull and that's a fact. Observe, sir, she flies no colour."

Burleigh was growing increasingly familiar with nautical slang. Colour meant flags in general, but could mean house flags, commission flags, or any of a variety of signal flags. No flags meant the ship could not be identified—always a bad sign. His lordship looked at the land looming ahead and at the ship behind, gauging the distance either way. The *Percheron* seemed to be poised roughly halfway between the two.

"The nearest port is Cape Trafalgar," continued Farrell, pointing to a small pale smudge of grey on the green coast showing on the horizon. "If we carried more sail, we might make the harbour in style. As it is, 'twill be a close-run race. That said, if they see us making for Trafalgar, that alone may be enough to convince them to keep their distance." He clamped the unlit pipe between his teeth. "The harbour guns, you see."

"Do your best, Captain," Burleigh told him. He went to the stern rail and stood for a time, observing the schooner. With twin masts, the schooner carried twice as much canvas as his brigantine. Low in the water, its sharp prow seemed not so much to cleave the waves as to bound over them, riding the swell and gaining with every surge.

He stood at the stern, pounding the rail with a fist, a sense of helplessness growing with every passing minute. Restless, he returned to his cabin for a drink, and when that failed to calm his nerves, he marched back up to the wheelhouse. "How soon before they overtake us?" he demanded.

"Not long now," replied Farrell. "Half a glass or so—if that. But we'll know her intentions sooner still."

"How so?"

He pointed to the hourglass in its stand beside the wheel. "We'll fall within reach of her guns before that glass is turned."

"Not long, then," surmised Burleigh.

"Not long, sir, no." The sailor gave a nod to the schooner and said, "When you can see the faces of the men at the rail, that is when you worry. Until then, 'tis a waste of ball and powder."

"What should we do? Break out the arms?"

"Aye, sir, if it should come to that," replied Farrell. "My seadogs know what to do. I'll have Mr. Garland tell the crew to stand to stations."

"Would you mind if I speak to my men? It might help for me to explain the situation to them."

"Seein' as how your fellas might need a little encouragement, I see no harm," allowed the captain. "Go ahead as you deem fit."

Having received the captain's blessing, Burleigh gathered his four ruffians from their various chores and took them to the gun room below. "We will not waste time moaning," he began. "There are privateers and pirates in these waters, and it appears that we have drawn the attention of some of them." He paused a moment to allow this to sink in. "Captain Farrell is making all speed for the nearest port, but the enemy will try to catch us before we come in range of the harbour cannon. If they succeed—as seems likely—there will be a fight and each of you will be required to do his part."

The men shifted in place and looked at one another. Only Tav spoke up. "What do you want us to do, boss?"

"I expect you to do whatever you're told," Burleigh answered. "Farrell's men are experienced and know the ropes. You are to obey them instantly and without question. Is that understood?"

All four nodded their heads as one.

"If we are taken, we will defend ourselves by any means possible— pistols, knives, swords, bare hands, and teeth if need be."

"Count on it, boss," said Mal. "I likes a good fight, me."

"You will be given weapons, and I expect each one of you to sell your lives dearly should it come to that."

"Aye, boss, we're with you there," said Tav, his voice taking on a savage note. "Come near us and we'll tear 'em limb from bloody limb." He turned to the other three. "Right, fellas?"

"Right-o!" they answered in ragged chorus.

"Don't you worry 'bout us, boss. We'll see 'em off or die tryin'."

"I expect no less," Burleigh concluded. "Acquit yourselves well and there will be something extra in it for you when we reach port."

Dismissing his men to their assigned stations, Burleigh returned to the quarterdeck to assess the state of affairs. The schooner was very much closer now and swiftly closing the distance. "They mean to overtake us," observed Burleigh as he stepped into the wheelhouse.

"Aye, so I expect," affirmed the captain. "They've had ample opportunity to slide off, but have not. They're on a course to intercept."

"We'll show them we're not for the taking," said Burleigh. "My men are spoiling for a fight."

"Let us not be o'er hasty, sir," Farrell cautioned. "I will run up a signal and see if we raise a reply—that's only fair. It may be they are making for port on our wake." With that, he summoned the first mate and instructed him to send aloft a signal requesting the stranger ship to identify itself and declare her captain's intentions. The seaman made a knuckle and hurried off to obey the captain's command. "Now we'll see where we stand," Farrell said.

Burleigh went to the stern and a few moments later heard a rippling sound behind him; he turned as the string of varicoloured pennant flags was hoisted aloft. They flew there in plain sight, and Burleigh turned to await a response from the schooner. "How long before they reply?" he called back to the crewman.

"Not long, my lord," answered the sailor, "if they know their business at all."

Burleigh observed the approaching ship and, indeed, within a minute or two, a flutter of colour appeared at the schooner's foremast. It was too far away to make out clearly, but the first mate came to the rail with his glass and took a reading.

"They say they are heading for port and will pass astern," he said slowly. He lowered the small brass telescope and handed it to Burleigh, who pressed it to his eye. He saw four small flags of different colours in a vertical row. The arrangement meant nothing to him.

"You do not sound convinced, Mr. Garland," Burleigh said, lowering the glass.

"No, my lord, I am not convinced." The mate pointed a finger at the schooner. "I asked her to identify and she declined to run up the ensign. As for the rest, anyone can see she means to pass astern. That is not what I asked."

"You think them up to no good."

"Aye, I fear so, my lord." The first mate spat over the rail. "Not to put too fine a point on it, I think them rogues and rascals, and I think they mean to take us."

"Then you best go inform the captain," said Burleigh.

"He already knows, sir."

CHAPTER 21

In Which an Unknown Mettle Is Tested

Do you trust me to see us through the thick?" demanded Captain Farrell. "Tell me aye or nay, for I will brook no second-guessing my commands once we engage."

"Aye, Captain," answered the first mate, and his ready answer was repeated by the rest of the crewmen arrayed behind him.

Farrell turned to the others looking on nervously. "Well? What say you, greengills?"

Tav spoke for all of them. "We're with you, guv'nor—Captain. No two ways about it."

"Then get you below to the gun room," Farrell commanded. To his own crew, he said, "To your stations, lads. And be ready for a fade and feint."

The men scattered, leaving Burleigh and the captain together at the rail. The schooner was almost within hailing distance. Burleigh raised the glass and swept the deck of the overtaking ship.

"They seem to be going about their business—just a few men on deck. I count eight gun ports, but no cannon in sight."

"Won't be cannon seen," Farrell told him. "Not yet. Their captain'll wait until the last moment to spring his trap. Once he's come up alongside we'll learn his intent. But I've got a surprise of my own."

"The fade and feint?" guessed Burleigh. "What is that?"

"As soon as they alter course to come onto us, I will douse the mainsail and throw the helm over hard—this will make our girl swing her stern and slack her sails. That's the fade."

"And the feint?"

"To an experienced seaman, it will look as if we were tryin' to make a break to open sea and misjudged the turn. They won't be able to match us—carryin' that speed—and will have a devil of a time to come about in short order."

"But won't we be a sitting duck?" wondered Burleigh.

"Aye, we will. But they'll have to come around if they want to broadside us or board us, and when they do . . ." Farrell gave a sly smile. "We open the gunports and let fly. At that close range we won't miss."

"What if they fire first?"

"Well, sir, it will be a test o' our mettle, no mistake," granted the captain. "But there's chance in every battle, aye? And we'll be countin' on the privateer's natural greed to see us through the worst."

"They want to keep the ship and cargo undamaged," mused Burleigh as the meaning came to him.

"Aye, what looks an easy prize is granted too great a license—I've seen such before."

"Do it, Mr. Farrell." He stuck out his hand and shook with the captain. "Good luck. Unless you have other duties for me, I'll go below and make ready the swords and pistols."

He had just started for the aft companionway when a blast echoed across the water. Burleigh looked up just in time to see a spray of water arch up a hundred metres or so before the bow. He raced back to the wheelhouse. "They fired on us!" he exclaimed. "It has started."

"Oh, it started some while back," observed Farrell philosophically. "They put a shot across our bow just now to advertise their business, nothing more. They hope that honest merchantmen like ourselves will consider our wives and families and surrender without bloodshed."

"Does such a ploy often work?"

"Often enough to make it worth tryin' of a time." The captain stepped from the helm to observe the schooner bearing ever closer on a course that would soon bring the two ships alongside one another. "It will not work this day, says I. It will not work with Bartholomew Farrell."

Cupping his hands to his mouth, he turned to shout an order to the sailors standing ready at the rigging. "Prepare to luff the mainsail!" he shouted. To Burleigh, he said, "Best get you below, sir, and stand ready to release the weapons." As the earl hurried away, he added, "Mind, tell Garland to open the gunports on my signal. Not a blink before!"

Belowdecks the men had heard the report of the enemy gun and were concerned. Burleigh explained what the captain had told him about their battle strategy. "Each of you get to your cannon and be ready for the signal."

Burleigh's men moved to their stations where, surrounded by small pyramids of cannon balls and stacks of powder cartridges, they picked up ramrods and waited for the seasoned crewmen to arrive. Burleigh positioned himself in the centre of the gun room near the bottom step of the companionway where he might more easily hear the captain's signal and, if necessary, dash up to the quarterdeck.

The momentary calm was abruptly shattered by another report of cannon fire. This time the men in the gun room heard the splash that followed. "Steady," intoned Burleigh. "They mean to frighten us into submission."

The words were scarcely out of his mouth when the cry echoed: "Luff the mainsail!"

At almost the same instant, the ship gave out a groan, and a shudder passed through the stout hull as Farrell spun the wheel hard. For a moment the *Percheron* seemed to rise in the water, then the floor beneath their feet tilted sharply—two ways at once: port to starboard and back to front. In the gun room, they heard water surge along the hull with the sound of a flood in full spate . . . followed quickly by footsteps pounding over the deck above and then down the companionway.

"Come on, you clew-footed rascals!" shouted the first mate, urging sailors to the guns. "Prime your cannon!"

The seamen leapt to the guns. Each gunner deftly shoved in a powder cartridge, rammed it home, and then, fed by Burleigh's men, rolled in a ball.

"Ready, Mr. Garland!" they shouted one by one as the four big guns were positioned in their cradles.

"You lot!" barked the first mate. "Put your hands to the port ropes and be ready to give an almighty heave."

Burleigh's gang did as they were told and stood gripping the braided cord that hung beside the covered porthole. The deck still tilted this way and that, but less dramatically as the ship settled and began to drift. All was quiet from above—so quiet they could hear seagulls keening as they wheeled in the air over the stern.

Then, in amongst the shriek of the gulls, there came another cry—that of a man's voice hailing them.

"What's he sayin', Mr. Garland?" asked one of the sailors.

"Don't speak French, do I?" snapped the first mate.

"He is ordering the captain to surrender," replied Burleigh from his place at the foot of the stairs.

"'Twon't be long now, lads," said the first mate. "Listen here—first shot will be blind, but we'll likely get in another before they know what hit 'em. Might not get more than that, so make it count."

There was another shout in French and an answering reply from Captain Farrell. This was followed a moment later by a dull, thudding clunk directly above their heads.

"Easy, boys," said Mr. Garland. "That'll be the grapple. They ent going to fire on us and risk damage to the ship and cargo. The Frenchies be getting ready to reel in the prize."

The *Percheron* gave another shudder and the deck tilted slightly to port.

"Ready . . ." Garland said, his voice low. "Wait for my count."

There followed an agonising wait . . . and silence . . .

A voice, low but firm, and speaking directly over the companionway shaft, called down to them. "On count of three, raise open ports and let fly!"

"There's the captain," said the first mate. "Ready at the ropes! On three count! One . . . two . . . PULL!"

All heaved at once, and the port covers flipped up and Burleigh glimpsed a banded expanse of black-and-white hull. The gunners, without pausing to shove the cannon forward into the port, simply pulled the firing chain, and there erupted a staccato burst of fire and smoke as the guns roared to life. Instantly the air filled with the corrosive stench of burning brimstone. The resulting concussion of sound hammered Burleigh's chest with the wallop of a horse's kick, rocking him back on his heels.

Into the silence that followed, he heard the screams and moans of wounded men.

Gasping, his ears ringing, the earl darted for the nearest gunport, fanning his way through the smoke. Pressing his face to the portal, he looked out to see that great gaping holes had appeared in the schooner's smooth flank. Smoke and fire belched from these ragged holes. Farrell's feint had succeeded in gouging a huge rent in the enemy ship's hull, taking out six of the eight cannon on the schooner's starboard side.

"Reload and fire at will!" shouted the first mate. "Let the salt rats have it!"

Before the guns could be reloaded, however, the schooner's two remaining cannon fired one after the other. The first ball struck the stern at an angle and sent a shudder through the ship. The second explosion punched a hole through the hull. The iron missile burst through in a blizzard of splinters—shards of oak, needle sharp, blasted through the air on a gust of smoke and fire.

"Destroy that gun!" screamed Garland. "Destroy it now!"

Dazed, deafened, Burleigh shook fine slivers of wood from his coat. His hand brushed his upper thigh and he felt a twinge, looked down, and saw a piece of oak the size of a dagger sticking out of his leg. Without thinking, he pulled it and instantly wished he had not been so hasty. Pain flashed through him with an intensity that stole his breath away. He staggered back and collapsed on the lower step of the companionway, suddenly light-headed and dizzy.

Across the room, everyone seemed to move with slow, lethargic nonchalance, as men in a dream, in timeless languid deliberation. He saw the sailor at the gun nearest the blast hole push the cannon carriage around and his man, Dex, shove in a cartridge and ram it home while the gunner pulled a lever to raise the elevation of the big gun's barrel. Dex pushed in a ball and the gunner pulled hard on the firing chain. The cannon lifted in its cradle as the explosion spewed fire. Smoke drifted from the barrel in backwards-curling billows. The resulting impact of the hurled iron piercing the wooden skin of the enemy ship resounded like a clap of thunder. And with that sound, Burleigh's normal sensation resumed.

Pain shot through him in throbbing waves and black spots danced before his eyes. His ears hurt and his head ached from the crown of his skull to his back teeth, and he realised he was clenching his jaw.

First Mate Garland dashed to the nearest gun port; he thrust in his head and assessed the damage inflicted on the enemy by the last shot. "Good work, lads!" he shouted. "That's slowed the buggers down."

Laying hands on the crewman nearest him, he pulled him away from the gun. "Thoms!" he cried. "You and Henderson get up top and mount the deck guns! Fire at will. The rest of you—follow me!"

Thoms and Henderson ran for the companionway and found it blocked by Burleigh sprawled on the steps holding his head. "Mr. Garland!" cried Thoms. "Sir is down!"

Garland hastened to the earl's aid. "Where are you hurt, sir?"

"My leg," growled Burleigh through his teeth. Blood spilled out from between his fingers where he gripped the wound.

The first mate bent to inspect the injury, then stood. To Thoms and Henderson, he said, "Get you up top and commence firing! Fly!" Bending once more to Burleigh he said, "Right, sir. We'll get you to your cabin. Dex, Mal—help his lordship—"

"The devil you will," growled Burleigh. "Lift me up." They raised him to his feet; he steadied himself and shouted, "Don't stand here gawking. Get to the weapons store and break out the pistols and blades. Then meet me on deck."

The men raced off and Burleigh struggled up the stairs to the quarterdeck, regaining strength and vigour with every step. The pain, though great, was bearable, and he limped onto the deck to find it awash in a fog of smoke. The schooner had attached itself to the *Percheron* with two grappling hooks—one below the bow and the other amidships—and enemy sailors were pulling on the cables to draw the two vessels closer together so that the prize could be boarded. Burleigh started for the bow, where crewman Thoms was priming a sixteen-pounder mounted on a swivel.

"There!" shouted Burleigh, tottering towards him. "Aim for the rail!"

"Aye, sir!" replied Thoms, ramming home the charge. Pulling the gun around, he lined up the shot and let fly. Fire and smoke issued from the slim mouth of the swivel-mounted gun, and the schooner's rail near the bow hook exploded in a hail of splinters. The enemy sailors dropped from sight and the ball careered on, smashing into a hatch housing in the centre of the deck.

"Keep firing!" shouted Burleigh. "Don't let up!"

"Your lordship!" called Garland. "Here!"

The earl turned as the first mate came running, a pair of pistols in one hand and two cutlasses in the other.

"I suggest you defend the gun, sir," said Garland, shoving a pistol into Burleigh's hand.

A desperate cry went up from the stern and Garland raced off.

"Right," muttered Burleigh, cocking the pistol. "Show your scabby faces, rogues. Let's make buzzard food."

A report resounded from the stern. Burleigh glanced back along the rail and saw the stern gun enveloped in smoke and a chunk of the schooner's railing pinwheeling through the air. Like his mate at the bow gun, Henderson was aiming for the sailors hauling on the grappling hook amidships.

As the smoke cleared, Captain Farrell appeared with a cutlass in hand, chopping at the hawser that secured the grappling hook. A hail of pistol fire spattered around him—one shot biting out a chunk of the rail near his hand. Burleigh scanned the schooner's rigging and saw three pirates clinging to the mast lines; two of them were reloading and the third was taking aim at Farrell.

Calmly, with practiced care, Burleigh raised his pistol, adjusted his angle, and pulled the trigger. The pistol kicked back with a reassuring clap and the ball sped to its mark. A sailor high in the rigging dropped his weapon and made a futile grab for the rope; then, one hand clutching his chest, the other flailing wildly, he dropped like a stone released from the rigging. His two comrades skittered down the webbing to safety. Burleigh saw his victim plummet, but no more, for the earl, ignoring the fire in his leg, was already running to Farrell's aid.

"What are you doing here?" shouted the captain. "Get back to the bow gun!"

"You need help," answered Burleigh, and began striking at the thick rope with quick slashing blows of the cutlass. The braided hemp resisted his first attempts, but then the sharp blade bit, fraying a little more with every strike. Again and again the blades rose and fell as the two men struggled to free the hook—and were about to succeed when out from behind the hatch housing came five enemy sailors, yelling, waving sabres and cutlasses. Burleigh gave a last swipe at the hawser and then turned his attention to the attackers as the first came scrambling up, his voice and cutlass raised.

The Frenchman leapt forward, leaning out over the rail across the gap separating the two ships, slashing wildly—not so much to wound as to keep Farrell and Burleigh away from the heavy grappling rope. Burleigh met the thrust of his assailant's broad blade with a sharp, downward parry, knocking the weapon aside. Two more blades instantly took its place as more sailors swarmed the rail, each one stretching, thrusting, jabbing in a frenzied effort to reach the lone defenders.

"Get you down, Captain!" shouted Henderson from the stern.

"Down!" shouted Farrell, pulling Burleigh to the deck beside him. "Cover your head."

The earl had time only to throw his free arm over his head when the stern gun gave out its strident clap. Bits of wood and rope showered over them. Farrell jumped to his feet. The attacking sailors were gone, and so was the grappling hook. "We're free!" he shouted. "Now the bow hook!"

Burleigh pushed himself up on his hands and knees and with some difficulty got his good leg under him. The captain, already dashing for the bow, glanced back and, seeing the earl struggling to stand, ran to take his arm and bear him to his feet. "You're wounded. Sit you down."

"It is nothing. Go! I am behind you."

Just as they reached the bow, enemy sailors came swarming across the deck of the schooner; several had pistols and fired across the rail at the running men. Farrell and Burleigh hit the deck and hid below the gunwale as shot peppered the deck and hatch housing around them. Thoms at the bow gun returned fire.

The pirates scattered and Thoms reloaded. Burleigh and the captain dived for the grappling hook secured to the bow rail and commenced hacking at the rope with their blades. Gunfire resumed. Shot spattered around them, and once more they ducked below the gunwale to wait for the shooters to reload.

Thoms hit the deck too, but an errant ball caught him on the way down. "Ah!" he cried as he fell. "I am shot!"

Farrell swam on his belly across the deck to the stricken gunner. Thoms, clutching his side, squirmed in pain.

"Easy, now," Farrell told him. "Let me see it." He pulled the seaman's bloody hands from the wound and lifted his shirt. "You're creased bad, Mr. Thoms," he announced. "We'll get you below as soon as we've cleared the bow line." Whirling around, he shouted to Burleigh, "See to the grapple, sir! I will man the gun."

The captain leapt up and primed the cannon as Burleigh hacked at the heavy rope once more. The strands gave way with maddening reluctance, but the captain kept the enemy sailors at bay by waving the bow cannon at them whenever they showed their heads above the rail.

Chopping like a lumberjack, the cutlass gripped in both hands, his arm rising and falling until his muscles burned, Burleigh at last succeeded in sawing his way through the hawser. "It is free!" he shouted. "The grapple is clear!"

"Well done!" cried Farrell. "Take over the gun!"

As Burleigh joined him at the cannon, the captain cried to his crewmen, "I need a gunhand here!"

"I'll do it," said Burleigh.

"You know how to charge a gun?"

"I have seen it done," replied Burleigh, limping to the swivel.

"Those go in first and get rammed down hard." The captain

pointed to the powder charges. "The ball goes in after. Aim high as the ball falls off sharp." He thrust a hand at the sail. "I'll get the sail up and see if I can give us some distance."

As Farrell darted off, an explosion rocked the *Percheron*, causing the deck to bounce and almost throwing Burleigh off his feet. He grabbed the rail and held on. Smoke billowed up from the hull in front of him. It was impossible to tell what had happened, but he heard shouting and the cries of wounded men.

Suddenly smoke was everywhere, boiling up out of the hatch behind him—and also from the forward hatch of the schooner. There were more shouts . . . followed by screams. Enemy seamen appeared on the schooner's deck, boiling up from the companionway, trailing smoke. One seaman's trouser leg was on fire, and he wailed in panic until one of his mates knocked him to the deck and threw sand from a canvas bucket over the flames. The others, waving sabres and cutlasses, stormed the bow where the ships were still close, shouting as they came; two of them climbed onto the rail and assayed a leap across the gap separating the two ships.

Burleigh fired the bow cannon. He missed the men but struck the webbing and brought down a tangle of rope and several blocks. He swivelled the gun and fell to reloading.

"Haul mainsail!" shouted Captain Farrell from the wheelhouse. Two crewmen ran to the capstan and began pulling the rope; the slack sail grew taut, caught the wind, rippled, and filled. The *Percheron* dipped a little and slowly began to move.

By the time the earl had the gun recharged and loaded, the gap separating the ships had grown to a dozen metres. The sails swelled and the prow bit into the oncoming waves as the captain brought the bow around. The distance between the two ships yawned and widened, and soon it was clear they were leaving the enemy vessel behind. Sporadic gunfire still rang from the schooner. Burleigh aimed a last shot at the schooner's helm and watched as the ball struck the deck, bounced, and caromed into a stack of barrels.

The *Percheron* gained speed, and the schooner receded. Smoke still hung in wispy tatters over the deck and in the rigging of the pirate ship, and some of the sailors stood at the rail watching their prize slip away. Burleigh raised his fist and shook it in their faces, then abandoned his gun and turned to help the wounded Thoms, who had dragged himself across the deck and was sitting against the forward hatch housing, his face blanched white as the sail canvas above his head.

The earl shouted for help, then fell back onto the deck, exhausted, his leg throbbing with pain.

It was almost dark by the time they entered the harbour mouth at Cape Trafalgar. Captain Farrell had run up the distress signal to enable swift passage and get help for Burleigh, Thoms, and O'Brien—another sailor injured by flying shrapnel when a lucky shot ignited the schooner's powder magazine. As the ship made its way into the bay, the high bluffs blushed with a ruddy purple glow. Never had Burleigh been so glad to see land, nor was he alone. Several of the men cheered when the harbourmaster sent out a launch to meet them and take the wounded to the port infirmary.

Burleigh, his own wound cleaned and bandaged, refused to leave the ship until he had spoken to the harbourmaster. "That was well done, Mr. Farrell," Burleigh said, watching the sailors being carried down the gangplank. "I salute you, Captain, and I intend to make a full report of the day's events to the authorities. Your bravery and that of your crew is exemplary and will not go unrewarded."

"All in a day's work, sir," replied the captain. "As a wise man once said—all's well that ends well. But we may be some time delayed, for it is my opinion that we must lay up here for repairs. It is a fair port and well-provisioned town. We might make Tarquinia in any case, but I think it best to see the ship right and give the wounded a chance to get back on their sea legs."

"I yield to your counsel, Mr. Farrell. Take all the time you need." Burleigh considered the generous harbour and the prosperous town rising on the hills above the bay and added, "I might as well tell you now—we are not going to Tarquinia, or Ostia."

"No, sir?" The captain turned, his eyebrows lifted in surprise. "Where then, if I may be so bold?"

"China, Mr. Farrell," Burleigh told him. "We must prepare for a lengthy voyage, for we are bound for the South China Sea."

PART FOUR

The Harrowing

CHAPTER 22

In Which Exploding Stars Are Harnessed

"Oh, come on!" protested Kit. "It is plain as paint what happened here—Haven has stolen the book and absconded."

"And Giles?" wondered Mina. "What about him?"

"She took him with her, of course," insisted Kit. "Who knows what she told him—some lie or other to get him to help her and keep it quiet."

"How would she even know where to look?"

"She searched the room, obviously." He thrust an accusatory finger at the chest standing open at the foot of his bed. His few items of clothing were tossed and rumpled—as if they had been rummaged through and then carelessly put back. "It wasn't difficult, was it—I mean, it's not as if there is a ton of stuff in here."

They were standing at the doorway to the upper room Kit and Gianni shared in the Grand Imperial. Kit had returned from a cruise around the marketplace to find the wooden chest where he kept his few belongings ransacked. He glanced at Gianni standing in the doorway, and then at Wilhelmina beside him, willing them to believe the evidence before their eyes. "The book was there, and now it isn't. Haven was here, and now she's gone. Coincidence? I don't think so."

"I'm not saying you're wrong," allowed Mina. "I just don't want to rush to any hasty conclusions. Let's wait and see."

"Fine. Whatever. But the fact remains—the book is gone. So what are we going to do about it?"

"I don't see anything we *can* do about it."

"This book," interrupted Gianni. "It is the same one you showed us, yes? You believe it may contain the key to the map. How did you come to possess this book? Explain, please."

"As I mentioned before, it is Sir Henry Fayth's personal journal," sighed Kit. "In its pages, Sir Henry recorded all his thoughts, speculations, and discoveries concerning ley lines and ley travel. Haven and I found the book in his study when he and Cosimo went missing. I've read it a couple times, or tried to, and to tell the truth I didn't understand most of it. But I think now that it might contain the information we need to help decipher the map. I was hoping that by putting the book and map together we could—" Kit broke off as a sudden thought occurred to him. He turned to Wilhelmina. "You *do* still have the map? Tell me you have it."

"Don't worry."

"I think we should check just to be sure," Kit insisted. "Haven is a devious, two-faced schemer, and if she's got her claws into that map—"

"Kit, it is safe. Relax."

"Go check."

"I have it under lock and key."

"I want to see the map right now."

"Oh, all right," Mina relented, "if it'll shut you up."

"We'll all go. Where is it?"

"If I showed you where it was, it wouldn't be secret anymore, would it?" she countered. "You two wait here—I'll be right back."

Wilhelmina scurried off down the corridor, and Kit returned to his survey of what he now considered the scene of the crime. "I know Haven took the green book," Kit said, returning to his current preoccupation. "She resented me having it in the first place."

"Why would she take it and run away?" asked Gianni. "Why not simply ask you for it?"

"Her ladyship is a law unto herself," replied Kit, bitterness creeping into his tone. "She does what she does for her own reasons and without regard for anyone else."

Gianni offered a sympathetic nod. "The world is only too full of such people."

Mina reappeared a few moments later with reassurances that, yes, their portion of the Skin Map was still safe and secure, along with the copy they had made. "Everything's okay," she told Kit. "All right? I've got a shop to run, so why don't you two go find something to do for now, and we'll all sit down later and discuss what to do about this."

"Are you trying to get rid of us?" asked Kit.

Mina was already moving through the door. "Something like that."

"I can tell when I'm not wanted," muttered Kit. "Come on, Gianni. Let's go grab a cup of coffee. We need to talk about our expedition to the Stone Age and what to do about that tree when we get there."

The priest demurred. "Nothing would delight me more—however, I must go see the potter before the market ends."

Kit, already royally cheesed off, rolled his eyes in disbelief. "Am I the only one anxious to get back to the chase?"

"Very sorry," said Gianni. "But today is the only day when the potter comes to market. I have made arrangements to meet him."

"Right. On your bike, then," replied Kit. "See you later." They parted company and Kit stuffed his belongings back into the chest, closed it, and kicked it back into place. Then he wandered downstairs to the main dining room of the coffeehouse. There were a few black-coated, bushy-bearded businessmen lining the benches against the back wall; they spoke in low tones and sipped their coffee from their own personal mugs, which Wilhelmina reserved for them. Three stately matrons with elaborately curled hair and satin dresses in green and blue occupied a table beneath the windows where the light was better and where they were sure to notice, and be noticed by, the passing foot traffic.

The afternoon trade had dwindled and the early evening crowd had yet to arrive, so the shop was relatively quiet—save for the clatter of pans and trays that emanated from the kitchen where Etzel and his helpers laboured to fill the void created in their stock of pastries by discerning palates. Dismissing the coffee idea, Kit decided instead to go see how Cass was getting along with the testing.

Leaving the Grand Imperial, he struck out across the market square. The buying and bartering were still in full cry, the square thronging with merchants in their stalls and shoppers cramming the narrow aisles. Wilhelmina had arranged for Cass to stay in a rented room above the *Apoteke*. Kit entered and called a greeting to Anya, the apothecary, a substantial widow who had worked the shop alone since the death of her husband years ago. *"Guten Tag!"* he chimed, raising a finger skyward. She nodded and he made his way upstairs.

Cass had set up a rudimentary lab on a cleared table she had moved to the bright space beneath the only window in the room. She was at work, humming to herself. The sight of her cheered him unexpectedly, and the sound of her soft, throaty singing charmed him. Pausing in the doorway, he allowed himself a second or two to savour the moment before knocking on the doorframe.

"Hey there!" he called. "How goes the battle?"

"Oh, hi, Kit," she replied, glancing quickly over her shoulder with a smile before turning back to the table. "Come on in and see for yourself."

In an effort to determine the identity of the mystery material that animated the shadow lamps, Cassandra had cracked open the shell of Kit's ruined device. "You can tell a lot about composition from the residue left behind when things burn out," she explained. "Ashes of all kinds have a chemical signature."

Kit nodded appreciatively. "What can you tell from this?" he asked, peering over her shoulder at what looked like an open clamshell made of brass.

"Nothing much yet. My equipment is not exactly state-of-the-art."

Cass had spread a clean white handkerchief on the table where the halves of the defunct ley lamp revealed a fairly simple internal mechanism—surprisingly simple, in fact. The guts of the gizmo seemed to consist almost entirely of a single large chamber containing the activating substance with smaller individual channels radiating out to the holes in the carapace from which the lights emanated. There were two or three other, much smaller compartments—it was difficult to say exactly because of the melting that had occurred during the power surge—as well as the remnants of a mechanism containing a spring, some baffles and channels, and what looked like a tiny bellows or diaphragm.

"Tell me again how this meltdown happened," said Cass. Using a large, curved upholstery needle with a flattened point, she carefully picked at a globule of molten stuff in the main chamber, scraping the charred, black remains into a neat little pile.

"We were in the Stone Age land I was telling you about," began Kit. "I wanted to show Mina and Brother Lazarus the Bone House, but instead—"

"The Bone House," murmured Cass, craning her neck to see him. "It sounds so . . . so Palaeolithic. Describe it for me."

"Well, it was the middle of winter. One day some of the younger men of River City Clan invited me to go out with them into the forest where they were building this amazing little hut—sort of like an igloo, but made entirely out of the bones of all these creatures—bison and rhinos and mammoths and elks, everything. The bones were gathered from a heap at the bottom of a cliff—"

"A kill zone," surmised Cass. "Some native tribes were known to do the same thing—chase animals off a cliff. It's a very efficient way to get meat."

Kit nodded. "So we pulled all these bones and antlers and skulls and things from the pile and dragged them to a clearing deep in the woods. I didn't know it then, but they were constructing this little hut right on top of a ley portal. The Old One—surely I mentioned *him*, didn't I? The clan chief? En-Ul was his name, and when the Bone House was finished, he crawled in and went into some kind of sleeping trance, or deep meditation, or I don't know what. Dreaming Time, he called it."

"Fascinating." Cass matched Kit's expression of awe with her own. "You *have* to take me to see this place. You promised, remember?"

"Sure, but there's just one small detail," Kit hedged. "When I took Mina and Gianni to the clearing in the forest, the Bone House was gone. Instead, we found this huge yew tree—a thousand years old at least, maybe older. That's the problem."

"A yew tree, huh?" Cass returned to picking at the black sooty ashes with the needle.

"Yeah, an absolutely gigantic yew tree," said Kit. "Why?"

"Well, you know, yew trees being associated with immortality and eternity—which also happens to be the subject of this quest everybody is always talking about." She glanced at Kit. "Didn't you know that? Lots of ancient cultures regard the yew as a sacred tree—probably because they're so fantastically long-lived. People thought yew trees lived forever, so they became a symbol of everlasting life. That's why you see them planted in churchyards so much." She gave a little half shrug. "It's an interesting coincidence, is all."

"Cassandra, my dear," said Kit, mimicking the old-fashioned, elevated tone of his late great-grandfather, "we should all very well know by now there is *no such thing* as coincidence."

Cass regarded him with a quizzical expression. "Okay . . ."

"It's something Cosimo and Sir Henry were always on about," he explained. "Anyway, back to the tree . . . So there we are, standing around in the forest looking at it and wondering what to do, and all of a sudden our lamps go crazy. We're just checking to see if the ley portal is still there, and they go all berserk—the shadow lamps, that is—and the silly things overheat."

"Just heat?" asked Cass, looking at the array of parts and materials before her. "Anything else?"

Kit thought a moment. "The little lights were blinking—no, not blinking, more like pulsing. Really bright—I'd never seen them so bright. And then suddenly the brass case got too hot to hold. Mina dropped hers first, and then I did. The gizmos gave off a funny little pop and white smoke came out, and *fzzt!* That was it."

"Hmm." Cass put down the needle and picked up a pair of tweezers, extracting a lump of charred material, which she dropped into a small glass bowl she'd borrowed from the coffeehouse. "So what happened next?"

"That's all," Kit said. "We came back here, and then you and Haven and Giles showed up. The rest you know."

Retrieving two more samples, Cass added each to a Grand Imperial cup. Into the first cup she added a drop of water; into the second, a smidge of vinegar; and into the bowl, a drop of something pale and yellow that stank of rotten eggs. "Crude, but we might be able to get a reaction from one of these reagents," Cass told him. "That is, *if* there is anything to react with anymore." She stirred the samples one at a time with the end of a glass writing pen and waited, frowning with concentration.

"Anything?" asked Kit after a moment.

"Nothing yet." She lengthened the wick on the table lamp and held one of the cups close to the intensified flame. "Sometimes a little heat can catalyse a reaction." She stirred the contents of the cup again, tilted it over the flame, waited, and then went on to the next. None of the samples displayed any discernible change.

"This might be a doomed project," she surmised, "but at least we're giving it a shot. If I had more sophisticated test equipment and more chemicals, we might get a little further." She turned back to her experiment. "I'll try a few more tests and see if I can advance things any. If not, I'll start in on the samples Gustavus supplied. But to tell you the truth, I'm getting near the end of my limited expertise."

"Right. You carry on," said Kit. "I'll go find Gianni."

"Hurry back."

Kit zoomed off in search of the Italian and, after a lengthy search through the aisles and avenues of the heaving marketplace, eventually located him at the far side of the square where the craftsmen generally set up their wares. Kit hailed him and joined him at a pottery stall. Gianni had drawn examples of what he wanted and, from what Kit could gather, was trying to convince the potter to make them for him. This entailed a lengthy discussion Kit could not follow, but which seemed to be satisfactorily concluded when the two shook hands.

"This time next week, God willing, I hope to begin my garden," he announced.

"May I?" asked Kit, indicating the drawing.

Gianni passed it to him, saying, "They do not have these here. Can you believe it?"

"Flowerpots?" wondered Kit, scanning the sketch. "That's what you needed to see the potter about?"

"Simple terra-cotta planters, yes. He kept saying that bowls are more useful. But I need something to grow herbs and vegetables."

"Whatever you say." Kit returned the drawing and said, "Cass and I were wondering if you could lend a hand with the testing. She's reached a roadblock."

Gianni sealed his deal with a small advance payment, and followed Kit to the upper room at the *Apoteke*.

"I have not induced a reaction to any of the test materials I have on hand," Cass explained. "I tested the residue as well as the raw material. No reaction whatsoever."

"It is not surprising. I suspect it would take more sophisticated tools and chemicals than you can find in this place and time—and

most likely will not be able to obtain for the next two hundred years."
Gianni pulled up a chair and took his place beside her. "But let us see
what we can do here and now. First, however, I would like to hear how
these little lamps . . . ah, function—is that right?"

Both turned their faces towards Kit. "How? But you've already *seen*
how they function."

"No, my friend, I have seen only how they *mis*function."

"Malfunction," Cass corrected lightly.

"Okay," said Kit, "it's really very simple. When the lamp comes
into contact with a ley line that happens to be active, the little holes
light up. They glow blue."

"I think there is maybe more to it than that," prodded the priest
physicist. "Please, describe what happens—from the beginning. Tell
us everything you can think of—even the smallest detail may prove
useful."

Kit gave a thoughtful nod and then embarked on a lengthy discussion of how the ley lamp worked and how it was used, everything
he could remember down to the colour of the lights and smell produced when it fizzled out. He concluded by saying, "Mina could tell
you more than I can—she's the expert. Also, her lamp was a newer
and more powerful model—more bells and whistles."

Gianni thanked him and then turned to his colleague in the next
chair. "Any ideas, Cassandra?"

"Rare earth," she said. "I've thought that from the start. Terbium,
maybe—or gadolinium."

"Possibly, possibly." Gianni pulled on his chin. "It could be
gadolinium—or one of its derivatives." He tapped his chin with a
finger. Then his eyes lit up. "I know! Europium!"

"Europium," echoed Cass. "That's a new one on me. But then, this is pretty far out of my field."

"Europium might be worth a closer look," Gianni asserted. "I think so. We should try gadolinium and terbium, also neodymium."

"I'm going to assume those are real things," Kit remarked. "You're not making them up?"

"Rare earth metals," Cass told him. "They are real, all right, very real—but also—well . . . very rare."

"I get it," said Kit.

"They are related members of a family of lanthanides—some of the heavier elements—produced in the nucleosynthesis of super-novae." Seeing Kit's eyes begin to glaze, she explained, "That means they are produced in the thermonuclear explosions of stars."

"Exploding stars," murmured Kit. "Of course."

"The elements produced can be used for all kinds of things," Cass continued. "They are useful to palaeontologists because they change over time, so we use them to help date fossils. They're also found in all sorts of high-tech devices such as lasers, X-ray machines, MRI scanners, nuclear batteries—things like that."

"Behold the glory of creation! Even exploding stars have their purpose," Gianni declared, allowing himself a little homily. "And that purpose can be harnessed by mankind."

"The lanthanides, as they are known, are likely candidates for these shadow lamps," Cass continued, "since many of them are sensitive to electromagnetic energy of various sorts—often exhibiting pronounced electron excitation resulting in abundant photon emission in the shorter wavelengths."

At Kit's puzzled expression, she added, "They glow."

"That would explain it," concluded Kit. He pointed at the dish of undistinguished grey granules. "Gustavus said that Burleigh brought the material to him, right? So where would Burleigh get this stuff if it is so very rare?"

"As we said before—when we know what it is, we'll know where it came from." Cass turned to Gianni. "China is my guess."

"That must be our first choice," he agreed.

"Why China?" asked Kit, feeling increasingly out of his depth and sinking fast.

"Simply because most of the world's supply of rare earth elements comes from there," she said. "Southern China is a rich area, geologically speaking."

Gianni picked up the glass vial containing a tiny bit of the raw material Gustavus had given them. "If we could narrow down our list of candidates, we might be able to design a more specific test. A few of these elements are halide reactive—some of them form stable compounds with chalcogenides . . ."

The discussion quickly plunged into deeper waters Kit could not navigate. He decided to go out, get some air, stretch his legs, and leave the technical talk to the experts. "You two carry on, I'm just popping out for a bit," he said, quietly removing himself from the discussion. Once outside, he strolled off across the square. Some of the merchants were striking their stalls and getting ready to head home, but there were still plenty of shoppers and vendors around doing last-minute deals. As he rounded a corner, he saw Engelbert disappearing into a side street with a bag over his shoulder; it put Kit in mind of Santa Claus making his rounds. Kit gave a halfhearted shout and a wave, but the baker was already gone.

Kit continued his window shopping; he sauntered here and there, idly examining the various wares on display and thinking, as he passed the iron monger and carpenter, what a monumental achievement the humble chisel represented. Among River City Clan even a simple saw would have been a marvel of technology. Take a saw, a sack full of nails, and a hammer or two back to River City and he would be thought a wonder-worker, a wizard of the first degree. Throw in a packet of needles and a pair of scissors and he would be hailed a king at least, maybe even a god.

Thinking about the clan cast Kit into a melancholy mood, which he misdiagnosed as impatience or frustrated purpose, but then realised was more properly a form of longing: he missed his friends, his people, the gentle giants of a more primitive age. Not least, he missed the person he was when he was with them. He missed the forthright simplicity, the innate compassion, the way the clan cared unstintingly for one another. He missed Dardok and the other members of the clan, the young Turks, the women and little ones; most of all, he missed the chieftain, En-Ul.

The Ancient One, in that mysterious way they all possessed, could read his thoughts almost as clearly as speech. Well, concluded Kit, if thoughts can be read across time and space, then read this, En-Ul: *I shall return.*

CHAPTER 23

In Which Tomb Robbing Is Encouraged

The desert heat struck Charles Flinders-Petrie with a force strong enough to peel paint. He imagined the soles of his shoes catching fire—or, worse, the searing rays of the white-hot sun igniting his hair and setting his head alight. If he had walked into a blast furnace it could not, he decided, have felt any hotter. Pausing only long enough to catch his breath and survey his surroundings, he patted the bone-white dust from his clothes and looked around. Beneath the sun-bleached empty sky, the distant hills danced in shimmering waves rising from the desert floor. But that was the only movement for miles in any direction. Stretching ahead of him, the ram-headed sphinxes lining the long avenue leading to the ruined temple remained, as ever, unmoved and unaffected by the scorching atmosphere.

Seeing that he was completely alone and unobserved, Charles allowed himself to relax a little; he pulled a length of linen cloth from the leather bag at his side and wound it around his head turban style. The pack—the same used by his father on his last visit to Egypt—contained all the things he imagined he would need on this, his most adventurous journey yet. The fact that he had Lord Burleigh to thank for his newfound enthusiasm for ley travel was not lost on Charles. For if not for the earl's insistent meddling all those years ago, he probably would never have given his grandfather's map a second thought.

With a tug on the long braided strap, he hitched up the pack and started off across country towards the gently wavering line of hills, leaving the double rank of silent statues behind. With only his father's description to guide him, Charles was soon wishing Benedict had thought to make a map of his own—or at least jotted down a few tricks of the family trade. Without such a guide, reconstructing the precise ley-leaping method used by Arthur had proven exceedingly difficult; it had taken Charles over five years and a few score attempts before he tumbled to a rough calibration method that would allow him to reach this place at this time—give or take a year, or even a generation or two. More work would refine his technique, but for that he would need the map. And the map was the reason for his visit.

Although he had never been to Egypt, from the time he was old enough to walk he had heard the family stories from his father and grandmother so often that he felt he knew the place—at least well enough to find his way around. He knew the Nile lay beyond the hills and that there would be a farming village or town somewhere on the riverbank nearby. He knew that beyond the river lay a wadi where, with perseverance and generous lashings of luck, he would find the tomb of Anen, his grandfather's friend and a high priest of what was now being called the Eighteenth Dynasty.

In the village he would find men he could hire to help with his reclamation project. This would, he expected, have serious consequences for future archaeology: he did not see how the desecration of the tomb could be prevented. For as soon as his erstwhile helpers discovered what Charles knew to be there, the looting would begin. Official documents from the time of Pharaoh Cheops spoke of "tomb robbers"—a particular scourge of the wealthier classes; consequently, Egyptologists tended to consider them a separate criminal class. They were not. In reality, the thieves were merely the poor local peasantry of whatever era who, in their hardscrabble need, simply helped themselves to whatever valuables they found lying around—often in burial chambers half hidden in the sand and long forgotten. No doubt the villagers would find plenty to please them in High Priest Anen's tomb; but so long as Charles got what he wanted, his hirelings were welcome to whatever they could carry away.

First, however, he had to reach the river and find the village. The walk was arduous to the point of absurdity, and by the time Charles reached the base of the hills, he was leaking water from every pore—but feeling no cooler for it. His sweat flash-dried the moment it seeped through the skin, leaving only a faint damp spot on the thin cloth of his linen shirt . . . and then that disappeared, evaporating into the arid desert air, leaving behind a deposit of his own salts. He shambled along the base of the nearest hill until finding a rock large enough to cast a shadow he might shelter in. When he came to it, he sat down in the shade; with his back to the stone, he withdrew his old-fashioned waterskin and allowed himself a good long drink. Then he closed his eyes and, leaning back against the stone, conjured cool, soothing thoughts until the sun, having reached its zenith, began its long, slow descent into the west.

While he rested, he reviewed the details of what he had been told about his family's connection with Egypt. He knew that Arthur, his grandfather, had lived some years there, studying the language and culture and making friends with a young priest named Anen. It was Anen who had looked after his father, Benedict, when tragedy struck and Arthur was killed during an uprising; and Anen also, in the end, provided a resting place for Arthur's linen-wrapped bones. He knew his grandmother, Xian-Li, and Benedict had returned at some later time to return the Skin Map to its owner.

This macabre object, born of a linguistic misunderstanding, had loomed large in the family lore ever since its creation. In fact, for Charles there was never a time when he could not remember knowing about his grandfather's storied map: how it had been made from Arthur's skin in order to save the tattoos that recorded the more important destinations his grandfather had discovered; and how, within the coded symbols, a fearful and wonderful secret lay hidden; and how his father had been made to give up interdimensional travel in order to better ensure the family's survival.

Well, Charles considered, the family had survived and even thrived, and his father's vow never again to use ley lines had not prevented him from talking about them and telling stories about Arthur's exploits and adventures. Before being made to give up ley travel, Benedict had shared some of his father's journeys, accompanying him on various trips through time and space, learning the secrets of ley travel first-hand. It was on such a trip to Egypt that the two had been caught in the uprising that took Arthur's life; young Benedict had met not one but two pharaohs, and it was he who had visited the high priest's tomb and deposited the map in his father's sarcophagus, thereby ending the familial preoccupation that Charles meant to revive.

When the shadow of the rock began to stretch long on the trail, Charles rose and began his climb over the hills above the Nile Valley. By the time he reached the top there were but two or three hours of daylight remaining. The little settlement, glimpsed as a dull smudge beside the great, glittering river, still lay some distance away. Owing to the heat and the need to rest, it had taken him longer to gain the heights than he had imagined; Charles doubted whether he could reach his destination before nightfall, and he reckoned a strange traveller arriving after dark would not find the sort of welcome he desired. No matter. He had come equipped for that eventuality. In his pack he carried a little food and a linen coverlet—something like a shroud—that would keep him warm when, perversely, the desert air grew chill in the hours before dawn.

Spending a night sleeping rough did not worry Charles in the least. It had been a regular, if not predictable, occurrence during his years at university: doorways, arches, church pews, market stall benches—these and others had sufficed for impromptu accommodations. Sleeping out under the stars would be a luxury by comparison. True, he was older now, but not so much older that he could not enjoy a night beneath the diamond-sprinkled spray of the Milky Way.

As the sun dropped below the western hills, flaming the sky with molten bronze, Charles found a stubby date palm at the edge of a sesame field and made his simple camp. After beating the surrounding shrubbery to drive out any resident snakes and scorpions, he piled a few dry palm branches together to make a reasonable bed and spread it with the cloth of his turban. He sat down with his back against the tree and rested, sipping a little water and listening to the cicadas and crickets and the calls of night-roosting birds. Slowly, slowly, the heat relinquished its grip on him and Charles felt his body relax. He opened his pack and brought out his supper—a feast of nuts and dried fruit, some hard biscuits, cured beef, and an apple. After the day's rigour, the simple fare would have satisfied the most jaded palate, and Charles savoured every bite.

Night stole in from the east, extinguishing the last embers of the day, drenching the lowlands in cool blue shadow. Charles stretched out and, using his pack for a pillow, fell asleep counting stars as they appeared in the slowly wheeling heavens. He slept well and deeply, but was awake again just before sunrise—roused from rest by the barking of dogs. As it would not do to arrive in the riverside hamlet too early, he took his time with his morning ablutions—splurging recklessly with a little of his precious water to wash his face and hands—combing his hair and brushing his clothes to make himself as presentable as possible. He ate another handful of nuts and fruit while he waited for the sun to rise above the surrounding fields.

He set off again, refreshed, into the silvery haze of a cloudless day. As he neared the village, he could smell the humid, earthy scent coming from the great unseen river. At the outskirts of the settlement he was greeted by a pack of dogs, who announced his arrival to their masters with noisy enthusiasm. By the time Charles reached the centre of the settlement, his yapping entourage had alerted everyone within earshot to the presence of a stranger in their midst. Knowing he was marked and watched, he proceeded to the communal well, drank, and refilled his waterskin while he waited to be received by the local headman or elder.

This was not long in coming. Naturally curious, the country folk could not abide the mystery of this visiting stranger in their midst. A white-haired man in a faded blue kaftan approached and stood leaning on his stick.

"Salaam alaikum," said Charles, holding out his hand.

"Alaikum salaam," replied the elder. He did not accept the offered hand but raised his own in welcome.

If Charles' Arabic was scant, his Egyptian was miniscule. Nevertheless, by dint of slow repetition and much gesturing, he was able to make himself understood. "I need men to help me," he told the old man in his patched-together Arabic. "I have money." He counted imaginary coins into his hand. "I can pay."

When his pantomime failed to communicate, Charles tried his schoolboy French. *"L'argent,"* he said. *"Je paie."*

"You pay," echoed the headman, nodding to himself. He turned around and, beckoning to Charles, led him to his house nearby. They were followed by most of the assembled villagers, who stood crowding the open door and windows of the dwelling to observe the negotiations. Hibiscus tea was produced by a serving boy, and after a haltingly slow negotiation, a deal was finally struck: five men with tools appropriate for digging, three donkeys to carry the necessaries, and provisions for a six-day expedition to a site Charles would show them on the western side of the river. Transportation for the men, animals, and cargo would be provided. Half the cost would be paid on commencement, and half on completion and return. Only the village headman would be entrusted with the money, and he would act as paymaster to anyone supplying provisions, transportation, or labour. The final amount was agreed, to which Charles offered to pay a bonus if the expedition met with smooth, uncomplicated success.

The deal was sealed over a glass of raw Egyptian wine, and the white-haired elder asked when Charles wished to embark. "As soon as men and supplies can be gathered," he answered. "Today, if it can be done."

The man shook his head. "Tomorrow." He patted the air with both hands. "You stay here. I make all things ready."

Charles regretted cooling his heels for an entire day but accepted the offer with good grace and used the time to draw a simple map of the place he hoped to find on the west bank. Thanks to Benedict's stories, Charles reckoned he had a pretty good idea where to look for the sarcophagus—providing he could find the wadi. This was the weakest part of his plan, he knew, but here he would trust local knowledge to lead him to the right place.

The next morning the expeditionary wheels began to turn—but slower and with many more halts and starts than Charles would have thought possible. Although the villagers expressed great interest in and enthusiasm for the project, this zeal failed to translate into speed. Moreover, there seemed to be no way to inspire in them the urgency Charles felt. The pace of progress in assembling the needed equipment and provisions was leisurely to the point of glacial.

After the fourth day, Charles gave up trying to hurry things along and simply sat under a date palm on the bank of the river, munching dried squash seeds and watching the wide green Nile roll by. This seemed by far the most sensible policy, since any interference on his part only served to slow things down further. On the sixth day, the headman came to where Charles had set up camp beneath the date palm and announced that tomorrow all preparations would be complete.

"Splendid!" cried Charles, leaping to his feet. "We will leave first thing in the morning."

"Next day," countered the village elder with a shake of his head. "I call my nephew."

Finally, eight days after his arrival in the village, all was ready and the expedition assembled on the riverbank to load the boats and set out. At the water's edge, the village elder placed his hand on the shoulder of a young man and indicated that he was to serve as the foreman of the expedition. "My nephew," the old man said. "He is guide."

"*Shukran,*" replied Charles. To the youth, he said, "What is your name?"

"He speaks no French. Only Arabic and Egyptian," the headman informed him. "Just call him Shakir."

"Well, Shakir," said Charles, "make ready to depart." He waved a hand at the boats and the few baskets yet remaining on the bank. "We go."

"Okay, *Sekrey!*" Shakir clapped his hands and hurried the workers to stow the last of the provisions onto the waiting boats.

"What is *sekrey?*" asked Charles, appreciating the young fellow's eagerness.

"It is captain," replied the village elder. "Boat, caravan, or men—all same." He offered a concluding bow. "*Salaam.*"

Shakir saw the last basket hauled aboard, then climbed into the lead vessel himself. He put out a narrow plank for Charles, who boarded and settled himself on a pile of rope in the bow, and the boat soon pushed off. The Nile was wide at this place, the water deep and easy-flowing, and the shallow-draft vessels drifted as they crossed, reaching the opposite shore a fair distance from the place where Charles wanted to disembark. The boats had to be slowly rowed back upstream to the landing place before they could be unloaded. Consequently, it was well past midday by the time the expedition was fully assembled—just in time for a lengthy rest through the hottest part of the day.

Though it chafed him to idle, Charles knew there was nothing for it but to endure the forced repose and stay on the good side of his crew. When at last the sun began to relinquish its fiery grip, they set off, reaching the farthest fringe of planted fields by sundown. Another night under the stars followed—this one much better supplied than the first—and they broke camp at dawn and set off, much refreshed, to begin the trek into the arid white wastes beyond the fertile green strip of planted fields.

Only one road ventured west into the desert, eventually bending around to run parallel to the escarpment of rocky hills and plateaux that stretched all the way to the Sahara. In places little more than a line scratched in the sun-blasted dirt, the naked track skirted the crumpled feet of the jagged barrens of the great limestone embankment that rose stark from the lower plain. Charles followed the trail, aided by a crude map he had concocted from the stories of his father, backed up by a book in the British Library detailing the geologic surveys of Emperor Napoleon's military engineers.

Holding this rough guide in one hand, his head swathed in his makeshift turban, Charles stumped along, scanning the unfolding hillscape as he walked, searching for two things: a towering triangular peak that, when viewed from a certain angle, resembled a pyramid; and a narrow crevice opening onto the valley floor and somewhat adjacent to the pyramid peak. This was the wadi, or dry gorge, leading into the heart of the hills.

The day, already hot, grew hotter and drier the farther away from the irrigated fields they went. Charles poured water on his turban and opened his shirt, which produced a fleeting relief. Within minutes he felt like a beast basting in its own juices; he could heartily commiserate with the poor skewered pig aroast on a turning spit—all he lacked was an apple in his mouth to make the sensation complete.

Nowhere in this blighted wasteland did he see even a twig, much less a tree, to provide the least scintilla of shade. Everywhere he looked, the same monochromatic landscape met his gaze—a world leached of colour until all that remained was a palette primed in shades of deathly white. Even the sky above had faded from blue to a ghastly hue the colour of old bones.

The air was not only stifling but immobile—too hot and heavy to move. Breathing was a chore that seemed to offer little reward for the effort. It would be, Charles considered, easier to simply give up the onerous work and suffocate than continue the exercise. Nevertheless, a higher purpose drove him on.

Eventually they came upon a massive standing slab and decided to stop for a rest until the heat began to dissipate. The stone was a monument in red granite marking the boundary of some pharaoh or other's domain.

The pause turned into a camp for the night since no one could muster either strength or will to continue the trek. Once the tents were erected and food began to cook, Charles allowed himself to entertain a more philosophical cast of mind. In the end, he decided, it was a fool's errand to count progress in miles covered. Rushing about in the desert could only result in sunstroke or worse.

His new attitude lasted until the next morning, when he charged off in search of the pyramid-shaped hilltop that marked the entrance to the hidden wadi. He sailed along the dusty track, paying little attention to the fact that he was quickly outdistancing his entourage—until, hearing shouts behind him, Charles turned to see that the donkey train was far behind him. He sighed and sat down to wait until they caught up.

As he waited he studied his hand-drawn map, comparing it against the surrounding landscape—absorbed in this survey until a shadow fell across the paper, jolting Charles from his appraisal. He looked up to see young Shakir standing over him, staring at the paper. Charles gave it to him and, climbing to his feet, indicated the line of high bluffs stretching into the distance; then he tapped the page.

Shakir's black eyes narrowed as his dark brow lowered with concentration. Charles pointed to his map, indicating the pyramid peak; next, he put his finger on the notch in the hill, which was meant to represent the hidden gorge leading to their destination.

Taking the map, the young man turned it this way and that, then darted off along the track. Charles called after him, then watched as Shakir paused, searched the hills, then came running back the other way, passing Charles and heading south.

"Okay, *Sekrey!*" announced the young man upon his return a few minutes later. Streaming sweat, but triumphant, Shakir tapped the paper and flung out his hand and pointed to the series of ragged outcrops looming over the trail to the south.

Accepting this assertion, Charles nodded and indicated that Shakir should lead the way. They resumed their march, moving along the bank of foothills, quickly reaching the place Shakir had identified. In little more than a quarter of a mile by Charles' rough estimation, he spotted a gap at the base of the rising bank of hills—not the breach Charles had imagined, more a simple overlapping, like the inward fold of a ruffled drapery. As this irregularity was the only candidate for investigation they had so far turned up, Charles decided to explore. Even before reaching the gap, however, he could see that it was indeed the entrance to a fair-sized wadi.

Closer, he discerned the smooth walls of wind- and water-sculptured stone rising sheer on either side to form the narrow gorge. Upon reaching the entrance, he stepped between the walls and was engulfed in blessed shadow. Charles sighed, wiped the sweat from his face, and ploughed on. With every step the air temperature seemed to fall as within the shaded realm the sun no longer ruled with impunity. Seeing a wider place a few metres ahead, he made directly for it and there, almost staggering with relief, he stopped and slid down the smooth stone to sit with his back against the wall, luxuriating as much in the escape from the searing sun as in the knowledge that he had found Anen's wadi.

Recovering the Skin Map was now very much in his grasp. In a few short days, the secret that Arthur Flinders-Petrie had long ago taken to his grave would at last belong to Charles and to Charles alone.

CHAPTER 24

In Which an Event of Great Significance Is Overlooked

Had he but known that the cosmic link between the shadow lamp and the Skin Map lay at his fingertips, Kit might have marked the day as one of the most significant in his life. But human consciousness is flighty, awareness fleeting, and important facts are often ignored; items of value remain unappreciated; vital information goes unremarked. In the heat of the moment, details of great significance are often overlooked. So it was that Kit failed to see what was right in front of him, and consequently the quest in which he and so many others were engaged failed to progress as it might have. Instead, this is what happened:

The day had faded to mellow gold and the sun had slipped behind the buildings surrounding the square. As the marketplace folded up around him, Kit returned to the upstairs room where he had left Gianni and Cassandra discussing the finer points of star-exploded elements. He gave the door a rap with his knuckles and received an "Enter if you dare" in reply.

"It's only me," he announced, pushing open the door. Gianni had gone, and Cass was resting on her bed. "Oh, sorry," he said. "I didn't know you were napping."

"Thinking, not napping," she said. "Come on in and make yourself at home."

Kit took a chair from the table and spun it around to face her as she struggled up out of the hollow in the centre of her feather bed. "Well? What did you decide?" he asked. "About the rare earth stuff, I mean. Any ideas?"

"We agreed that we won't be able to tell anything at all with the equipment we have on hand, and we dare not waste the material we've got trying things that probably won't work," she told him. "Our sample needs analysing with pretty sophisticated gear if we're going to get a definitive result."

"Why am I not surprised?"

"Fortunately, Gianni knows a place where we can get it tested properly."

"Here?"

"Not hardly. He wants to take it to Rome." At Kit's raised eyebrows she laughed and said, "The Vatican."

"The pope has a microscope?"

"I doubt the pope has much experience with exotic thermonuclear materials—if he does, he's definitely hiding his light under a bushel. But the Vatican maintains a state-of-the-art lab, and Gianni knows how to get there in the twenty-first century, which is essential."

"Being a priest probably doesn't hurt either," Kit surmised.

Cass nodded. "He can get access there faster than probably anywhere else and no questions asked. So we're good to go."

"That Gianni." Kit shook his head in admiration. "He's a pip!"

She laughed again. "I like you, Kit."

"I like you too." He smiled and then ran out of things to say. "So, um—want to head over to the coffeehouse and see what everybody else is up to?"

Cass swung her legs off the bed and gracefully angled one stockinged foot into an empty shoe.

"We'd best take this with us," said Kit, reaching around to retrieve the glass vial of rare earth from the table behind him. Preoccupied by the sight of a young lady's shapely leg, his hand failed to connect with the little jar and instead upset the brass carapace of the shadow lamp containing the powdery residue of the burnt-out material. Black dust scattered over the handkerchief Cass had spread out as a work area.

"Oops! Sorry. No harm done," he said and began sweeping the grainy ash back into the half shell of the lamp. When he had retrieved as much as he could, he shook the powdery remainder off the white square of fine-woven cloth.

It was at this moment that Kit might have noticed something extraordinary. Had he not been distracted, he would have seen that the grey smudge left on the handkerchief had formed a highly distinctive design: a spiral whorl with an unaccountably straight line directly through the centre and three separate dots along the outer edge.

The image, though faint, was well defined and far too precise to be the result of mere chance. Yet in the waning afternoon light stealing through the room's single window, the inimitable pattern—which would have fitted perfectly with those Kit had seen scrawled on the wall of a Stone Age cave, painstakingly rendered in the inner burial chamber of High Priest Anen's tomb, and, most notably, tattooed on the half-bare torso of Arthur Flinders-Petrie at the Spirit Well—remained unregarded and unrecognised.

And so Kit simply shook out the handkerchief and handed it to Cass, who promptly tucked it into the cuff of her blouse as she finished putting on her shoes. Then, blithely unaware of the secret they now possessed, Kit pocketed the ruined shadow lamp and vial of rare earth and escorted Cass from the *Apoteke*. Alas.

The two started across the market square, the crowd rapidly thinning as twilight deepened and lights began to glow in windows. Silvery smoke threaded from the chimneys clustered on the rooftops all around, tinting the air with an autumnal scent. Halfway to the coffeehouse, they met Wilhelmina coming the other way. "Hey, you two—I was just coming to find you."

"Did you see Gianni?"

"Yes, he told me the jury is still out on the mystery powder."

"He wants to take the sample to Rome for testing," Kit told her.

"That's what I hear. I think it's a good idea." As she was speaking, the church bells began ringing. She paused to listen.

"What church is that?" Cass asked, turning her eyes towards the dark façade of the imposing gothic church fronting the square.

"That's Týn Church," Mina told her. "Vespers is just starting. Actually, I was on my way to the service. Would you like to come along?"

"I'd love to," said Cass.

"Let's all go." Wilhelmina continued across the square; Cass fell into step beside her and Kit followed. "I like it—especially when I've had a busy day and I need some peace. Etzel hardly ever misses a service. In fact, I wouldn't be surprised if we see him there tonight."

"Speaking of bumping into Etzel, I saw him today." Kit went on to relate how he had seen the big baker in the square with a bag slung over his shoulder.

"He was probably on one of his missions. There are a lot of needy people in the back streets around here. Etzel is always doing something to try to help out—his *Seele arbeitet*, as he calls it."

"His *soul works?*" wondered Cass.

"You know German?"

"Not really," she allowed. "I run into it in an academic way from time to time, that's all."

"I'm impressed," remarked Kit. "You also know how to test chemicals and read Latin. Is there anything you *can't* do?"

"Cook." She gave him a sunny smile.

Týn Church loomed from the shadows, its twin multi-spired towers rising heavenward, each finger-thin pinnacle topped with a cross glinting in the last of the day's dying light like golden stars. The lower panes of the enormous centre window, an elongated gothic design, shone with the ruddy glow of candlelight, and torches on either side of the imposing black iron-studded doors pooled light around the entrance. Kit cracked open the smaller door set in the larger one, and the three entered the venerable old church.

The service was well attended. "Standing room only, I see," Kit quipped, then realised it was *always* SRO because there were no pews—only a row of chairs ringing the expansive sanctuary for the older members of the congregation. Mina shot him a stern glance. "Sorry," he said. "I'll behave."

They pushed in among those gathered at the back. The attending priests were chanting the voluntary. Though the service was an amalgam of Latin with a few instructions in German, it was fairly easy to follow, and Kit, who was not so well versed in religious rites, found the service at least unobjectionable if not actually enjoyable. One look at Mina, whose face gently illumined by candlelight appeared reverent, beatific even, gave Kit to know that she was enraptured by the majestic movements of liturgy and song. Posing as a nun at Montserrat Abbey, he concluded, had no doubt quickened in Wilhelmina a deeper appreciation.

For Cassandra, however, it was something more.

As the psalms and hymns echoed up through the great vaulted darkness and the incense rose in sweet, pungent clouds before the altar, Cass grew at first quiet, then pensive, and finally markedly subdued—head bowed and eyes not so much closed as clenched, her whole body tense, almost rigid. Finally, as the final notes of the great pipe organ rang in the air, Kit leaned close and whispered, "Are you okay?"

Cass nodded but did not lift her head; her hands remained clenched tightly over her chest. Worshippers began disbanding and streaming away around them, but she did not move.

Wilhelmina put her arm around the young woman's shoulders. "What's wrong, Cassandra?"

When she failed to respond, Kit gently urged, "You can tell us. We're here for you. Is it homesickness?"

"No," Cass breathed at last. "Nothing like that." She raised her face, and Kit saw she had been crying. "I don't think I've told anyone what happened to me in Damascus."

Kit and Mina exchanged a glance. "You don't have to say anything if you don't want to," Wilhelmina told her. "It's okay. We'll understand."

"It's the reason I'm here," said Cass, smudging away the wet tracks down her cheeks with the heels of her hands. "I saw something that scared me—a vision—and it frightened me so much I ran to the nearest shelter I could find, and that was in the Sisters of Tekla chapel."

"What did you see?" asked Kit. Mina gave him a cautionary glance and he quickly added, "That is, if you want to share . . . or not."

"No, it's all right. I can tell you." Cassandra drew a long breath and said, "I guess you could say I saw the destruction of the entire universe. That's the only way to describe it." She went on to relate more details of the terrifying vision—the insatiable, all-devouring darkness, the vast and mindless hatred of light and its manifold expressions, the pitiless obliteration of all creatures possessing the spark of life, the relentless desolating rush towards oblivion—that had driven her from sleep and into the embrace of the Zetetic Society. She finished, saying, "I sat there praying until it got light enough outside to see, and then I ran as fast as I could to join the society." She glanced up with a sad, almost rueful smile. "I guess I have been running ever since. This is the first time I have actually had a chance to stop and reflect on what happened. The service tonight was beautiful, but it brought it all back to me." She glanced from one to the other of them and drew a long, shaky breath. "I don't really understand any of this."

"Never mind." Mina gave her shoulders a squeeze. "There's a lot going on that none of us understand, but we're all in this together."

"All for one and one for all," Kit added. "And we're not about to let anything happen to you." It was a brave but silly thing to say—an ultimately empty promise—and Kit knew it the moment the words left his mouth. Cosimo was right, this ley travelling was an exceedingly perilous business indulged at great personal risk—and there was nothing he or anyone else could do about that.

Cass seemed to understand but accepted the solace of his words all the same. "Thanks," she sighed. "You're both very kind." She gave an embarrassed little laugh. "I'm not usually such a basket case, honest."

They joined the congregation making its way out of the church. Passing through the heavy oaken doors, they moved off towards the Grand Imperial Kaffeehaus across the way. Save for the departing worshippers, the marketplace was nearly deserted; the last of the day traders were tying down the coverings on their fully laden wagons. The great square was cast in darkness now, and the bright needle-points of stars were shining in a clear sky.

"How are you feeling now?" asked Kit.

"A little better," answered Cass. "Still . . ."

"That must have been some bad vision to scare you like that," remarked Kit.

"It was . . . harrowing." Cass shivered at the memory, which even now had the power to chill her heart.

"If it would help to talk about it," offered Wilhelmina, "I'd be happy to listen. That is . . ." She trailed off as she noticed that Kit had stopped walking. Both women glanced around to see him stock-still, as if rooted to the spot. He was staring into the middle distance as if he had just seen a ghost.

"Kit?" gasped Mina. "For Pete's sake, what is it?"

"Burleigh is back," he spat, his voice a low, rasping whisper. "I just saw a Burley Man."

CHAPTER 25

In Which Corpse-Pickers Raise the Alarm

The once-peaceful valley was transformed into a killing field as the fire arrows screamed overhead, each one streaking to earth to erupt in a gout of flame and searing metal, slaughtering the terrified victims by the score. The desperate race flowed around them—horses, cattle, people—all of them blind with terror and in full flight. Giles clutched Haven's hand in a strong, unyielding grip and pulled her with him into the wild and reckless flood.

Filling the heavens with their bloodless shriek, the fiery salvos sliced through the darkened skies, striking again and again in a lethal rain. The torrent of humanity raced on, streaming over the bodies of the dead and dying; the slower ones were caught and crushed by those coming behind, pulled under by the unstoppable human tide surging through the valley.

From their very first steps, Giles knew they were in a race for their lives. Though it meant hard scrambling along the sharply tilting slope of the hill, Giles was determined to keep himself and Haven at the farthest edge of the flood and away from the chaotic, killing crush of the centre. Over the sloping ground they ran. Time and again Haven slipped, and each time Giles was there to bear her up and put her back on her feet.

The dazzling fireballs fell all around them. With each shattering impact, bodies were smashed and torn apart. What the impact did not destroy, the inevitable eruption obliterated. Thick and fast they fell, howling as they came. The soft earth shuddered with the explosions, spewing flame and searing gases to singe the air.

Soon Giles and Haven were running through a fog of bitter smoke that stung the nostrils and obscured the way ahead. They gulped air and felt the burn in their lungs. Coughing, eyes streaming, they ran blindly on.

Directly ahead, one of the infernal things slammed into the hillside, obliterating bodies and sending up a deadly shower of cinders and molten metal and carving a crater in the soft earth. Giles saw the hole too late and tumbled into it, pulling Haven down with him. Fragments of hot metal and scorched dirt smouldered in the hole. The air stank of singed hair and charred flesh. Giles rolled onto a piece of glowing shrapnel, burning holes in his shirt and trousers. He gasped and squirmed away, brushing burning cinders from his arm and leg. Haven landed hard on her side and felt the heat of scorched earth through her clothing.

She struggled onto her knees and made to rise. A fleeing rider loomed out of the smoke. Galloping hard, he saw the hole and prepared to jump. As Haven's torso appeared above the smouldering embankment, the horse spooked and tried to veer away. Caught between a leap and a swerve, the terrified animal's forelegs tangled, and it plunged headlong into the embankment. Haven ducked below the protecting rim of earth and the rider threw himself from the saddle. The injured animal thrashed on the ground, its legs kicking. It screamed once and then fell still. As another missile screamed down through the haze of smoke, the warrior abandoned his ruined mount and ran.

Haven started up once more, but Giles pulled her back. "Stay down! We are safer here." The body of the dead horse, like a boulder in a stream, caused the fleeing hordes to part. Hunkered down in the bottom of the hole, they could stay out of the onrushing turmoil.

After a time the fireballs ceased, but the desperate retreat continued. On and on the people came, passing in a blur of smoke and motion before disappearing into the night. Giles and Haven lay in the bottom of the crater, occasionally stirring to gauge the flood until exhaustion overcame them and they slept.

When Giles stirred again, the sun was rising, and with it came the advance scouts of the invading forces: men on horseback riding fast along the river course to vanish in the early morning mist rising from the water. The forerunners were followed by a small force of scavengers—old men and women who picked their way among the scattered dead to collect weapons and valuables, clothes and boots and armour. Some carried long leather bags that trailed after them on the ground; others, in twos and threes, dragged wicker baskets, and still others pulled small handcarts.

Into the bags, baskets, and carts they tossed belongings of which the dead had no further use. Some corpses were stripped bare, others lost only hats or belts. A rare few lost nothing at all, but all were examined and their material goods evaluated and, for the most part, confiscated.

The scavengers worked efficiently, but without undue hurry, moving from body to body among the dead scattered across the wide bowl of the valley on both sides of the river. Giles and Haven watched the grim undertaking as it moved methodically closer to their earthen bunker.

"I fear we must move, my lady," observed Giles. "It would be best if we were not found here."

"I agree," said Haven, her voice ragged. "But where can we go?"

"If we climb the slope, they will not come up there, I think, and we can watch to see what is to happen." He paused, looking off towards the river. "I do not care to move far beyond the sight of water."

"Nor do I," replied Haven. "Lead on, Giles. I am content to follow."

While the corpse-pickers were still some way off, the two travellers quit their refuge and quickly as possible climbed the nearest slope. They had almost reached the top when the shouting began—first one lone voice, and then others raised the alarm. Giles cast a hasty glance over his shoulder. Some four or five scavengers had stopped working and were now making urgent gestures in their direction.

"They've seen us!" said Giles. "Run!"

Up the hill they fled, scrambling the last few yards to the top and flinging themselves over the crest, where they ducked out of direct sight from the valley. They threw themselves down in the long grass and lay panting, hoping against hope they would not be followed. When he had recovered his breath somewhat, Giles rolled onto his stomach and began crawling up to the hilltop.

"Giles! Stay down. They will see you!"

"I must know what they are doing," he whispered tersely. "We may be in danger yet."

He edged up and up until he could peer over the top of the hill and down into the valley. The shouts of the scavengers had brought outriders to their aid; three mounted warriors with spears were even now making their way towards the hillside up which Haven and Giles had fled.

He slid back down to where Haven was anxiously waiting. She saw the expression on his face and said, "Tell me."

"Riders." Giles wiped sweat from his eyes. "We've been seen. They're coming for us."

"How many?"

"Three of them—armed."

Haven bit her lip. "Giles, we cannot hope to outrun them."

"Not together, no. But I will draw them away, and as soon as they give chase, you run the other way. You may be able to find a place to hide."

"What will you do?"

"I will keep going as far as I can."

"That will not be far," she told him.

"I need only divert them long enough for you to escape."

"But you will be caught."

"That does not matter."

"It matters to me!" she spat. She took his hand in both of hers and pressed it tightly. "No. We will face them together come what may. I will not abandon you to your fate."

"Then I fear you will share it," he said. "Please, my lady. It is for the best."

"The best ceased to interest me some time ago," she replied, and offering a sad, hopeful smile, said, "Come, we have no time to argue. Let us be resolved in this."

Giles regarded the woman before him. Something had changed in her demeanour—something he would have given much to discover. Alas, it was too late. Raising the hands that still clenched his, he pressed them to his lips.

"I am sorry, my lady." With that, he leapt to his feet and fled the grassy hollow. "God be with you."

"Giles!" She lunged after him, but he was already up and away. Squirming to the edge of the shallow depression, she raised herself up to see him running fast along the top of the hill.

The first rider crested the hill, paused, gazed around, saw Giles, and bolted after him, shouting as he slapped his mount to speed. The other two riders appeared an instant later and, seeing their comrade giving chase, joined the pursuit. Haven waited only a moment longer and, seeing the riders commit to their courses, rose and fled in the opposite direction, running as fast as she could, the long grass pulling at her feet.

She scanned the hilltop as she ran, searching for another hiding place. The smooth incline of the treeless hills offered nothing. Over the gently mounded slope she flew, growing more desperate with each fleeting step. She risked a backwards glance at the pursuit unfolding behind her. Giles and the horsemen had passed from view. She was alone on the hillside—but not for long.

Just as she turned her gaze to the slope before her, there appeared the head of a rider, followed instantly by the head and neck of his mount and then the rest of the animal. Heart beating furiously, she threw herself down in the grass and prayed he had not seen her.

It was a prayer that died in the air. The rider's shout reached her even as she struck the ground. She lay in the grass only a moment, then scrambled up and darted away, heading down the slope this time, her feet flying as momentum carried her faster and faster.

The horse was faster still—as Haven knew it would be. Her plan was simply to put a little distance between herself and the chase so that when she turned she might have a heartbeat or two in which to position herself to strike.

Haven could hear the hooves pounding nearer and, judging the moment had come, she halted and turned directly into the path of the oncoming beast. It took every scrap of nerve and all her knowledge of horses to hold her ground. At the very last moment she dodged deftly to the left of the rider, seized the bridle as the horse sped past, and held on for all she was worth.

The impact nearly tore her arm from the socket, but she refused to let go. The horse's head slewed sideways and down. The rest of the beast followed its head. The churning legs stumbled. The horse fell. The rider was thrown wide as his mount rolled onto its side.

Quick as a blink, Haven grabbed for the empty saddle. Reins still in hand, she threw her leg over the horse's back and urged the struggling beast to its feet once more. The animal obeyed, lifting itself and Haven along with it. She kicked its flanks and slapped the reins, urging it away.

The horse reared and, when it could not throw her, leapt away, resuming its downhill race. From his vantage point on the ground, the stunned rider saw his mount being expertly stolen and shook his head. Pushing himself to his knees, he gave out a shrill whistle.

Haven heard the whistle and so did her mount, for the animal seemed to pause in midstride, then slowed and, despite her best efforts to whip it into motion, stopped. The warrior whistled again, and the animal swung around and trotted back to where its owner waited. The well-trained horse stopped obediently in front of its master and lowered its head to crop the grass while Haven was hauled from the saddle.

By the time Haven's feet were on the ground again, three more riders had joined the first. The newcomers must have seen what she had done, for all three stared at her as if at a feisty Goddess of the Hunt come down to earth to steal their horses.

One of the mounted warriors spoke a brief command to his fellow on the ground and then wheeled his mount and started back the way they had come.

Haven expected to be dragged back along with them, but to her surprise, she was taken up and placed in the saddle once more. The warrior whose mount she had requisitioned, albeit briefly, swung up behind her and, with his comrades close beside, returned to the valley.

By the time they reached the bank of the river, the first wave of the invading army was just emerging from the early morning mist—led by a double rank of the most incredible creatures Haven had ever seen.

CHAPTER 26

In Which a Smattering
of Latin Finds a Use

Big as houses, the enormous grey beasts moved with a stately grace that belied their ungainly proportions. Startling, almost ridiculous in aspect, there was yet something tremendously attractive about them. Huge to the point of absurdity, they were also quiet, moving through the river mist as silent as ghosts—as if possessed of an otherworldly composure, a calmness and dignity commensurate to their size.

Haven recognised them from a bestiary she had pored over as a child whiling away many a rainy afternoon in her father's library, though in the flesh she was at first sight repulsed by their outrageous appearance: vast, flapping ears on a colossal, high-domed head from which sprouted great curving scimitars of pale bone—similar to the tusks of a wild boar, but the size of tree limbs; hideous baggy skin that was naked, hairless, and the colour of the grave, skin so wrinkled and creased and folded it seemed ancient; giant pillars for legs that had no feet, but ended in flat, round pads as broad and rotund and expansive as the bulwark of a ship. Most startling of all was the snout, which, instead of tapering tastefully to a modest, rounded muzzle or even the rootling snub of a pig, instead went on and on to form a preposterously long appendage that, apparently, had the insidious self-will of a snake, coiling and questing of its own accord. Lastly, there was the mountainous hump of its back, which descended to an insignificant afterthought of a tail, a mere bare stub sprouting a paltry handful of bristles.

Though she found them repugnant, Haven could not tear her eyes from the abhorrent creatures. The longer she watched as they marched with their slow, swaying gait, the more she found herself affected by them. Within minutes revulsion had turned to fascination, and fascination to charm. By the time they had approached close enough for her to see their large, luminous, knowing eyes with their fringe of dark lashes, she thought them inexplicably endearing.

Lost in wonder, all thought of her capture and likely fate flew right out of her head.

Elephants! Who would have believed it?

It was said that King Henry III had kept one during his reign and housed it in the Tower of London, and someone in the court of Elizabeth reported seeing one in Portugal, of all places. As they passed, Haven could only gape and stare, strangely moved and enthralled by the sight.

All too soon the reality of her situation reasserted itself. The elephant phalanx passed and she saw, some little distance behind them, a spiky forest of pikes and spears and blood-red banners. The army moved slowly, inexorably, spreading across the valley like an indelible stain.

Haven's captors halted, perching themselves up on the hillside so as not to obstruct the forward progress of the troops. They dismounted and permitted Haven to sit down; when they drank, they passed the leather flask to her.

From her place on the hillside, Haven had an excellent view of the warriors as they paraded, rank upon rank, in seemingly inexhaustible numbers. Most were foot soldiers, but there were divisions of mounted warriors too, and all advanced with the dour relentlessness of a machine in motion.

Although similar in most respects to the harried mass of people Giles and Haven had first met, these invaders were different enough in appearance to constitute a distinct race. On the whole the men were thick through the shoulders and chest, but short-legged—Haven herself was taller than anyone she saw. Yet, possessing neither lofty stature nor great bulk, they nevertheless gave the impression of being stubbornly durable in the way of tree stumps or foundation stones. Their flesh was sallow or fair; many had red hair, though most had brown. In contrast to their ruddy, black-haired, moon-faced enemy whom they pursued through the valley, the newcomers' features were broad and open; they had large, round eyes and generous, full-lipped mouths. Most everyone was dressed in either leather or a heavy, loose-woven cloth; and all bristled with blades of every kind: swords, spears, long-shafted pikes, daggers, and broad knives. They also carried tiny round shields of leather on their backs, and some wore bows and quivers of arrows across their broad chests.

Early morning slowly gave way to midday and still they came. When the last of the soldiers had passed, then came the baggage train: lightweight vehicles constructed of wicker with large wooden wheels and pack mules in long lines, each piled high with sacks and bundles.

Trailing the supply caravan were the camp followers: women for the most part, many with infants and young children whose blond curls had been bleached almost white by the sun. These were the wives and children of the soldiers, Haven decided. Scattered in amongst the women were men with horses or wagons piled high with bags, sacks, and barrels of various kinds—merchants, perhaps? Haven did not know.

As the sun reached its zenith, the final wave of invaders appeared in the form of flocks of sheep, goats, geese, and small herds of shaggy cows. The air soon reeked of fresh dung. The shepherds and herders kept their animals moving, allowing them to snatch only the barest mouthful of grass or drink of water from the river before the flick of a staff or switch urged them on.

Tired from sitting in the sun so long and exhausted by lack of sleep, Haven's head grew heavy and she closed her eyes on the straggling remnant of the great procession. In her sleep she heard a familiar voice chiding her. "Asleep at midday? That is not like you, my lady."

The sound snapped her awake at once. She glanced around quickly but saw only the horses grazing and their riders still reclining where they had sat all morning. There was no one else around. Deciding she must have dreamed it, she closed her eyes again and nodded off . . . only to be awakened a moment later by the arrival of another group of riders. The newcomers greeted their comrades noisily and, Haven thought, with some merriment—as if sharing a jest—as they dismounted.

And then she saw the reason for their amusement: one of their number exhibited a black eye and there was blood on his face beneath his nose. He had, very obviously, come off the worse in a fistfight. And judging from the frown on the fellow's besmeared face, he did not much appreciate the banter of his comrades.

Grumbling, the battered fellow slid from the saddle and laboriously reeled in a rope and, tied to the trailing end, his subdued opponent.

"Giles!" cried Haven, leaping to her feet. Before anyone could stop her, she had run to him.

"My lady," he said wearily.

"You are safe." She fumbled at the knot that bound his hands. "Are you well? Are you injured?"

The warrior shoved her aside and proceeded to untie his captive; then, coiling his rope, he pushed them both back up the hill and made them sit down together, giving them to know they were to stay put. Without any further fuss, he left them to themselves and marched off to join his comrades.

"He was bruised and bloody," said Haven as the fellow moved away. "Did you do that?"

"I did," admitted Giles. "I expected to be killed outright—he had weapons and I did not. As I think on it now, I do not believe he meant me any harm."

"You could not know that," she countered. "I am only glad you are hale and well. I thank heaven no greater ill has befallen us."

"I think they are scouts or outriders," Giles surmised. He glanced around at the warriors who were now reclining on the ground. "Have you been here long?"

"I have been sitting here all morning," she said and then told him about the passing parade—elephants and all. "The most extraordinary creatures I believe I have ever seen."

"I know," Giles said, "I saw them too . . ." He hesitated, then admitted, "Though I did not know what manner of beast they were."

As the long afternoon wore on, they discussed what they thought had happened during the night and who the invaders might be. Then, as the last of the herds and herdsmen passed, the lounging scouts rose from their rest. They passed waterskins around and brought one to their captives; when all had drunk, they took to their saddles once more. Giles and Haven were each tied at the hands and the ropes secured to the saddle of a rider.

The captives were led along the bank of the shallow river at a plodding pace. There seemed to be no hurry and, if not for being tied to a horse, the two walkers might have considered it a pleasant riverside stroll. This lasted until, as the glowing orange disc of the sun began its plunge behind the ridge of hills to the west, the scouting party arrived at the outskirts of a veritable city made of tents.

Having halted its march for the day, the invading army set about making camp. Everywhere, people were busy: erecting shelters, corralling livestock, carrying water from the river, lighting charcoal for fires. The early evening air rang with a lively cacophony of voices, barking dogs, lowing cattle, chattering children. The speech that bubbled all around the strangers had a sibilant, swishy sound like that of wind through the grass, and it was uttered in a rush of merging syllables—sounds only, not words at all.

The riders and their prisoners passed among the outlying tents, moving deeper into the encampment. They had not gone far before the two tall, strangely clothed strangers were observed and word began to spread. Haven and Giles heard the change in the voices as curiosity rippled around them. Interested onlookers abandoned their chores and joined the march; the ranks swelled, becoming a procession as it went along.

Upon reaching the heart of the tent city, the two captives were conducted along an avenue of sorts formed by dwellings of a more elaborate design, constructed of a dark, bulky material with high sides and roofs that peaked at a single central pole. Banners in red and yellow flew from the centre poles of a few tents; others displayed flags planted outside the entrance or draping the sides.

At the end of this avenue stood a tented dwelling much like the others, but made very much larger by the simple expedient of joining several smaller tents together to form a cluster, around which stood a ring of torches in iron stanchions. The impromptu procession marched directly to this dwelling, where the outriders dismounted and their leader ran to the entrance, where he pulled on a woven band that hung beside the heavy flap that served as the door. The light tinkling of a bell sounded and a man in a yellow satin robe appeared, took one look at the crowd assembled before him, and ducked back inside. A moment later, from the same doorway emerged a colossal warrior. Brawny, broad-shouldered, with the muscled torso of a wrestler, his robust body encased in armour made of boiled, hardened leather, he towered like a giant above his more diminutive countrymen and surveyed the crowd with a solemn, forbidding gaze.

Everyone fell silent beneath that baleful stare, and when all was quiet, the hulking Goliath pulled aside the door flap. The yellow-robed figure reappeared leading another—elegantly clothed in a robe of crimson and blue that shimmered and winked in the light of the encircling torches. This fellow, almost as tall as his enormous bodyguard, shared the same light skin as those around him, and his hair hung in long curls pale as spun gold. He wore a brimless cap with a high crown made of the same glistening material as his robe. As he stepped from the tent, the scout waiting at the door immediately flattened himself to the ground and all the rest of the assembled throng bowed low, their faces horizontal to the earth.

Giles and Haven felt heavy hands on their shoulders, forcing them down. Clearly they were in the presence of greatness and required to show their respect too. They readily complied, rising again only when the man in the crimson robe took his place before them. He appeared fascinated, studying them intently, his expression imperious but not unkind. Then, his inspection concluded, he slowly raised a hand and in a loud, clear voice addressed the captives in the airy, untethered language of the steppes.

When that failed to produce any response, he spoke again in another tongue—different from the first, but just as incomprehensible to Haven and Giles. The two merely returned his gaze with a puzzled expression. The nobleman frowned and seemed about to turn away when the man in the yellow robe approached and whispered something in his ear.

The crimson-robed one nodded and in clear, bell-like tones said, *"Pax vobiscum."*

The familiar words spoken in this primitive place were such a surprise that it took Haven a moment to collect her wits. *"Pax vobiscum,"* she echoed.

The kingly one smiled and, with a gesture to his yellow-robed assistant, retreated to his tent. Giles cast a sideways glance at Haven. "My lady?"

"It is Latin," she replied in a whisper. "I command a smattering—from Uncle Henry and, of course, from the Mass."

The crimson-clad nobleman paused at the entrance to his dwelling. His giant bodyguard motioned to the leader of the scouting party that had captured the strangers; the scout hastened to his captives and, pointing to the entrance of the nobleman's tent, indicated they were to follow. The great man's dwelling was a veritable palace among tents, adorned with costly wall coverings in jewel-coloured silk and thick rugs on the floor with chairs of tooled leather and small octagonal tables of rosewood inlaid with ivory. The sumptuous interior was suffused with the heavy, sweet scent of frankincense that hazed the air and dimmed the warm, honeyed light from dozens of tiny golden lamps hanging from the roof struts by golden chains. Three young serving men in white tunics and voluminous white breeches stood by to receive their lord and his guests; one advanced with a chair and another with a golden cup.

As soon as the nobleman was seated on his chair, the cup was placed in his hands. Raising it to his guests, he drank and then passed the cup to the servant in the yellow robe, who offered it to Giles, indicating that he should drink. When Giles tried to pass the cup first to Haven, the fellow shook his head gravely and wagged his finger. Giles drank, then returned the cup; only then was it offered to Lady Fayth.

She clutched the cup gratefully and swallowed down a deep draught of a sweet liquor that tasted of plums. Upon returning the cup to the servant, she tapped the cup and said, *"Aqua, orare."*

The nobleman appeared surprised but clicked his fingers at an idle servant and issued a command. The youth bowed and disappeared into one of the other rooms. Giles glanced at Haven for an explanation. "I just begged him for some water," she said, then added, "At least, I hope that is what I did."

The white-robed youth returned with two silver chalices filled with water and gave one each to Giles and Haven. They drank in great greedy gulps under the fascinated gaze of their host. When Haven lowered the cup again, she smiled and said, *"Meus gratis, dominus."* Pointing to herself and Giles, she added, *"Sitis moribundus."*

The nobleman clapped his hands. He spoke a question to the scout, who offered a short reply, then bowed and hastened from the tent. Meanwhile, the white-garbed servants produced small folding stools that they placed behind the visitors, then took up stations to one side. Putting out a hand to his guests, the crimson-robed man announced—so far as Haven's smattering of Latin could follow: "I am called Simeon. I am khan of this people. Be welcome in my home."

There were words Haven did not understand—*khan*, foremost among them. She repeated the word aloud as a question.

"Ah!" he replied. "Khan is *Rex*."

"I give you good greeting, Khan Simeon," she said, dipping her head. They were in the presence of a king. He looked at her expectantly.

"I am called Lady Fayth," she answered, "and this is . . ." She hesitated, then, with a glance at Giles, said, "my friend and protector, Giles Standfast."

She spoke with slow deliberation, working it out as she went. "We are *peregrinatori*," she said, meaning to indicate that they were travellers.

"Peregrinatori?" wondered the khan, raising his eyebrows in amazement. "Without horses, or tents, or supplies——" He pointed to the chalices in their hands. "Without water even?"

Haven held his gaze and nodded. "It is so, Khan. We have lost our way."

The khan threw back his head and laughed. "Truly, you are lost."

"Truly, my lord," agreed Haven, failing to see the humour. No doubt she had misspoken.

"The scout told me he found you hiding among the dead of the Yellow Horde."

"It is so." Haven hesitated, trying to think of a version of the truth that would satisfy both the facts and her inquisitor. "We were . . ." She hesitated, then lunged for *"captivus."*

"Captivus," echoed the khan, nodding.

"We were captive and made to run with them. The attack came and we hid ourselves."

Khan Simeon accepted this with a thoughtful nod. "I am persuaded that all travellers have come from someplace. Where is your home?"

It took a little longer for Haven to work out what he was asking. "What did he say?" whispered Giles. "My lady?"

"Shh! Let me think." To the waiting king, she said, "We have come from England . . ." Haven began, then paused and corrected herself. "A land called *Britannia.*"

"Truly?" wondered the khan. "I have heard of this Prytannia, but I have never met anyone who travelled there."

"It is very far away," Haven told him. She paused and relayed to the bewildered Giles what had been said. Then, turning back to the khan, asked, "My lord khan, allow me to ask how you know of my land?"

"As a child I was schooled in Constantinople," answered Simeon. "There were many Gauls and Saxons in the city. Is it true that your Prytannia is a land of endless water?"

"It is so," said Haven. "It is an island surrounded by a sea and watered by much rain."

"Your sheep and cattle must be very fat."

"Very fat, my lord."

"What is he saying?" whispered Giles.

"I think he says Britain must have fat sheep."

Mystified, Giles merely shook his head.

"Have you travelled to Constantinople?" asked Khan Simeon. His voice took on a coaxing tone.

"No, my lord khan. We have not," she replied. Sensing something more was required, she added, "God willing, we hope to visit there one day."

This last part was not strictly true, but she hoped it might satisfy whatever unspoken expectation the king held.

It must have worked, for the king cried, "God wills!" Then, with a clap of his hands, he signalled an end to the audience. "Your wish is soon granted. We are even now on our way to Constantinople."

The king rose, and his servants produced silk slippers to replace his fine leather boots. "You will come with us," Khan Simeon decreed, stepping into the silk shoes. He regarded his two guests with an expression that invited no questions and concluded, "I have spoken."

With that he turned and strode from the room, accompanied by his silent bodyguard and the two white-clad servants, leaving Giles and Haven in the care of the yellow-garbed one, who led them from the tent.

"My lady?" asked Giles as they moved to the entrance. "What has happened here?"

"I believe the king is taking us to Constantinople."

CHAPTER 27

In Which a Rendezvous Is Arranged

D id he see you?" asked Mina, surreptitiously scanning the near-empty square.

"Don't turn around," said Kit. "Keep your head down."

"Which one is it?"

"I don't know. The smart one—Tav, I think. We can't go back to the coffeehouse. That's the first place they'll look."

"I agree," said Wilhelmina. "How about Cass' place?"

"Okay. Turn around slowly and let's move along."

"We'll have to get word to Gianni to meet us there."

"I could go get him," offered Cass. "So far as I know, none of these Burley Men have ever seen me."

"I don't know," hedged Kit. "It's better we don't get separated. We can send someone with a note." He risked a furtive look around. "That might be safer."

Mina and Cass anxiously watched his face. "Anything?" asked Cass.

"Still just the one. But you know he's not alone."

"What's he doing?" said Mina. "Has he spotted us?"

"Not yet. He seems to be watching the coffee shop." Kit turned his face away and lowered his head. "Come on, we've got to move—walk, don't run. Last thing we want is to draw attention to ourselves." Kit glanced at Cass' stricken expression and put a reassuring hand on her arm. "It's going to be all right. Ready? Whatever happens, just keep moving. Let's go."

The shop fronted the same side of the square as the church, so the three changed course, retreating slowly towards the church and then moving quietly along the row of buildings to the *Apoteke*. They slipped in quietly and filed silently upstairs to Cass' room and closed the door.

"I'll light the candle," offered Cass.

"Wait," said Kit. "Let's not show anyone we're around."

"That was close," sighed Wilhelmina. "I hate running into those guys. Burleigh won't be far away."

"We can't stay here," said Kit, moving to the room's single window; he closed the shutters quietly and stepped away again. "We've got to get out of town—the sooner the better."

"How dangerous are these Burley Men really?" wondered Cass.

"Dangerous enough."

"Kit's right. We should clear out as soon as possible," said Mina.

"Where do we go?" Cass looked from Mina to Kit, their faces pale and shadowed in the darkness.

"That's the question." Kit stepped away from the window. "I'm thinking that since we want to test the sample for the shadow lamps, we should head to Rome where we can make use of Gianni's contacts." He glanced at the others in the dim light. "Make sense?"

"Fine with me," agreed Cass. "But could I make one suggestion? I need to get to the Zetetic Society—they're waiting for me to report on what I've found out." She brightened as a new thought occurred to her. "Also, they have all those books and manuscripts—who knows? Maybe they could help us find out what to make of those symbols in the photographs."

"Good idea," said Mina. "You should definitely go there."

"Splitting up . . ." Kit pursed his lips in a frown. "I don't know."

"We'll be much harder to track that way," Mina pointed out. "I definitely think you and Cass should head to Damascus, and I'll go with Gianni to Rome and get the stuff tested. We'll catch up with you in Damascus when we're done."

"Sounds good to me," said Cass.

"Then Damascus and Rome, here we come," agreed Kit. To Cass he said, "Are you sure you can find your way back?"

Cass nodded firmly. "Brendan gave me detailed directions. I've still got them. But—" She paused uncertainly. "I'm afraid we have to go by way of London—that's the only way I know. But if you can get us there . . ."

"Not to worry," Kit replied lightly. "I know how to get to London, no problem—it's where all this began."

"Right," said Mina. "You two stay here. I'll go arrange for a message to be taken over to Gianni right away." She left the room, saying, "We'll need some money too and . . ."

When they were alone, Kit said, "It's going to be fine. Really, it is."

"Don't worry about me, I'm okay. I'm still trying to get used to this, is all." Cass forced a brave smile. "It can be a little overwhelming."

"Tell me about it." He crossed to the window and cracked open the shutters and put his eye to the slit.

"See anyone?"

"No." He closed the shutter again. "Just a kid and a dog."

There was a soft tap on the door and Wilhelmina reentered. "Okay, I sent little Hans over to the shop with a message for Gianni, telling him to wait ten minutes after Hans leaves and tell Etzel we've all had to leave for a few days. Then Gianni will make his way down to the Rathaus. We'll head that way ourselves."

"That's too risky," said Kit. The image of what happened the last time he tried to flee the city sprang instantly to mind. Getting chased out of town and pistol shot held no appeal. "We've got to expect that one of Burleigh's goons is watching the square. They're probably watching the gate as well."

"We'll take the wagon," Mina countered. "We can hide in the back and get Etzel or someone to drive us out."

"Not Etzel—that would make them suspicious. Who else?"

Mina paused for a second to think. "I know! The wagon is at the hostler's—we'll get Albert to drive us out."

Kit frowned, assessing the viability of this hastily concocted plan. "Okay, but what about Gianni?"

"I'll have Albert stop and pick up Gianni—as if he's offering a lift," replied Mina. "That should work."

A few minutes later they heard the *Apoteke* door close and went downstairs where Hans, the apothecary's boy, stood with a tin box in his hands. Wilhelmina met him, took the box, and exchanged a few words; she thanked him and, opening the box, fished out a shiny coin, which she dropped into his hand.

"*Vielen Dank,*" she told the boy, then turned to the others. "Message delivered. I've got money." She rattled the coins in the box. "We're good to go."

At the back of the shop, Wilhelmina called for the apothecary. The two spoke briefly, embraced, and Mina turned to the others. "If anyone comes sniffing around here, our secret is safe. Anya will see to that."

They left the shop by the back door and hurried down a very dark alleyway, moving as quickly and quietly as possible along a passage that was not only exceedingly narrow but filled with all manner of rubbish: empty crates and boxes, cast-off furniture, heaps of mouldering garbage, broken glass and crockery. They went single file, edging their way around the obstacles until coming to the entrance to the alley in a side street off the main square. After a quick check to confirm that there were no sharp-eyed Burley Men lurking about, they entered the street and, using one back street after another, proceeded to the hostler, who kept a stable and mews in the street at the far end of the Old Town square.

The stable doors were barred and locked, and the little yard was dark and quiet. The hostler's cottage formed one side of the yard; no light showed in the single window, but Wilhelmina hurried to the door, knocked, and kept knocking until the summons was answered.

"*Es tut mir leid, Albert. Sie zu wecken,*" she said. "*Wir brauchen die Wagen— und Sie.*"

"*Jetzt? Es ist Nacht!*"

Kit glanced at Cass, who whispered, "I'm not entirely sure, but I think she just apologised for waking him and told us we need the wagon and she wants him to drive it." She listened to the following exchange and added, "Mina's telling him that she'll pay three times . . . something . . . I didn't get the rest."

The exchange ended with Albert the hostler disappearing inside to put on his work clothes and ready the team and wagon.

"He'll do it," Mina reported, returning to Kit and Cass. "No questions asked."

Engelbert's wagon was soon ready—a big, boxy, high-sided vehicle that tonight would be pulled by two heavy-footed mares; the size was surplus to requirements, to be sure, but Wilhelmina explained, "The gatemen know Albert and they know the wagon. And if we hunch up together near the front of the box and scatter the straw sparsely around the back it will appear emptier—in case anyone takes an interest."

This is what they did, throwing a few bundles of fresh straw into the box before climbing in themselves. Kit covered Wilhelmina and Cass with straw in one corner of the front wall, then concealed himself in the other. He banged on the box to signal that they were ready, and the wagon rumbled out of the yard and into the empty street. By the time they passed in front of the Rathaus, Gianni was there, waiting. Huddled under the straw, the passengers felt the vehicle stop and heard the conversation between the priest and the driver; a pause, a snap of the reins, and the wagon trundled off once more.

Kit felt the wagon bed tilt slightly as the vehicle started down the long slope that ended at Prague's main gate and held his breath as it rolled to a halt at the guardhouse. "Quiet, everybody," he heard Mina whisper. There was a brief word with the night guard, and then the wheels were turning and they were out of the city. After what he estimated to be a suitable interval, Kit risked a look out the back of the wagon, but all he saw was the dark mass of the outer wall rising like a featureless cliff behind them. There was no one else on the road that he could see from his limited vantage point.

"Gianni," he called, keeping his voice low. "Don't turn around. Just tell me if you see anyone on the road."

"I see no one anywhere, my friend," came the reply a few moments later. "I think it is safe to come out."

The three emerged from hiding, brushing straw from their hair and clothes. Wilhelmina stood up and conducted a quick survey of the road and countryside to assure herself they were not being followed. Leaning over the wagon box between the driver and his bench mate, she thanked Albert for getting them safely out of the city, then addressed Gianni in English. "I hope we didn't scare you with that note. I'm sorry we couldn't give you more notice. I'll explain later."

"You must have no concern for me," the priest reassured her. "We know each other well enough, I think—if you say the need is urgent and dangerous, then I believe and obey."

"You're a prince, Gianni," she told him and gave him a peck on the cheek.

The passengers settled back to endure a ride that lurched and jostled so much that none of them could relax, much less sleep. In time the moon appeared, illuminating the world with a thin, watery light. The countryside seemed quiet; they had the road to themselves. They talked a bit, planning strategy, maintaining a wary watch all the while. But no Burley Men swooped down from the hills or raced from the city on horseback to cut off their escape. By the time Albert reined the horses to a halt, they were miles outside the city in the quiet countryside.

Wilhelmina paid and thanked Albert, warning him to say nothing to anyone about the journey, and then waited while he turned the wagon and rumbled off back to the city. "The ley is beyond that hill," she said. "It is the one I've discovered most recently and one of the best—it's saved me all kinds of time on the England route. It shouldn't take you more than a day to get to London—providing you calibrate it correctly."

By the light of the moon the four travellers climbed the hill, moving easily through the lower meadows to the upper grazing lands. The night was still and bright, the air cool but not uncomfortable, and the walking easy. As Mina had indicated, the ley was contained in a low fold between two hills and ran east to west. An old stone well marked one end, and the other lay a kilometre or more from where they stood.

"This is it?" asked Kit.

"This is the place," Wilhelmina confirmed.

"Remarkable," observed Gianni. "As if the earth has shaped itself to accommodate the line." He walked a few paces away and knelt, putting his hands flat on the ground. "Or perhaps it is the work of human agents." He strolled away, examining the physical manifestation of the ley.

"Okay, so where do we go from here?" Kit gazed down the length of the line. "Give us directions."

"Starting from the well head, count off fifty steps and jump," instructed Mina. "You'll end up in a forested hill path somewhere on the southern Polish border—depending on what year you arrive, of course—but if you have timed it correctly, it should be Poland. Then walk out of the hills towards the south until you come to a plain with lots of farms and smallholdings. There is a road leading to the village of Podbrdy. The ley line is beyond the village to the west—the road follows it for a while. You can't miss it. The best time to make the leap is early morning, although the evening works okay too. Make the leap anywhere between thirty-three and forty-three paces and you'll end up in Stane Way." She regarded Kit and Cass. "Any questions?"

"However did you find this Polish ley?" wondered Kit.

"Because, dear heart"—she patted his cheek—"that is where I ended up the first time you tried to show me how to make a ley leap." She smiled with mock sincerity. "Remember that little incident?"

"Am I ever likely to be allowed to forget?"

"What about you guys?" asked Cass.

"We'll head up the line towards the other end of the ley and make our jump from there. That will take us near another ley that leads to the southern Alps. From there we can get a post coach to Italy and work our way down to Rome."

Wilhelmina opened the tin box and divided up the money, dropping coins into each outstretched hand. "There," she said, closing the lid with a snap. "Don't spend it all in one place."

Kit looked at his handful of loot: silver coins of various sizes, and quite a few gold coins mixed in as well. "Why do I feel like a schoolboy who's just been handed his lunch money?"

"Lunch and then some," Mina told him. "That should be enough to get you around the world and back with change left over. You'll be surprised how far it goes."

"Thanks, Mina," said Cass, pocketing her share.

"It's nothing." Mina stashed the box beside the base of the well. "Now all that remains is for you to tell us how to get to Damascus." She turned and called, "Gianni, you should listen to this so you can help me remember."

He returned, and the three put their heads together and conferred over the directions. "Okay, got it," declared Wilhelmina after a moment. "We'll meet you in Damascus."

"God willing," added Gianni.

Wilhelmina noticed Cass' wrinkled brow. "Don't worry. You'll have Kit if you get into difficulty." She pressed Cass' hand in a sisterly gesture. "You'll be all right." Then, turning to Gianni, she said, "We'd best be on our way. Our jump-off point is a mile or so farther along the line." She gave Kit and Cass a wave and, taking Gianni's arm, started walking along the crease between the hills.

"See ya," called Kit. "Bring us back a bag of magic pixie dust."

"Good luck, you two."

"Vaya con Dios!" added Gianni.

Kit and Cass watched the two moonlit shapes fade into the night, then turned to one another. "We might as well find a place to sit down and make ourselves comfortable," said Kit. "We've got a few hours yet."

"Will you know when the ley is active?" wondered Cass, rubbing her arms.

"Yeah, I can most often feel it—like a tingle on the skin. Are you cold?" He moved to the well and sat down, patting the ground beside him. "Here, sit next to me and we'll keep each other warm—like they do in the Stone Age."

Cass eased herself down beside him, and Kit put his arm around her and pulled her close. "You can sleep if you want. I'll keep watch and wake you when it's time to go."

"I couldn't sleep if you paid me," she said, snuggling in a little closer. "Tell me about the Stone Age people you were with. I want to meet them in person when . . ." She paused. "I guess, when all this is over. You promised, remember—and I mean to hold you to it."

"Of course. We have a solemn, sacred deal."

"A sacred, solemn deal," she corrected.

Huddled together at the base of the well, they talked until the stars began to fade, watching the sky slowly brighten. When at last the eastern horizon showed a blush of pink, Kit determined the time was drawing near.

"It won't be long now," he said, rising. "I'll measure off the steps and mark the spot so we can judge the jump more accurately. Mina didn't allow us much margin for error."

Cass scraped up a suitable rock and followed Kit to the place where he stopped counting his strides. She placed the rock at the spot he indicated, then looked around for two more stones to add to the pile for good measure. "There. We won't misjudge that."

Walking back to the well, she asked, "Do you feel anything?"

"Hunger. We seem to have skipped supper last night. I could do with some breakfast. How about you?"

"Now that you mention it—absolutely."

"We'll get something as soon as we get to London. I know this excellent little place . . ." He paused, remembering. "Oh, it won't be open yet."

"At six in the morning?"

"Not in 1666. We'll have to wait a few hundred years maybe."

Cass frowned. "I don't think I can wait that long."

"Then we'll grab a pie on the street. That'll hold us until we get to Clarimond House. We'll tell Villiers to have the cook whip up a full English breakfast—eggs, bacon, sausage, mushrooms, black pudding, toast—the works."

Upon reaching the well, Kit turned and held out his hand. "It's best if you hold on to me. That little mistake cost me one girlfriend; I don't want to lose another."

Cass took the offered hand. "Am I your girlfriend now?"

Smiling, Kit started down the centre of the ley.

"Absolutely."

CHAPTER 28

In Which Trust
Is Cruelly Tested

Archelaeus Burleigh stood outside the Grand Imperial Kaffeehaus, gazing through the steamy windows at the activity within. The shop was quiet; only a few remaining customers lingered over their cups. He could see the serving girls in their green-and-white uniforms bearing trays of cups and pots and plates to the kitchen. Business was winding down for the evening.

Outwardly innocent and inviting—a simple coffee shop with a line of tasty pastries. What could be more innocuous? But that was the genius of it, decided the earl. That inoffensive appearance was itself a façade of falsehood. The Grand Imperial was, the earl now believed, a veritable hotbed of plots and subterfuge.

Loitering in the wide-open plaza, Burleigh took the opportunity for a good long look around. He would miss Prague. Despite the language limitations and its pokey, straight-laced Bohemian ways, he had grown quite fond of the stately old dame. Nevertheless, he had leeched all he needed from the place, and it was time to move on.

Will I ever come back? Possibly, he decided, but unlikely. The city had been useful to him, there was no denying that; his contacts among the alchemists had proven invaluable. But the place was also a source of continuing irritation, and he itched to be able to concentrate his full attention on the quest for the Skin Map. Before leaving Prague, however, he had a conspiracy to crush.

He heard a dog bark across the square and the fluttery chatter of folk as they hurried home for the night. Down at the far end of the square the clock tower chimed the quarter hour. Burleigh breathed in the cool evening air tinged with the rich scent of woodsmoke. Yes, he would miss the old girl. Once the quest was completed, however, and everything had changed, perhaps he would come back and take over the palace—make it one of his summer homes, or revive the old empire. He could become Emperor Archelaeus I. The thought made him smile.

He was still smiling when three customers emerged from the coffeehouse. Tav appeared in the doorway a few moments later; he raised a hand and tapped his nose with a forefinger.

As Burleigh proceeded towards the door, Con and Mal, who had been watching from another corner of the square, came running to meet him. "All clear, Boss," said Con.

"Good. You go 'round the back and watch the door. I don't want anyone running off."

The thin-faced man nodded and darted away again.

"Mal, you watch the front door. Don't let anyone into the shop."

"What if somebody comes along?" asked Mal.

"Just say, '*Kaffeehaus geschlossen*'—got it?"

"Yes, Boss."

Upon reaching the Grand Imperial, Burleigh pulled Tav to him and, in a low voice, said, "Come with me—in case our friend needs a little persuading."

Putting his hand to the door, Burleigh pushed it open and stepped into the shop. The air was warm and heavy with the scent of fresh-baked bread and coffee. He made a swift survey of the large room; as he expected all the tables were empty . . . save one in the far corner at which two men still sat head to head in close conversation over their cups. The earl cast a sharp, disapproving look at Tav.

"Sorry, Boss, I thought they left." Glancing at the two dawdlers—businessmen of middling age and little consequence—he said, "Want me to get rid of them?"

"Too late now. Just keep an eye on them." Burleigh moved towards the counter separating the main room from the kitchen behind. He moved quickly around the counter and into the work area. There the oven was the baker, stooping to tend the fire, banking the coals for the night. Burleigh gave a silent nod to Tav, who took up his position, and stepping around the end of the counter entered the kitchen.

"*Entschuldigen Sie mich,*" he said softly. "*Ein Wort, bitte.*"

Engelbert turned and straightened, his pleasant round face red from the heat of the oven. "*Hallo,*" he replied with a smile. "*Wie kann ich Ihnen helfen?*"

"*Sprechen Sie Englisch?*"

"*Nein,*" replied the baker. He smiled and shrugged. "*Es tut mir leid.*"

Burleigh nodded. He disliked this Old Deutsche and always struggled to make himself understood when forced, as now, to use it. "No matter," he said, mentally adjusting to the language, "I will not trouble you. I have only a question."

"Please," said the baker; he closed the door of the oven and then turned to his visitor. "My name is Engelbert. How can I help?"

"Your partner—Wilhelmina, is that her name?—I would please to speak to her."

"I am sorry, she is not here."

"No? I thought I saw her earlier this evening." Actually, it was Tav who thought he had seen her, but lost her in the crowd coming from church.

"Yes, she was here. But she had to go away," explained Engelbert.

"That was sudden," observed Burleigh. "Where did she go?"

"She should return in a day or two. You could speak to her then."

"That is not what I asked." Burleigh moved a step closer. "I must to know where she went."

The baker stared at his visitor for a long moment, then said, "She has gone away on business of her own."

"I understand that. I must know where Wilhelmina has gone."

"Why should this concern you?"

"I have information for her," Burleigh lied. "It is important that I find her." He patted the breast pocket of his coat as if it might contain something of value. "It is a message that will be of great benefit to her. Please to tell me where is she?"

"Perhaps if you tell me this information, I will be able to assist you," suggested the baker.

"It is a simple question," said Burleigh. "Why do you refuse to answer?"

"I tell you she has gone away on business. She sometimes does this. What more can I say?"

Burleigh's smile faded and his eyes narrowed. "But that will not do, my friend," he said, his voice taking on an edge. "You must try harder." He moved into the room and lowered his voice. "Your associate has involved herself in my business and I want to know why. I want to know everything."

Concern wrinkled the baker's placid brow. "I do not understand."

"My German is not so good." Burleigh stepped closer. "I will try to explain. The *Fräulein* is interfering in my affairs. I want to know why. In fact, I want to know everything."

"I think you should go now," replied Engelbert, crossing his arms across his massive chest. "There is nothing more I wish to say to you."

"We are not finished," said Burleigh. He called to Tav, who stepped around the counter and into the kitchen. "He refuses to talk. See if you can loosen his tongue."

"Right, Boss." Tav quickly took up a position in front of Etzel. He cocked his head to one side and then glanced away. With cat-like quickness, his hand flashed out, seizing his victim by the throat. "Listen, you ignorant oaf," he said, his voice a grating whisper in the startled baker's ear. "My boss here asked you a question. I suggest you tell him what he wants to know. Or this could get messy."

"He doesn't speak English," Burleigh observed mildly, leaning back against the table.

"Oh, I think he got the message," replied Tav, releasing his grip.

Engelbert fell back, rubbing his neck. "I will tell you nothing," he said. "You must leave now."

The words were barely out of his mouth when Tav's fist smashed into his jaw, snapping his head to the side.

"As I have explained," said Burleigh, "you will tell me what I want to know."

The baker, glaring at his attackers from below lowered brows, rubbed his jaw and shook his head. "I will tell you nothing."

"We shall see." Burleigh nodded at Tav, who reached into a coat pocket and produced a set of brass knuckles, making a show of fitting them to his hand and making a fist.

"You think to hurt me?" said Engelbert. "You think maybe that if you hurt me this will make me tell you something? Is this what you are thinking?"

"I give you one last chance," said Burleigh.

Tav slammed his armoured fist down on the wooden tabletop beside him. The resulting crack sounded like bones breaking.

"Shame on you," said Engelbert, with a defiant thrust of his chin. "I will tell you nothing."

Tav lunged forward, plunging his fist into the big man's stomach. Engelbert staggered back, hit the oven, and fell onto his hands and knees. The Burley Man lashed out with his boot, striking again at the baker's round stomach.

Etzel loosed a gasp of pain. He gulped air and held his side. "Yes, you can hurt me," he said, his voice tight and strained. "Still, I say nothing."

"We're just getting started, you and me," Tav told him. His next blow caught the baker on the side of the head, opening a gash above his eye. Blood spurted from the cut and splashed down the baker's round, cherubic face.

Engelbert, gasping in pain, shook his head from side to side to clear his vision.

"Get up," snarled Burleigh. "On your feet."

"You can knock me down until I get up no more," Etzel said, dragging himself upright. "But still I tell you nothing."

By way of reply, Tav threw a vicious uppercut, catching the baker on the chin and opening another deep cut. Blood flowed down his white shirt and onto his apron. "Anything to say yet?" demanded Tav.

Glaring defiantly at his attackers, Etzel declared, "As Wilhelmina has placed her trust in me, I place my trust in God." He cupped his broken chin. "God is my refuge and my strength."

"God?" snarled Burleigh. Rage shot through him. "You dare speak to me of God? Blind, stupid fool! There is no God!"

The baker just stared at him with a pitying expression.

"Did you hear me?" shouted Burleigh. "There is no God!"

Tav swung his fist again, catching the big man on the jaw; the brass knuckles sliced into the soft flesh. There was a crack as teeth and bone gave way.

Engelbert moaned and sank once more to his knees.

"Where is this God of yours?" Burleigh sneered savagely. He put out a hand to stay Tav and, standing over his groaning victim, shouted, "Where is your mighty refuge now?"

From the dining room came the sound of a chair scraping across the floor. A moment later a sharp-featured man with a pointed beard and green hat appeared at the end of the counter. "What is going on here?" he demanded.

"None of your business," snapped Burleigh without looking around. "The baker and I are having a discussion."

"Etzel?" asked the man. "Is this so?" Glancing around, he found Engelbert on the floor, took one look at the baker's bloody face, and gasped. "Etzel! Look at you!"

"Stay back!" growled Burleigh, turning on the man. "I told you this is none of your business."

"I make it my business," countered the man, moving around the counter and into the room. "I am Herr Arnostovi and I own this building." He stepped quickly to Engelbert's side and turned to face Burleigh. "You, on the other hand, are a ruffian and a criminal."

"Tell me what I want to know," shouted Burleigh, ignoring the landlord. "Tell me—and it is finished. I will leave you alone."

"Tell him nothing, Etzel," said the landlord. "He now has Jakub Arnostovi with whom to deal."

"Keep your big nose out of it, Jew!" snapped Burleigh. Tav adjusted the brass knuckles on his fist and prepared to swing again. "Talk, baker, or this time we break your skull."

Arnostovi drew a deep breath and shouted into the dining room. "Ruprecht!" he cried, calling for the man who had been sitting with him. A face appeared at the counter. "Trouble!" cried the landlord. "Run for the *Wachtmeister!*"

"*Jawohl!*" came the reply. Before anyone could move, he disappeared and the door slammed from the dining room.

"Now we see who will be talking," sneered Arnostovi. He put a protective hand on Engelbert's shoulder and passed him a large linen handkerchief. "Put this on your eye to stop the blood. I will send Ruprecht for the doctor as soon as he returns." To Burleigh he said, "I have powerful friends. You will be arrested."

"Take them down," Burleigh instructed. Tav stepped forward, readying himself to strike.

Just then the front door slammed and another voice called from the dining room, "Boss! Better hurry!" It was Mal. "They've called out the guard!"

Though he spoke in English, there was no mistaking the urgency in his voice. Arnostovi smiled. "Eh? See? You will spend the night in irons."

Burleigh backed away. Tav turned and followed, snatching a cloth from a serving tray as he passed; he rubbed the blood from the brass knuckles, removed the weapon, and stuffed it back into his pocket.

With a last defiant snarl, he threw the cloth at Etzel, then hurried after Burleigh and out the door.

Burleigh grabbed Tav and Mal in the doorway. "Where is Baby?"

"In her cage behind the stable," answered Mal.

"Get her and meet us at the gates." Burleigh pushed his henchman away. "Go." He glanced out across the square to see armed men running towards them. To Tav he said, "Go get Con and Dex, but stay out of sight. Head for the gate and wait for me outside the walls. I'll collect my things and meet you there."

"What's happening, Boss?"

Moving into the shadows, Burleigh said, "We're leaving."

Burleigh put his head down and started walking, quickly passing the three guardsmen running for the coffeehouse. Two of the soldiers wore steel helmets and carried short pikes with hooked blades. Burleigh turned his face away and melted into the darkness of the empty city square.

PART FIVE

The End of Everything

CHAPTER 29

In Which There Is No Smoke Without Fire

It was difficult to know how much time was passing. Each day was so very much the same as the one before, they bled into one another, piling up in an undifferentiated accumulation. They began with ablutions and a simple breakfast of rusks, watered wine, and fruit; this was followed by the appearance of the royal scribe who served as their language instructor. Douglas would then devote the next several hours to the study and application of the mind-numbingly intricate Etruscan language, which, so far as he could tell, was a mix of proto-Latin and Phrygian, or Persian, or something equally baffling. For Douglas, who had learned passable medieval Latin, it might as well have been proto-Eskimo or Venusian. The language of Etruria was slippery and obtuse, complicated and unyielding to rational expectation. Some might have found it inspiring—if what one was seeking to inspire was despair.

Snipe was spared the interminable lessons, because—after one particularly harrowing session involving the ink pot and quills—their royal tutor deemed the lad beyond instruction, or even restraint, and dismissed him to his own devices. Douglas was not so lucky.

After the lesson a servant would arrive to cook a meal or bring one. Douglas and Snipe would eat and then be left to themselves for a while. Sometimes they walked about the surrounding vineyards— in the unobtrusive company of one or both of their guards—and sometimes they, like good Etruscans, napped through the heat of the day. In the evening Pacha, the royal chamberlain, would arrive to review what had been accomplished by way of the day's instruction. Occasionally Pacha expressed approval of Douglas' progress; most often he went away shaking his head in dismay.

Advancement was slight, each step a battle against an uncompromising adversary, yet ground was gained and Douglas eventually managed to string a few simple words together and have them make the intended sense. Though he felt like a tongue-tied stutterer, he could, after a fashion, make himself understood—in basic matters anyway. The effort was grinding, and lately depression seemed to hang on his elbow and drag at his heels. He had given up trying to keep Snipe occupied and out of trouble. Now he simply let the guards deal with the wayward child, thinking that so long as they were always on duty, they might as well make themselves useful.

This morning Douglas awoke suddenly and with the instant awareness that something had changed. He lay on his pallet trying to discern in the dim morning light what had brought him so abruptly from sleep. Senses alive, he lay listening but heard nothing that would explain his abrupt arousal. Yet even as he strained into the silence, it occurred to him that perhaps the silence itself had quickened him; less a quietude, it was more a stultifying stillness, an oppressive force that sat heavily on him, making every breath a chore. Here at last was something different.

Throwing aside the thin coverlet, he rose and cast a quick glance around the room. Snipe still slept, curled up like a cat in his corner; why the strange lad preferred sleeping that way Douglas had never discovered. He moved into the main room of the guesthouse—nothing altered or out of place there—and continued to the door, opened it, and stepped outside onto the vine-covered portico that fronted the little house.

The air, though cool, was humid and unmoving; the sun had not yet risen, though the eastern sky was glowing with a dull and baleful light the colour of a bad oyster. The vineyards were quiet, the leaves glistening with dew. Oddly, the dog-and-rooster chorus that greeted every dawn was mute. Nor had the guards arrived. They were regular as sunrise; Douglas had never known them to appear later than a few minutes after the sun broke the horizon—a convention that puzzled him, as if the royal guests, chafing under their confinement, would not think of escaping during the night. That Douglas and Snipe had not fled already was due not to lack of opportunity, but to Douglas' driving desire to penetrate the mystery of the map. To achieve that end, he was willing to endure much—including house arrest.

As he stood gazing out over the vines and the gentle hills beyond, swathed in blue morning mist, he caught the scent of smoke on the air: not at all unusual, as most of the folk round about cooked over charcoal and used olive wood and old grapevine cuttings to fire their ovens. But this scent possessed a different, darker signature Douglas thought significant.

In a little while the sun peeped above the eastern hills like a swollen red eye. And still the guards had not appeared. Dressed only in the thin tunic he slept in, Douglas left the portico and walked a short way down the trail, but did not see anyone coming. The unnatural calm pervading the land persisted; if anything it had deepened to a cloying, almost suffocating closeness. The air felt leaden, dead, thick—like breathing treacle.

A storm must be in the offing, Douglas decided, and returned to the house. He climbed the portico steps, and as his hand reached for the door he heard a shout—a short, sharp, wordless cry—distant, yet stark in the all-pervading silence. Instinctively he turned towards the sound and paused, listening. That first cry did not repeat, but as he opened the door to the guest lodge, another shout reached him: a different voice, and much closer.

Douglas made an about-face and headed down the trail once more. This time he went as far as the king's residence—meeting no one on the way—and started down the long ceremonial avenue leading to the main road at the bottom of the hill. He could see a section of the road as it passed between the cypress trees on either side of the avenue; even as he watched he saw a figure on the only visible part of the road—moving quickly, a fleeting glimpse and then gone.

Before he had taken three more steps he saw two more people. Like the first, they were looking neither right nor left, hurrying west in the direction of the sea. The other thing Douglas noticed was that the closer he came to the road, the stronger the scent of smoke.

Upon reaching the road he looked in the direction the fleeing figures had gone. The first had disappeared around a bend in the road, and the second pair was just reaching the same bend. Turning the opposite way, Douglas was amazed and a little shocked by what he saw: a dozen or more people running towards him—men, women, and children, family groups, hurrying as fast as they could, quietly, but with visible urgency. Behind them a low, spreading cloud darkened the air above the road: a filthy, dun-coloured pall that stained the sky.

The cloud was some little distance to the north and building slowly. It took Douglas a moment before he realised that he was looking at smoke. The ghastly stench of hot tar that followed this realisation removed any lingering doubt. He hurried towards the people in the road and called out to them as they came within earshot. "What is? What is?" he shouted in his stunted pidgin Etruscan.

The first group passed him in a rush; they looked at him but made no effort to reply.

Another knot of fleeing people reached him. "What is?" he called, pointing to the dirty smoke cloud. "Fire?"

"Yes, fire!" replied an old man. He cast a hasty glance behind him and threw a backwards gesture. "It is the Latins!"

Before Douglas could work out what the fellow meant by such an assertion, the old man beetled off, leaving Douglas to ponder the significance of his words. *The Latins . . . what?* Then it came to him, and he cursed his slow wit. The Romans were coming.

Before the next clump of frightened refugees confirmed his suspicion, Douglas was already running back up the long avenue towards the guesthouse. As he moved past the king's palace at the top of the hill, he paused; there was still no sign of life within, so he continued on to the guesthouse and woke the sleeping Snipe.

"Get up!" He shook the lad roughly by the shoulder. "Snipe, get up!"

The boy came awake with a snarl.

"Stop it," Douglas growled. "Get dressed. We're leaving. This place is under attack. We're getting out of here."

While the sullen Snipe pulled on his tunic, trousers, and boots,

Douglas dressed quickly and took a last look around their rooms. Aside from his linguistic notes and two small curios he thought might be worth selling at auction, there was nothing to be taken away. Pocketing the iron figurines, he stuffed the sheaf of notes into his shirt and called, "Here, Snipe! Let's go."

A moment later they were pounding back down the long avenue through the double rank of cypress trees. They reached the road to find there were now many more refugees on it, and all were fleeing west towards the coast. For Douglas, however, escape led in the opposite direction. The Sacred Road carved into the tufa stone beneath the soil lay to the east. He had no choice but to face the oncoming traffic—weaving his way through, dodging right and left around obstacles human and, increasingly, animal, as more country folk with livestock joined the flight.

Douglas and Snipe muscled through the ever-increasing throng. Progress slowed. Frustration rose. Desperation intensified as it became harder and harder to force their way along. The whole countryside must be on the move, Douglas decided, and all of them going the wrong way.

By the time they reached the fording place in the road, their forward progress had slowed to fits and starts. A step at a time, they waded through the water, and as they started up the bank on the other side there arose a tremendous cry. People began flinging themselves into the water and scaling the steep banks on either side of the road, scattering in all directions.

Douglas halted. Watching the chaos, he saw a break and made up his mind. "This way, Snipe!" he shouted, diving into the melee. "Snipe! Hurry!"

Where was that boy?

Douglas whirled around and scanned the confusion. He shouted again, trying to make himself heard above the screams and cries all around. "Snipe! Here! This way!"

Terrified people streamed past him, collided with him, knocked him back a step or two at a time, blocking his path. "Get out of my way!" he shouted. Frustrated, Douglas seized one confused, stumbling fellow by the arm. "Fool! Get out of my—" He stopped short. The man was bleeding from a vicious cut to his forehead; blood was streaming down his face and into his eyes. The man could not see where he was going. Releasing the man, Douglas shoved ahead and the oncoming mob parted before him.

He darted into the gap to find himself face-to-face with another man—this one on horseback. At first glance Douglas thought him another refugee, but a second look told him otherwise. The man, naked from the waist up, his face daubed with yellow stripes on his cheeks and forehead, held a spear with a wicked spike-shaped blade. Another rider followed close behind.

Latins!

That thought had scarcely registered when a third raider appeared. Like the first two, he wore the yellow paint and carried a spear. Unlike the others, he did not hesitate when confronted by Douglas standing in the middle of the road. He drove on, his spear levelled.

"No!" screamed Douglas. Holding up his hands, he cried, "Not Etruscan! English! I am English!"

This distinction failed to deter the warrior. The raider charged ahead.

Douglas threw his hands before him and shouted. The horse swerved at the last instant to avoid Douglas, but the spear slashed forward. The blow struck Douglas on the side, spun him around, and hurled him backwards.

Even as he was falling, he looked down and saw the long, lethal blade piercing his flesh just below his ribs on the left side. And then the ground came up, knocking the breath from his lungs. For one awful instant, he lay pinned to the ground, the spear still in place. Douglas saw the look of fierce hatred on the Latin's face, saw his arm tense as he made to withdraw the blade and strike again.

But before the spear could fall, the horse leaped away, carrying the raider beyond easy reach of his victim. Douglas squirmed on the ground. Dust kicked up by the horse's hooves rose in clouds around him. Choking, he rolled up onto his knees and pressed his hand to his side. Blood spilled in a crimson cascade through his fingers.

Clutching the wound to staunch the blood, he tried to rise. The pain hit him then with the force of a bludgeon to the head. His stomach heaved and, dry, heaved again. His nostrils filled with the sickening scent of his own blood and bile and faeces, and he slumped forward onto one hand, gagging for breath. Pain clouded his vision. He pushed himself up onto his knees once more. He glanced around for Snipe, who was nowhere to be seen.

Another Latin raider thundered by and took a swing at Douglas as he passed. The blow was haphazard and only grazed Douglas, striking him on the side of the head. Not enough to hurt him, but enough to knock him down again.

Unable to sustain the effort to rise, he rolled onto his back. He gazed up into the smoke-stained sky and announced to whoever might be listening, "This is not supposed to happen."

Time seemed to slow. He could hear shouts and screams all around him, but they faded to a trivial annoyance. He could feel his wound throbbing with agonising urgency, but this also was of no concern. His eyesight, still sharp, gained focus even as his field of vision narrowed down to a hard little circle of light against an encroaching field of darkness.

The last thing he saw was the round moon face of Snipe smiling down at him.

CHAPTER 30

In Which the Future of
the Future Is Considered

F or argument's sake," suggested Brendan, "if we grant that the expansion of the universe is a fact—whatever the cause may be—and that the extremely fast outward expansion is actually slowing, what do you think would be the effect if that expansion began to reverse?"

"I don't have to think about it," replied Tony. "I already know exactly what would happen."

They had been walking in the cool of the day, and now evening was descending over the Old Quarter as Damascus settled in for a peaceful night. The two men were stopped in the middle of a cobbled lane beneath the spreading boughs of a great cedar tree in which doves were taking roost. The doves, the gentle twilight, the soft evening air, music from the nearby tea shop—all contributed to an atmosphere of tranquillity.

But for Tony Clarke, the discussion had just taken a dark, disturbing turn and he was feeling far from tranquil. He contemplated a horror that had, for reasons he could not presently define, suddenly become a real and present danger.

Brendan was waiting for an answer. "Well then?"

"It would be the end of everything."

"Define the *end of everything*," suggested Brendan. "In layman's terms, what do you mean?"

"The EoE, or End of Everything theory, is the systematic annihilation of all that exists," replied Tony matter-of-factly. "In a nutshell."

"Everything in the universe known and unknown utterly and completely destroyed," said Brendan, nodding in agreement. "Yes, that would be my understanding."

Tony gave a mirthless smile. "Friend, you're just not thinking big enough."

"Enlighten me." They slowly resumed their stroll, working their way back to the Zetetic Society headquarters, their way lit now by the intermittent light spilling from nearby windows.

"When a scientist talks about the EoE, he is talking about something far greater than mere destruction," Tony explained. "Destruction implies damage, demolition, wreckage—there is debris, bits and pieces of stuff left over, along with energy, light, heat, sound, that sort of thing. This allows some possibility, however small, of reconstituting or rebuilding—as following an earthquake or tornado, for example. But with *annihilation* there is *nothing* left over. All matter—each and every molecule and atom, as well as energy, light, heat, and the rest—*everything* that ever existed is consumed in the ultimate cataclysm."

"Including time?" asked Brendan.

"Including time and space, for sure. Whatever future may have been is snuffed out, the present grinds to a halt, and the past unravels and disperses like mist on the wind." He made an airy gesture with his hands. "There are various theories about how time might be affected during the cataclysm," he continued after a moment. "Some suggest that the flow of time reverses like a river suddenly changing its course, and we all live our lives backwards to the moment of the Big Bang. Others think that time simply evaporates like a drop of water splashed onto a hot iron. Nobody really knows what form it would take, but most agree that all time—past, present, and future—would cease . . . along with everything else that came into existence at the first moment of creation.

"Think of all the galaxies and star systems spinning into an all-devouring void; light shutting down, heat dissipating into a cold beyond description; the whole spectrum of energy simply radiating away and ceasing; each and every photon suddenly winking out; all atomic particles—even those in the quantum vacuum—disappearing one by one with ever-increasing speed; the rocks and trees and oceans and the earth beneath our feet dissolving and each flying into its constituent molecules—our bodies likewise—and those molecules simply fizzling away into nothingness . . . everything returning to the primeval void from which it sprang in the instant of creation. Worse still, there would be conscious, living, breathing, thinking entities to watch it happen and suffer its unimaginable horrors." Tony shook his head at the magnitude of the terror. "We would be alive to witness our own obliteration."

In the silence that followed this grim pronouncement, Brendan drew a breath and let it out slowly. "Put like that," he said, "*cataclysm* does not seem a large enough word to describe it."

"Not by a long shot," agreed Tony. "Fortunately, there is no hard evidence that the outward expansion of the universe is slowing."

Brendan said nothing. Tony cast a sideways glance at his lanky companion whose gaze seemed remote, as if fixed on a distant yet distinctly unsettling prospect.

As if compelled, Tony insisted, "The best scientific evidence we have from close and continual observation shows that the expansion of the universe is continuing full tilt—despite rumours to the contrary."

"And it will continue," observed Brendan glumly, "until something disrupts that expansion and brings it to a halt."

"This is . . . correct," Tony confirmed hesitantly. He studied Brendan's knitted brow and dour expression. "But if the JVLA data you mentioned was to be confirmed . . . well, that would certainly throw a wrench into the works."

Brendan's downcast eyes shifted to his companion. "Do not misunderstand," he said. "I have no hard evidence. For me, it is more in the way of a premonition, a feeling of impending doom I cannot explain—and I am fairly certain it derives from the nature of our work at the society. Almost since its very inception, our members have been puzzling over one of the most frustrating riddles of ley travel."

"Only one?" quipped Tony, trying to lighten the mood. "I'm still struggling with ley lines, multidimensional space, alternative time— the whole enchilada. What is your riddle?"

"Why is it that no one ever travels to the future?"

"Oh boy," sighed Tony. "By *future*, I assume you mean the absolute future—not the relative future—because, obviously, some travellers could conceivably journey to places where times were in advance of their own. That is, they would experience a time in advance of their own, yet still somewhat removed from the absolute future of the cosmos."

"Quite right," Brendan confirmed. "Sir Henry Fayth, for example, came here on many occasions. For him, a man born in 1620-something, this was the future, but not for me. I was born in 1958. For me—as for you—*this*"—Brendan waved a hand at their surroundings—"this is the past. But why am I unable to travel to the future of my own world?"

Tony considered this for a moment, then offered, "Presumably because the future has not happened yet."

Brendan steepled his fingers beneath his chin and gazed down at the darkness pooling around his feet. "That, or some slight variation of it, has always been our official interpretation," he said slowly. "You cannot reach a destination by train unless the rails have been laid to take you there—that is what we have always told ourselves. Even so, that description has never satisfied, and many of our members have tried to find a better, more rewarding explanation. None have ever succeeded."

"Your lack of success in finding a better explanation may be due to a faulty hypothesis," observed Tony. "It is a well-known bane of science."

"Meaning if we adjusted our assumptions about the future the facts might fit better?"

"Adjusting your assumptions not only about the future but about time itself. For example, you assume that time has a flow—moving from past through the present to the future, which is how it looks and feels to us in our normal, everyday experience. But what if time's flow actually moves the other way? What if it moves from a very fluid future into a much less malleable present before hardening into a solid-set past?" He glanced at his companion to see if he was following and saw a broad grin on his face. "What?" He stopped. "What have I said? Why are you smiling?"

"I am just happy you suggested this alternative view yourself without prompting from me," Brendan told him, "because it will make what I have to say that much easier."

"Go on, then. Hit me—I'm a physicist, I can take it."

"Suppose that time flows from the future towards the past," replied Brendan. He turned down another street; Tony fell into step beside him. "If so, then it would follow that anything—I repeat *anything*—that threatens the future inevitably endangers the present as well, and the present is where life as we know it is lived."

"True. I see that," Tony replied. "What I do *not* see is what this has to do with ley lines and multiple dimensions that we were talking about earlier."

"It is my belief that the future is even now under threat," declared Brendan in a solemn tone. "The knock-on effect of that threat, if allowed to continue, will cause the expansion of the universe to slow and ultimately reverse . . ."

"Resulting in a chain reaction that will bring about the annihilation of life, the universe, and everything," concluded Tony, once again sinking beneath a sense of utter calamity. "It would be as if absolutely nothing had ever existed." He glanced at Brendan, silent beside him. "You do realise what you're saying?"

"How long would it take to reach the end?" asked Brendan. "How much time would we have before the final cataclysm overtook us?"

Tony turned his gaze to the sky where the first stars were shining as dim pinpoints in a clean, cloudless expanse. He saw only a blot of blackness spreading like an ink stain over the heavens as he made rough calculations in his head, checked them, and then at last announced, "Depending on when the reversal actually began, such a scenario would unfold in a matter of months. Annihilation would be complete within a year—two at most."

"That soon?" Brendan cast a hand towards the heavens where Tony's gaze was directed. "Considering that it has taken the universe so many billions of years to expand to the present size, I would have thought that reversing it—"

"Would take a similar amount of time?" Tony finished the thought. "If only that were the case." He shook his head. "No. You seem to have forgotten the increased mass and its effect on momentum. See, the megaverse is so very much larger now. And once all that mass begins moving backwards, so to speak, the speed of that reversal will increase exponentially—much, much faster than the initial acceleration. It would all come crashing down very, very quickly indeed. Months, not years. I'd need instrumentation to be more precise, but there it is."

Brendan gave him a grim smile. "I knew you'd understand."

They turned down another street. The lights of a tiny café spilled out onto the cobbled stones in a splash of liquid gold. Laughter erupted from the men gathered around the boxy radio in the corner.

Tony noticed none of this. His mind was churning with possibilities, all of them dire. "Let us accept, for the sake of argument, that this threat is real," continued the physicist. "To what do you attribute this threat? What form does it take? Where is it? More to the point—can we test it? Can we prove it?"

"It is my belief—my hypothesis, if you like—that the Great Reversal, as I think of it, is linked in some way to the very mechanisms we've been discussing."

"By that you mean consciousness and its interaction with electromagnetic forces?"

"Those very mechanisms, yes. I believe something has happened, or is happening now, to render that interaction unstable. It is this instability that poses the threat to the ongoing function of the universe."

Tony nodded thoughtfully. "Any idea what has caused the system to become unstable?"

Brendan drew a deep breath and then blew it out. "Not really, no—nothing concrete. Only a wild speculation."

"Often the best kind," said Tony. "Go ahead, speculate away."

"I suspect that it has to do with the map," replied Brendan, directing his feet onto another darkened byway. "Perhaps a better way to say it is that once we have discovered the secret of the map, we will better understand the source and nature of the threat."

"Whoa! Hold on. What map are we talking about?"

Brendan glanced around. "The Skin Map."

Tony returned a blank stare. "Pardon?"

"Sorry, I thought you knew," said Brendan, who then explained, "The Skin Map is a chart of the routes and destinations of various ley lines scattered throughout the cosmos. It belonged to a ley explorer named Arthur Flinders-Petrie. In fact, it *was* a man named Arthur Flinders-Petrie."

Brendan went on to describe the map, how it was made and where, and what it was thought to contain—a treasure of unrivalled significance. He gave a curious little laugh. "To tell the truth, we're still a bit hazy about that. We don't really know what old Arthur found."

"Best guess?"

"There are those among us who believe that what Flinders-Petrie found is none other than the legendary Well of Souls or, as we call it, the Spirit Well."

"Now, *that* at least I *have* heard about," said Tony. "It is a common Middle Eastern myth, if I remember from my school days." He glanced at Brendan to gauge his reaction. "Are you telling me you believe the Spirit Well is an actual, physical place?"

"We have good reason to believe it exists, yes. Our *genizah* contains all sorts of wonders. After dinner, if you're interested—"

"Consider me interested," said Tony. "I'd very much like to see this Skin Map you mentioned too."

"Ah, well," said Brendan. "There's the rub. We don't have the map in our possession. At some point in the past it was divided up into four or five sections. Those pieces were hidden in places scattered far and wide through time and space. For over two hundred years it has been the work of our society to find the missing pieces and put them back together. All we have is a poorly rendered copy made by an artist who knew very little of the map's true significance. He thought it a map of the Faery Realms."

They had retraced their steps to the Zetetic Society headquarters. Brendan drew out his keys, and Tony glanced up at the night sky and the faint sprinkling of stars. "Thanks for the walk, Brendan," he said. "It was . . . harrowing."

Brendan gave a sympathetic laugh; he opened the black door and ushered in his guest. "Perhaps if you are not too very harrowed, you wouldn't mind continuing our discussion after dinner? Talking things out helps me crystallise my thoughts."

Tony stepped into the cosy book-lined reception room—light-years away from the doom-laden multiverse they had so recently envisioned. It took him a moment to realise that Mrs. Peelstick was there, and she was welcoming two newly arrived visitors—a young couple whose backs were to him.

"Oh, here you are!" she called as the returning men came through the door. "We were just talking about you, Dr. Clarke."

"About me? Well, I—" He halted as the young couple turned to meet him. "Cassie!"

"Hello, Daddy," she said, holding out her arms for a hug. "Fancy meeting you here."

CHAPTER 31

In Which a Question of Payment Arises

Burleigh walked from the coffeehouse casually but with purpose as the three guardsmen pounded towards him across the square towards the Grand Imperial Kaffeehaus. One of the soldiers glanced at him as they passed, but ran on. Quickening his pace, the earl made directly for the inn, where he quickly changed into his tall boots and put on his greatcoat. He lingered long enough to gather the designs for the new ley detectors he had been intending to commission from the palace alchemists. Regrettably, that would have to wait until the next visit. Then, pausing to swallow down a fortifying bolt of brandy from the decanter on his table, he grabbed his hat and took a last glance around the room. Silent as a shadow, he slipped into the corridor, down the stairs, and out of the building unseen.

With the brisk, efficient strides of a man in a hurry, heels tapping the paving stones in quick staccato, the earl made his way along darkened streets towards the city gates. Avoiding the main square took a little longer, but it would be, he thought, better to avoid any awkward confrontations with pike-wielding guardsmen.

Despite his many visits, Burleigh did not know the old city as well as he might have liked, and his already convoluted route became even more so when he took a wrong turn; he realised his mistake only after the street ended in a tiny plaza fronted by a church. Retracing his steps took him some time, and it was a relief when he at last entered a darkened lane and the city gates loomed into view. Torches had been lit on either side of the entrance and outside the gatehouse—shining like beacons to guide him to his destination. One of the imposing iron-banded doors was already shut for the night, but the other was still open to allow any late-arriving travellers through. He steamed ahead, slowing his pace only slightly as he approached the yet-open doorway, glancing around for his men. Where were they? Tav and Dex should have been there waiting for him. Con and Mal—where were they? Perhaps, owing to Baby's increasingly problematic presence—the bigger it grew, the more difficult the Stone Age beast was to control—his men had already slipped through and were waiting for him outside the walls.

That oversized cat has become more of a burden than an asset, he thought, stepping into the wavering circle of torchlight. *Perhaps it is time to set the creature free.*

Burleigh passed the gatehouse and caught a movement out of the corner of his eye. Two guards in helmets and breastplates appeared in the doorway. One of them called to him. *"Halten, Sie!"*

Pretending not to have heard, Burleigh continued towards the open gate. The guard put up his hand and shouted again, a little louder, *"Sie da! Halt!"*

Burleigh half turned to look behind him; he slowed his pace but kept walking. "Problem?" he asked, forcing a smile.

"Halt!" The two guards hurried after him—drawing their short-bladed swords as they came. *"Ihr Name, bitte?"*

"My name?" he repeated in German. "I am Lord Burleigh, Earl of Sutherland and friend of the royal court."

The foremost guard appeared unimpressed. "You must come with us," he said.

"I do not understand," replied Burleigh. Still smiling. Still edging towards the open gate. "Is there some difficulty? I have important business elsewhere tonight."

"That is him!" The voice came from the guardhouse, and the figure of Jakub Arnostovi burst from the guardhouse onto the steps. He thrust a finger at Burleigh. "That is the man who attacked Herr Stiffelbeam. Seize him!"

"You are arrested." The guard swung his sword up to Burleigh's chest. His companion lowered his pike. "You will please come with us."

"You have made a mistake," protested Burleigh, estimating the distance to the gate. If he could make it through the door, he could call on Tav and Dex to release the cat. Baby would keep the guards busy long enough to get away. "I do not understand . . ." He edged closer to the open gate and to freedom. "I am a friend of the court. I have the freedom of the city."

"Your days of freedom are finished, rogue," shouted Arnostovi hotly. To the guards, he urged, "Seize him at once! See that he does not get away!"

The guards stepped forward. Burleigh put up a hand to halt them and called over his shoulder for help. "Tav! Dex!" he cried, shouting behind him. "Hurry!"

There was a shuffle of movement beyond the gate. Burleigh took another step towards the door and the blackness beyond. "Release

Baby! Release her now——" he cried. The words died in his throat as four more armed guards appeared, shoving Tav and Dex before them. Mal and Con, looking raw and unhappy and much the worse for wear, shuffled after.

Baby was nowhere to be seen.

"Sorry, Boss," muttered Tav grimly. "We're nicked."

"Well done, Captain," crowed Arnostovi, fairly dancing with triumph. "The city council will hear a glowing report of your bravery and resourcefulness."

Burleigh spun back to his accusers. "This is intolerable! I demand to speak to the emperor!"

"Be quiet," said the captain of the town guard. "You will have your chance to speak before the magistrate."

The nearest guard put a rough hand to Burleigh's shoulder and gave him a push. "Get moving."

"I will see you flogged in the square for what you did to Engelbert," sneered Arnostovi.

"You snivelling little man," snarled Burleigh as he passed, his face a rictus of frozen rage and frustration. "You think you can stop me? Nobody crosses Archelaeus Burleigh. There will be hell to pay!"

"We will see who pays," replied Arnostovi. He made an airy flick of his hand. "Take them away."

Fuming with frustration and indignation, Lord Burleigh and his men were led away under armed guard. As it was late and the magistrate's offices were closed for the night, they were taken directly to the gaol and locked up until formal charges could be made and the case placed before the court. Until then, they would remain in Prague's mouldering dungeon in the lower depths of the Rathaus.

CHAPTER 32

In Which Time Is of the Essence

Distinguished members of the Zetetic Society, welcome to the Seventy-Second All-Society Convocation," announced Mrs. Peelstick, taking her place at the tabletop podium. "As moderator of tonight's session, I want to thank you all for coming on such short notice. Please know that we would not have summoned you so urgently if need had not dictated haste."

Her tone, softened by the beguiling lilt of her Scottish accent, gave no hint of the crisis that had brought the Zetetics together—eighteen venerable members assembled from places and times representing fifteen different world realms, or dimensions. Kit was still trying to get his head around that as he passed his gaze over the audience gathered in the *genizah*; the large upper room had been prepared for the special meeting, its centre cleared of books and manuscripts, and a double ring of chairs set up around an octagonal table; sharing the table with the podium were four unlit candles, a Bible, and a speaker's gavel. Kit could not imagine that tempers ever became so elevated that the wooden hammer was required to quiet things down; judging from the advanced age of most of the participants, he would have been surprised if they could raise anything more strenuous than geraniums.

He and Cass had been in Damascus five days, during which time he had got to know Brendan, Mrs. Peelstick, and Cass' father, Tony Clarke. They had been joined two days ago by Gianni and Wilhelmina who, having finished their work in Rome, had then made their way to Damascus. Kit had noticed a change in the normally sanguine priest's demeanour. "What happened in Rome?" Kit asked Wilhelmina when, after their initial greetings, Gianni had excused himself and made a beeline for Tony Clarke.

"I wouldn't call it a complete waste of time," Mina had reported. "The Vatican lab was very helpful and we learned a few things—Gianni especially—but we didn't get a definitive analysis of the rare earth. We still don't know what fuels the shadow lamps."

"So what's with our friend?" wondered Kit. "The poor guy looks like he's carrying the weight of the world."

"I'm not sure. Whatever it is, it's something he heard from his buddies at the observatory. I've never seen him so upset."

The introduction of Gianni and Tony—like flame meeting fuse—touched off a series of sombre and anxious closed-door discussions. The others did not know what they discussed, but whatever it was must have been worrying enough to warrant Brendan's sudden decision to convene an all-society gathering—a convergence of minds, as he put it. "We cannot do this alone," Brendan had been heard to say. "We need the support of our members."

The very next morning the Zetetics had begun arriving. How they had been summoned Kit never discovered, but over the next two days the members who could make the journey descended on Damascus.

As he met them one by one, Kit had quickly become impressed with how very much alike they all were in temperament, hardihood, and outlook—spirited, adventurous, wise, and a little cranky: very much, in fact, like his dear departed great-grandfather, Cosimo.

As to that, news of the deaths of Cosimo and Sir Henry had been received with dismay and heartfelt sympathy. One member—an elderly firebrand named Tess—took it upon herself to organise a memorial service for them. That had taken place at evensong in the nearby chapel of St. Tekla's convent where most of the Zetetics were staying. The service was simple and sincere, and during the prayers Kit found himself moved beyond mere affection. When Brendan stood up to say a closing prayer, grief such as Kit had never known surged up from somewhere deep within and overwhelmed him. With his head bowed, tears flowed down his cheeks to splash onto his clasped hands. He had not really known Cosimo all that long, but the blood tie was strong, and for the first time since his great-grandfather's untimely demise—murder, actually—Kit allowed himself to mourn; the long-pent feelings of sorrow and regret spilled over his natural defences and the tears flowed in bittersweet remembrance.

If I had been more alert, acted sooner, Kit thought, *I could have done something to prevent Burleigh from killing him. If I had been a better friend to him, Cosimo would still be alive—and Sir Henry too.*

The service in the little convent chapel—spare to the point of spartan, but more potent for its simplicity—proved an affecting and fitting tribute to the memories of two good men so cruelly cut down. After the service there followed a light supper, and then the opening session of the gathering to which the Zetetics had all been summoned.

"Before I officially convene this special assembly," Mrs. Peelstick was saying, "in observance of society bylaws and protocol, we have new members to induct. Brother Gianni Becarria, Christopher Livingstone, Wilhelmina Klug, Dr. Anthony Clarke—would you four step up here, please?"

Kit and Wilhelmina passed a fleeting glance to one another, and Kit could not help thinking that she looked very much in her element: fairly glowing with pleasure and anticipation as she took her place between him and Gianni, who appeared to be a natural participant; only he and Tony seemed nervous and out of place.

"I will ask Director Hanno to do the honours." Mrs. Peelstick yielded the floor and Brendan took her place.

"Fellow members, friends," he said, opening his arms to include them all, "many of you will recognise this moment as an answer to prayer for new blood to enrich and strengthen our society." He put out a hand to indicate the unlit candles on the table. "Tonight we rejoice in lighting not one but four candles to mark the induction of four new members into our fellowship."

He went on to introduce each one, giving a concise appraisal of the skills and resources each candidate brought to the society, and then moved on to a brief ceremony that somehow managed to be both pithy and profound. By the time Brendan got to the part of the pledge where he enjoined the candidates "to fight valiantly against evil in all its insidious forms to the glory of the Creator who made and—by perpetual loving care—continually sustains the Omniverse and everything that lives, moves, and has being within it," for the second time that night Kit found himself deeply touched. He had fully entered the spirit of not only the ritual but the society itself, and when Brendan grasped his hand in official welcome, Kit actually grew misty-eyed with a sudden surge of emotion.

As the newly minted members returned to their seats, he sighed under his breath. "Whew, I didn't see that coming." When Wilhelmina failed to answer, he glanced at her to see her eyes closed, head bowed, and hands folded in her lap.

"Thank you, Brendan," said Mrs. Peelstick, returning to the podium. "I'm certain we would all like nothing more than to give our new members a fitting welcome, but that will have to wait for another time. This convocation has been called to address a matter of utmost importance." She wasted no time breaking the bad news. "It has been brought to the attention of this directorship that the world as we know it teeters on the threshold of a cataclysm of unimaginable magnitude . . ."

This bald pronouncement sent a wave of alarm coursing through the listeners. One or two voices called for clarification, others asked for greater detail, and still others demanded to know the source of this information. Not one to be easily derailed, Mrs. Peelstick banged the gavel on the podium. "The tidings are fraught enough without everyone flying off the handle," she said, her austere Scottish character coming to the fore. "And the situation won't be helped by bleating like woolly-headed sheep." She passed a stern eye over the assembly, daring anyone to speak before continuing. "To begin, we have asked Brother Gianni to present a little background on the nature of the threat. We will then entertain questions and motions on how best to proceed." Still holding the gavel, she extended her hand to the Italian priest. "Brother Gianni, would you please come up?"

Dressed in his ubiquitous black suit, his beard freshly trimmed, his expression open and engaging, he looked the image of everyone's favourite natty uncle—if said stylish relation happened to be an Italian priest. He thanked Mrs. Peelstick and Brendan for allowing him to address the society and begged the members' kind indulgence if his English was not adequate to the task. He then launched into a concise discourse on creation that soon had everyone struggling to keep up.

"In my years as a priest and a scientist, I have been guided by two allied principles," Gianni began. "One, that the universe was created for a purpose. And two, that the purpose for which it was created was guided by a loving Creator who desired that its purpose should be fulfilled." He held up two fingers as if exhibiting proof of this assertion. "From these two principles all things under heaven and earth derive their meaning.

"From these two simple principles, we gain our understanding of Creation. The first thing we see is that creation is not an event that took place only once at the beginning of time—instead, it is the relation of every moment of time to the eternal reality of the Creator, who continually nurtures and sustains His creation out of His desire that its purpose may be achieved.

"From this we may discern the active, ongoing involvement of a wise and benevolent Creator directly engaged in the work He has ordained in bringing every part of His creation to its fullest fruition in relation to the Divine purpose.

"We may pause a moment to ask ourselves, what is this purpose for Creation that God desires? In other words, to what end is the universe directed?" Gianni gazed slowly around the room, the round rims of his glasses glinting in the candlelight. Posing the question again, he then supplied the answer himself: "We believe that the universe was created in order to produce conscious agents who can share in the apprehension and appreciation of Divine goodness, which is the nature of God; Divine beauty, which is the delight of God; and

Divine truth, which is the wisdom of God. Further, we believe that the purpose of the universe in bringing about independent conscious agents is directed towards the ultimate aim of uniting all creation with the Divine Life."

Gianni began pacing slowly back and forth along the front row of chairs, reminding Kit of a professor lecturing a class. Kit also realised that what had just been said was so freighted with meaning that the implications would take some time to unpack, and he wasn't sure he had the proper tools.

"Thus it follows that human beings are central to the ongoing purpose and function of the universe. As the objects of Divine intention, we are entangled with the cosmos from the beginning. Our very bodies are made of the elements forged in stars that were born and lived and died in far distant galaxies billions of years ago. We are, literally, stardust. All is as it had to be in order to bring us into existence. We are not flukes, or accidents, or trivial and inconsequential parasites who have arisen by chance only to disappear into nothingness when our survival is exhausted.

"Rather, we are the beneficiaries of complex processes that began before the Big Bang—the Alpha Point, yes?—processes that were put in place to produce active and independent conscious agents able to respond to their Creator in love. Thus, it follows that we are the *reason* for Creation's very existence. Consequently, the destiny of the cosmos and human destiny are bound closely together from before the beginning—the Alpha Point."

Gianni paced to the other side of the room, hitting his stride as he warmed to his thesis, his hands describing complex Italianate gestures in the air. "As there was a beginning, so there will be an end. In this, we believe that the Creator desires for time to run its course and *not* merely end at some arbitrary point short of the final completion He desires—a destination known as the Omega Point—which is the perfected, harmonious, and joyful unity of all Creation in Him for the purpose of engaging in the ongoing creative activity of a redeemed and transformed universe—forever." Gianni raised a finger in the classic style of a teacher beginning a quote. "For as the author of Ephesians, having glimpsed this, was moved to write, 'He has made known to us the mystery of his will, . . . a plan for the fullness of time, to gather up all things in him, things in heaven and things on earth.' Again, the Omega Point."

Returning to the podium, he took a moment to collect his thoughts before starting in again. "A plan for the fullness of time," he said, repeating the ancient words. "Let us consider what this means, for time is, after all, an essential quality of our existence. From the human perspective, time is a linear progression consisting of a swiftly retreating past that can never be altered or recovered, an ever-moving present that consists of a fleeting moment that can never be fully grasped and held, and an unformed future that consists of many possible outcomes to any action or event, only one of which will pass into actuality. Is this how we see it?"

There were nods all around the room.

"But from the Divine perspective, time may be very different. For the Creator, the past is never lost, never beyond recovery—because it can always be reclaimed by weaving it into a wider pattern of ultimate goodness so that even the most horrendous disasters of life may come to play a significant part in achieving the intended purpose of Creation. In this way, the past can be redeemed.

"From the Divine perspective," the priest said, "the present is not a fleeting moment—here for an instant, then gone. For the Creator, the present is a malleable substance that may be held, nurtured, and guided towards a realisation of its fullest potential as a vehicle for the expression of goodness, beauty, and truth and therefore a reflection of the Divine.

"And the *future*"—Gianni paused as he drew out that word—"the future is a most marvellous creation. For in it lies all the mystery of raw potentiality—a boundless reservoir of all that could be—formed by the illimitable interactions of conscious human beings with their individual environments, circumstances, and conditions, and in concert with their fellow humans. Here we pause to ask ourselves—does the Creator control this process of interaction? Does our Wise and Benevolent Sustainer direct these interactions that produce the fabric of actuality that we know as reality?"

The physicist priest passed his gaze around the room; every eye was on him and many a brow furrowed in thought. "A moment's reflection should tell you that He does not. To control the interactions of those agents would be to negate the purpose for which those agents were created. If proof of this assertion is needed, we have only to look at ourselves, because each and every one of us in this room has experienced not only the wonder and beauty of ley travel but also its intriguing limitations.

"In our travels, we move about from place to place, inhabiting different dimensions, participating in times not our own. In each place and time, we are caught up in the life and events of that particular destination—is this not so?" There were nods all around. "Yes, we may bring our intellect and understanding with us—that is only to be expected—but we do not float above or move outside the reality of that alternate existence. Indeed, wherever we travel we are caught up in the life of the world we visit in precisely the same way as those for whom that reality forms their only experience of the world. We live with them, subject to the same basic structures of life as they know it, whatever our prior experiences may have been in the world into which we ourselves were born. In other words, we live a common life with them and—as we have been so poignantly reminded earlier this evening in the memorial service for Cosimo and Sir Henry—we may share a common death with them.

"Nothing about our ability to leap across the dimensions of our universe insulates us from life and death, nor from the unfolding reality of the places we visit, and that, we further note, is always, always some variation on the past of our home world. For all our expertise in manipulating the ley lines, we acknowledge our inability to separate ourselves from participation in the ongoing reality of the multiverse. Each and every one of us has pondered the mystery of our powerlessness to reach, much less influence, the future.

"All our travels and experiences have brought us no closer to an explanation of why this should be so." He spread his hands, inviting each member to consider the conundrum. "So, I ask again—does our Wise Creator alone control the future?"

He let the question hang as he returned to his place at the podium. "No." Gianni shook his head slowly. "It is my belief that the future is not controlled in any way. To control the future would impose a deterministic outcome on the created order, thereby destroying both the freedom and independence of the freely interacting creatures it is meant to produce and, likewise, negating the very purpose for which the future and even time itself was created!"

Gianni spoke with easy confidence, his speech betraying none of the linguistic defects he confessed. Rather, it seemed to Kit that the priest went from strength to strength, his fluency matching the clarity of his mind. For the second time in his life Kit had the uncanny awareness of being told a truth he had always known instinctively, but which had always remained just beyond his ability to articulate. Hearing it now, spoken aloud in this place by a man of unquestioned passion and commitment, produced the sensation of standing too near an open flame—as if he lingered any longer in proximity to the source of this sacred knowledge he would be consumed.

"We must remind ourselves," the priest was saying, "of the repository of pure potential; it is that place in which the myriad possibilities of each and every action reside, where the infinite outcomes of our participation in creation are generated. The future exists to allow the created order to achieve the highest expression of goodness, beauty, and truth, in harmonious and joyful unity with the Creator. And while the Creator intends our free and willing participation in the ongoing realisation of His desires, and aids us in bringing about His purposes, He does not control the results of our participation. We know this because the result the Creator desires—that is, the active creation of new and higher forms and expressions of goodness, beauty, and truth—is one of the primary reasons for our existence in the first place.

"Thus it follows—if the future is to be that realm where possibility becomes actuality—any interference or alteration would produce catastrophic results for the entire created order. Anomalies would creep in, discrepancies would proliferate, irregularities would arise and subvert the natural course—all these things producing swiftly multiplying contradictions that would ripple backwards through the cosmos like a tsunami that gathers force as it travels over many miles across the deeps to wreak unimaginable destruction when it finally breaks upon a distant shore. Any interference in or tampering with the future would wreak untold destruction at every level of creation."

Gianni rested his hands on the podium and leaned forward with the air of a man imparting a terrible secret. "My friends, it is with the most profound foreboding that I inform you that the future— our future, the future of the cosmos, and even time itself—even now stands under threat. Indisputably, it is the greatest threat humankind has ever faced . . ." He paused as if unwilling to make himself say the words. The whole room seemed to hold its breath, awaiting the dire pronouncement. ". . . The wholesale collapse of the universe."

There were puzzled expressions and glances all around. Kit, too, felt a queasy uncertainty about what this meant. Before he could wonder about it further, Gianni continued, saying, "Dr. Clarke and I have been in consultation over preliminary data obtained from the Vatican observatory that indicates that the expansion of the universe may be slowing. This initial finding is now being investigated by the Jansky Very Large Array telescope in New Mexico, and according to our preliminary calculations, if the deceleration were to be confirmed, the outward expansion would eventually halt and a reversal or contraction would begin."

From the frowns and muttering following that announcement, it was clear few of the listeners understood the implications of this singular discovery. Several hands went up. "Could you tell us what they saw—through the telescopes, I mean? What did they see to make them think the universe is shrinking?"

Gianni nodded, thinking how best to explain. "Measuring the outward expansion of the universe is a fairly simple routine procedure these days. Data is collected from sensors that measure high-energy frequencies coming from various sectors, and by comparing recent measurements with data taken a few weeks ago, JVLA astronomers have been able to detect a slight but significant alteration in what is known as the cosmological redshift velocity—the speed at which distant galaxies are moving away from us. For the first time since these measurements began, the redshift velocity has lessened. Obviously, more measurements from other observatories will be required to confirm this, but early indications are that the expansion is indeed slowing. Like a rubber band stretched to the limit, once expansion stops, contraction begins."

Here he paused to see that most of his small audience was keeping up. "Understandably, this discovery is very worrying, and more data will have to be collected over the coming weeks and months, but the early evidence indicates that we may be witnessing an unprecedented phenomenon. In other words, the ever-accelerating expansion of the universe that we have been measuring for the past fifteen years or so, but that has existed for the past fifteen billion years, may at last be slowing.

"If unchecked, this could trigger a reversal that could result in what is euphemistically called the Big Crunch—a poor choice of words for what is, in reality, nothing less than the utter annihilation of the universe and the entire created order. Everything that exists or has ever existed will be obliterated." His voice trailed off. "Existence itself will cease . . ."

It would be the end of everything.

There was nothing more to say.

CHAPTER 33

In Which Family Lore Is Fully Explored

The wadi was much as Charles imagined it: a dry channel cut through solid limestone by eons of water runoff from the surrounding hills. It was, however, far deeper than he expected. The smoothly undulating walls rose on either side to a height of twenty metres or more in great curves of banded stone like a giant curtain. In some places, however, the walls towered above the floor as high as thirty metres. The width varied too; sometimes the gap was so narrow the men and cargo-laden donkeys had to go single file; other times the corridor widened to stretches where an army could have marched ten abreast. The narrows were regions of cool shadow; the wider areas, where the sun reached all the way to the valley floor, were stifling hot. The air did not move much in the wadi.

Some of Charles' earliest memories involved the story of the Skin Map and how it had been carried back to Egypt to be reunited with its owner—"in the wadi tomb where the three branches met." It was not much to go on, and as he led his little expedition down along the winding corridor of the wadi, he desperately hoped it would be enough.

Deeper into the gorge, the expedition began to pass curious rectangular niches carved into the soft stone. Some of these had inscriptions above or below the recess in a language Charles did not recognise; others were adorned with odd images: winged beasts and men, pomegranates, disembodied heads with oversized eyes, braided cords, the outlines of flowers, meaningless abstract designs involving lightning bolt zigzags or bands of wavy lines. Farther along what had become an unending gallery, these hewn alcoves became more elaborate, more highly decorated—often with human figures in togas or flowing robes. Most of these bore inscriptions in Latin, and from this Charles guessed they were tombs or memorials to deceased aristocrats of the Roman occupation.

On they went, pausing at midday to eat and rest in the pools of shade provided by the rim of overhanging rock until the sun crossed the gap and the shadows began creeping up the wadi wall. It was not long after resuming their trek that they reached a place that matched the description of the location Charles had received from his father over the years. And Charles knew it the moment he saw it.

He had seen the wall ahead for some time and, as they drew nearer, he saw revealed the elaborately carved doorway of a large tomb or, perhaps, funerary temple. Upon reaching this imposing structure some minutes later, Charles saw that it lay across a wide expanse—a bowl of sorts—created by a second large ravine running perpendicular to the main gorge to form a fair-sized Y-junction . . . the place where three branches met.

"We stop here for the night," Charles told Shakir in his pidgin Arabic. "Make camp."

Leaving the details in the capable hands of his young assistant, Charles undertook a preliminary investigation of the area. Unfortunately, there was not much to see. Whatever signs he hoped to detect that might lead him to the tomb entrance were nowhere to be found. Aside from a scattering of shallow funerary niches carved into soft stone and the cavernous hollow of the ruined temple, or whatever it was, there was not so much as a crack or seam in the walls anywhere.

Charles made a lengthy survey of each branch of the wadi, but saw nothing he thought might indicate the presence of a tomb. While annoying, certainly, it was not entirely unexpected. He had come prepared with tools for excavation, after all. He went to sleep under the diamond-spangled heavens that night, certain that tomorrow he would locate Anen's final resting place . . . and was still brimming with certainty the next morning when he quit his bedroll, pulled on his boots, and began a proper systematic search. He strode about the junction fizzing with anticipation and thumping the sides and floor of the gorge with a long iron rod. With each tap and thump he listened for a change in the sound that might betray a hollow or change in the makeup of the rock.

The workers—having risen, tended the animals, and breakfasted— now sat under their turbans watching him stalk the wadi like a thief knocking on the walls of a house to find a secret nook. This was, of course, exactly what he was doing.

When the sun rose high enough to begin pouring hot light down onto the floor of the wadi, Shakir approached with a bowl of mashed prunes mixed with pine nuts and a cup of water, beseeching his employer to eat and rest a little. Discouraged by his lack of success, Charles reluctantly agreed and went to sit in the shade of one of the low tents that now lined the eastern wall. As he munched his porridge and sipped his water, he regarded the nearly flat floor of gravel and pebbles and sand. It occurred to him that four thousand years of time and weather had conspired to alter the configuration of the wadi—subtly perhaps, but enough to thwart easy access to its secreted treasures. Clearly, a new tactic of discovery was necessary.

He finished his breakfast and summoned Shakir to join him at the west-facing wall. The young man watched as Charles, beginning at the junction corner, marched off a dozen paces and then a dozen more. Using his iron rod as an oversized stylus, he then etched two deep lines in the loose grit of the ravine floor—a short one of a metre or so perpendicular to the curtain, and a slightly longer one running parallel to it. Then, pointing to the space he had just defined, he pantomimed digging and said, "I want this all cleared away." He grabbed a handful of loose rubble from inside his described box and threw it aside. "See? I want to dig a hole."

Shakir likewise scooped up a handful of dry grit and tossed it away to show he understood. He then turned and called a command to the labourers, who gathered their tools and, upon receiving the boss's orders, began to dig. Charles, his head now swathed in a makeshift white turban, stood by, watching as the hole deepened. At a depth of around one metre they reached bedrock, or at least the stony bottom of the gorge.

"Good! Excellent! Now take it that way," Charles cried. Using the rod once more, he extended the line along the wadi face another metre or so. This was duly excavated and the hole cleared—at which point Charles extended the length yet again. The work continued, and slowly the trench took shape. He drew more lines in the opposite direction, whereupon the workers downed tools and returned to the tents.

"Come back!" called Charles. "We must make it bigger!"

"*Laa, laa, Sekrey,*" said Shakir, frowning and shaking his head. He pointed to the sky, shielded his eyes, and then wiped sweat from his face, all the while saying, "No."

"Okay, okay," relented Charles, waving his hands. "I understand, Shakir. We rest and eat." He mimed eating, then pointed to the sun standing directly overhead and traced an arc towards the west. "We dig more later."

The young Egyptian hurried away and ordered the midday meal to be prepared. While the others were thus occupied, Charles climbed down into the narrow trench and walked its length, tapping every few inches with the rod. The exercise did nothing to advance the project, and after a while Charles gave up and went to join his men in a meal and a nap during the hottest part of the day. When he awakened again the shadows had begun to gather in the wadi; he roused the men and directed them to extend the trench a few more metres—which was all that could be accomplished that day.

The next day was an almost exact repeat of the day before, as was the one after that. Progress was achieved, but at a pace Charles considered painfully slow. Though maddening, the lack of speed was understandable. The soaring heat meant that, at best, only six hours of actual labour could be maintained: three hours in the morning and three in the evening before the sun set. And while in England the luscious, lingering twilight hours might make up for an afternoon's idleness, sunset in Egypt was an abrupt, truncated affair. Darkness descended with a rapidity that Charles found disconcerting—the drawing of a curtain, or snuffing of a candle.

Five days after the first pick struck the rubble, Charles had a handsome trench but little else to show for the effort, and supplies were getting low. He called Shakir to the cook tent. "We need more food and water," he said, gesturing to the bags and skins heaped in the corner. "More men too."

The youth nodded sagely. "Okay, *Sekrey*."

Outside, Charles pointed to the mules. "You take beasts and one man," he said, taxing his Arabic to the breaking point. "Get food. Get water." He held up his palm, fingers spread. "Get five men— workers. Five." Charles then mimed counting coins into his hand. "I give you money. Okay?"

"Okay. I go."

Shakir and one of the younger labourers departed after the mid-day meal, taking the animals with them. It would be five more days before they returned, bringing with them enough supplies to replenish the stores and more besides. Also added to the number were five more men. Although two of the newcomers were scarcely more than teenagers, Charles was grateful for the help and put the younger ones in charge of the kitchen and menial chores, thus freeing three others to join the digging crews.

Life in camp settled into a daily round of work and rest, punctuated by meals and sleep. Every fortnight Shakir and one other would make the journey to secure more supplies, and the round began again— disturbed only by the occasional mishap: a heavy stone dropped on a bare foot; a swollen hand from a scorpion bite; food poisoning from inadequately salted fish; and, for Charles, prostration due to sunburn when he foolishly removed his shirt one day to allow it to be washed.

The trench gained length from both ends and a new excavation was begun on the opposite side of the wadi. But with each passing day, hope of finding the tomb dimmed a little more. Until one day, almost two months into the dig and with optimism and funds at their lowest ebb, Charles was stirred from his tent by urgent shouts.

"*Sekrey! Sekrey!*" cried one of the workers, and the summons was taken up by others. Charles emerged from the tent to see men gesturing wildly for him to come and see.

He hurried over to where the diggers were clearing the rubble from a narrow crevice little more than a crack in the stone—but a crack that ran perpendicular to the wall and straight as a ruler: a join that could only be man-made.

"Splendid!" cried Charles. "Clear it away!" He scratched a box in the dirt, indicating the area to be excavated. "Clear it all away!"

Work proceeded to expand the narrow ditch, following the line in the stone until the hole stretched halfway across the floor of the gorge. At times both labour and labourers were obscured by the heavy clouds of dust that hung in the dead, unmoving air. Bit by bit, as the blades of picks and shovels, rakes and hoes laid bare the base, certainty grew that they had found a series of hand-cut stones—blocks used to cover an opening.

Once the dust cleared, the extent of the brickwork was revealed; Charles estimated that they were looking at a sealed opening roughly two metres wide and about three metres long. "This is it!" he cried, fairly hopping from one foot to the other in his excitement. "This has got to be the place. Well done!"

The enforced rest through the afternoon heat was difficult to endure, but digging resumed in the shadow of the gorge and ceased only when it finally grew too dark to see. When the last digger crawled from the hole, Charles thrust in his torch to verify that they had succeeded in prying up most of the capstones to reveal a staircase; it angled down and into the base of the wadi wall. "Well done, Shakir," he said. "Well done, everybody. We'll begin again in the morning."

The men, exhausted and hungry, dragged back to the tents for a well-earned supper and rest. Everyone slept soundly that night and rose the next morning to a day already stifling. The sky was parched white; the air lay heavy upon them—not enough movement to even stir the dust that billowed up with each basket of rubble cleared from the doorway. By midmorning the entrance stood revealed: a narrow doorway sealed with mortared stone. Charles, who had spent most of the morning down in the hole, called for a pick to begin chipping away at the blocks.

With each blow the stonework gave slightly, tumbling inward after only a few hefty swings of the pick. The bricks collapsed with a deep resonant clatter that sounded like thunder. It happened so fast, Charles stood for a moment listening to the echo and peering into the darkness yawning before him. "We're in!" he called up the steps to Shakir, who was waiting at the top. "Bring torches. I need light."

He was still speaking when there came another low rumble. It sounded so very much like another crumbling wall that Charles glanced back into the void half expecting to see the doorway collapsing. But all was as it had been moments before. He looked back up to Shakir and saw the young man and several of the workers gazing skyward.

"What was that?" he called from the hole. Cupping a hand to his ear, he shouted, "Shakir—that sound. What was that sound?"

Even as he spoke, the sky lit up with a flash of lightning; a few seconds later the low rumble echoed through the gorge. Thunder, unmistakably. A storm was on its way. A rare event in one of the driest regions in the world, it nevertheless happened. And it was about to happen now.

"The torches!" shouted Charles again. "Bring torches. No time to lose!"

He stepped into the yawning entrance of the tomb. Slowly, his light-dazzled eyes adjusted to the darkness. He began to make out the obscure bulk of objects, their edges outlined by the light slanting in from outside. He was about to call again when Shakir appeared in the doorway and thrust a torch into his hand.

Turning once more to the chamber, the flickering glow revealed an untidy mess of junk heaped in careless, haphazard piles, all of it covered with a hoary coat of dust. Charles had seen such a jumble before, in his own much-neglected attic. But where Charles' loft contained tea chests full of old clothes, books, obsolete furniture, seasonal bedding, and the like, this chamber contained chairs and beds and lampstands, the slender wheels of several disassembled chariots and the chariot cars themselves, spears and rods and bows with quivers of arrows, painted screens, chests made of stone and wood, and numerous small statues. And everywhere: jars. All shapes and sizes of vessels in obsessive perfusion from tiny delicate alabaster unguent pots with the heads of goddesses on the lids to titanic terra-cotta grain jars that would have taken half a dozen men to shift.

The walls were decorated with the paintings—elaborate scenes of life on the Nile lovingly rendered in exquisite detail—recording a time and culture now at least three thousand years distant, yet still as fresh as wet paint. The colour, the immediacy, the intimacy, were breathtaking.

Charles observed all this in a single prolonged gape of enraptured astonishment. So many wonderful things! The depth and extent of the treasure was staggering. He had grown up hearing about the wealth of the ancients, but he had never imagined it amassed in heaps for the taking. Here it was, spread before him, untouched since the day it had gone into the tomb.

He moved into the treasure house of objects, his torch revealing more and still more wonderful things—many of them glinting warmly gold in the fluttering light. Yet the more he saw, the more concerned he became. With a sinking heart he realised he did not see the one object he had counted on finding. Nowhere amidst the bewildering welter of objects was there a sarcophagus.

As Charles gazed around, dismay grew. Where was the great burial vault containing the earthly remains of High Priest Anen? More to the point, where was the casket of his grandfather Arthur?

He was puzzling over this when a sharp cry from the stairway outside drew Shakir from the chamber. Ignoring the commotion, Charles moved farther into the tomb and made another sweeping examination; holding his torch high, he searched the room corner to corner and side to side.

There was no sarcophagus or coffin to be seen.

As large as they were, the great stone burial vaults could be neither missed nor confused with anything else. The grave of Arthur Flinders-Petrie was simply not there.

CHAPTER 34

In Which Hindsight
Yields Perfect Vision

ekrey! Sekrey!" The shout came first, and a moment later Shakir thrust his head through the doorway of the tomb. *"Sekrey!"* he cried again, pointing to something outside. "You come now."

Returning to the entrance, Charles followed the youth up the stairs to find the workmen milling about in a state of agitated alarm. The donkeys were braying and pulling at their tether lines. Directly overhead, the dull white sky was now the colour of an angry bruise— blue-black and swollen with low, ominous clouds. The air was much cooler and surging on an erratically gusting wind. Charles could smell the rich, spicy scent produced by rain on dry desert soil, mingled with ozone. Even as he watched, a streak of forked lightning arced from west to east in a blinding flash. The crash of thunder that followed trembled the ground and quivered through the entrails.

"Sekrey!" shouted Shakir, pointing down the ravine where a thin

snake of something dark and sinuous was meandering down the bottom of the gorge. *"Heset!"*

Charles stared at it for a few seconds before realising that it was, in fact, water—a probing, muddy tendril of filthy liquid blindly groping its way along the bone-dry wadi floor.

"You!" Charles pointed to a nearby worker. "You and you! Come with me," he commanded, retracing his steps to the tomb. "You and you! Bring tools. Follow me."

Darting back into the chamber, he moved to the far wall and, holding his torch close to the surface, quickly located a section of brickwork behind one of the mural paintings. Though it had been sealed with plaster, he could still make out the bricks beneath and, pointing to the wall, he said, "Take it down."

The labourers stared at him. Seizing a pick, he swung it against the wall—once . . . twice . . . three times. Paint and plaster crumbled away, revealing the brickwork beneath. "Take it down!" he repeated.

The workers fell to, and the close air of the tomb was soon white with dust as the ancient painting disappeared in a pile of chips and chunks, revealing the shape of a door. Charles, his heart beating quicker, wasted not a moment ordering that to be taken down as well.

He ran to the stairway. "Shakir! More torches!" he called, then darted back to the wreckage being performed on the sealed door. A few well-placed blows soon had the blocks tumbling. After the first few, all the rest came down in a rush and he was looking at the entrance to a hidden chamber.

Shakir appeared with the torches and, in a rush of Arabic, tried to tell Charles something that Charles failed to comprehend. He dismissed the youth and ducked into the inner room. As revealed by the light of his torch, the chamber was smaller and spare, built to contain not one, but two sarcophagi. Only a few jars and wicker baskets lined the walls—but what walls! All four surfaces and the ceiling, too, were painted, and the artwork here was more colourful, more detailed, and much more lifelike than that in the first room. As magnificent as they were, Charles had eyes for only one: a scene in which a chubby, bald man—the priest Anen?—stood with one hand pointing to a star in the sky whilst the other held a flat object on which was rendered a collection of tiny blue symbols. Both the object and the symbols were known to Charles as the Skin Map.

"*Sekrey*," called Shakir, his voice urgent, plaintive. "You come."

Ignoring him, Charles moved to the first and largest of two burial vaults. It was red granite and richly carved with a stylised likeness of its occupant and decorated head to toe with hieroglyphs. Turning away, Charles moved to the smaller sarcophagus; it was white limestone and adorned with a single strip of glyphs down the centre. "Open it," he ordered.

"*Sekrey!*" shouted Shakir, his voice growing more shrill. "You come now!"

"Open it!" commanded Charles.

His five helpers moved to the vault with some reluctance. Using their picks and shovels, they succeeded in edging the heavy cover an inch or so to one side. "Open it now," Charles repeated.

His words were swallowed by the sudden roar and rattle of thunder that blasted through the stillness of the tomb. Shakir disappeared into the other room, but Charles stood his ground. "Open it!" he shouted, pointing at the great stone casket.

The workers looked at one another and reluctantly applied their tools. They had succeeded in moving the lid another few inches when Charles felt an odd sensation: wet feet. He looked down. A questing snake of water was oozing through the door. It had already reached him and was flattening and spreading across the floor.

"Hurry!" shouted Charles. "Get it open."

But the workers had seen the water. They threw down their tools and fled the tomb.

Thrusting the torch into the crevice between the lid and side, Charles snatched up the nearest pick and began prying at the heavy top. He swiftly found the right leverage and managed to increase the gap another centimetre or so. Meanwhile, the water rose higher. By the time the crack was wide enough to thrust in his hand, the water covered the floor and was rising quickly to his ankles. Charles continued. Working with a desperate frenzy, he leaned on the pick handle, straining every nerve and sinew. Sweat ran down his face, stinging his eyes. The massive lid shifted—ever so slightly, but just enough.

The water seeping into the chamber had now risen over the tops of his shoes.

Charles shoved his hand inside the vault and discerned the stiff, dry outline of the linen-wrapped mummy. He held the torch close as he dared but could see little. Touch told him that there were no objects buried with his grandfather's corpse. He felt along the chest and head—nothing there. He put his hand under the mummy and discovered a flattened, cloth-wrapped bundle at one end. His fingers closed on a corner of the parcel and pulled. A second pull freed the packet but sent the torch spinning to the floor where it expired with a sputter and hiss of steam. Darkness thick and deep descended instantly.

Clutching the bundle, Charles felt his way to the foot of the sarcophagus. Like a blind man, waving his hand before him, he fumbled his way to the ragged opening in the wall, breathing a sigh of relief when his fingers snagged the edge. He stepped through, lost his footing on the rubble littering the floor in front of the breach, and fell headlong into the next room and into the water that now covered the floor, barely managing to maintain his grip on his prize.

Spluttering and wet, Charles hauled himself to his feet and glimpsed the dim outline of the outer doorway; he splashed his way to it, dodging grave furniture, knocking over jars, and scattering priceless objects in his wake. He reached the stairway, which had become a cascade of successive waterfalls, and scrambled up the steps and into the dim, lurid light.

The sky was wine-coloured, virulent and angry; the wind whipped through the gorge, shrieking as it shredded itself on the rocks. The men and animals were gone. Charles started across the encampment to his tent to retrieve his leather bag—only to be intercepted by Shakir, who grabbed him by the arm and pulled him away, pointing down the main channel of the wadi where the last of the labourers were just then disappearing into the storm-darkened wadi. "You come now, *Sekrey!*"

"My bag—I must have my bag!" insisted Charles.

But Shakir did not release his grip. "No, *Sekrey!* No!" He pointed down the smaller branch of the Y-shaped junction where the stream of water now coursing along the valley floor was met by another coming from the opposite branch. The combined flow swirled, gathering force and volume as it entered the main channel. Fed by a multitude of runnels and rivulets off the surrounding hills and high places, the water level rose even as he watched. Alarmed by the speed with which the gully was filling, Charles stuffed the precious parcel into his shirt next to his skin and splashed after Shakir. Within three heartbeats, he was running for his life.

Down through the undulating corridor of stone he fled, legs

churning, arms pumping. The water and debris underfoot did not make for easy running; his feet dragged and skidded. Shakir, by contrast, flew. Younger and quicker, he seemed to skim the surface, barely touching the ground. The distance between them increased.

Around the winding curves of the wadi they ran. The air temperature dropped and rain began to fall in large, round drops big as grapes, slowly at first and then faster. The wind gusted from the north, hurling rain in sheets with such force that the oversized drops seemed to bounce off the stony, hard-baked ground. Charles, soaked to the skin, dashed water out of his eyes and ran half-blind through the canyon. Shakir disappeared around a bend and Charles ran on alone. Meanwhile, the angry water gathered volume and force behind him. It was now an onrushing wall sweeping along the wadi, a churning mass of muck—dead acacia branches and dry brush ripped from the upper slopes of distant hills, desiccated weeds, rubble, and mud—racing ever nearer with the rumbling, grinding sound of a great millstone freewheeling down a cobbled road.

The leading edge of this torrent caught Charles, and before he knew it he was running in water to his knees. A few more steps and he was in up to his thighs. He fought on, water swirling around him, slowing him, rising with every step. Above the roar of the water he heard a higher-pitched wail: the sound of savage wind ripping down through the empty heights. Risking a glance over his shoulder, he glimpsed the terrible wave-wall sluicing up either side of the canyon walls to a depth three times his own height.

The mighty gush of air driven before the wave struck him, hurling him forward. Charles was thrown headfirst into the water. An instant later the wave crashed over him, swamping him, submerging him, crushing him down against the rocky floor and holding him there.

Caught in the ferocious current, unable to resist, Charles was spun up like a cork in a torrent. Twisting, tumbling, he bumped along the bottom of the ravine, careening into rocks, pummelled by stones. Vainly he tried to right himself, to fight his way to the surface. The gulp of air he had snatched before the wave took him was not enough. His lungs burned. Desperate to find the surface, he opened his eyes in the murk but could see nothing. He kicked his legs and flailed his arms in the forlorn hope of contacting something solid—to no avail.

His lungs ached to the point of bursting and he could feel his consciousness beginning to slip, his awareness growing muzzy. Then, just as he released the last of his spent air, his chest smacked against the wadi floor. Gathering his feet under him, he shoved with every ounce of his remaining strength and shot upward. He breached the surface just as his exhausted lungs inhaled.

Water poured down his throat and he choked on it. But his head was above the surface now and he fought hard to stay atop the churning waves. Branches poked him, stones torn from their moorings pounded him—Charles ignored the bumps and thumps, flailing his arms and legs to keep his head above water, refusing to allow the current to drag him under again.

This strategy came at a price. For as the flood hurtled around the sinuous bends of the wadi, slamming first into one side and then the other, Charles was tossed along with it. With every twist and turn, the wild water heaved him closer to the walls. There was no avoiding a collision.

Charles slammed against the curtain of stone and the impact drove the breath from his body. He gulped and gagged and downed a mouthful of water before he could breathe again. The flood surged around the next bend and, as the raging water impelled him into the next bank, he tried to brace himself for the impact. He put out his hands to fend off the brunt of the blow, but the angle was too sharp and the wadi wall came up too fast. His left arm grazed the edge of a projecting slab and he was spun sideways into the wall, his right arm taking the full force. He felt the jolt through his entire frame and his arm snapped, the bones giving way like kindling.

Pain shot through him and his head went under. Gritting his teeth, Charles fought to the surface once more, but without the use of his right arm he could only just keep his head above the lashing chaos of the waves. Pain consumed him. He could not see. He could not think. Dazed and confused, he felt a sense-dulling numbness creeping through him.

He flailed with his good arm, trying to return to the centre of the channel. On one of his strokes, his hand made contact with something—a yielding mass that seemed to be covered in hair. Without thinking, he grabbed for it and pulled himself to it and found himself holding on to the carcass of a dead donkey.

Charles wrapped his arms around the poor drowned creature's neck and held on. Together the two of them were swept along, and Charles was able to remain afloat by clinging to the animal's buoyant corpse. How long he could hold on, he did not know.

Around one bend and another, the two were swept. Charles lost his grip on the donkey when it hurtled into a wall, but regained his hold, throwing his good arm around the animal's neck. He felt himself slipping. He sensed darkness looming on the edge of his vision and knew he would not be able to remain conscious much longer.

"Sekrey!"

The shout was only barely audible above the sound of the crashing water. Charles thought he imagined it—until it came again.

"*Sekrey!*"

He craned his head around, scanning the walls of the gorge as they sped by him. And then he saw a hand sticking out from the wall; swirling swiftly closer, he caught a glimpse of a dark head of hair and Shakir's face beneath it. The youth was leaning out of a crevice in the wall, leaning out and reaching for him.

Charles released his hold on the donkey and flung himself at Shakir, willing himself across the gap. Their hands grabbed, snatched, and fingers scrabbled for a hold. With a tremendous cry, the young Egyptian seized him and held on, slowly dragging Charles to the side, out of the direct pull of the current. Shakir was not powerful enough to haul Charles bodily out of the water, and Charles could not fight free of the current. He felt his hand slipping and he was dragged from Shakir's grasp.

Charles saw the look of horror on the young face, his mouth round with the shout. "*Sekrey!*"

Consigning himself to his fate, he floated now, not bothering to fight or swim, allowing the flood to have its way. He bumped against the donkey carcass again and flung his good arm around the dead creature's neck, relaxed, and let the water take him.

Sometime later and farther downstream, the fearsome intensity seemed to drain from the current; the level of the water began to fall. And with each successive drop in depth, the level fell faster——like a jar overturned, releasing the last of its substance in a rush. In this way, Charles was lowered to the ravine floor. Soon he was able to get his feet under him and to stand, bracing himself against the stream.

Directly ahead of him he saw daylight through the gap between the walls. A few dozen yards later Charles walked out of the wadi and into the desert. The torrent had cut deep gashes in the soft desert earth—a spread of finger channels that still ran full, draining water away into the dry emptiness of the empty flatlands beyond the hills. The storm howled away across the desert, spending its fury on the desolate wastes. Charles waded out onto one of the little sandbars in this delta and collapsed, cradling his broken arm. "Thank God," he whispered with every pulse of blood through his veins. He felt the cloth-wrapped bundle beneath his shirt. "Thank God."

Shakir found him a short while later and helped Charles to his feet; the two started off on the long road back to the river. They had not gone far when they heard a shout, and three of the workmen came running to meet them; four others stood with the remaining donkeys.

His relief soon gave way to regret, however; two men were missing and would not be seen again. The walk gave Charles ample time to reflect on what had happened and his part in it; with every step his guilt and shame burned hotter. Two men drowned because of his stubbornness. Remorse overwhelmed him.

Three days later, his arm set and bandaged, he sat on the riverbank waiting for the boat, penitent, consumed with guilt. He had achieved the object of his quest—the map was undamaged and safely tucked away—but he had failed. With the crystal clarity of hindsight, he could see it now: arrogance, stupidity, pride, ignorance had all played their nefarious part in this disaster. But the chief culprit surely was pride. Charles the Great had swanned into Egypt expecting the lowly natives to come running to his beck and call, serve his every whim, bend their backs to boost him to his glory as he collected his prize.

Yet he knew no language other than mammon, knew no culture other than that of the marketplace. In his heart he had trumpeted: *I am a Flinders-Petrie!* What more was needed?

The shame of those ludicrous assumptions made his face burn, which was only a dim outward reflection of the fire of humiliation raging in his soul. He had been a pompous, haughty fool; a rude, stubborn, unthinking ninny; an utterly self-absorbed, self-obsessed, self-determined, selfish yob—and he had the broken arm, and broken spirit, to prove it. In the circumstances, Charles decided, he was lucky to have escaped with a mere injury, painful as it might be. Bones could heal. He was not sure there was a cure for hubris, for the blind, arrogant pride that leads inexorably to destruction of its human vessels.

He was sunk in the slough of shame when an unexpected thought occurred to him: perhaps his narrow escape had been granted by an All-Wise Providence in order to allow him a second chance, to put matters right, to make amends, to change. Very well. If amends could be made, he would make them. He would humble himself and learn what was needed, whatever that might be. The language and culture of the people? The geography of land and climate? He would take time to study them, master them. Whatever the cost of obtaining this knowledge—or, as he saw it, this new humility—he would cheerfully pay it.

Over the next few days, as he visited the families of the men who had lost their lives and made offerings of money to the widows—with promises of more to come—the conviction hardened in Charles that not only could he change, but the necessary change had already begun. It had started with the realisation that a new and contrite heart was needed. And, having made a beginning, he would now devote himself to this revolution in his soul. He would become the leader of the insurgency. Moreover, he would earn the right to the title *Sekrey*.

The next time he mounted an expedition, wherever the Skin Map might lead him, he would be captain indeed.

CHAPTER 35

In Which Confession Is Good for the Quest

"The problem as I see it is a matter of redressing the balance." Brendan Hanno paused to judge the mood of his gathered listeners. Hollow-eyed, haggard, their expressions tight, they met his declaration without a crumb of enthusiasm. The day had not gone well, and everyone was tired and out of sorts. "It is as simple as that," he added, instantly wishing he had not.

Tony Clarke was quick to reply. "If it is that simple, what are we doing here?"

"Simple it may be," answered Brendan, his tone weary, "I did not say it would be *easy*. God knows it won't be easy."

"You have put it most succinctly, my friends," offered Gianni, trying to soothe frayed tempers. "The next step must be to discover what has caused this imbalance. Once we know that, we will be able to judge what may be done to put things right."

"*That* could be a complete waste of precious time," snapped Tony, irritation making his voice sharp. "We end up in a futile search for a *cause* that may turn out to be totally irrelevant, when what we really need is to pursue a *remedy*."

"Treating symptoms without addressing the disease is bad medicine," observed one of the elder Zetetics.

"You would know, Richard," sniped another. This comment was met with hoots of derision from other members.

"Gentlemen, please!" piped Mrs. Peelstick. "Remember your manners. We are all friends here. We are all struggling to come to terms with very difficult information, and we are all doing the best we can. Let us at least be civil to one another."

The gathered Zetetics lapsed into bristling silence.

Kit, slumped and stiff in his chair, felt the tension coursing around the stuffy room and knew its source. Brother Gianni's brilliant and masterful exposition on the nature of the crisis looming over them had produced an almost giddy sense of camaraderie, of a fellowship of courageous warriors united to repel a stealthy and deadly foe. By turns inspiring and frightening, the priest astronomer had delivered a concise lecture on the nature of time and the glorious purpose of Creation, and the threat that both now faced. He explained that both the Vatican observatory at Castel Gondolfo and the Jansky Very Large Array radio telescope in New Mexico had reported data anomalies indicating universal deceleration. Lest any members wonder at the significance of this event, he defined the hidden connection between the shrinking of the universe—which he likened to a collapsing soufflé—and the unravelling of matter to its constituent parts, a cosmological cataclysm he termed the End of Everything.

Roused by a clear and urgent call to arms, the Seventy-Second

All-Society Convocation of the Zetetic Society had taken up the challenge; they would champion the cause and save the universe and everything in it from total annihilation or die in the attempt. On the heady wave of an adrenaline rush, each and every one had pledged to work tirelessly, faithfully, heroically to restore order to the cosmos. Gianni's speech had duly ignited the flame. But where dazzling fireworks had been called for, the result was a damp squib. Like the others, Kit had gone to bed in a state of highly charged nervous excitement. Overnight, however, the exhilaration bled away; a dull, numbing dread had settled in its place.

No one had slept very well and breakfast had been a sombre affair. The morning session had been spent in useless hand wringing, and now the afternoon gathering was proving restive and contrary. Everyone seemed distinctly ill disposed to plunge headlong into another round of gloom and destruction, and thrashing out a solution to what was arguably the most extreme dilemma ever to face the human race seemed more remote than ever. Where did one even begin? Kit could feel the frustration bubbling away beneath the surface, and it was breaking out in petty arguments and bickering.

Brendan, clearly discouraged, banged his gavel and, when he had reclaimed the attention of the group, said, "This is getting us nowhere. I am going to suggest we take a break to cool off a little."

Tony raised his hand. "Perhaps I might make a suggestion? Sometimes when faced with a difficult problem in committee, we split up into smaller working groups to tackle the issues from different angles. It can yield good results."

"I agree," put in Tess. "It is worth a try. We're not accomplishing anything this way."

Brendan passed his gaze around the ring of unhappy faces. "How does that sit with everybody?" Hearing no dissent, he tapped the tabletop with the flat of his hand. "Okay then, let's give it a go."

Thus it was agreed and four groups were formed—each to meet in a different part of the society's headquarters, and each to work on a different approach to the dual problem of what could possibly have happened to bring about the impending calamity and what, if anything, might be done about it.

"If we're all happy with the arrangements, we will gather again this evening after dinner for progress reports from each committee." He banged the gavel one last time, very loudly. "We are adjourned. Let's get busy."

The various groups drifted off to their appointed locations. Brother Gianni led his crew of four down to the courtyard. Mrs. Peelstick paused on the threshold and said, "You carry on. I'll just get the tea going—shan't be a moment."

"I'll help," said Mina. "I could use a break."

The two disappeared into the kitchen; Kit and Gianni continued to the sun-drenched courtyard. Surrounded by its high walls, half shaded by its striped canvas awning and potted palm, and soothed by the gentle play of water in the central fountain, the simple walled garden seemed a veritable paradise: a world away from the creeping horrors they had been discussing only moments before. As Gianni started for the table under the umbrella in the corner, Kit tugged him on the sleeve. "Before we get started, I need to ask you something . . ." He hesitated, then added quickly, "As a priest."

"Certainly, my friend. You would like to make a confession?"

"Something like that."

"This way." Gianni indicated a corner of the courtyard. "We can talk over there."

Kit followed the priest and stepped into the shade of the potted palm. "Do you believe in eternal life?" Before Gianni could reply, he corrected himself. "Of course you do. You're a priest. I mean, do you think it's possible for people to come back to life?"

Gianni smiled. "Well, our Lord Jesus came back to life, of course, and he raised others—Lazarus, for example. He showed us that it is possible."

"Right," agreed Kit. "But besides him. Ordinary people, I mean—would it be possible for a dead person to be brought back to life?"

The priest regarded Kit with a curious expression. "I suppose," began the priest thoughtfully, "it would very much depend on the particular circumstances. I suspect you have a particular circumstance in mind?"

Kit nodded. "Your talk last night about time and how it flows—and how the future contains all possibilities and potentials and all that—well, it got me thinking about Cosimo's untimely death."

"Ah, yes." Gianni glimpsed the connection. "Because of the memorial service, no doubt."

"I was there when Cosimo died, see." Kit went on to give a brief description of being caught by Burleigh and locked in the desert tomb where Cosimo and Sir Henry were already imprisoned, sick and dying. "If Giles and I hadn't been rescued by Mina, we would have died there too. But I have always wondered if I could have done something about it. Or if there is something that could *still* be done about it. I remember asking Mina at the time, and she seemed to think that it might be possible to reverse what happened somehow—using ley lines and the Spirit Well and all that. Maybe they could be rescued—brought back to life." He finished, casting a hopeful glance at the priest. "What do *you* think?"

Gianni looked down at his clasped hands. "I think," he said after a moment's consideration, "that it would be dangerous in the extreme." He raised his glance to meet Kit's surprised expression. "This is not what you expected."

"To be honest? No, it is not what I expected you to say at all."

"The reason has to do with my belief in the supreme sovereignty of God and His ongoing work to bring His creation to its ultimate fruition in unity with Him."

"The Omega Point you mentioned last night," said Kit.

"All things that happen to us happen for a reason," Gianni continued. "No, that is too simple too—how do you say?—ah, like a *formula*."

"Formulaic," Kit supplied the word. "Why too simple?"

"Let us say that all things that happen must be somehow woven into the emerging pattern of God's ultimate design. Even the stray and errant threads can be used—or, perhaps, *especially* the stray and errant threads may be required for a particular purpose that, because of our limited human view and understanding, we cannot possibly see or know." He offered Kit a hopeful smile. "*Capisci?*"

"I guess," Kit allowed. There was no mistaking the reluctance in his tone.

"And yet you doubt," observed the priest. "I can well understand your wanting to overturn a wickedness and set matters right. But reversing or attempting to reverse what has happened in the ongoing flow of events can have serious and long-ranging effects that we cannot possibly foresee."

Kit produced a puzzled frown. "You're saying that it would be like pulling a thread on a jumper—once you start pulling, the whole thing might unravel . . . Is that it?"

"Unweaving the tapestry, yes," agreed Gianni. "Because removing even a small portion of the design creates gaps and holes that multiply and spread as more of the fabric becomes involved. This is one reason, perhaps, why time moves only in one direction."

"So even if I *could* somehow go and bring Cosimo and Sir Henry back to life, it would be wrong to do it," concluded Kit.

"Wrong in the sense that it could possibly create even worse problems—catastrophes, perhaps—elsewhere," Gianni confirmed. "Thus, even if it could be done, I could in no way condone it."

"But what about Jesus? He came back to life. He was dead, and God brought Him back to life, didn't He?"

"Ah, yes!" Gianni smiled. "What is the expression? It is the one . . . ah, *l'esclusione* that confirms the rule."

"The exception that proves the rule," corrected Kit. "Okay, but if Jesus coming back to life upset the created order and brought about this cascade of catastrophe for all time and everything . . ." Kit paused as the meaning began to sink in. "Unless," he continued, "that is what God wanted."

"It is beyond doubt what God intended—not a catastrophe, but a *eucatastrophe*—a glorious upheaval of the created order for the ultimate good of all creation."

Gianni caught the glint of understanding beginning to quicken in Kit's eyes. "Yes, you see it now? The resurrection of Jesus sent shock waves backwards and forwards throughout the cosmos and affected all time—past, present, and future—forever. Because of the resurrection, everything changed. *Everything!* Nothing could ever be the same again. It was a rescue mission on a cosmic scale."

Kit was nodding. "But since we're not God, we can't know or guess what changes we might unleash if we tried the same thing."

"That is correct most assuredly."

"Then I guess Arthur Flinders-Petrie was wrong to use the Spirit Well to bring that woman back to life," Kit concluded.

Gianni's demeanour changed completely. His face froze, eyes wide with horror.

"What did I say?"

"You said . . ." Gianni opened and closed his mouth, working at the words. ". . . that Arthur used the Spirit Well . . ." Gianni reached out and clutched Kit by the arm, digging his fingers into his flesh. "What did you mean?"

"Well, I—I'm not sure I know what—" Kit stuttered, alarmed by his companion's stricken expression.

"Tell me what you saw!" Gianni's grip tightened. "Please, it is of paramount importance. I need to hear it all—every last detail—exactly as it happened."

Startled by his companion's reaction to his innocent confession, Kit swallowed hard. "Okay. Let's see . . ."

He collected himself, drew a breath, and began. "It goes back to when I was with River City Clan. One winter they built the Bone House—in fact, I helped them build it—and when it was finished, En-Ul, the clan chief, took me with him. I don't know why." Kit shrugged. "Maybe to watch over him while he slept, or maybe just to be there in case something happened.

"We were there a long time—hours anyway—and something *did* happen. My shadow lamp woke up. I had it in this pouch I made in my shirt, where I kept the green book too, and I felt the lamp grow warm. When I took it out, the little blue lights were glowing like crazy. I didn't know what to make of it—after being inactive for so long. It surprised me and I got up. I started to step over En-Ul and fell through the floor of the Bone House." Kit regarded the priest, who had closed his eyes and bowed his head. "Are you okay?"

"I am." Gianni seemed to have mastered himself once more. "Continue, please."

"Well, I took a step, and the next thing I knew I was flying through space—not like a regular ley jump," Kit told him. "This leap seemed to just go on and on. And when I thought it wasn't going to end, I landed on a beach—white sand, blue water, balmy ocean breeze, all of that. I'd arrived at the most incredible place I've ever seen. It was beautiful beyond description—the plants, the colours, even the quality of the light and air was different, more vivid somehow. A paradise—that's what I thought. It was paradise."

"What did you do?"

"I started walking inland and sort of stumbled onto this path, so I followed it—no idea where I was going. I just followed the path into this awesome jungle and eventually came to a pool." Kit paused to consider. "That's the only way to describe it, really—it was a pool in the middle of this clearing. But it wasn't water in the pool—it was more like light."

"Light?"

Kit nodded. "Liquid light—as if you could somehow distil all the sunlight and concentrate it in a pool, that's what it would look like." Kit's eyes grew slightly unfocused as he remembered the extraordinary experience.

"What happened there?" prodded Gianni gently.

"I was just standing there, looking at the light, and heard a sound—someone was coming. I don't know why, but I decided to hide. It seemed like a good idea, so I ducked down behind some ferny things, and a second later I see this man pushing through the undergrowth. He's coming to the pool and he's carrying a body in his arms—a woman . . ."

"What do you mean—*body?*"

"Just that," replied Kit. "She's dead—limp as a rag doll. This guy is carrying a corpse in his arms." Kit gave a firm nod for emphasis. "The man sort of pauses, like he's taking a deep breath, and then he steps into the glowing stuff. He keeps walking until he's completely submerged, dead body and all. He was under the surface for, I don't know, maybe a few seconds, and the liquid light changes colour—it goes from golden yellow to this bright, glowing red-orange—and a huge bubble forms in the middle of the pool, growing bigger and bigger until . . . it breaks. And there is the man again. He's still holding the woman, only this time, she's alive!"

Glasses glittering in the reflected sunlight, Gianni held Kit in his gaze. "You are certain?" asked Gianni at last, his voice soft, trembling. "There can be no doubt?"

Kit was already shaking his head. "No doubt whatever. I can still see it like it happened yesterday. I saw her move when the man carried her out and put her on the bank. That's when I saw who it was."

"How? What did you see?"

"The tattoos on the man's chest. All the symbols—his shirt is open and there they are. In bright blue. The same symbols that are on the map, only they're on him. It is Arthur."

"You are certain of this?"

"It was Arthur—blue tattoos and all. I don't know who the woman was, but she was dead going into the pool and alive coming out. And whatever it was he did, it was Arthur who did it."

Gianni, head lowered, hands clasped beneath his chin, remained silent.

Kit watched him for a moment, unwilling to interrupt the priest's meditations.

"Tea, gentlemen!" called Wilhelmina from across the courtyard.

The two men reluctantly moved towards the table where Mina was setting out a bowl filled with mint leaves and plates of tangerines and apricots. Cass followed with a platter of almond, sesame, and pistachio sweets, which she placed in the centre of the table.

Halfway across the courtyard, Brother Gianni halted in his tracks. He looked up quickly and then slapped his forehead with the flat of his hand. *"Stupido!"* he cried and dashed for the open doors. On the threshold he paused, flung out a hand towards Kit and Mina as if gesturing for them to stay put. *"Uno momento!"* he shouted as he dashed away.

"What was that about?" asked Mina, staring at the door through which the priest had disappeared.

"We were having a discussion, and it took a bit of an odd turn."

"It must have been a pretty intense conversation. I've never seen him like that. What on earth did you say to him?"

"I just happened to mention what I saw at the Spirit Well. Apparently he thinks it might be important."

Mrs. Peelstick appeared just then with a tray containing tea things—a pot, glasses, and a plate of sesame biscuits. "What is important, dear?"

Kit hesitated.

"Go on, Kit, tell her," nudged Wilhelmina. "Tell her what you told Gianni."

"Okay, okay," replied Kit. To Mrs. Peelstick he said, "I told Gianni that I saw Arthur Flinders-Petrie bring a dead woman back to life in the Spirit Well."

At first she seemed not to have heard. She continued to the table, then stopped. Her head snapped upright. "Oh, dear Lord in heaven!" she gasped.

As she spoke these words, time seemed to pause. Its relentless headlong race slowed, the brief duration of a moment lengthened and protracted to a leisurely, lingering dawdle. Kit watched the colour slowly ebb from Mrs. Peelstick's face, ruddy flesh bleaching by degrees to the pallor of old parchment. Her eyes grew round and wide in apprehension, and the tray in her hands wavered, wobbled, and at last began to unbalance.

The glasses on the board jiggled and, as the tray tilted from horizontal, the large flowered teapot began to slide—slowly at first, but as friction gave way the heavy container slewed sideways across the surface of the board, contacting the glasses in its path, knocking them down, scattering them like bowling pins. The rolling glasses reached the edge, slammed into the shallow side rail, bounced against it, and, driven by the oncoming mass of the teapot, were forced over the side, first one and then another until all were spinning through the air in free fall.

The pot came next, crashing into the wooden edge of the tray, increasing the imbalance further. Mrs. Peelstick's left hand lost its grip and her right hand proved unable to control the weight. The board angled sharply away, launching the pot into a majestic, spinning trajectory. Centrifugal force lifted the lid, which spun clear of the pot, releasing the freshly brewed tea in an orderly, crown-shaped splash. Hot liquid spewed from the curved spout in a graceful arc of disconnected drops, each one forming itself into a perfect brown sphere as it rose, hung, and then fell towards the courtyard floor. The pot itself continued on its downward journey, rotating lazily about an unseen axis, handle over spout over handle, each slow revolution throwing more tea into the air.

The first glass reached the stone paving, struck, and bounced. As it rebounded, cracks appeared throughout the fragile, transparent body. By the time the vessel met the second glass coming down, the cracks had widened and the shards were already flying apart. The second glass completed the process, smashing through the fractured debris of the first to strike the pavement, renewing the cycle of demolition as the remaining glasses rained down around it.

Kit watched with a kind of dread wonder as the squat globe of the teapot completed its third rotation just as it reached the courtyard floor; its rounded side simply collapsed on contact with the stone, disappearing completely beneath the curved bulk of the pot. As with the glasses, a network of cracks appeared on the surface of the ceramic, widened, and separated; velocity and momentum combined to propel each individual fragment back into the air. The hot tea, suddenly liberated from the constraining walls of the pot, rushed outward, a circle of liquid fingers as the broken shards of stoneware turned and tumbled in the air, glinting in the sunlight.

Tea, glass, pottery, the black dregs of spent tea leaves—all of it, for one splendid, perfect instant, seemed to hang in the air, caught between rising and falling, each droplet and sliver and speck suspended, at rest. Then gravity took over once more and all resumed their inevitable descent, striking the stone paving in a cacophonous concert that reached Kit's ears in a chaotic clatter of orchestrated destruction.

All this unfolded in stately progression with the uncompromised clarity of a dream. And in that long, unhurried instant, as the shards and splashes spun and collided in the air and on the ground, Kit glimpsed something of the slender, elusive nature of reality . . . of the deeply entangled, sublime unity of Creation and the manifest physical effects of unseen forces . . .

Kit saw, and understood, what it would be like to witness the End of Everything.

He sensed a movement to his right and Cass was beside him. Even before the shattered fragments had finished their chaotic dance and come to rest, she was in motion. Her hand entered his field of vision, and he saw that she clutched her handkerchief and, bending towards the wreckage, that she intended to use it to wipe away spatters of hot tea.

With the same clarity of vision, Kit watched the crumpled square of white in her hand ease and unfurl, and he remembered the last time that same cloth had been used—to catch the spilled substance of the shadow lamps. As this realization arced through his mind, he glimpsed the pale-grey smudge of rare earth as Cass spread the cloth to lay it flat over the brown liquid on the marble floor. Her fingers flexed to release the cloth and Kit grabbed her wrist.

He straightened, pulling Cass with him. Still gripping her wrist, he gently withdrew the handkerchief from her unresisting grasp and held it to the light so they both could view what had been fleetingly revealed in that split second before it would surely have been obliterated: a spiral whorl with a straight line directly through the centre and three separate circular dots spaced evenly along the outer edge of the spiral's curve.

They gazed upon the symbol and their thoughts were as one, as if there was but a single consciousness between them: truly, there was no chance, no coincidence. From the lowliest atom in a grain of sand at the bottom of the deepest sea to the most far-flung galaxy, the universe, the entire created cosmos, was a seamless, unified, and interwoven whole.

Epilogue

*W*ater oozed down the slime-covered walls and dripped from the tiny iron grate in the ceiling of the subterranean keep. The stagnant air was a rank and fetid stew laced with the odours of human excrement, rotting straw, and rodent droppings. The light from the slit in the wall that served as both window and air shaft did nothing to ease the gloom; if anything, it only made the murk worse by offering the illusion of illumination. The cell was a large square room steeped in perpetual chill from the seeping water, its stone walls tinted a sickly green.

Archelaeus Burleigh had been incarcerated before, briefly, following an incident where a maimed pickpocket in Florence had met the sharp end of his lordship's pig-sticker cane. In that instance, the Florentine *polizia* had taken the view that excessive violence had been used in what, to them, was a minor infraction of propriety. The harried Italian magistrate concurred, and the earl was summarily sentenced to sixty days in the chokey. That he actually spent fewer than three days in gaol before Con and Dex showed up to spring him was entirely beside the point.

Yet the gaol in Florence had been a luxury suite compared

to this one: a disused storage cellar beneath the Rathaus that the Prague city officials used to warehouse miscreants. And this time Burleigh could not anticipate a swift rescue, because all four of his Burley Men were locked up with him. To make matters worse, after five days in detention, hunger was dangerously sliding into starvation, owing to the fact that prisoners awaiting trial were required to purchase their own food, clothing, and necessaries or have them provided by relatives. Most prisoners were locals with plenty of friends and family on the outside who could be counted on to supply what was needed; Burleigh, however, had no one. No one, that is, aside from the alchemist Bazalgette and, perhaps, Emperor Rudolf himself—both of whom might as well have lived on the moon for the apparent impossibility of getting a message to them. Thus his sole recourse was to the grudging cooperation of the turnkey, who provided Burleigh and his men with the barest minimum of grossly inferior foodstuffs for which he reimbursed himself liberally from Burleigh's purse.

Accordingly, they had been given a pan of stale bread, three wizened apples to share among them, several handfuls of rancid walnuts, and two hunks of mouldy cheese—at the cost of a feast at one of Prague's best eating houses. That was two days ago, and the victuals—if that was a word that could be applied to the poor fare they received—had only served to stoke their hunger, not to sate it. In the meantime, Burleigh had tirelessly campaigned to have his case brought to trial at once. This request fell on deaf ears. In Prague, there seemed to be no way to compel a magistrate, judge, or anyone else to bring a case to court that he was not inclined to process. Five days had passed, and with no word of any impending proceedings, hope for a speedy trial had dissipated.

"We're going to rot in this stinking hole," grumbled Dex, "if we don't die of plague first."

"Instead of moaning all the time," suggested Con, "I say we try and tunnel our way out. That's the only way we're going to get free."

"Ent you the bright one!" hooted Mal. "Dig ourselves through solid stone! You got a magic shovel, then?"

"It's better than sitting here in the muck and stink," challenged Con.

"'Twouldn't stink so much if ya wasn't 'ere," replied Mal.

"Shut your gob!" growled Tav. "Both of you put a cork in it. Boss is working on getting us out. He's got a plan—just see if he don't."

Truth be told, however, Lord Burleigh did *not* have a plan. Their arrest had been so precipitous and unexpected, the possibility so unimaginably remote, that for once he was literally taken unawares. There was no alternate plan, no way out. And lacking the ability to get a message to anyone on the outside who could apply the influence needed to move matters along, digging their way out, however unrealistic, did seem to offer their best and likely *only* hope of escape.

"Is that so, Boss?" asked Con. "Tell us, then. Tell us the plan."

"We've sat 'ere long enough," grumbled Mal.

"We wouldn't be here at all if *you*—" started Tav.

"Enough, all of you!" snarled Burleigh, rousing himself from his corner. "Listen!"

Into the sudden silence they heard the distinctive clack of the gaoler's hobnail boots on the stone flagging. Presently the footsteps stopped and there was the rattle of a key in the lock, a loud *clack*, and then a low groan as the iron-clad door swung slowly open. Light spilled into the cell, dazzling the prisoners, who could not abide the radiance that suddenly pierced the gloom. They blinked and shielded their eyes as out of the light emerged a towering giant with broad shoulders, a shapeless head, and a weirdly hunched back.

Thinking the torturer had come, the Burley Men shrank back into the shadows. The oversize figure entered the cell and looked around, the gaoler moving in to stand behind him. As the prisoners' eyes adjusted to the light, they saw that their visitor was not a hulking rack-master come to torment them——it was the big baker from the coffee shop. A green hat lopped over his round head, and on his back he carried a bulging cloth sack; his ample middle was swathed in a green apron dusted in floury smudges. He said nothing——merely stood taking in the dank atmosphere of the prison, his expression, if he had one, difficult to read because his face looked as if it had been trampled by horses. Puffy and inflamed, covered in liver-coloured welts; one eye a painful purple slit and the other rimmed in black; his lips split, distended; and his nose cut and swollen . . . he stood in towering silence, exuding the warm, homey scent of the bakery from which he had just come. The prisoners caught the scent and it made their empty stomachs squirm.

Lord Burleigh roused himself from his corner. "You," he said coldly, his voice a hateful slur. "Come to gloat, have you?" He drew himself up. "Come to see me grovel?" He spat in the baker's direction. "I won't give you the satisfaction."

How much of this Etzel understood was unclear. He merely nodded and moved farther into the room, swinging the bag off his shoulder and placing it between his feet on the floor, where he opened it to reveal a number of loaves of fresh bread, a half round of soft cheese, ten green pears, a bunch of carrots, and two large sausages. Turning, he gestured to the gaoler hovering in the doorway, who entered bearing a pitcher of dark ale and a bucket of fresh water.

Burleigh stared at the food and drink, then raised his eyes to Engelbert. He pointed at the little heap of food. *"Was ist das?"* he asked in German.

"I am sorry it is not more," replied Etzel, speaking slowly and with some obvious discomfort through his ruined lips.

How was it that the man's jaw was not broken? wondered Burleigh. "What is this?" he asked again.

"Herr Arnostovi told me only this morning that you were here."

"Look at all that grub!" said Con, edging towards the heap of food. "I could eat the lot, I could."

"Get back!" warned Tav. "Not 'til Boss says it's okay. There's some trick here—I smell it. Right, Boss? It's a trick, ain't it?"

To Etzel, Burleigh said, "What's your game, then, baker?" He thrust an accusing finger at the food sack. "What does this mean?"

"It is for you," replied the baker simply. *"Zum Essen . . .* for eating."

Burleigh gazed at the pudgy dumpling of a face—battered and bloated and damaged from the beating he had received at their hands. "I can see that," said Burleigh. "What do you—ah . . ." He searched for the German words. *"Was woollen Sie?"*

"You ask what do I want?" wondered Etzel. "I want nothing."

The Burley Men had edged close around the bag of food, and though they could not follow the conversation, they were mightily interested in the outcome. Con, unable to wait, reached for one of the little loaves of fresh bread. Tav swatted his hand away and gave him a warning glance.

"Ha! Then you will get *nothing* from me," crowed Burleigh, his voice strident and hollow. "You hear, baker? *Nichts!"*

Engelbert shook his head and backed away. "Tomorrow is Sunday, but I will be able to bring more in two days."

With that, he was gone. The gaoler retreated, pulled shut the door, locked it, and departed. In a moment, their footsteps could no longer be heard. Only then did Burleigh stir. He moved to stand over the pile of food, then prodded it with an exploratory toe. It was what it appeared to be: fresh bread, fruit, cheese, sausage, and a few vegetables.

Burleigh stood for a moment, gazing at what in this place amounted to a banquet, and then raised his eyes to the door once more. He turned away and moved back to his place in the driest corner of the cell.

Tav called after him, "Boss?"

There was no reply, so he tried again. "Boss, what should we do with the food?"

Still Burleigh made no reply—so Con tried, saying, "The food, Boss—what do you want us to do with it?"

"Divide it up," muttered Burleigh finally. "Divide it fair and square—each man responsible for his own stash."

Tav fell to with a will and the others crowded close around, keen to make certain the division was done fairly. Burleigh watched from a little distance, a deep frown creasing his countenance as he tried to discern what cruel-but-subtle game the baker was playing, or what advantage he hoped to gain from this remarkable deception.

For deception it was—of that Burleigh was certain. A master of deceit himself, he could smell it from a distance. However, this particular ruse took a form he had never before encountered, and it would take some thought to crack it. But he would—oh yes, he would discover the treachery, and when he did, he would wield his knowledge like a weapon.

As the food was being shared out, Dex voiced aloud what the rest of them were thinking. "Why is he doing this?" He looked around. "Boss? I don't get it. What does the big oaf want?"

Burleigh lifted his head and gave a ragged laugh. "I don't know yet, but I will find out," he replied. "Mark me, all of you—I *will* find out." His voice rang hollow in the cell. "And when I do, that fool of a baker will curse high heaven that he was ever born."

The Great Divide

AN ESSAY BY STEPHEN R. LAWHEAD

During a recent visit to Rome, in the sweltering month of May, I took refuge in the coolness in Santa Maria degli Angeli, that glorious mash-up of a church designed by Michelangelo and built within the surviving walls of the ancient Baths of Diocletian, a Roman emperor not known for his kindness to Christians. The huge, cavernous space is a haven from the noise and heat of the modern city, and I could feel my body temperature and blood pressure slowly drop as I strolled into the vast hall and began to look at the inscriptions, shrines, and architectural details that naturally capture one's attention.

It was quite a surprise to turn a corner in the nave and come face-to-face with a magnificent statue of that great heretic, Galileo. And what's this? An elaborate historical exhibit dedicated to the man who was maligned by the church simply for insisting, on the basis of evidence obtained through his telescope, that the earth and all the other planets of our solar system are actually orbiting around the sun. His insistence, as everyone knows, challenged the prevailing view that the earth—God's chosen venue for His story of creation and redemption—was also the physical centre of the universe: an important theological point at the time. An earth that moved around a stationary sun was an unacceptable, possibly dangerous proposition.

And so Galileo fell foul of the church, was arrested, tried for heresy, convicted, and summarily excommunicated. Galileo went on, of course, to become the poster boy for the Church-versus-science debate, his experience most often cited as illustrating the great divide between science and religion. Yet here he was, in all his bronze glory, honoured in Rome (the location of his humiliation) and in a Christian church. Had I got the story wrong?

As a scientist, Galileo Galilei (1564–1642) was engaged in the great ferment of scientific and philosophic inquiry of late sixteenth- and early seventeenth-century Europe. Well known and respected, and himself a priest, he initially enjoyed strong support from within the Church. Pope Urban VIII was a close personal friend and early defender not only of Galileo but of scientific endeavour in general. In fact, Urban was so enamoured with Galileo's ideas that he wanted to be seen as aiding his friend and championing the new theories. To this end, Urban wrote a little essay ("Dialogue Concerning the Two Chief World Systems") to be included in Galileo's page-turner on planetary motion and the flow of tides. This is where Galileo's trouble actually began.

The pope, for all his enthusiasm, was perhaps not the best one to expound on the intricacies of the daring new theories under consideration; as a scientist, his work was not quite up to standard. Moreover, it rankled Galileo to have anyone—even his very powerful and influential friend, Urban—sharing any portion of the limelight with him. Reluctantly, however, he agreed to include the pope's essay—how could he refuse? But in a startlingly ill-advised move, Galileo cast a portion of his new book in the form of a dialogue among several characters: chiefly, a wise, knowledgeable scientist called the Academician, who elucidated all the brilliant cutting-edge ideas, and a nincompoop named Simplicio who spouted archaic nonsense. No prizes for guessing who the scientist character represented, and whose thoughts the moron mouthed.

Naturally, when Urban read the result he was furious. Here this man Galileo, whom he had befriended and defended, was mocking him before the world, calling him a simpleton and holding up his ideas to universal ridicule. Urban, his enormous papal dignity abused, turned to Cardinal Bellarmine for aid and advice. The cardinal, a devoted scholar and theologian, naturally sided with his superior. There were forces about that were deeply critical of Galileo—not so much for his science, but for his noisy insistence on making theological pronouncements that exceeded his expertise on such issues. So a case was brought against Galileo. No hasty kangaroo court, much less a rush to judgement, the case proceeded at a slow snail's pace, lasting almost a decade. In the end, without the pope's patronage and protection, Galileo was at last called before the Inquisition to answer multiple allegations. Unable to mount a coherent defence, he was found guilty of heresy. (It is worth pointing out that Galileo was considered by many to be a scientific heretic long before the Church got involved in the controversy. Colleagues who clung to old views and theories censured him, not for his theology, but for his *science*. Flying in the face of scientific orthodoxy can be every bit as dangerous as flouting religious convention.)

In exacting punishment the Church showed remarkable leniency:

there would be no execution, and no incarceration as such. Galileo would be confined to his residence and prevented from teaching or giving public lectures. Still, many of his sympathetic fellow scientist-priests continued to visit him and correspond. In fact, he spent a year of his "imprisonment" in the home of the archbishop of Sienna, another friend and supporter, and he published one of his finest works during the period. Thus science continued to be advanced with the aid of the Church, and Galileo's contributions were openly discussed and refined.

Obviously, in the case of Galileo and the Inquisition there is more than enough pomposity, arrogance, and shame to go around. But, interestingly, while the court of public opinion roundly condemns the Church for what it considers the suppression of science, Galileo is rarely held to account for the hubristic pride, disloyalty, and self-centred spite he brought to the matter. In truth, neither Urban nor Galileo covered himself in glory by acting pettily and seeking to serve his own ego when much larger issues were at stake.

Has anything changed? From what I read of the New Atheists and the Creationist Fundamentalists—and I read quite a bit—it seems not. Turf wars continue to be fought loudly and stridently in the public arena, in the academy, in the arts, and on the political stage, and the statements made are often self-serving and one-sided. Cheap shots are taken and facts obscured, ignored, or distorted.

When a loudly outspoken evolutionary biologist declares absolutely that religion is a mental delusion . . . or a prize-winning physicist claims to have proven there is no God . . . we might take a step back and reflect that these men are simply repeating Galileo's mistake: pontificating on matters outside their field and beyond their understanding. And when religious fundamentalists refuse to consider evidence that challenges the likelihood of a preposterously young universe . . . or ignore perfectly credible fossil evidence . . . we might pause to consider that creating pseudo-science to support dogmatic beliefs does great violence not only to realities that are ultimately beyond time and space, but also to any reasonable ability we might ever have to comprehend them.

It is a fact that the Roman Catholic Church has continually pursued a policy of active involvement in scientific inquiry and advancement, quite notably through the Vatican Observatory that is headquartered where the pope spends his summer vacation, in Castel Gandolfo, Italy.

And so it was to the College of Rome that Gianni, my very own scientist-priest, repaired when he needed vital information on the state of the universe. He might as easily have visited the Mount Graham Observatory nearer to Cass' base of operation in Arizona—and consulted the world-class scientists working there with the Vatican Advanced Technology Telescope.

Stephen Lawhead
Oxford, 2013

Acknowledgments

The author wishes to thank the following people:

Those who guided me through foreign and exotic lands: Wael El-Aidy, Nabile Mallah, Adrian Woodford, and Scott and Kelli Lawhead.

Those who corrected my Spanish, French, Latin, Italian, and German dialogue: Michael and Martina Potts, Danuta Kluz, Richard Rodriguez, Hailey Johnson Burgess, Matthew Knell, Daniele Basile, Sabine Biskup, and Bettina Heynes.

Those who advised on various historical, cultural, and technical matters: Clare Backhouse, Suzanna Lipscomb, Drake Lawhead, and Andrew Hodder-Williams.

Those who edited and consulted: Amanda Bostic, LB Norton, Jessica Tinker, and Ross Lawhead.

Any mistakes are my own.

An excerpt from

The Paradise War

I t all began with the aurochs.

We were having breakfast in our rooms at college. Simon was presiding over the table with his accustomed critique on the world as evidenced by the morning's paper. "Oh, splendid," he sniffed. "It looks as if we have been invaded by a pack of free-loading foreign photographers keen on exposing their film——and who knows what else——to the exotic delights of Dear Old Blighty. Lock up your daughters, Bognor Regis! European paparazzi are loose in the land!"

He rambled on a while and then announced: "Hold on! Have a gawk at this!" He snapped the paper sharp and sat up straight——an uncommon posture for Simon.

"Gawk at what?" I asked idly. This thing of his——reading the paper aloud to a running commentary of facile contempt, scorn, and sarcasm, well mixed and peppered with his own unique blend of cynicism——had long since ceased to amuse me. I had learned to grunt agreeably while eating my egg and toast. This saved having to pay attention to his tirades, eloquent though they often were.

"Some bewildered Scotsman has found an aurochs in his patch."

"You don't say." I dipped a corner of toast triangle into the molten center of a soft-boiled egg and read an item about a disgruntled driver on the London Underground refusing to stop to let off passengers, thereby compelling a train full of frantic commuters to ride the Circle Line for over five hours. "That's interesting."

"Apparently the beast wandered out of a nearby wood and collapsed in the middle of a hay field twenty miles or so east of Inverness." Simon lowered the paper and gazed at me over the top. "Did you hear what I just said?"

"Every word. Wandered out of the forest and fell down next to Inverness—probably from boredom," I replied. "I know just how he felt."

Simon stared at me. "Don't you realize what this means?"

"It means that the local branch of the RSPCA gets a phone call. Big deal." I took a sip of coffee and returned to the sports page before me. "I wouldn't call it news exactly."

"You don't know what an aurochs is, do you?" he accused. "You haven't a clue."

"A beast of some sort—you said so yourself just now," I protested. "Really, Simon, the papers you read—" I flicked his upraised tabloid with a disdainful finger. "Look at these so-called headlines: 'Princess Linked to Alien Sex Scheme!' and 'Shock Horror Weekend for Bishop with Massage Parlor Turk!' Honestly, you only read those rags to fuel your pessimism."

He was not moved. "You haven't the slightest notion what an aurochs is. Go on, Lewis, admit it."

I took a wild stab. "It's a breed of pig."

"Nice try!" Simon tossed his head back and laughed. He had a nasty little fox-bark that he used when he wanted to deride someone's ignorance. Simon was extremely adept at derision—a master of disdain, mockery, and ridicule in general.

I refused to be drawn. I returned to my paper and stuffed the toast into my mouth.

"A pig? Is that what you said?" He laughed again.

"Okay, okay! What, pray tell, is an aurochs, Professor Rawnson?"

Simon folded the paper in half and then in quarters. He creased it and held it before me. "An aurochs is a sort of ox."

"Why, think of that," I gasped in feigned astonishment. "An ox, you say? It fell down? Oh my, what won't they think of next?" I yawned. "Give me a break."

"Put like that it doesn't sound like much," Simon allowed. Then he added, "Only it just so happens that this particular ox is an ice-age creature which has been extinct for the last two thousand years."

"Extinct." I shook my head slowly. "Where do they get this malarkey? If you ask me, the only thing that's extinct around here is your native skepticism."

"It seems the last aurochs died out in Britain sometime before the Romans landed—although a few may have survived on the continent into the sixth century or so."

"Fascinating," I replied.

Simon shoved the folded paper under my nose. I saw a grainy, badly printed photo of a huge black mound that might or might not have been mammalian in nature. Standing next to this ill-defined mass was a grim-looking middle-aged man holding a very long, curved object in his hands, roughly the size and shape of an old-fashioned scythe. The object appeared to be attached in some way to the black bulk beside him.

"How bucolic! A man standing next to a manure heap with a farm implement in his hands. How utterly homespun," I scoffed in a fair imitation of Simon himself.

"That manure heap, as you call it, is the aurochs, and the implement in the farmer's hands is one of the animal's horns."

I looked at the photo again and could almost make out the animal's head below the great slope of its shoulders. Judging by the size of the horn, the animal would have been enormous—easily three or four times the size of a normal cow. "Trick photography," I declared.

Simon clucked his tongue. "I am disappointed in you, Lewis. So cynical for one so young."

"You don't actually believe this"—I jabbed the paper with my finger—"this trumped-up tripe, do you? They make it up by the yard—manufacture it by the carload!"

"Well," Simon admitted, picking up his teacup and gazing into it, "you're probably right."

"You bet I'm right," I crowed. Prematurely, as it turned out. I should have known better.

"Still, it wouldn't hurt to check it out." He lifted the cup, swirled the tea, and drained it. Then, as if his mind were made up, he placed both hands flat on the tabletop and stood.

I saw the sly set of his eyes. It was a look I knew well and dreaded. "You can't be serious."

"But I am perfectly serious."

"Forget it."

"Come on. It will be an adventure."

"I've got a meeting with my adviser this afternoon. That's more than enough adventure for me."

"I want you with me," Simon insisted.

"What about Susannah?" I countered. "I thought you were supposed to meet her for lunch."

"Susannah will understand." He turned abruptly. "We'll take my car."

"No. Really. Listen, Simon, we can't go chasing after this ox thing. It's ridiculous. It's nothing. It's like those fairy rings in the cornfields that had everybody all worked up last year. It's a hoax. Besides, I can't go—I've got work to do, and so have you."

"A drive in the country will do you a world of good. Fresh air. Clear the cobwebs. Nourish the inner man." He walked briskly into the next room. I could hear him dialing the phone, and a moment later he said, "Listen, Susannah, about today . . . terribly sorry, dear heart, something's come up . . . Yes, just as soon as I get back . . . Later . . . Yes, Sunday, I won't forget . . . cross my heart and hope to die. Cheers!" He replaced the receiver and dialed again. "Rawnson here. I'll be needing the car this morning . . . Fifteen minutes. Right. Thanks, awfully."

"Simon!" I shouted. "I refuse!"

This is how I came to be standing in St. Aldate's on a rainy Friday morning in the third week of Michaelmas term, drizzle dripping off my nose, waiting for Simon's car to be brought around, wondering how he did it.

We were both graduate students, Simon and I. We shared rooms, in fact. But where Simon had only to whisper into the phone and his car arrived when and where he wanted it, I couldn't even get the porter to let me lean my poor, battered bicycle against the gate for half a minute while I checked my mail. Rank hath its privileges, I guess.

Nor did the gulf between us end there. While I was little above medium height, with a build that, before the mirror, could only be described as weedy, Simon was tall and regally slim, well muscled yet trim—the build of an Olympic fencer. The face I displayed to the world boasted plain, somewhat lumpen features, crowned with a lackluster mat the color of old walnut shells. Simon's features were sharp, well cut, and clean; he had the kind of thick, dark, curly hair women admire and openly covet. My eyes were mouse gray; his were hazel. My chin drooped; his jutted.

The effect when we appeared in public together was, I imagine, much in the order of a live before-and-after advertisement for Nature's Own Wonder Vitamins & Handsome Tonic. He had good looks to burn and the sort of rugged and ruthless masculinity both sexes find appealing. I had the kind of looks that often improve with age, although it was doubtful that I should live so long.

A lesser man would have been jealous of Simon's bounteous good fortune. However, I accepted my lot and was content. All right, I was jealous too—but it was a very contented jealousy.

Anyway, there we were, the two of us, standing in the rain, traffic whizzing by, buses disgorging soggy passengers on the busy pavement around us, and me muttering in lame protest. "This is dumb. It's stupid. It's childish and irresponsible, that's what it is. It's nuts."

"You're right, of course," he agreed affably. Rain pearled on his driving cap and trickled down his waxed-cotton shooting jacket.

"We can't just drop everything and go racing around the country on a whim." I crossed my arms inside my plastic poncho. "I don't know how I let you talk me into these things."

"It's my utterly irresistible charm, old son." He grinned disarmingly. "We Rawnsons have bags of it."

"Yeah, sure."

"Where's your spirit of adventure?" My lack of adventurous spirit was something he always threw at me whenever he wanted me to go along with one of his lunatic exploits. I preferred to see myself as stable, steady-handed, a both-feet-on-the-ground, practical-as-pie realist through and through.

"It's not that," I quibbled. "I just don't need to lose four days of work for nothing."

"It's Friday," he reminded me. "It's the weekend. We'll be back on Monday in plenty of time for your precious work."

"We haven't even packed toothbrushes or a change of under-wear," I pointed out.

"Very well," he sighed, as if I had beaten him down at last, "you've made your point. If you don't wish to go, I won't force you."

"Good."

"I'll go alone." He stepped into the street just as a gray Jaguar Sovereign purred to a halt in front of him. A man in a black bowler hat scrambled from the driver's seat and held the door for him.

"Thank you, Mr. Bates," Simon said. The man touched the brim of his hat and hurried away to the porters' lodge. Simon glanced at me across the rain-beaded roof of the sleek automobile and smiled. "Well, chum? Going to let me have all the fun alone?"

"Curse you, Simon!" I shouted, yanked the door open, and ducked in. "I don't need this!"

Laughing, Simon slid in and slammed the door. He shifted into gear, then punched the accelerator to the floor. The tires squealed on the wet pavement as the car leapt forward. Simon yanked the wheel and executed a highly illegal U-turn in the middle of the street, to the blaring of bus horns and the curses of cyclists.

Heaven help us, we were off.

The story continues in *The Paradise War* by Stephen R. Lawhead.

About the Author

Photo by Alice Lawhead

Stephen R. Lawhead is an internationally acclaimed author of mythic history and imaginative fiction. He is the author of such epics as the King Raven, Song of Albion, and Dragon King trilogies. Lawhead makes his home in Oxford, England, with his wife.